BAPT

David Hewson is a former journalist with *The Times*, the *Sunday Times* and the *Independent*. He is the author of more than twenty-five novels including his Rome-based Nic Costa series, which has been published in fifteen languages. He has also written three acclaimed adaptations of the Danish TV series *The Killing*, and the Arnold Clover mysteries set in Venice.

BAPTISTE

THE BLADE MUST FALL

DAVID HEWSON

ORION

First published in Great Britain in 2024 by Orion Fiction,
an imprint of The Orion Publishing Group Ltd.,
Carmelite House, 50 Victoria Embankment
London EC4Y 0DZ

An Hachette UK Company

1 3 5 7 9 10 8 6 4 2

A CIP catalogue record for this book is
available from the British Library.

ISBN (Paperback) 978 1 3987 1804 3
ISBN (eBook) 978 1 3987 1805 0

Typeset by Input Data Services Ltd, Bridgwater, Somerset

Printed in Great Britain by Clays Ltd, Elcograf, S.p.A.

www.orionbooks.co.uk

Un héros, c'est celui qui fait ce qu'il peut.
A hero is a man who does what he can.

L'Adolescent, Romain Rolland.

Part One:

Summons to an Execution

1

10:05 a.m. Douai Prison, Monday, 15 November 1976

Baptiste lit his seventh Disque Bleu of the morning and cast his eyes over the guillotine. There were only two or three still working in the whole of France. This one, a warder told him, was shipped by truck from Dijon three days before. The man who held the title of Chief Executioner had arrived early that morning and left it to a couple of workmen to assemble in the prison courtyard. It was smaller than Baptiste expected, perhaps because the only images he'd seen before were in history books. Marie Antoinette and the victims of the Terror meeting their ends on a public platform, severed heads held high by a triumphant *sans-culotte* to amuse a cheering crowd.

There was no stage for the rudimentary mechanism that was meant to take the life of Gilles Mailloux. No sense of theatre or much of an audience, though a small crowd of protesters had begun to assemble outside the high jail gates, calling for an end to state executions, singing songs, kneeling on the grubby cobbles and saying prayers. Capital punishment was rare, and probably soon to be abandoned given slow shifts in public opinion. Mailloux might be its last victim, in no small part due to his bizarre behaviour in court. That and Baptiste's dogged handiwork in the case of the missing Noémie Augustin, raped

1

and murdered at Mailloux's hand the court decided, not that they yet had a body.

He couldn't take his eyes off the guillotine. It seemed more like a piece of ancient farm machinery liberated from an agricultural museum than an instrument of death in the employ of the Ministry of Justice. A wooden frame like a giant child's toy, ropes to raise the angled blade, sharpened and shining in the wan winter sun, a low plank bed for the prisoner to lie on, a half-moon cut out for his neck. Maybe there was a wicker basket somewhere, just like they had two centuries before during the Terror. There would be blood too, surely. Lots. And, waiting in one of the prison storerooms, a cheap pine coffin that would be brought out before the condemned man's final moments.

One of the workmen yelled, 'Hey, Marcel. Here's to you!' He had a cabbage, a big one, green and leafy, and was lobbing it through the air to his colleague. The other man caught it like a rugby player receiving a pass.

'Trial run,' he cried and placed it on the neck rest beneath the shadow of the frame. The other one pulled on the rope. The gleaming blade rose then locked in position at the summit. '*Fais gaffe!*'

One quick pull on the lever and they stepped back, laughing as the keen edge tumbled down with a squeal and screech, slammed into the cabbage, cleaved it in two.

'*Bon appetit.*' The one who worked the rope picked up half and threw it to his mate.

Baptiste finished his cigarette then threw it to the cobbled ground. One last time to plead with Gilles Mailloux. For some news, however grim, of the young woman he never once denied killing, not from the moment they took him into custody.

It only occurred to him when he reached the cell that there'd been an added act of cruelty on the part of the jail authorities. The guillotine was just a short walk from the barred window.

2

The man who might soon die there could listen to the instrument of his end being assembled, tested, made ready for the final act. There was the hammering again. Nails. Wood. The scrape of metal on metal, that cruel blade being sharpened once more, cackles and jokes from the two workmen arguing over who got the largest share of the severed cabbage.

Gilles Mailloux looked much as he did that strange hot summer when Clermiers turned from a sleepy, little-noticed town in northern France into a hotbed of rumour, misery, and death. Tall and skinny as a bent scarecrow, with a gaunt face, sallow complexion, a little yellow over high cheekbones. Bulging bright blue eyes and unkempt greasy hair clinging to his scalp. The grey prison jacket and trousers they'd given him were a couple of sizes too big.

He nodded at the window: six bars, grubby with soot, paltry daylight barely filtering through, a spider starting to build its silky web in the corner.

'*Bonjour*, Julien.' Mailloux lounged back on his cell bed. 'How goes it?'

Baptiste sat down on the cane chair set against the outside wall. He'd no idea how many hours were left before the sentence might be carried out, but he was determined not to leave empty-handed. Though, looking at Mailloux, he wondered if he was fooling himself. For a man on the verge of execution, he seemed remarkably calm.

The hammering ceased for a moment and one of the workmen barked out a nasty crack about whose job it might be to sweep up the blood.

'It's meant to be a kindness.' Mailloux shuffled on the narrow, hard cell bed then stretched his skinny arms up against the brick wall painted a scruffy shade of olive. 'Better than hanging. Or shooting. Or . . . I don't know. I read they used to garrotte people, strangle them, in some places.'

'I can never conceive that killing someone might be construed as a kindness, Gilles. Surely, you can't be serious.'

Mailloux had turned twenty-three in jail, but one of the many oddities about him was how he looked so young yet sounded much older. Something in his background, not that Baptiste could imagine what that was. He'd managed to keep much of his true character, whatever demons drove him, well hidden, not just from the police but the one psychiatrist who'd tried to penetrate that hard, opaque shell and met little but silence and small talk. It was not a lack of intelligence. More likely a surfeit of it, derailed somehow. What learning Mailloux had was from his own efforts, not the school that had abandoned him at the age of fifteen, left him to survive as best he could on the grimy, impoverished Boulliers estate that sat on the wrong side of the river Chaume.

"You forget. I am the Monster of *Merdeville*. The Beast of Shit Town. I am serious. Deadly so, with every right to be. You know your history?'

'History was my subject at university.'

'Why? Why choose that?'

A good question. Mailloux always had them when he wanted. It was ridiculous that the best job he could find was working behind the counter of a petrol station at night, the ghost shift where, for hours it seemed, he did little but study books and read poetry.

'I think because it helps me try to see where things go wrong. Where there's a tear, a wound in the world, and how that wound might sometimes be healed, and occasionally made much worse. How, in the end, we turn towards good, though not easily on occasion, and not forever.'

Mailloux grimaced. 'You sound like a priest. I didn't summon one of them. I never would.'

'I am no priest, I assure you,' Baptiste said with the faintest of smiles.

'Good. History. During the Revolution, the days of terror, the masters in Clermiers, the important men you understand, they'd drown people. Those icy grey waters. They'd herd them

4

onto a boat, tie them down, then hole it midstream and sit back to enjoy the spectacle. The *Noyades* they called it.'

'I believe that was Nantes.'

Mailloux laughed and shook his head.

Baptiste took out his pack of cigarettes. Almost half gone already, and he was glad there was a spare in his jacket pocket. He shuffled one out and offered it across the cell.

'I don't smoke. Surely you know that?'

'I just thought. Now . . .'

'Bad for you. Kick that habit, Julien. They may tell you it makes you look like a man. The truth is you smell. And maybe one day you'll wake up and find there's cancer running round your bones, raising tumours everywhere.'

Baptiste lit one anyway and immediately had a coughing fit. 'Thank you for your concern.'

'It's not concern. It's a statement of fact. Something Clermiers doesn't much like. That place is good at keeping its secrets. Better than you know. History. Like I said, they drowned them in the Chaume. How much kinder to chop off a man's head.' His scrawny pale fist came down with force on his bony knees. 'Bam! And they're gone. Though . . .'

He hesitated and for a second or two Baptiste thought: *Gilles Mailloux is scared.*

'Though what?'

'I wonder if you die the moment the blade has done its work. Or live on a second or two after, watching the ground rise up to meet you.'

'Who could know?'

He grinned, yellow teeth, sharp, vulpine. 'The dead, of course. Don't worry. I won't come back to haunt you. To whisper secrets into your ear one dark, cold, lonely night. Tell you what I saw, what I felt in those last few moments. Ideas like that are for fairy tales, told in fairy palaces.'

'There are more practical matters I'd rather hear right now.'

'I'm sure there are. But you're the one who put me here. That blade will rise at your bidding and . . .'

He drew a flat hand across his neck.

'I don't believe in executing people, Gilles. You wouldn't be facing this impasse had you offered a little in the way of cooperation, of sympathy, of regret. And who knows? Perhaps it won't happen. We'll hear one way or the other soon enough.'

Mailloux's face fell, all the fake mirth gone. 'Those bleeding hearts should mind their business.'

It was a civil rights group that had petitioned the Élysée Palace for clemency, not the prisoner himself. He'd turned down the offer of legal representation, just as he'd refused to explain himself to the police and the court itself. All the same, the petition was lodged. An answer from the office of the President, Valéry Giscard d'Estaing, was expected any hour. Gilles Mailloux's life hung on nothing more than a telegram, a few words on a sheet of paper.

'If that corrupt idiot is fool enough to sanction a so-called reprieve, he only sentences me to a different kind of death. A worse one.' He nodded at the bars. 'You think I'd survive one week if they let me wander among the animals out there?'

He'd been in solitary ever since his arrest. Given the publicity, much of it lurid, the authorities felt there'd be an attempt on his life were he to mix with other prisoners.

'You've said nothing about Noémie Augustin since I arrested you. Now you ask to see me. Why?'

A shrug. 'I was bored. A man on death row has the right to make a few demands.'

'It's not too late. Were you to shed some light on Noémie's fate I could call the Élysée and tell them you were cooperating. That might carry some weight. They could delay matters until we've investigated further. A few more days, weeks. Months even. There's always hope.'

Gilles Mailloux leaned forward. 'Where does blood come from?'

6

'I'm sorry . . .'

He looked at Baptiste as if he were an idiot. 'Where does blood come from? What was it before?'

'I don't—'

'From some kind of heaven? Or nowhere? Or maybe that's the same.'

'Gilles—'

A wry and knowing smile. 'And where, in the end, does it go? Down a gutter. Into a drain. Is that where I'm headed?'

Baptiste wanted to spend the rest of this dismal day letting the fumes of a Disque Bleu circulate around his lungs. Then get a drink, red wine and cognac after. All that seemed distant, irrelevant at that moment. The image of the guillotine had been pushed from his head by another: Mailloux's one outburst in court, after days of smirking, laughing, yawning and making faces at the judge and jury. He'd offered nothing in his defence, let alone a word of denial. There was just a single moment of furious speech, over something as ridiculous as a comic book. Mailloux had got to his feet in the dock and bawled out, 'If this world had a heart, I'd reach through its ribs and tear the bloody thing to shreds.' Then held out his hands like talons, ripping apart some invisible organ, laughing all the while, like the villain in a cheap noir movie.

It was a performance, an obvious piece of theatre, one Baptiste had watched in silent despair, understanding at that moment that Mailloux was surely headed for the guillotine.

'The world does have a heart, Gilles.'

A moment, then, 'Not for the likes of me.'

'Just tell me where you left Noémie Augustin. Where we might find her. Give her mother the proper grief of a funeral. Release her from the hell you've sent her to. What reason could you have not to tell me now?' He paused and wondered if any of this was going in. 'Let me make that call. There's still time.'

Mailloux threw up both hands in despair. 'If only matters were that simple.' He pointed at the door. 'I would like a hot chocolate. A good one. And a croissant. With butter and strawberry jam. Something proper from a café, not the crap the canteen puts on tin plates here.'

'I'm not a waiter.'

'True. But you are a man who wants something.' A weak wave of those skeletal arms. 'Which, who knows, I may offer.' That strange, unworldly smile. 'If only you promise to stay with me to the end. The very end. To watch. To see me leave this shitty circus for good.'

2

Clermiers, Sunday, 18 July 1976

The tennis courts were by the river, three of them, changing rooms and a small shop. They belonged to the charitable organisation, *Les Amis Dans L'Adversité*, Friends in Adversity, based in its own clubhouse on the rise above. A villa from the late nineteenth century with a private restaurant, bar and lounge. A focal point where the men of Clermiers, the important ones, would meet to discuss business, talk politics and local affairs. Then, as the name suggested, feed a little support and money to the neighbourhood poor, mostly the wrong side of the river, before retiring to drink and dine to their hearts' content.

Noémie Augustin, just turned nineteen, worked for the club as a waitress, lunchtimes and occasionally for their night events. The money was rotten but all she could find in the two months since she'd moved to the town. Still, they let her use the tennis courts for free, the one privilege that came with the uniforms the girls had to wear to work for the *Amis*.

Daniel Murray had to pay. He was an outsider, an English exchange student her parents had taken in as a brief lodger. One year older, a nice boy her mother thought, and her mother was usually right about things when she was allowed an opinion.

Daniel didn't seem to care her father was black, an immigrant from Martinique. Or that she had inherited a good deal of his looks. Clermiers wasn't Paris. There were few immigrants in town. The fact her mother was white didn't make much difference. Apart from her, the only other person of immigrant stock she'd got to know in the previous two months was Gilles Mailloux. Half-Algerian, his father long vanished, his mother scarcely at home much, Gilles was the local oddball. Likeable, always talking about books he'd read while working as the night attendant at the one petrol station on the edge of town. But tall and spindly, almost academic, not sporting at all. Never someone to join her at tennis.

She lined up to serve, right-handed, strong legs apart the way her idol, Evonne Goolagong, stood. That must have been why she sent an ace flying past Daniel on the far side of the court.

'Not fair!' he shrieked as the ball shot past him into the hedge behind.

'Game, set, and match. Are the English all sore losers?'

'This one is. I didn't stand a chance!'

'Of course you did. You just couldn't take it.'

He squinted at her, shook a fist, then burst out laughing. Funny and good-looking as well. She'd started to wonder if there was a girlfriend back home. Someone he'd return to soon and forget about sorry little Clermiers where he lived briefly in a cramped spare bedroom for which he was paying an extortionate rent.

Not that he ever complained. He picked the ball out of the privet hedge, grabbed his racket and bag, and hopped over the net, catching his foot so he nearly fell flat on his face.

'Clown. You did that deliberately.'

'Got a smile out of you, didn't it? Haven't seen that for a day or two.'

He was perceptive, too. Right then, Noémie wished he wasn't.

She watched as he picked up the rest of the balls. Back turned so she couldn't see the long windows of the clubhouse lounge, or care if there were curious faces there.

'What is it?' he asked.

Everything was tidied away. He was as quick as he was relentlessly cheerful.

'What's what?'

'You keep looking at that place back there.'

'Do I?'

Daniel had only been in France ten days and seemed quite shy. He hadn't talked much at all, but she'd got the impression Clermiers wasn't what he expected. Her part anyway. Noémie Augustin's family had landed up on the Boulliers estate, the wrong side of town. Before, they'd lived in a public housing flat in Calais while her father got his accountancy qualifications. At the end of the previous year, he'd been offered a job in Clermiers. It was an odd interview. She was called to it along with her mother, sitting through an anodyne bunch of questions in front of a man called Bruno Laurent and his elegant wife Véronique. Laurent seemed to own most of Clermiers and was willing to offer her father work on condition he start immediately, living in a bachelor flat the company provided. Family accommodation was harder to find, and it was only down to the generosity of his employer that she and her mother were finally able to join him that May, in a small house vacated, she learned, through a death.

Parts of Boulliers, a few worker's cottages, dated back a century or more. Gilles Mailloux lived in a semi-detached among them, along with his mother when she was around. But most people were crammed into ugly concrete terraces and a few low apartment blocks put up by shoddy builders in the Fifties. Theirs was one of the few detached homes, a three-bedroom house, or, more accurately, two and a half, that belonged to Bruno Laurent, naturally.

Hauteville, the oldest part of Clermiers, set on the low

hill on the left bank of the Chaume, was so much grander, almost a different place altogether. Elegant buildings, a neat town square, even a small theatre converted into a cinema, all built on the wealth of agriculture and the industries that once flourished in this grey part of northern France. A lot of that money had vanished, at least as far as the workers of Clermiers were concerned. But the traditional families of Hauteville still ran everything, owned most of the properties, owned people like her father too. That, Charles Augustin insisted, was the way of the world. The rich were always there, just like the poor. No point in trying to deny it, best to knuckle down, tug the forelock and hope for advancement somewhere along the way.

Ambition. Aspiration. Hope. Three things her father clung to. Three things many on the Boulliers estate would despise, along with those who sought them. They had their own name for the place: *Merdeville*. Shit Town. She hated hearing that. It wasn't the place they were talking about. It was themselves.

Daniel sat down on the bench at the side of the court and patted the empty space next to him. 'One more time. What is it?'

'It's nothing.'

'Do you have any idea how infuriating you can be at times?'

'That's a bit cheeky from a lodger.'

'A lodger who's a friend . . .'

The walk from the club to home took nearly half an hour. The distance wasn't so far but the route was blocked by the shuttered estate of the Château de Mortery, a local landmark long gone to ruin. This wasn't the kind of château she'd read about in books, elegant, fancy, aristocratic. What little was visible behind the walls from the path outside looked like a castle of old, rugged, a fortress once.

After the château she'd cross the bridge over the broad and sluggish waters of the Chaume, then do her best to avoid the rougher parts of Boulliers. The week before, she'd engineered an excuse to leave her bike at home so the two of them could go that way together. She'd pumped the reticent Daniel for information, all of which came easily. He was from a middle-class home on the other side of *La Manche*, Folkestone. Father was a barrister, his mother had taught French at the local grammar school which was why his was so good. His sister Celia, two years older, worked for a travel company the family owned. All very different from the life Noémie and her family led. Charles Augustin was a hungry man, a bookkeeper by training though Laurent seemed to use him as a general dogsbody. It was for his family's benefit, Charles Augustin always said, that he worked so hard, night and day, vanishing in the small hours for reasons he never explained with any conviction. In that case, she thought, he was a martyr for little purpose. There was never enough money, not that her mother complained. Martine Augustin seemed happy enough, content as she always said to 'know her place'.

'Nothing's wrong. Nothing I can't handle. Can we just leave it there?'

She opened her tennis bag and stuffed the racket inside.

'What's that?'

Damn, she thought. *He saw.*

'What's what?'

'It looked like a black dress. Shiny. Like . . . you're going dancing? And . . .' He scratched his head. 'Bananas?'

'Have you been peeking in my bedroom, Daniel Murray?'

He was affronted. 'Certainly not. I wouldn't dream of it.'

She zipped the bag, stood up and shimmied for a moment, hips swaying side to side. 'How very English you are. Maybe I do like to dance at times? Don't you?'

He laughed. 'Two left feet.'

'I'm sorry?'

'It's an English expression. Probably doesn't work in French.'

She didn't move. Noémie seemed uncertain of something.

'Are you OK walking back?' he asked. 'I thought you'd have brought your bike—'

'Flat tyre.'

'Oh. I assumed . . .'

'I can walk. Those kids on the estate aren't so bad.'

Daniel said nothing. She suspected he'd had a run-in with them somewhere along the way. A few nights before he'd come back from a walk looking flushed, grazes on his knuckles. Stumbled on a slippery path, or so he claimed, not that there'd been any rain. It was the hottest summer in years the weather people kept saying. Water shortages, bans on hosepipes. Hard to imagine someone losing their footing.

'I'd come with you,' he said. 'But I can't.'

'It doesn't matter!'

'Someone's over from England. I've got to meet them . . .' He glanced at his watch. 'Twenty minutes ago.'

'Mustn't be late for your girlfriend. Not if she's travelled all this way.'

He groaned, folded his arms and gazed at her so directly she felt the blood rush to her cheeks.

'Sorry. Didn't mean to . . . be nosey.'

'Of course not.'

'Best be off then. You're late.'

'Maybe I could learn to dance,' he said, getting up. 'If I knew someone who could teach me.' Then, not looking at her, he added, 'We could give it a try. If you have the time. Talk about it over pizza. I'll pay. I mean . . . only if you want . . . it's up to you. Not pushing—'

'Like a date, you mean?'

'If . . . if . . .' He was blushing. 'If you'd like to see it that way.'

She grabbed the tennis bag and glanced back at the club-house. 'See you back home. Whenever. I just . . .' Noémie hesitated, and smiled, a little awkwardly. Then did the little dance again, more vivid, more enticing this time. 'I'm just going to stay here for a little while. So hot. I need a shower.'

Daniel Murray headed off to town, puzzled, intrigued, perhaps disappointed. Maybe she'd led him on too much. Not that she was playing with him. Another day she'd have said yes. Gone for a pizza. Perhaps followed her feelings and let him get closer. Tried dancing, curing those two left feet. He'd be a good pupil, and a pupil was what she needed, more than a boyfriend just then. She'd learned enough already from the books she'd secretly bought online and borrowed from the town library. Now it was time to put all that into practice.

With Daniel.

A nice idea.

If only . . .

But nice ideas were fairytales in Boulliers. In *Merdeville*.

Mostly the place lived on airy fantasies and sometimes outright lies.

Furtive, whispered half-truths, like saying she needed a shower. Which she did. But that, Noémie Augustin knew, was only the start. The prelude to something she didn't quite understand. A secret appointment that, whatever she'd been promised, had begun to fill her with dread.

3

There were five men watching the end of the tennis match from the comfort of the clubhouse dining room. The executive committee of *Les Amis Dans L'Adversité*. Fabrice Blanc, town mayor and chairman, next to him Philippe Dupont, the captain in charge of Clermiers' small police station. Across the table Christian Chauvin, priest at the Église Saint-Vivien, and Louis Gaillard, local member of the Picardy assembly in Amiens. Bruno Laurent took the seat at the end as usual. He was the closest the town had to a local magnate, owner of a sugar beet refinery and two farms through inheritance, then, with canny and aggressive investment, the freehold of most commercial properties in Hauteville along with many residential homes across the region. In recent years Laurent had added property development and hotels to his portfolio. He was the one who kept the *Amis* alive with modest donations from his personal fortune, a generosity that had won him the thanks of national politicians and the occasional half-grudging gratitude of those his trickle-down of riches aided. The poor, it seemed to him, were rarely thankful, perhaps because they blamed him for their impoverishment in the first place. Still, it was an investment that paid dividends from time to time.

'The business was acceptable,' Blanc announced, closing the folder in front of him. 'As usual, we've no need of minutes.'

Laurent groaned and rolled his eyes. 'It seems to me all you people need is my money. How much have I shelled out for those losers in Boulliers today?'

'Twenty thousand francs,' Dupont said. 'You'll scarcely notice it, and most you'll set against tax in any case.'

'And all for an excellent cause,' the priest added. 'The young are the future of this world. They deserve all the help they can get.'

Dupont finished his glass of Evian then poured himself a calvados from the flask on the table and lit a cigarette. 'If the young of Boulliers are the future then truly we're fucked. Still, if you want to put up a hut and call it a youth centre so be it. Somewhere they can smoke and deal and shift whatever stolen goods they've liberated along the way. At least I'll know where to look.'

Silence until Chauvin broke it in a voice that was just a couple of tones below that of a sermon. 'I know you deal with their problems on a different level to ours, Philippe. Nevertheless, if we can divert them from their nefarious activities with a little sport and culture . . .'

'I doubt a priest understands their definition of culture,' Dupont sneered. 'Doing good is a fine and decent thing, Father, but let's not pretend it's an activity on their behalf alone. Although . . .' He nodded at the window. 'I gather from your probing eyes that pretty black girl on the tennis court would be welcome to a little charity if it were available.'

Blanc tapped the mayoral chain around his neck. 'Remember where you are and who you're talking to. I noticed you taking a good look as well.'

'That kind is not to my taste,' Dupont replied and downed his glass.

'I gather you have a new colleague.'

'Who the hell told you that?'

'It doesn't matter who. What matters is . . . why? We've no crime of any interest here.'

'This is true. We are and always have been a town of saints and petty, insignificant sinners.'

'Enough of that. You've someone coming from Paris. Why?'

Dupont waved his hand in the air with a nonchalant sweep. Cigarette smoke pooled around the table like a tiny storm cloud. 'It's a temporary posting. That's all. I'm captain. The fellow will do as I tell him for a few weeks then disappear back to his office none the wiser.' He leaned forward and jabbed a finger round the table. 'He'll see what I allow. That's all you need to know.'

'Please, Philippe,' said the priest. 'What you say here will never travel beyond these four walls. You know that. Your friends have the right to know.'

'If this is anything to do with . . . digging . . .' Gaillard had a high-pitched voice, often mocked. And always the last to speak.

'Digging?' Dupont demanded. 'I haven't a clue what you mean.'

'Must I say it out loud?'

'Useful if you want people to understand what you're whining about.'

'You know damn well. What's the point of our meeting like this if—?'

Dupont was squeaking like a mouse . . . *eek, eek, eek,* the volume growing ever louder until Gaillard fell silent.

'Oh, for god's sake, man. Cut it out. The police force of Clermiers is me and that porky idiot Bonnay at the moment. Chastain is on vacation in his stupid caravan and won't be back for two weeks. Allemand is in the nut hutch screaming at the walls how I've been beastly to him.'

'You drive your men hard, Philippe,' the mayor said.

'That's how I've been keeping this town tame for fifteen years! Think that's going to change because some idiot from Paris who's never set foot outside in the rain or put his boots in cow shit saw the staffing level here and came up with this hare-brained scheme?'

They waited. Dupont stubbed out his cigarette in the brimming ashtray in front of him. 'It's a new idea one of those idiots on high had. Dispatch some desk-bound clown from the city out to the sticks to see what he can learn. His name is Julien Baptiste. A university type. Probably thinks you do policing from a textbook. Sitting behind a desk.'

Laurent laughed. 'You don't step out much from behind yours, do you?'

Dupont picked up his pack of cigarettes and his lighter. 'That, my friend, is because Clermiers is a peaceful place. And it will be as long as I keep the creatures over the river in check and make sure they never cross the bridge to disturb good folk like you. Have I failed you there?'

'No,' said Blanc. 'You have not. I tell you that as mayor. As your friend also. All the same . . . you understand our concerns?'

The police captain got to his feet. 'You really think I can't handle a man like that for a few weeks? Besides, your information is incomplete. It's not just this Baptiste fellow. They're sending me another. A junior on probation.'

'What?' Blanc cried. 'From Paris?'

'No. Marseille. Étienne Fatoussi. *Pied-noir* father I guess. So maybe little Étienne is bent already.' He grinned. 'You might want to keep him, huh?'

They went quiet until Blanc shuffled his papers together. 'Then this is all in your capable hands. We've nothing to worry about.'

'You never do. I'll give the Marseille kid something to fuck up then send him on his way. Same with this Baptiste character. What goes through the heads of those idiots in Paris is quite beyond me.' He nodded at the window. 'Now you can get back to staring at that black girl. Planning the rest of your pleasant Sunday.'

They all looked.

'We can't,' said Christian Chauvin. 'She's gone.'

4

The only garage in Clermiers lay on the outskirts past the high walls of the abandoned Château de Mortery. Three pumps, a cabin, a corrugated iron workshop at the back. Baptiste's mother was driving him in her little city Citroën and none too happy about it.

'Jesus,' she muttered as they pulled into the forecourt, 'we're nearly in Belgium. Who in God's name wants to go to Belgium? What must your bosses in Paris think? Dispatching you to a dump like this?'

Marie Le Gall had never been anywhere near Clermiers, or possessed the faintest idea what the place was like. Nor had Baptiste beyond what he'd read in the files.

He took out his wallet. 'I go where they tell me. That's how it works in most jobs.'

'If your father could see this . . .'

Frederic Baptiste had been a lecturer at the Sorbonne,

economics with a Marxist bent. He'd died of a heart attack during the riots of May 1968, picking up a rubbish bin to lob at the ranks of baton-wielding police in the Latin Quarter. Marie – the two had never married, since matrimony was deemed a pointless bourgeois institution – was in London at the time giving a series of fiery talks to students at the LSE. She only heard the news a day later, broken in a phone call by Julien, then eighteen, a quiet, awkward youth, rebellious too, but after his own fashion. In some odd, illogical way she resented him for being the bearer of ill tidings, and both knew it.

There came that awkward silence they both knew from the moment Frederic's name was mentioned. Then a skinny young man, sick-looking, though perhaps that was the light from the filling station's fluorescent tubes, shambled out to meet them and began to fill the Citroën without being asked. She followed Baptiste out of the car to watch. The drive from Paris had taken almost four hours, the last part on minor roads so twisting and frequently unmarked they'd had to retrace their steps three times before finally seeing a sign marked 'Clermiers'. Baptiste had offered to drive but, as he'd expected, she'd refused. It was her car after all. His only mode of transport was his racing bike now strapped to the boot.

'You're new,' the petrol attendant said. 'Haven't seen you around before.'

Baptiste held out his hand and said, 'Julien Baptiste. I'm moving here for a little while.'

The man glanced at his own hand, stained with petrol, and didn't shake. 'Why?'

'Because,' Marie jumped in, '*les flics* have ordered it. And being a slave to his masters in Paris he must do as he's told.'

'Police.' He drained off the last of the petrol, shook the pump, replaced it, rubbed his hands on his overalls. 'Gilles Mailloux. I live in Boulliers.'

'Where's that?'

Mailloux laughed. 'You'll find out soon enough. Probably the only place you'll end up going. Money please.'

Marie stuck her hands in her pockets. Baptiste handed over the cash as he'd planned.

Mailloux walked round to the boot. 'You have a bicycle.'

'It's his only form of transport,' Marie said. 'He gave his car to his ex-girlfriend who dumped him after he found out she'd been sleeping around.'

Baptiste took a deep breath. 'Thanks, *Maman*. Like I said. It was the only way she could get into work.'

'Too snooty for a bus then.'

'There are no buses.'

'There are always buses. Why couldn't you take up with one of those nice girls from the flower shop next door? The sisters.'

'Chloé and Elise are hardly girls.'

'That explains it then. Can't expect a grown woman to want you.'

'They own the flower shop by the way. The whole building.'

'All the more reason to take up with one of them. They both like you. Elise, especially, finds you funny, I think. That's a start. For a fellow like you. Being amusing. Breaks the ice.'

The garage man just grinned, embarrassed.

'How do you intend to get around this place when I'm gone, Julien?'

'I have the bike. Also, the job comes with a car.'

'A marked car, I'll bet. At least they don't make you wear a uniform in Paris. How common. My son riding round with the word "Police" stamped on the door.'

'I already said. I don't know. I won't. Not till I check in.'

'The shame of it.'

She was a short woman, still slender, still pretty her son thought even if she no longer showed any interest in men. Baptiste took after his late father, tall, upright, athletic if he'd been interested.

Gilles Mailloux appeared amused by this brief and testy

exchange. 'You know where you're going from here?'

Baptiste pulled out his notepad and showed him the address Paris had provided. 'It's police accommodation.'

'They own you,' Marie muttered. 'You've sold them your soul.'

'Temporary,' Baptiste added. 'Just for a few months.'

'Three kilometres away. Drive past the old château', said Mailloux. 'Take a left up the hill through Hauteville, then keep going on the road north. Not much round there except a few houses. You'll be needing that bike to get to the shops.'

'As I said . . . I get a car.'

Mailloux pointed at the bike. 'Best lock that up. People round here sometimes take a liberal view of private property. Not just those of us from Boulliers either.' Finally, his hand came out. Baptiste took it. 'Welcome to Clermiers, Officer Baptiste. And consider yourself lucky too.'

'He's never lucky,' Marie said. 'Why do you say that?'

Mailloux turned and pointed at the filling station clock. 'Because it's ten past nine. Sunday. I'm here all night Monday to Friday. But weekends we shut at nine. Once I've cleared up, I'm gone. *Bonne nuit.*'

5

The cottage Charles Augustin had rented from his boss Laurent two months before lay on the edge of Boulliers, but he'd soon learned it was near enough to the public housing blocks and terraces to make him and his wife cautious of an evening. Always lock up. Always keep a light on outside. Never leave anything easily stealable lying around.

A couple of weeks before, Augustin had found Didier Hubert, one of the gang kids, hanging round watching Noémie leave for a stint in the *Amis* clubhouse. He hadn't taken to one of the boy's remarks, or the way he looked at her. Augustin was a powerful man in his early forties who'd done a little amateur boxing when he was younger. He wasn't above using his fists when he needed to. All the same, Hubert's father Eric was known to be an evil bastard, feared by pretty much everyone on the estate. Rumoured to deal in dope, pornography and stolen goods, poaching deer and pheasant on the side. It was enough to warn the young Hubert off with a few sharp words, to make sure he knew there'd be consequences if he came too close to the Augustins' only daughter.

Who was now late back from her evening with the English lodger, Daniel Murray, to her mother's annoyance.

'Where did they plan to go?' Martine asked. 'Did she tell you?'

The dinner plates were still on the table. That night's beef stew half-eaten. He normally cleaned the plate. Maybe the food wasn't so good.

'She's nineteen. What do you think?'

'I think they've been gone a long time.'

He shrugged and kept quiet.

'He likes her,' Martine added. 'I think he lacks the courage to say so.'

Augustin took his wife's hand. 'Best we stay out of the lives of teenagers. It's still the weekend. They deserve a little freedom. More than we ever had. Now . . .'

He got up and took the car keys off the sideboard.

'Oh, for pity's sake, Charles. Not on a Sunday. Does Bruno Laurent think you're his slave?'

She winced. That was badly put. Charles Augustin may have spent six months in Clermiers on his own, but he was still acutely aware he was one of the few black faces around. He'd been grateful Laurent had given him a job in the first place. No one else was offering anything like the kind of contract Laurent had in mind, and accommodation too, even though Augustin had accountancy qualifications as good as anyone's. If the hours were flexible and on occasion long, so be it.

22

'There's a stock take at the Hermitage.' The hotel restaurant Laurent owned ten kilometres out of town. A fancy place, somewhere the man had never invited them. 'It's got to be done overnight.'

'When will you be back?'

'Depends . . .'

'How long am I supposed to wait before I get worried about Noémie?'

Augustin smiled, took her in his arms and kissed her. 'You're her mother. You never stop worrying.'

She tapped her watch. 'Gone ten. She should be here. She—'

There was a knock on the door, loud. It made her jump.

'Hello!' cried a young English voice.

Daniel Murray was on the step, smiling, a little woozy-looking.

Her husband scowled at him. 'You've been drinking, young man.'

'Just a little wine.' He grinned, face flushed. 'I am in France after all.'

Martine Augustin barged her way to the step and looked around. It was pitch dark. Somewhere there were voices. The local kids, she guessed. They were always flitting through the shadows. 'Where's Noémie?'

The question seemed to baffle him. 'I don't know. She went off after we played tennis. I met . . . someone I knew. We had pizza.' He stopped, seemed to detect something in her attitude. 'Isn't she back yet?'

'Did she say where she was going?'

'She said she needed a shower. It was so hot.' He looked worried suddenly. 'She hasn't been home at all?'

'Charles . . .' Martine stepped out into the street and bawled out her daughter's name. No reply except a cackle of male laughter from somewhere out in the dark pool of night. 'Something's not right.'

'I'll have a word with her when she gets back,' he said.

'No. I really think—'

He turned on her, suddenly furious. 'What is it now? Is there anything in this house that's not down to me? Am I responsible for everything?'

She was taken aback by that unexpected outburst. 'I didn't say you were responsible at all, did I?'

'You don't need to. It's always me. Not now. She's nineteen. There's a boy or something out there. Let her have her own life. It doesn't belong to you. Enough . . .' He picked up his jacket. 'I've work to do.'

There was a full moon, so bright it bathed Boulliers in a flattering silver light.

Charles Augustin ignored his wife's continued bleating and headed for his car.

6

The police house was a two-storey building half a kilometre out of town, lights on in the right-hand half, music blaring out of the open windows. Springsteen, 'Born to Run'. A shiny Alfa Romeo Spider stood on the drive. His mother made a savage remark about the impracticality of two-seater sports cars then parked alongside an ancient green Citroën *deux chevaux* next to it. What should have been lawn was a dense thicket of tall, parched grass, clearly unmown in months.

'You want me to ask about a hotel?' he said as he got out. They hadn't talked much about the practicalities of the trip. He'd only decided he was leaving his Renault 5 with Charlotte that morning when she came round and burst into tears about work, about feeling guilty, how she wasn't sure she was making the right decision leaving him at all. That last part had been easy to resolve: she was, he told her, and handed over the keys. Then called his mother, who was, as he expected, quite furious.

The front door was open, the keys to the apartment in an envelope with his name. His new temporary home seemed spacious but only because there was so little in it. A living room with a sofa, a bedroom, a bathroom, a small kitchen.

His mother pointed at the sofa and said it was his.

While she headed off, flip flops clattering on the linoleum floor, Baptiste bounced on the cushions like a teenager, said a quiet 'ouch' and wondered how much sleep he was likely to get. He watched his mother throw off her sandals and fall on the mattress in the bedroom, then followed her in. Before long they could hear the couple next door.

'That girl's loud,' Marie said. 'Doesn't sound like she's faking it either.'

'I'll take your word on that.'

'I do hope they won't be at it all night long.'

He closed the door behind him. It didn't make much difference.

'The sofa, Julien. I told you.'

'I know. I will. But there's something that needs saying.'

She folded her arms and gave him a motherly scowl. 'Oh dear. That does sound ominous.'

'You need to accept this is what I do. All this . . . carping and criticism. It's pointless.'

'Why?'

'Because it doesn't bother me anymore. I've lived with your disapproval most of my adult life. You hated me joining the police. You disliked Charlotte because you thought her a snob.'

'She is a snob.'

'A snob would surely never have been with me, would she?'

She waved that away. 'Pedantry.'

'Now you complain she's left me for someone else, as if it's my fault.'

'Isn't it?'

'Possibly.' He came and sat on the edge of the bed. 'But if that's the case it's my business, not yours.'

The woman next door screamed out loud, with such force it almost seemed to shake the walls. Then cried out an obscenity.

Marie laughed. 'That's a new one on me.'

'Me too. We have to accept we are who we are. I won't change. You won't change me either.' He smiled, then patted the bed clothes. 'Nor would I waste a minute dreaming I might change you.'

'You mean crazy? And old?'

'You're fifty.'

'Fifty-one.'

'That's not old.'

She shuffled up against the wall, reached over and took his hands. Hers were wrinkled, scaly, a nervous complaint or so he thought. Not that she talked about her health, about herself much at all.

'I'll get there soon enough. This is how it ends, isn't it? Your offspring sitting on the edge of the bed, the way I used to when I came in to read you stories back home. Positions reversed. The first sign the decline is now in train.'

There were so many memories there. 'It was always you. Not Dad. Telling the stories.'

'Ha! Your father always had too many big things going round his head to waste time on fairy tales. Those big things were fairy tales too, of course. He just didn't realise. Or if he did, he never let on. We met as students, idealistic, engrossed in one another. I suspect we never really progressed from there.'

'We had plenty of good times, me and him. In the park. Playing football. Doing men things.'

She nodded. 'Then one day he was gone and a part of me went with him. It's a cliché, naturally, but then grief usually is. Everything that could be said has been. I wonder if we inherit it. From others. Books and the cinema. More fairy tales. That we feel this way because we believe we're supposed to. Whatever, I've been lonely ever since, which seems real and perhaps it shouldn't. Doesn't matter. It's like I lost a limb, and I could still sense the ghost of it, the way they say you do when they amputate a leg or an arm. Was it obvious?'

They never had this kind of conversation. Something must have been building all the way through that long and torturous car ride from Paris, windows open trying to dissipate the enervating heat.

'We're both tired. In the morning . . .'

'In the morning you'll be going to your new job. I'm sorry I take things out on you. It's mean. It's pointless. You deserve better than a cranky old woman on your back.'

Baptiste shrugged. 'I didn't have anyone else to drive me out here.'

She laughed. 'That's my son. Always going for the practical solution.'

'I suppose I hoped you'd find someone else.'

That got a snort, half anger, half amusement. 'One man like your father's quite enough for one lifetime, thank you. Frederic was as stubborn, as clever and, yes, as sly as you can be. Gentle as a lamb mostly, and then suddenly, out of nothing at all, there'd be that sudden, fiery temper. I was never frightened of him. Not quite. Sometimes I knew exactly where we stood. Others . . . I didn't have a clue. No idea where he might be going, what he might do, what he was thinking.' She prodded her son in the chest with a forefinger. 'I see all that in you, and it worries me. It makes me remember that day we lost him. Dead through trying to pick up a rubbish bin to throw at some idiot cop in a helmet, a shield in front of him, a baton in his hand. For what?'

He squeezed her hand. 'The doctors said his heart was weak. He never knew.'

'Balls. He just never told me. Never wanted me to worry, I guess. I only found out later when he was gone.'

Baptiste didn't say a word. She glared at him.

'But I see this isn't news.'

'He was going to the doctor quite often, wasn't he? I

27

remember that.' A shrug, a smile. 'It's not hard to work out. Dad was no fool.'

'He was a rebel. He hated to be told what to do. Where he belonged. What he should think. How he ought to behave.' She sighed. 'Arrogant, impulsive and selfish when he felt like it as well. Just like you. Who now rebels against your rebellious parents even though your father is long in the grave.'

She took his face in her wrinkled hands. 'Oh god, Julien. The trouble with men like you is they're so good at seeing into others and incapable of recognising themselves. The trouble with women like me is it's the other way round. I keep staring inside at the darkness and take out what I see there on whoever happens to be nearest. You, usually.'

He frowned. 'I'm used to it. We never pretended we were the perfect family.'

'We didn't. Sometimes there's so much of him in you it's like he's not dead at all. That sharpness you can turn on like a tap. Then that anger that just happens and you never realise it's mostly aimed at yourself. The endless, dogged curiosity. The decency and the cunning. I watch and, just as I did with your father, I wonder what you're not telling me. What you might do when I'm not there. Also . . .' She patted his jacket where he kept the constant pack of Disque Bleu. 'You smoke too much. Just like him.'

Baptiste laughed. 'I'm twenty-six. The fledgling has to fly the nest.'

'I know. I know. But I'm still your mother. You never stop wondering where that fledgling might be headed.' She bent his head down and kissed him once over the brow, just as she'd done when he was little, at the end of a bedtime story. 'I suppose you want me to go back to Paris tomorrow?'

He didn't know what to say.

'Yes or no?'

'I could maybe find you a hotel if you really think—'

'You don't want me here.'

'I didn't say that!'

'Clermiers can't be a total dump. That funny young chap at the petrol station said something about a château. Nowhere can be completely without interest, can it?'

The noises started up again next door. A loud and pulsing performance, this time in perfect rhythm with the squealing bed springs.

'Jesus,' Marie Le Gall said between moans. 'No worries. Decision made. You can deal with this madhouse yourself. Just remember to call your crazy old mother now and again if you please.'

7

Clermiers, Monday, 19 July 1976

Mornings in Clermiers police station were rarely busy. Just one officer in reception that day, Pascal Bonnay, thirty-five, unambitious, with a wife seven months pregnant whose constant complaints always sent him out of the house early. Dupont, the station captain, was long divorced, kept a couple of mistresses at a distance out of town and rarely arrived before nine. But he was there at his desk in his private office when Bonnay turned up that morning, a black look on his narrow, scowling face. When the captain, never the sunniest of men, told him to deal with anything that happened himself, he had calls to make and two newcomers to deal with shortly, Bonnay was only too happy to oblige.

Then the Augustins marched through the door along with an English kid who'd been boarding with them. Bonnay knew they were newcomers. Word had got round before Christmas that Bruno Laurent had found himself a black man as a new employee. The mother and girl turned up early that summer and didn't seem to go out much, let alone make friends. Bonnay

29

listened to a minute of their whines, got out his notepad and pen, made them sit down and asked if they wanted coffee.

'To hell with coffee,' Martine Augustin snapped back. 'Our girl's vanished.'

He thought about making one for himself but instead began to take notes. Slowly. This issue would, he felt sure, wind up on Dupont's desk, to the captain's intense disgust. The more Bonnay could delay that moment, the less vile Dupont's temper might be when he was disturbed.

Bonnay scribbled down the date and time and looked up from his notebook. 'You say your daughter's missing?'

'Jesus Christ,' the mother cried. 'How many times do we have to tell you?'

'We've been out all night looking,' her husband added.

'Daniel and me anyway.' She cast him a sour look. 'We didn't see you till what . . . four?'

'I told you . . . I was working.'

'No one answered the phone. In a hotel.'

He grimaced. 'Closed for the stock take. Like I said.'

'We went all over the estate,' the English kid added, trying to cool things down. 'No one saw her come back to Boulliers.'

'No one *said* they saw her come back,' Bonnay pointed out. 'What if you were out? And she couldn't get in?'

The wife looked ready to lose it. 'Noémie's got a key! We're not idiots.'

The husband seemed almost embarrassed. Who wouldn't be with a hysterical wife like her? Something clerical in Laurent's sprawling empire, a gofer. No trouble to the police, which was smart of him. Dupont wasn't keen on foreigners.

First he needed names, addresses, dates of birth. Daniel Murray didn't have his passport with him which in itself, Bonnay said, was a breach of the law, one he would, on that occasion, ignore.

Still, he scribbled down the details with a painstaking sluggishness.

The mother watched, close to tears, of fury more than anything. 'This is outrageous. She's out there somewhere. While you sit on your fat arse asking stupid questions.'

Bonnay put down the pen and scratched his cheek. 'She's nineteen. How many nineteen-year-old girls don't bunk off with a boy now and again? Then slink back later, head down, praying to be forgiven.'

'Noémie isn't like that.'

'You've no idea how many times I've had a parent say that very thing, madame. What would you suggest we do? How do we start?' He waved an arm around the empty station. 'I have one colleague on holiday, another sick. I'm forbidden from leaving this desk. Our replacement officers have yet to arrive. First, we establish the facts then embark upon the correct course of action. Do you think I can pick up the phone and summon a helicopter or something?'

'Why not?' Murray asked.

'Because this is Clermiers. Not Paris. Not London. Not one of those cities where people go missing for no good reason. A quiet little town where occasionally teenagers take themselves off. Usually out of boredom.' He stared at the parents. 'Am I wrong?'

'You are,' said Martine Augustin. 'Completely. Here.'

She passed over a photo. Bonnay looked at it and groaned.

'Oh. Yes. Her. She's quite the looker.'

'Her?' the mother roared. 'My daughter has a name. Noémie Augustin.'

She was smiling for the camera, outside in a garden somewhere. White shirt. Long neat hair, quite straight. Bright, smart eyes. 'The black girl. I noticed her riding her bike the other day.' He passed the photo back. 'When did you last see her? Where do you think she might have gone?'

8

Baptiste and his mother woke early, disturbed again by sounds next door. Voices this time, happy, and lots of carefree laughter. Then silence. He'd been expecting his mother to wade in against their neighbour. Just after seven thirty, she flip-flopped out to the front of the house where their neighbours had parked themselves by a table and chairs and her frown soon vanished. The couple there were all smiles and charm. They had fresh pastries on the table, croissants, butter, jam. Coffee, a big pot for four.

Étienne Fatoussi was another young officer dispatched to the provinces as part of the new training development scheme. He'd driven up from Marseille two days before. A new Alfa Romeo didn't seem to be the usual car for a junior cop, but Baptiste kept that to himself as Fatoussi introduced his friend, Bernadette, poured coffee, and offered round the pastries he'd bought from the town bakery that morning.

Bernadette, it seemed, was a local girl he'd met the day before after parking his glittering Alfa outside a café in town. She didn't say much but she smiled at him a lot. Étienne Fatoussi had dark Mediterranean looks, neat black hair, the kind of eyes some people called 'soulful', neat, well-cut blue shirt and trousers, made to measure maybe. He reminded Baptiste of the actor Sami Frey, so much he wondered if he'd be enough of a cinephile to be able to do the Madison dance from *Bande à part*. Baptiste, who thought little of his own appearance, and regarded clothes as practical matters to be judged on comfort and cost, found Fatoussi one of the most unlikely cops he'd ever encountered.

'How long's your incarceration in Clermiers, Julien?'

'They didn't say exactly.'

Fatoussi held up two fingers. 'Two months in purgatory. That's what I told them. Two months in the north is as much as I stomach. After that it's back to Marseille. To civilisation.'

'Can I come?' Bernadette asked.

He raised his glass and winked. 'We shall see, sweetie. Who knows . . . in two months if you'd really want to?'

Baptiste tapped his watch. Time to go.

Fatoussi sighed and began helping Bernadette clear away the breakfast things. The ready, charming smile was gone. 'Just so you know . . . I popped in to see our new colleagues when I arrived. There was only the captain there and some chubby chap who looked like he'd just fallen off the turnip truck. The captain's name is Dupont. He thinks he's a tough piece of work.' Fatoussi grinned. 'We'd eat him for breakfast in Marseille, bones and all. But maybe in this weird little dump he can think he's king. All the same, we need to watch out there, Julien. That man does not want a pair of strangers here. Welcome we are not.'

9

Véronique Laurent woke to the smell of burning. She was, as usual lately, in the guest quarters, a bungalow in the grounds of the Laurent family mansion. There'd be a divorce at some point, when she agreed to it, when Bruno came up with enough money. No kids, thank god. That was one subject on which they'd both seen eye to eye. And anyway, fate had decided otherwise to seal the deal.

She threw on some clothes and wandered outside. The Laurents had lived on the same estate for almost two centuries, Clermiers aristocracy. Unlike most of their peers – old families that had withered away into bankruptcy or worse, moved down to middle-class mediocrity – the Laurents had prospered through her husband's aggressive pursuit of business and financial opportunities, especially when it came to picking up failing enterprises at a bargain price. All the more reason he could bring the farce of their twelve-year marriage to an end with a generous settlement.

The day was already too hot, the air, flecked with black flakes from a fire somewhere, so dry it made her throat hurt. She found him round the corner behind the empty stables. He was in the old khaki boiler suit he wore when he wanted to pretend to be a simple farmer, poking at the dying embers of a small bonfire with a pitchfork.

'I didn't hear you come back,' she said.

He turned and scowled at her. The smoke was so thick and black it had marked his face. Still handsome, she thought, still the man she fell for. She'd just ignored the warning signs and hoped he might one day change.

'Does that matter?'

'I am allowed to worry about you, Bruno. This is a failed marriage. Not a war.'

He grunted something inaudible.

'Is it really wise to start a fire at a time like this? Everywhere's so dry. It's a tinder box.' She swiped away a smouldering fleck of something black floating through the air. It stank. 'Fire can fly. If you started something in this weather even Dupont might not be able to keep you out of the papers . . .'

He stopped, came over. Close up, he looked tired, hung-over maybe. There was the smell of booze still about him. 'I've started nothing. How did your night go?'

Véronique Laurent shrugged and said nothing. What business was it of his?

They stood there, the angry silence building between them. Then she said, 'I imagine it's pointless asking what you're burning and why.'

'Papers. Documents I no longer need. Or wish to share with others.'

'You really are a man of mystery at times, Bruno. I'm going shopping.'

'That makes a change.'

'Anything I can get you?' She felt the collar of his grubby boiler suit. 'Clean clothes?'

34

Dupont expected them in the station by nine. That, to Baptiste, meant they ought to be early. Bernadette was fussing over Fatoussi when he rapped on the door across the hall.

'Ready as I'll ever be, Julien.' He was in uniform, smart and neatly pressed, and stared at Baptiste who wore the plainest of plain clothes.

'My son dislikes formal wear,' Marie Le Gall said, leaning on the corridor wall, ready to leave. 'One of his few saving graces.'

'They never told me I was to be in uniform. So . . . why?'

Fatoussi held open the door and let Bernadette out. One peck on the cheek and a few affectionate words between them. Then all four were outside, staring at the searing day. The bugs, the mosquitoes, the midges were swarming all around. Insects risen from the dead, dry fields and the miasmic waters of the Chaume.

Baptiste looked at his mother's car and cursed himself. The bike, so carefully locked to the holder he'd bought for the boot, was gone. Just as the petrol station man, Mailloux, had predicted. He'd been too tired, too occupied, to remember to stash it somewhere safe the night before.

'Thieving little bastards,' Fatoussi said when he realised. 'It'll be the dregs from that estate of theirs. The fat guy in the station said that was the only place they got trouble.' He turned and looked back at the house. Overnight someone had painted a few words of obscene graffiti on the side wall. Something less than complimentary about the police. 'Perhaps we have more work to do here than we expected, my friend.'

'All yours,' Marie Le Gall said and set off through the thicket of parched grass towards her car.

'Wait . . .' Baptiste was taking in the graffiti, the theft of the bike. Some locals had clearly been busy during the night. To what extent . . .

A scream, his mother's angry high voice. Then she was rolling on the ground, shrieking obscenities.

He was there first, Bernadette close behind.

'Watch out!' his mother screamed. 'There's glass. All over the place.'

Baptiste picked his way carefully across the thicket of overgrown lawn. There was what looked like a smashed wine bottle, maybe two, hidden in the grass. His mother had stumbled on some pieces, fallen, got cut some more. Blood was seeping around her ankles, staining the ancient plastic flip-flops as she lay back gasping in the scorched tall grass, insects buzzing all round them.

'We have to get her to the hospital,' Bernadette said. 'Douai.'

That got a quick response.

'I don't want to go to any damned hospital.'

With a gentle, practised skill, Bernadette bent down, looked at the wound, ran her fingers around the blood and the cut. 'Listen. I'm a nurse. When I say you need to get this looked at, I mean it. You may need stitches. When did you last have a tetanus shot?'

'A what?'

His mother had always hated doctors, hospitals, anything to do with medicine.

'This isn't an accident,' Fatoussi muttered. 'Some evil bastard put that there. If I find the son of a bitch he'll be sorry as hell.'

'Welcome to Clermiers,' Bernadette said with a quick, grim smile. 'You'll live, Marie. You just won't be playing football for a while. Come on, love. I'll drive you there. I doubt they'll keep you in, especially if you continue mouthing off like now.'

Baptiste took his mother's hand. 'I'll come with you.'

'Oh please.' She clutched at her ankle. 'It's not that bad. You've got a new job to start. Why the hell did I leave Paris?'

'When they kick you out, take my place. I can move upstairs,' Fatoussi said. 'The rooms up there are empty. The keys are in the door.'

A moment, then Marie Le Gall said, 'Can you please make sure I'm not beneath you two? I need my beauty sleep.'

Bernadette snorted, loud and ribald. 'Done. Besides I'm working nights from now on. You'll have Étienne all to yourselves.'

Not a word.

'Won't they?' she added, puzzled by the evasive silence.

'*Naturellement, chérie* . . .' he said in the end.

Baptiste helped his mother to her feet, half carried her to the battered green *deux chevaux* Bernadette indicated was hers. She winced with pain as they eased her into the flimsy passenger seat.

'I'm coming with you,' he said. 'To hell with work. No arguments.'

'Don't be ridiculous,' his mother replied then slammed the door and told Bernadette to drive.

The old car vanished up the road puffing blue smoke in its wake.

Étienne Fatoussi was walking round his bright red Alfa, shaking a fist. There was a deep scratch mark running the length of the driver's side from the bonnet to the boot. 'I'm going to call my cousin and get him to drive this home. Can't leave anything decent in this dump. If I get hold of those bastards—'

Baptiste trudged round the tall dry grass, dragging his feet, carving out a safe path. There was no more broken glass elsewhere as far as he could see.

'Leave that to me,' he said then climbed into Fatoussi's car.

11

Ten minutes later Baptiste was introducing himself to the lone officer on duty, Bonnay, the one he'd heard about. Fatoussi was on the phone to his cousin in Lille asking him to pick up the

Alfa and keep it safe for a while. Clermiers police station was small, empty and could do with a good clean.

A door opened and Dupont came out, a grizzled man in his late forties, sour-faced and balding, his uniform creased and worn. Fatoussi came off the phone and saluted.

'Cut that crap,' Dupont said. 'Let's get this straight. I didn't ask for you two. Just because I've got one of my idiots on vacation and the other in a straitjacket doesn't mean we can't cope.'

Baptiste had a habit of judging people instantly, one he was trying to lose. But not at that moment. 'If you want us to leave, Captain . . .'

'I'd say so. You're the one from Paris then? I imagine you think you know it all. Parisians usually do. Won't wash here.' He stared out of the window at the red Alfa. 'I told you yesterday a car like that's not welcome in Clermiers. Especially if you're in the job.'

'As I discovered,' Fatoussi said. 'It'll be gone by this afternoon.'

Dupont reached into his pocket and threw him some keys. 'Good. And don't wear that uniform again. I want you both in plain clothes. Don't draw attention.'

Fatoussi didn't like that. 'In Marseille, attention is what deters them.'

'Really? You get an eight-year-old Simca. Don't bring it back with more dents than it's got already. Also . . . Bonnay . . . is the radio working yet?'

'Allemand usually does the batteries.'

Dupont walked over and placed a hand on his shoulder. It was not a friendly gesture. 'Allemand is eating flies in the chuckle factory and if you don't buck up you'll join him. Find some and give them to our guests here. Who knows? Maybe it works for a change.'

'They painted stuff on the police house and left broken glass hidden on the lawn,' said Fatoussi. 'His mother walked into it.'

The captain scowled at Baptiste. 'Why's *he* telling me this? Is she hurt?'

'Not so bad,' Baptiste said. 'She's at the hospital. If you've got nothing for us we can go looking for the little shits who did it.'

Dupont laughed. 'Jesus Christ you pair have a few things to learn. There are two sides to Clermiers. This part, Hauteville, which is quiet and decent, and we'll keep it that way. Mostly by making sure the pond scum from Boulliers don't cross the river and trouble us here.'

The door opened. The skinny young man from the petrol station walked in.

'Oh look,' said Dupont. 'There's one here already. What do *you* want?'

'Baptiste,' Mailloux said, with a quick smile. 'At work already.'

'Not exactly—'

'Talk to me!' Dupont yelled. 'What is it?'

To his credit, Baptiste thought, Gilles Mailloux didn't seem in awe of the thuggish captain.

'I heard Noémie was missing. Has she turned up yet?'

'What business is it of yours?' asked Dupont.

'She's a neighbour. Is she OK?'

Fatoussi and Baptiste shared puzzled glances. Bonnay had his head down, staring at the desk.

'The parents were in here with that English kid,' Dupont said. 'I told them to get themselves home and wait for her to turn up. Teenagers go walkabout all the time. It's nothing. Not worth wasting our time.'

'It's just . . .' Mailloux stopped.

'Just what?' Baptiste asked.

'When I was closing up last night . . . there were noises, lights, round the old château boathouse. I just thought it was odd.'

'Don't be ridiculous,' Dupont snapped. 'No one's used

39

that place in years. What's this got to do with some girl from Boulliers?'

'Sometimes the kids from round my way go there. To smoke. Do stuff. I just thought—'

'You're wasting our time.'

'Maybe. But if you want to let me finish . . .'

'Tell us, Gilles,' said Baptiste.

'I thought I heard someone screaming. I'm not sure. And there are sounds you can . . . misinterpret let's say.'

Bonnay looked up from the desk. 'You could have got in touch if it was that serious.'

Mailloux stood his ground. 'I don't know if it was, do I? Besides, if I'd called you out for nothing on a Sunday night . . . how would that work out for me?'

Baptiste rattled the keys to the station Simca. 'We could take a look. If someone showed us the way—'

'I'll do that.' Mailloux looked keen. 'I like Noémie. She's nice. Kind.' He beamed then. 'She's pretty too. Really striking. I don't think she's the sort who'd just walk off and not tell her mum and dad.'

Dupont nodded at the door. 'The kid's from Boulliers. Go waste your time. Chances are she'll be home crying her eyes out, broke and hungry, before long.'

To Baptiste's astonishment, that was it. 'Have you got a name and address for the girl? A statement?'

'Ah.' Bonnay woke up, tore off some pages from his notebook. 'I talked to them. Well, the mother mostly. The black guy looked as if he didn't want to be here. There was an English kid with them too. Didn't come in with his passport. I kicked his arse for that.'

'Good work,' said Baptiste.

'Thank you!' Bonnay was obviously unfamiliar with sarcasm. He'd located some batteries in the desk drawer and fed them into the radio. 'Take this too. I hope you can read my writing.'

The Simca was round the corner, old, filthy, spotted with

rust. Baptiste got in the driver's seat, Mailloux the back. Fatoussi climbed in the passenger side and ducked down beneath the dusty dashboard.

'What is it?' Baptiste asked.

'My cousin Vincent is turning up to take the Alfa. If he sees me in a shitheap like this, I'll never hear the end of it.'

Mailloux pointed at the road down the hill on the opposite side of the square. The Simca started on the third try, the engine in the back wheezing like an asthmatic old man as it came to life.

'Please god, Vincent, don't look,' Fatoussi begged as they bumped off across the cobbles.

12

Martine and Charles Augustin sat in the front room, lost for words, drained of emotion. Daniel Murray had gone out to look for Noémie again. They hadn't asked where or how.

'You want a coffee?' Charles said in the end.

Theirs was a happy marriage mostly, rarely marred by arguments. She just wished he didn't work so hard, didn't have to spend so much time out of the house, at night too often. It didn't seem to fit with what she thought of as accountancy.

'I called and called,' she said. 'No one answered.'

'Oh god!' He threw up his arms in despair. 'How many times do I have to say it? I was on my own. The hotel was closed for maintenance. The stock is mostly in the storeroom out the back. I didn't hear the phone. I'm sorry.'

She wasn't having that. 'Did you argue with her? About waitressing for those stuck-up men who think they own us? *Les Amis?*'

He grimaced. 'Waitressing. That's all she did. Not exactly like sending her down a mine or something, is it? I had worse at her age.'

41

'Did you argue?'

He went to get himself a coffee. When he came back, she was upstairs. He could guess where.

Noémie's bedroom was tidy as always, all her things from Calais neatly stashed away, a magazine open on the little desk alongside her pens.

'Did you argue, Charles?'

'No. I said if she wanted to quit working for them it was up to her. I just suggested she keep going until she found something else. She wanted the money. I didn't have any to spare.'

'What did she need money for?'

'Everyone wants money. Maybe she hated it here and didn't want to say. Two months. She's hardly got any friends except that English boy.'

Martine began to cry. He tried to wipe away her tears but they came too fast.

'Where is she?' Martine whispered.

'We'll find her. Maybe . . . maybe Daniel will.'

'And where,' she asked, 'is he?'

13

'You've heard of the Château de Mortery?' Mailloux asked, cramped in the back of the battered car.

'Can't say I have,' Baptiste replied.

'Used to be a big baron's lair. Centuries back. I always thought they might take us there on a visit when I was at school. But no . . . I had to read about it down the library.'

Fatoussi stuck his head over the dashboard, trying to make sure they were clear of the square and anyone who might see. 'Nice of you to turn up like that, Gilles. From what the captain says you don't get many bookish types round your way. Or folk who like to help the police.'

Mailloux shrugged. 'I speak for myself, not the population of Boulliers.'

Mortery was in the hands of the same ancient family for centuries, he said. Shortly after the First World War they went bust, and the place had been left to go to ruin ever since. The estate was vast, running from the foot of the hill on which Hauteville stood down to the river Chaume where a dilapidated boathouse sat on the southern bank.

'The one piece of juicy history I found out at the library . . .' Mailloux waited to make sure they were listening. 'The Marquis de Sade was a secret guest of the hosts for several months, after he escaped from prison in Savoy. Need I say more?'

'You do for me,' Fatoussi said. 'Who was he again?'

Baptiste was aghast. 'The Marquis de Sade. Did you never do history at school?'

A wave of the hand then, '*Bof.* Every lesson. Doesn't mean I was listening.'

'There were the customary depravities of their class,' Mailloux went on. 'Prostitutes, male and female, many complaining of being assaulted, wounded with knives even. In the end the hosts kicked him out and de Sade was arrested once more and sent back to jail.'

They drove past the petrol station. A man in a greasy boiler suit was in the shop looking bored. The walls of the castle, snaggle-toothed but still forbidding, rose on the left as the car wound down the hill.

'When did you hear this commotion?' Baptiste asked.

'Around eleven.'

'You told us last night you were closing at nine.'

A pause, and then Mailloux said, 'I was closing the petrol station. The work doesn't end when I stop pumping fuel. Some maintenance on the tanks. Got to do the books. Clean up. Customer records. Bruno Laurent is a stickler for that.'

'Another guy I've never heard of,' Fatoussi said.

'Bruno Laurent.' Mailloux waved his hand back at Haute-ville. 'He owns most of this. Most of the people too.'

Baptiste was trying to think straight. Rural France was so different. 'Customer records?'

'The visitors we get.'

'You mean you write down the number plate of every car that stops for fuel?'

'Laurent insists on it and he's the boss. Wants to make sure no one's ripping him off. Quite a few people are on an account with us, so Sundays I have to add it all up. Is this important? There! The lane on the left.'

It was little more than a narrow track half-hidden by the branches of wilting elder bushes on both sides. Baptiste edged the Simca off the road and onto the dirt, clay by the looks of it. The suspension groaned as they rolled down towards the river, broad, muddy, quite low, judging by the depth of bank that was visible on the far side. There was a clearing at the end and a building, brick and timber, half in ruins, most of the roof missing, the remains of a small pier jutting out over the water. As they turned into the open space they could see the wrecked hull of a holed and capsized rowing boat at the outer edge of the boathouse.

Baptiste parked by the bushes and stepped out onto ground so hard, so parched it might have been concrete. A winding path of broken bricks led back up the hill, finishing at a high wall green with moss and algae. There was a red door there, half open.

'What exactly did you hear?'

'I was about to go home. Voices. People. Maybe music.' He looked apologetic. 'I'm probably wasting your time. I'm sorry. It's just . . . I really like Noémie. She's kind. Thoughtful. Different. Dupont may be a total bastard but he's not wrong when he says there aren't many in Boulliers like that.'

Fatoussi was hunting around already. The two of them followed. By the riverbank there were wine and beer bottles.

Discarded dog-ends. He picked one up, sniffed it, scowled. 'That's not Gauloises, for sure. You got a lot of dope on this estate of yours?'

'I keep my head down, my mouth shut, and my eyes closed,' Mailloux said. 'It's easier that way. I could get a kicking if some of them saw me talking to you two right now.'

There were a couple of syringes too and a cassette tape, clearly broken, the guts spilling out of the shattered plastic: Aerosmith, *Rocks*.

Nothing to suggest Noémie Augustin had been there as far as Baptiste could see. He was about to follow Fatoussi into the boathouse when there was the sound of a vehicle coming down the track.

14

Fabrice Blanc had been mayor of Clermiers for five years. His predecessor, Louis Gaillard, held the post for six, then won a seat on the regional council. It was a well-trodden path in local government in the area, one that led to cosy connections and access to money, both public and private. Blanc had no such ambitions. Ruling Clermiers was enough. His job was to be seen to govern well, to keep the town safe and, at least in Hauteville, presentable and prosperous. The drip feed of funds into Boulliers, cash that came mostly from Bruno Laurent's deep pockets, went some way to silencing the wails of the underprivileged there. But there was always a mutinous murmur on that side of the river, one the local press was wise enough to ignore. One Blanc was always keen to suppress.

The priest, Chauvin, arrived when summoned, bearing a bag of rich butter croissants from the baker down the street.

'I bought three,' he said, placing the pastries on the desk. 'I thought Louis was coming.'

So did Blanc. 'I can't raise him. Do you know where he might be?'

Chauvin looked almost offended by the question. 'Why should I? I was getting through paperwork this morning when you called. Then Dupont too. Both of you being infuriatingly oblique. Has something happened?'

Blanc scoffed. 'A teenage girl's missing. Hardly the end of the world. These two temporary officers who've been dumped on Dupont . . . they're out looking by the river.'

Chauvin tore his croissant to pieces, spilling flakes of pastry everywhere. 'Louis said they might be trouble.'

'Louis Gaillard's an old woman. He takes fright at a fly.'

The priest didn't argue. 'What are we supposed to do?'

Blanc wrinkled his pale and fleshy nose. 'Nothing. Dupont will deal with it as usual. Now . . . is there anything you wish to tell me? If so, say it. I need to know. I can only bury bodies, not ghosts.'

'There are no ghosts on my conscience,' Chauvin replied, quite puzzled. 'Or bodies. What on earth do you mean?'

Blanc patted his hand. 'As they say, ignorance is bliss, Christian. It usually is in your case.' He grabbed a croissant for himself. 'All the same I think we tread carefully for now. No more meetings of the *Amis* unless it's absolutely necessary. Until this Augustin girl returns home. How are you coping with this weather? Have we ever known it so hot and dry for so long?'

15

Dupont was driving an unmarked Renault, sparkling clean and recent. He parked it next to the Simca, rolled out, marched over, glared at Gilles Mailloux, and asked what, if anything, they'd found.

Baptiste pointed to the joint butts, the bottles, the syringes.

Dupont sniffed and walked along the bank, kicking them into the river.

'We may have needed them, sir,' Baptiste said.

'For what? To tell us the kids on Boulliers come here to smoke dope, pump poison into themselves and drink till they're stupider than usual? Do you think I don't know that already? This is one of their playgrounds. Nothing here I wouldn't expect.'

Mailloux stepped back and said nothing.

'What's that look for?' Dupont demanded. 'Well . . .? Is there anything to suggest this black kid was here?'

Étienne Fatoussi emerged from the boathouse carrying something. A thin strip of black fabric, shiny like fake silk.

'Found this on the ground by that path. I read Bonnay's notes. The English kid told him he saw a black dress in the girl's tennis bag.'

'*Thought* he saw. The kid also said some shit about bananas. Found any bananas?'

'No bananas, sir. But there was this.'

He unrolled the scrap of material to reveal a condom inside, used, leaking grey fluid onto the material.

Dupont burst out laughing. 'A miracle! Some Boulliers aphid who takes precautions.' He clicked his fingers. 'Give.'

Fatoussi glanced at Baptiste.

'I'm captain here,' Dupont snarled. 'You do what I say. Not him. Give.'

He snatched the ragged piece of cloth, maybe a hand wide, three times that long, scowled at the thing then threw it into the river. The four men watched it drift away on the sluggish current.

'Couldn't we have made some . . . some use of that?' Fatoussi asked.

Dupont paused and stared at the two of them. 'Do you have any reason to believe something actually happened here?'

'We've hardly started looking,' said Baptiste.

'Anything to suggest this isn't one more teenager bunking

47

off with a boy? Having a row with her parents? Or deciding quiet little Clermiers is just too boring to bear?'

Baptiste looked at the river, the black rag of dress disappearing on the muddy surface, a thin grey smear in its wake. 'We might have had . . .'

'It's spunk,' Dupont cried. 'That's all. Listen, both of you. I've lived here all my life. I've worked in that police station, from cadet to captain. I know this place better than the likes of you ever will. If there's anything wrong, it's down to the lowlifes of Boulliers. Or her parents.'

Baptiste took a couple of steps up the path. 'Gilles said he heard some noises from there. The château.'

'I think so,' Mailloux agreed.

'Nonsense.' Dupont took out his car keys. 'No one's been in that dump for years. Look. This girl's going to turn up before long, shame-faced and apologetic. You go round and see her parents. Talk to that English kid again. Ask around the estate. If she isn't back by tonight, I'll log her as a missing person. Put a description on the wires. She's probably on a bus or a train somewhere. Trying to pluck up the courage to come home.'

He pointed at each of them in turn. 'What I don't want is for you to make more of this than it is. You're not in Paris. Or Marseille. We don't do dramas in Clermiers, and I don't want you two starting one.'

They watched him leave.

Mailloux headed for the track. 'I can walk back, thanks.'

'You're working already?' said Baptiste.

'No. Sorry. I'm not going to be seen going into Boulliers with you guys.' He stopped for a moment. 'Please find Noémie. I used to see her dancing sometimes, on her own, when she thought no one was looking. A rose among our thorns.'

Baptiste had taken down the number of the police house. One phone in the hall for all four flats. He scribbled it out and passed it over. 'I'm grateful for your help, Gilles. We may need to call on you again. If you think of anything . . .'

Mailloux glanced at Dupont's car vanishing up the track. 'I'd really rather not get involved . . .'

'You don't need to talk to him. Talk to me. This is my number. I'll be discreet.'

He waved his hand, no. Still Baptiste held out the note.

'You'll be the death of me,' Mailloux said, then took it.

Part Two:

The Secret Dancer

16

11:50 a.m. Douai Prison, 15 November 1976

The executioner was a middle-aged man with a jowly, florid face, a walrus moustache, glassy eyes that never seemed to blink. He stood in the prison courtyard watching the workmen check over the assembly of the guillotine once more. A perfectionist, Baptiste thought, determined the final act would be carried out as quickly and efficiently as his masters demanded.

Gilles Mailloux had clammed up after picking at a croissant from a bakery down the road. Baptiste said he needed the toilet, dismissed the young man's offer to use the pot beneath his cell bed, and went outside. A cigarette was necessary too. The smoke from his Disque Bleu mingled with that of the executioner's pipe as they stood together beneath a grey winter sky. The man was called Perreault, a farmer from near Pontoise. The job had run through his family for three generations. When he was needed, he left the farm to his son and went wherever the Ministry of Justice demanded.

Perreault gestured at the guillotine. 'This thing is a piece of cake. Any idiot could do it. My father had to hang Nazis at Nuremberg. Now *that* . . .' He waved the stinking pipe in Baptiste's face '. . . is something else. You need to weigh your customers. Measure their height. Get it wrong and the

50

results . . . well, best left unsaid. I've never had to hang a man and I'm glad of that.'

Baptiste had to ask. 'If the message comes through from the Elysée to go ahead . . . how quickly . . .?'

'Minutes. Seconds if I had my way. No point in prolonging the process. Mailloux has refused a priest. All he wanted, I gather, was you. Do you know why?'

'I've no idea.'

'Well, we mustn't keep him waiting. I'll be in there swiftly with some men, we bind his hands, we lead him to the machine, take off his jacket, make sure the neck's clear. Blindfold him, strap him down and . . .' The pipe was out. He sniffed and tapped it on the wall, scattering blackened tobacco ashes on the filthy cobbles. 'If it takes more than five minutes, I haven't done my job.'

Baptiste was lost for words.

'You disapprove, I suspect.'

'Nothing personal. I don't believe there's a case for killing people, whatever they've done. It's judicial murder. Does nothing to deter. Nothing to deliver justice. Only vengeance.'

Perreault nodded. 'Maybe he's the last. The mood's turning. Your friend in there behaved so badly in court people were screaming for his blood. But that will fade. We won't be executing anyone much longer. I hope so, anyway. It's barbaric.'

This took Baptiste aback. 'Why do it then?'

The question seemed to puzzle him. 'Someone has to. Like I said, my father did this. My grandfather. Why should I pass on that burden to someone else?'

'You sleep at night?'

'Very well. All I do is lead a man to his death then pull a lever. I didn't put him there. He did. And you, Baptiste. I read up on the case. Do *you* sleep at night?'

'Not much.' He shrugged. 'But I never did before. Sleeping's not in my nature.'

51

'One must never mistake responsibility for blame. You did your job. As I'll do mine.'

The man assumed there would be no reprieve. He was probably correct in that, unless Baptiste could persuade Mailloux to talk.

'I understand why you look melancholy,' Perreault added. 'This is a miserable day for a miserable task. But you must leave your sorrow in this courtyard. Take it with you and that black dog could follow you through life. Believe me. I speak of something I know.'

The executioner packed his pipe away and came a little closer, spoke quietly so the men across the yard might not hear. 'Unless there's more to this than meets the eye.'

Say it, Baptiste thought. Someone needed to hear.

'I have my doubts.'

'We all have doubts. A man with nothing but certainties is more than likely a fool.'

'I don't think I made myself clear. I worked to put Gilles Mailloux in the dock. I did everything I could to find that poor girl. But Noémie Augustin's still lost—'

'That's not your fault.'

'Perhaps you're right.'

'Mailloux wouldn't speak! He wouldn't even have a lawyer! It's as if the creature wants to die.'

'It's that exactly.'

'Guilt,' Perreault went on. 'It eats away at a man. Rots his soul.' A nod at the cells. 'That fellow in there understands he's lost and wants the world to know it too.' He hesitated. 'You don't look convinced.'

Baptiste nodded. 'I brought the man to this fate. I never thought he'd be headed for the guillotine. If he'd talked, told us where she was. What had happened. All this would be different.'

'Quite.'

The cigarette had burned down so much it had reached his

52

nicotine-stained fingers. Baptiste threw the stub to the cobbles and ground it with his foot. 'The trouble is I'm not sure he can. Tell us, that is. I'm not sure he knows. All the story anyway. The more I turn it over in my mind, I'm not convinced Gilles Mailloux deserves to be headed for that blade of yours at all. There . . .' He patted Perreault's arm. The man looked shell-shocked. 'I'm sharing with you my present lack of sleep. This is unforgivable. The burden should be mine alone.'

There was a pack of guards waiting outside the cell door when he got back. The officers who would seize Mailloux by the arms and lead him to the guillotine, under Perreault's supervision. They didn't look in the least troubled by the job.

'No news from Paris?' he asked.

'If there was,' said the first, 'we wouldn't be standing here, would we?'

'You were very slow, Julien. If you don't mind me saying.'

Baptiste was on another cigarette. He couldn't stop himself listening for that knock on the door and the letter that might lead Gilles Mailloux to another cell for life, or that short walk to the blade outside.

'I was very stupid, I agree. I made many mistakes. Noémie Augustin's disappearance was an extraordinary case. I hope I never meet one like it again.'

'You can't let it go, can you?'

That was true. He wasn't sure that strange, scorching summer would ever leave him.

'Anyway. I didn't mean slow in that sense. I meant *slow*. Noémie goes missing some time during the night. You lot were barely waking up to that fact a day later.'

Baptiste had thought about that a lot. 'Blame Dupont. The man really didn't want all this on his doorstep.'

Mailloux sat back on his bed, raised an eyebrow, said nothing. The anaemic sun had shifted position. Now it was full on him, and Baptiste realised his first impression was mistaken.

53

He wasn't the same as before. In the summer he'd just seemed a skinny, pasty-faced young man, a little hunched, careworn. Something had happened since and perhaps it was his incarceration, the solitary confinement designed to keep him safe from other prisoners. His skin was more pallid, he'd lost weight to the point of being skeletal. In other circumstances Baptiste would have wanted him to see a doctor. But that was something else Gilles Mailloux had turned down.

'Even if Dupont hadn't dragged his feet,' Baptiste went on, 'it's not like you see in the movies. Not in a place like Clermiers. The man had a point as well. Usually when someone vanishes there's a rational explanation. An argument. A breakdown maybe. I think Dupont was hoping to convince himself things like that didn't happen in his sleepy little town . . .'

'He knew better than that, Baptiste. You're no fool. You do too, don't you?'

'All the same, you hope whoever's vanished will walk back through the door a few hours later. Apologies, hugs, tears.'

'There was very little usual about this, was there?'

'Still isn't—'

'Could you please stop smoking? Just for a little while. It's getting on my lungs.'

There was a rattle and the door opened suddenly. Baptiste's heart leapt into his mouth. One of the jailers was there, grinning.

'Canteen wants to know if the prisoner has any request for lunch. Choice is lamb stew or couscous.'

Mailloux grinned. 'Ah, my lifelong friend, Joel.'

'Good to see you keeping up your spirits, lad. Not long to wait now.'

'I was under the impression a condemned man got whatever he wanted.'

'Not here you don't. Lamb or couscous.'

'I'll pass. Baptiste?'

He shook his head and the door slammed shut.

'I'm going to keep on asking, Gilles. If you tell me where to look, I can be on the phone to Paris straight away. Maybe they'll reconsider. Think of the mother. Hasn't she been through enough?'

'Don't blame me for that!'

Not the answer Baptiste expected. 'Then who should I blame?'

He was barely listening, mind somewhere else altogether.

'You're the detective,' Mailloux said finally. He turned and stared at Baptiste. 'You tell me.'

The door burst open again, this time with a noisy violence that made them both jump. It was the same jailer. He had an envelope in his right hand, his left behind his back. He waved the letter and said, 'Oh, sorry, Gilles. That's not for you.' He switched the hands and revealed a small plate of biscuits in his left, walked in and placed them on the bed.

'Compliments of the canteen lady. She reckons it's bad to sit around waiting on things with an empty stomach.'

'*Merci*, Joel,' Mailloux said and held out the plate. 'But I'm trying to cut down on sugar. You have them. Please.'

'Just one.'

He grabbed a couple then, just as noisily as before, banged the door shut.

'Have they been pulling these tricks all along?'

'Joel, mostly. The rest are either surly or occasionally kind. It amuses him to bait the condemned man. I'm at one with it.'

'I could say something—'

'Why? What does it matter? Talk to me about Clermiers, Julien. I wish to know what you did that first day. After I took you down to the river and Fatoussi found that scrap of black dress and a condom. I meant it when I said I couldn't hang around. It would look bad and Boulliers is not the place for that. Do tell. Who knows?' He smiled, crooked teeth, a little yellow. 'Perhaps I will have that cigarette.'

17

Clermiers, Monday, 19 July

Baptiste drove past the garage where Gilles Mailloux worked nights, took the Simca down the hill to the river, crossed a modern and ugly concrete bridge and found himself in the kind of grim, grey post-war estate that had sprung up on the edge of so many towns and cities over the past few decades. The apartment blocks were low, three or four storeys, and looked poorly maintained. Signs of decay were everywhere, rubbish strewn on the street, bins toppled over, walls half-ruined, windows broken and blacked out.

Someone lobbed a stone as he crossed a junction. It clattered on the engine at the rear, got Fatoussi swearing again, promising to give someone a good kicking before long. Who threw it they couldn't see. The narrow alleys between the blocks were made for hiding and rapid escapes. Baptiste had worked in just such a neighbourhood in one of the rougher areas on the outskirts of Paris soon after he signed up for the police. He knew how hard it was to extract hard information in places like this. Anyone in a uniform was distrusted. On a more general level, he'd come to feel this kind of brutalist architecture fed into the local psyche. Men and women, particularly the young, made to live in an environment composed of rat runs, physical detritus, shadows, and places to hide, inevitably took on habits to match.

The radio crackled. Pascal Bonnay in the station saying his mother had been in touch. She was out of hospital, not badly hurt, but unable to walk far. Bernadette had taken her back to the police house and was helping her move into the downstairs apartment.

'That's good news,' Fatoussi said. 'I like your mum.'

'And she likes you . . .'

'That kid from the garage . . .'

'What about him?'

Fatoussi shrugged then pulled a face. 'I don't know. Always makes me feel uncomfortable when people just stand up all helpful and that. Most of them hate us. Why do it?'

Baptiste was astonished by the question. 'Maybe because he likes that girl and wants her found?'

'Yeah. He likes her.' He glanced across the car. 'Thinks she's pretty too. Striking. Still . . . what do I know?'

Ahead was the Avenue Laval, a long, straight road that ran parallel to the low bank of the Chaume. On the Hauteville side of the river willows wept into the grey water; on the other, the avenues and dead ends of Boulliers led into the estate. At the very end stood a few older houses, farm cottages from the days the area was purely agricultural. With a little imagination he could see how the place was once quiet and bucolic. Then a figure came out of nowhere to the left. Baptiste jammed his foot on the brakes, puny things that squealed and kicked back as he fought to stop the car.

Too weak, they crashed into a kid on a bike, sent him flying into the road as the car rolled on, something beneath its wheels.

Fatoussi was out in a flash, Baptiste behind them. A boy of maybe twelve was on the ground, crying, holding his elbow. Scruffy little urchin, cursing like a marine, most of it aimed in their direction. Scraped elbow, grazed arm, face as guilty as hell when he saw the car was police.

'You want to watch where you're going,' Fatoussi said. 'Another time you might be dead.'

He said nothing, just looked at Baptiste. Who went back to the car, reversed, got out and then pulled free the mangled frame of the bike that had fallen under its wheels.

His bike. The one that had vanished the night before.

Fatoussi had clocked that already, was getting a name out of the kid: Didier Hubert, lived with his dad in Dumas two streets away. Fourteen, older than he appeared. Like Mailloux, he had a weaselly look about him, feral.

'This bike . . .' Baptiste came over and stared into Hubert's scared, defiant face. 'Belonged to me. Someone stole it from the police house last night. Someone put broken glass in the front of our place. My mother stepped into it. She's just coming out of hospital.'

Hubert's eyes grew wide with terror. 'Wasn't me.'

'What?' Fatoussi asked. 'Stealing things? Scattering broken glass? Ruining the paintwork on my nice car—'

'Wasn't me!'

Baptiste took the kid by the collar. 'How did you get the bike, Didier?'

'Found it.'

Fatoussi laughed, loud and hollow. 'Jesus. If I had a *sou* every time I heard that . . .'

Baptiste tightened his grip. 'I don't like people hurting my mother. Where were you last night?'

He was scared. 'I didn't hurt no one. We were in Lille. Me and Dad. We went to see the football. Stayed at Uncle Franc's.'

'We'll check.'

'It's true!'

'The bike.'

The story came out piecemeal, stuttered, with a reluctance designed to make it seem true. That morning Hubert had gone for a walk by the river, got to the boathouse, found the bike abandoned.

'I didn't know it was stolen. I was just keeping it to see whose it was. I . . .' Now he was struggling. 'I was going to ride it into the police station and hand it over. That's where I was going. When you hit me. When you ran me over.' He scowled, found a grain of courage somewhere, brandished his bleeding arm at them. 'My dad won't like that when I tell him. You don't want to be on the wrong side of him.'

Baptiste gave him the lightest of slaps around the head. Hubert glared back. 'I'll tell him about that too.'

'Tell him what you like.'

The kid looked shiftier than ever.

'Why did you walk down the river? Why the boathouse? Why there?'

'Just did.'

The two men waited.

'Sometimes there's a party down there. Just wanted a look. Drunks throw up. Do stuff. Lose things. Money.' He scowled at the ruined bike. 'Not seen one of them before.'

Baptiste went over, picked it up and threw it in Hubert's direction.

'All yours, Didier. If I find one word you told me is a lie . . .' He grinned, winked. 'I promise I'll make your sorry life hell. Now get out of here and take this thing with you.'

They watched him slink off, dragging the mangled remains of the bike.

Baptiste lit another cigarette. 'Fourteen. Looks twelve. Did you see his arms?'

'He got scraped when we hit him.'

'He did. But he had bruises. Some recent. Some old. The kind you get when you're beaten about. At home usually.' He hesitated. 'Maybe I shouldn't have come on so heavy. I just thought . . .'

'You thought he left that broken glass. Understandable. I didn't see that coming. You turning like that. Scared him good.' He nudged Baptiste's elbow. 'Scared me a little.' He winked. 'You've hidden depths, my friend.'

There was a dent on the front of the car where it hit the bike. Fatoussi wiped away the dust and dirt. It wasn't much at all. Then the two of them climbed in and carried on down the Avenue Laval. The house was small, detached, set on its own at the end of a cul-de-sac. The mother was at the window staring out as they turned up.

'Guess Noémie hasn't come home,' Fatoussi said as Baptiste parked on the gravel drive behind a recent black Citroën saloon bearing a sign in gold lettering on the doors: *Compagnie Laurent*.

18

Marie Le Gall was rearranging her things as best she could when the front doorbell rang. All her few belongings from the apartment next door were now in Fatoussi's old rooms. Bernadette had done what she could, but then she had to return to the hospital to start her shift. Short of clothes, of coffee, of so many things. Her son was going to have to go down the shops before long and fix that.

'Julien!' she cried. 'It's open. Let yourself in. I can't walk, remember?'

But it wasn't him. A middle-aged officer was there in a scruffy, creased uniform, a supermarket bag from Auchan in his hand.

She stayed firmly on the sofa, wishing the wound in her foot didn't itch, and stared at him. 'Is this all the police of Clermiers have to do? Deliver groceries?'

He laughed. 'Marie Le Gall. Philippe Dupont. Captain of the quiet little police station in quiet little Clermiers. If I wish to deliver groceries, it's entirely up to me. You're a special case, madame. How are you?'

'My foot hurts, I've no idea how or when I'll get home. It seems my son and I will be spending more time in one another's hair than we might wish. Pretty shitty if you ask me.'

A swift scowl replaced the smile. 'I can't say how furious I am that you should be greeted this way. We'll find the culprit responsible. He will pay.'

'My stupid fault for wearing flip-flops. But this weather . . . did you bring coffee?'

He opened the bag and started to take out the contents. Milk, wine, cheese, ham, butter, a baguette, pâté, and some tins of soup. 'Instant only, I regret,' Dupont added, taking out a jar. 'The old police houses are surplus to requirements, to be disposed of soon. Somewhat short of amenities.'

The kitchen had a kettle though and within a few minutes Dupont was back with two mugs of coffee and a tray with bread, biscuits and food, cutlery and kitchen knives so that she could, he said, prepare her own meals until her son came home.

'And when will that be?'

Dupont took the chair opposite. 'Oh, by the end of the afternoon I imagine. There's a small matter of a young girl who's run away from home. I doubt it will detain him. Usually, they come back of their own accord.'

'The young . . .' Marie grumbled.

'We were all young once. Some of the things I got up to round here . . . let's say I'm lucky they never came up when I applied for a job in the police.'

She didn't seem convinced. 'I find it hard to imagine there were many avenues for temptation in Clermiers. Or that a man of dubious character would rise within the ranks.'

He chuckled. 'It required a little effort on my part I must admit. Now, is there anything else you need? I thought of food and drink only. But I gather you may be here for a little while. If you wish, I can contact Paris and ask someone to bring things from your apartment. We will need a key . . .'

She scribbled a few words on a scrap of paper and passed it over. 'Monique is the *gardienne* of my apartment block. If you pass this on, she can do the rest. Send an officer round to see her. She hates the phone.'

'I'll have it done as soon as I can. A gardener will mow the front lawn this afternoon and make sure there's nothing else of danger around here. Bonnay, one of my officers, will keep an eye on the place. As will your son, I'm sure. And Fatoussi. An attack such as this in Clermiers. I'm speechless . . .'

'You seem quite talkative I'd say.'

61

He grinned and waved a finger: *got me*. 'It's the hoodlums from Boulliers. They are . . . uncontrollable.'

'I'm not a fan of the police.'

'Few people are. We're a necessary evil, not here to be popular. Yet your son is one of us now.'

'Without my blessing.'

'I understand. Tell me about him, please. I've had so little information from Paris. I like to get to know the officers I work with, even if it's for the briefest of periods.'

The request puzzled her. 'Tell you what?'

'What brought him here? Why Clermiers?'

She reached out for a biscuit. 'As far as I know, he had no choice. He's donated his soul to the police and so must go wherever they dictate. As I understand it, they said some city officers had to spend time out in the boondocks as the Americans say. A learning exercise. Julien's name came out of the hat for Clermiers.'

'Has he always been in Paris?'

'Why yes. Don't you—'

'What sort of work interests him? Theft? Drugs? Social matters?'

'Questions for him, I'd suggest.'

'Ah.' He winced. 'I'm afraid he caught me at the wrong time this morning. I was rather besieged by bureaucratic matters and may have been a little curt.'

'Huh. Water off a duck's back. You're lucky you didn't get the same in return.'

'How might we make his stay in Clermiers of use to him and to me? His special talents . . .'

Surely, she thought, the police were sufficiently well-organised to be able to pass on such information internally, even at the considerable distance from Paris to Clermiers. But no. It seemed Dupont was mostly ignorant of Baptiste's background and work, the departments he'd moved through since joining the police after university.

'His special talent,' she said, 'is that he's Julien Baptiste. A versatile fellow, perhaps too clever for his own good. A mother can say that. As to where he's headed in the police, I've no idea. Everything seems to interest him – science, the law, the psychology of offenders. He's good with people when he wants to be. Can argue the hind leg off a donkey and get you to agree to things you never wanted. In his head I believe he thinks he'll go far. A rising star, smarter than everyone and determined not to show his cards until he deems it worthwhile. Whether his colleagues agree is another matter. Frankly, what little he says about work bores me.'

Dupont nodded and rested his chin on his hand. 'I am, unfortunately, given to rapid judgements. Your son strikes me as a more incisive, cleverer fellow, than the young officer they sent me from Marseille.'

'And it strikes *me* that Étienne Fatoussi is a rather more amenable human being. A bit . . . twitchy for some reason perhaps.'

He raised his finger again. 'We need all kinds in the police. A mix of talents. Much of what we do is tedious, I'm afraid. But required too.' He raised his coffee cup. 'Do bore me with talk of your son, please.'

She grimaced. 'As for his love life, if you can call it that . . .'

Philippe Dupont looked at his watch. 'I've twenty minutes to spare. Another coffee, perhaps?'

She nodded at the baguette. 'Cut me some of that cheese as well.'

19

Charles Augustin was heavily built with a broad and handsome face, an exotic accent and the cheap business suit and shiny shoes Baptiste associated with travelling salesmen. His wife had the pale, white complexion of a northerner and looked a little older, more drawn. Fifi, Noémie's beloved pet, a lively one-year-old terrier, wire-haired, kept sniffing round her ankles.

The house was small and modestly decorated, with pictures of the region on the walls, a photo of Paris with the three of them, Noémie no more than ten or twelve, smiling and pointing at the Eiffel Tower behind in that pose that made her look just as tall. A couple of packing cases were still in the hall. Two months was all mother and daughter had spent in Boulliers after joining Augustin from Calais. He'd been working there alone since before Christmas. Not everything had found its place.

Martine Augustin spoke more than her husband. Or perhaps he couldn't get a word in. It was hard to judge. Baptiste did most of the questioning, Fatoussi made notes and was happy to chip in from time to time. The story hadn't changed much from the one they told Bonnay in the station that morning. Noémie was still missing. They'd asked around Boulliers for hours since leaving the station. No one had heard or seen anything of her since the day before when she set off for a tennis match with their English lodger. Daniel Murray had gone out again to search for Noémie. He couldn't stay in the house and do nothing, it seemed. Though where he might have gone to look, they'd no idea.

Noémie had left college in Calais early to move to Clermiers. She was still trying to work out what to do next. A trainee in a clerical position in one of the local factories, if she could find the work, her father said. She'd been getting bored with so little to occupy her. The one girlfriend she'd made wasn't close and hadn't got any closer when Noémie turned down an invitation to join her on holiday somewhere on the Côte d'Azur. The Augustins just didn't have the money to pay her share.

'Was she mad about that?' Baptiste asked.

'Noémie wasn't mad at all,' the mother said, patting the dog, trying to make it sit. 'She knew we couldn't afford it. She understood. The friend was . . .' Her words drifted off.

'The girl took up with Noémie because she thought it was entertaining to have a black friend,' Charles Augustin added. 'It happens. Noémie knew damned well what was going on.'

All the same, Baptiste said, they needed a name for the family and would contact them to see if they'd heard from her.

'You're not listening to me any more than Dupont did this morning,' Martine Augustin told him. 'Noémie had no intention of going on that holiday after we told her. She's not the kind of girl who wants things that are beyond us.'

'She was a good kid,' Fatoussi said.

Silence. The two of them glared at him.

'Present tense, Étienne,' Baptiste said quietly. 'She is a good kid, I'm sure. We'll find her.'

'You say that very easily,' the woman pointed out.

'Most . . . mostly these cases end well. Boys?'

She sighed and they went through exactly what they'd told Bonnay. Noémie briefly had a boyfriend back in Calais, but he'd dumped her when she said she was moving to Clermiers. She hadn't seemed bothered. All that, Noémie thought, could wait. Better to spend her time on sport: tennis and swimming, and earning pocket money working as a waitress for the *Amis* society that owned the courts and paid for charity work around town.

'She never hung around with people on the estate?' asked Fatoussi.

'Noémie's too sensible for that,' her mother insisted. 'The boys here are mostly trouble. It's not their fault. It comes from their parents, and the fact no one's got much. Noémie wants out one day.'

'Where?' Baptiste wondered.

'Lille. Paris. Some big city,' the father said. 'But that wasn't for now. She plans to wait until the summer's over, try and get a job locally. Then, when she has the experience, look for something better.'

'Noémie's smart enough for university,' the mother added.

'She just thinks she needs to earn some money to help us. That's how she is.'

Fatoussi glanced Baptiste's way. They were running out of questions. Out of avenues to pursue.

'The English boy—' Baptiste began.

'She liked him,' Martine Augustin cut in. 'A lot, I think. I wondered if maybe something . . .' A wan smile. 'It could never have worked. He's due to go home in a week or so. His family have money. Lawyers. Businesses as well, travel or something.'

'They thought it could never work for us two as well,' the husband said and clutched at his wife's hand.

Martine Augustin's eyes shone with a glassy lustre just short of tears. 'What will you do now?'

'Does Daniel Murray have a car?'

'No,' said Augustin. 'I had to pick him up from the station in Douai. The buses here are terrible.'

Baptiste made a note, then went through the routine for Étienne Fatoussi out loud. Get the best photos of Noémie they could find, recent, headshots preferably, and clear. They could be distributed to the missing persons offices in all the large cities. The names and addresses for anyone she might have associated with from school, teachers and pupils. Anything else that the parents thought might be useful.

'I would like to look around her room if I can,' he added.

'She's very private,' the mother said. 'Doesn't like people going in there. Keeps it all clean and tidy herself.'

'All the same, while my colleague is taking these important details . . .'

She sighed and nodded at the stairs.

20

Teenagers.

Baptiste's experience of them was limited, and his own

experience at that age marred by the sudden death of his father. A blank time in his life, one he couldn't wait to leave behind. His room in the family apartment in the 7th arrondissement in Paris was small and bare, with little more than a single bed and a desk for work and his books.

Noémie Augustin's couldn't be more different. The bed was neatly made with nothing but a pink sheet to cover it, understandable in the baking weather. The curtains were pink too, frilly, closed, though so thin and cheap they let through the light. There was a desk here as well, a tiny one that must have been meant for a young child. The walls were covered with posters, a couple featuring the tennis player, Evonne Goolagong, the rest for films, and not the popular recent kind Baptiste might have expected. These were old Hollywood musicals: *Singin' in the Rain*, *The Wizard of Oz*, *West Side Story*, *Calamity Jane*. Beneath a poster for *The Sound of Music* was a framed photo of Noémie imitating the dancing Julie Andrews, a bag in one hand, a guitar in the other. The same instrument, cheap and scratched, was leaning in a corner of the room. He stroked the strings. It sounded in tune.

Baptiste sat on the bed, tried to think about what he'd heard downstairs, and what he hadn't. The Augustins seemed a close couple, perhaps made more so by his colour, something that might have been noticed but infrequently remarked upon in metropolitan Paris though not Clermiers. They loved their daughter. They were agonising over her disappearance, and appeared willing to offer up all the information they could to help find her. All the same there was a kind of distance between them, one that meant they rarely looked at each other directly. Charles held her hand. She failed to squeeze his in return. And the eyes . . . Baptiste was developing his own theories and methods when it came to talking to people, trying to judge whether what they said was the truth, a part of it, or simply a lie. He didn't feel the Augustins were distorting the facts. He did wonder whether they were saying all they knew.

And what story would their daughter tell if she were found? *If.* He'd been improvising downstairs when he spoke so glibly of being certain they could find her. Martine Augustin had spotted that instantly. Her husband surely noticed too though perhaps he was better at keeping his emotions in check.

'More,' Baptiste whispered to himself. 'There has to be more.'

He went to the desk and opened the drawer. A diary maybe. An address book, that might help. But there was instead a scrapbook and on the cover a photo he dimly recognised from somewhere: a black woman smiling for the camera, posed as if about to dance. Seemingly naked except for a beaded neck-lace, heavy earrings and a string of large and clearly artificial bananas slung beneath her navel. It was a tantalising pose side-on, close to pornographic but not quite there.

A name came to him: *Josephine Baker.*

Baptiste sat down on the bed and began to flick through the scrapbook. It was all there, cuttings from newspapers, photos of the woman over the years, a drawing of her almost naked, being offered a bouquet of flowers by a beaming cheetah beneath a sign for the Casino de Paris. The skimpy costumes and the illustrations all seemed to make out she was African. Though the cuttings told a different tale, of an impoverished American girl who'd barely escaped with her life in the race riots of St Louis, left school and worked as a waitress at a 'gentleman's club', lived in the street, begged for food, married at thirteen, divorced at fourteen, found work as a vaudeville dancer. Then sailed to Paris when she was just nineteen and found a place in the chorus line of a show called *la Revue nègre* at the Théâtre des Champs-Élysées.

No one had danced so daringly before, as good as naked, alive with a brazen eroticism. Josephine Baker was soon a sensation, a spy for the Allies in occupied France during the war, returning in triumph to star at the Folies Bergère. She became rich and bought a château in the Dordogne, lost it through financial problems, only to be offered an apartment in Monaco by Princess Grace and a revival of her career in a review bank-rolled by Prince Rainier, his wife and Jackie Onassis.

An early supporter of the civil rights movement, success-ful, universally adored, she'd died in Paris the year before. Baptiste remembered the day of her funeral at L'église Sainte-Marie-Madeleine. The event had attracted so many mourners – twenty thousand, according to the cutting from *Le Figaro* Noémie had snipped – the police had to bring in street control measures to cope.

It was an extraordinary life. One that would have seemed even more so to a young black girl in Clermiers who must have sorely wished to escape the straitjacket of the grim and miser-able estate where she'd landed in something close to poverty.

There was that one curious line in Bonnay's notes of his conversation with the English kid, Daniel Murray. He thought he'd seen bananas and a black dress in Noémie's tennis bag.

Something else was just visible at the back of the drawer, tucked away. He had to reach deep inside to get finger and thumb on the edge then pull it out. A small diary, a childish drawing of a grinning cat on the plastic cover, a scribble on the side like a padlock, then in black felt tip: *Noémie Augustin's Private Thoughts and Wishes KEEP OUT!*

The door opened. Baptiste stuffed the diary into his jacket pocket before anyone could see. Martine Augustin marched in, Fatoussi too, shrugging as if to say he couldn't stop it. The terrier ran straight up to the bed and seemed puzzled it was empty.

'Have you found something?'

Her husband was behind her and he looked worried.

'This,' Baptiste said and held up the scrapbook.

She shook her head and came and took it.

'Bananas!' Fatoussi cried, seeing the photo.

'Did you know your daughter wanted to be a dancer?' Bap-tiste asked.

Martine Augustin looked lost for words.

Baptiste didn't wait for an answer. He nodded at Fatoussi to make a note. 'We must include all the dance halls in Paris when we circulate her photo. It's clear she idolised this woman, Josephine Baker. She was black. Came from nothing. The gutter. Made her name in Paris. Found fame. Riches for a while. It seems to me this is a very specific dream, and one we must think about. Charles? May I call you that?'

He nodded.

'Did you know about this obsession of your daughter's? Had you any idea?'

'No,' the mother said.

'It was just a dream,' added Charles Augustin. 'Nothing more.'

She stared at him, baffled.

'Perhaps.' Baptiste placed the scrapbook on the bed. 'But a very organised one. We must get her photo circulated, as I said. If there's nothing more . . .'

The couple glanced at one another and kept quiet. The dog began to whine.

'We will, of course, keep you informed when there are any developments.'

Baptiste got behind the wheel of the Simca. Fatoussi fell in the other side. The two men looked at each other.

'Well?' said Baptiste.

'Something odd there, boss.'

'I'm not your boss! We're equals.'

'No,' Fatoussi insisted. 'I just watched and listened. And . . .' He tapped the pocket of Baptiste's jacket. 'I saw you nick something too. Trust me. I'm just a street cop. A chaser of villains. You're . . . different. Equal, we're not.'

He was barely listening.

'What next?'

Baptiste started the car. 'You have a good photo?' Fatoussi held up three, headshots, clear, Noémie smiling in all of them.

70

'Good. Bonnay can get them on the wires. We pass on the details of this girl in the south who offered Noémie a holiday. And . . .'

'And what?'

'Mostly,' said Baptiste, 'we hope Dupont is right. The kid's swanned off for some reason. And sometime soon will swan right back.'

'Right ...'

The doubt in Fatoussi's voice was obvious.

'But first we talk to this English boy.'

'Where do we look?'

'Close by. He has no car. No means of transport. You heard Augustin. The buses here are terrible. How hard can he be to find?'

21

Twenty minutes and a stroke of good fortune was all it took. Daniel Murray was on his own in a café on the southern edge of town, sitting by the window, an empty cup in front of him. He didn't see the police car pull up. Didn't look pleased when Baptiste and Fatoussi came through the door, ordered coffee, asked at the counter if there'd been any English customers, a young man in particular, of late. The waiter just nodded at the table. The cops got their drinks, sat down, folded their arms, smiled.

'Have you found her?' Daniel Murray asked.

'No,' said Baptiste. 'Have you?'

'I wish.'

'Not much chance you'll come upon her in a café, is there?' Fatoussi said. 'The Augustins told us you were so upset you couldn't stay with them. You had to be out here.'

He looked offended by that. 'I've been everywhere I could think of.'

'The boathouse? Near the old château?'

A moment of hesitation. 'Something seemed to have happened there. I stopped by the garage. The man there said you'd been looking.'

Baptiste nodded. 'Did he tell you we found a scrap of a black dress? And a used condom?'

Again, that pause. 'No.'

'Did you know Noémie was obsessed with a dancer called Josephine Baker? A black American woman, quite a star in Paris and elsewhere. She died last year.'

Fatoussi looked baffled. 'Who?'

'Josephine Baker. Noémie kept a scrapbook. Photos. Her obituary. Perhaps she dreamed of following in her footsteps.'

'I know who Josephine Baker was,' Murray said. 'I read about her in the papers.'

'Do you remember she used to dance almost naked, nothing but a necklace and a string of fake bananas round her waist?'

He shook his head.

'But you saw something like bananas, and a black dress, in her tennis bag?'

'I thought so.'

'And you never made the connection?'

He was getting cross, and Baptiste was fine with that. 'We weren't that close. She said she liked to dance. And no, I never made the connection. We'd just played tennis. I thought she was going to walk home. She said she needed a shower. It was really hot.'

Fatoussi leaned across the table. 'Did you want to be more than just friends, Daniel? Did you ask her for a date?'

No answer. He was starting to go red.

'Where were you last night?' Baptiste asked. 'Down by the boathouse?'

'I wasn't with Noémie, if that's what you mean.'

'I wanted to know where you were. Not where you weren't.'

He went quiet, eyes on the other side of the room. A woman

was walking out of what Baptiste assumed to be the toilet. Mid-twenties, dressed for a hike by the looks of it, jeans, a white cotton shirt, curly fair hair casually tied back in a makeshift ponytail.

She came and sat down on the spare chair at the table, smiled at them briefly and said, 'Daniel. You have new friends?'

Baptiste pulled out his police card and said, 'And you are?'

'Julien Baptiste. What an interesting name.' She pronounced it correctly, silent 'p', something the English rarely did in his experience. 'Celia Murray. Daniel's big sister. Can I help?'

'We're looking for Noémie Augustin.'

'Oh god.' The smile was gone. 'Is she still missing? Do you have any idea what's happened to her? Those poor parents. I haven't met them, but Dan says they're lovely.'

'We wanted to know where your brother was last night,' said Baptiste.

She blinked. 'Why?'

'Because we do. It's a simple enough question.'

'It is,' she agreed. 'I'm sorry. I understand. Dan was with me. We got a takeaway pizza and ate it in my camper van. The petrol station chap let us park behind the place for free.'

'Gilles Mailloux?'

'Is that his name? We drank rather too much wine. Bit of a thick head this morning. Still slightly grumpy. Apologies.'

'What time—?'

'I met Dan after he played tennis with her. About six. Still down in the dumps because she'd thrashed him apparently. We got food, went back to the camper. He staggered out around nine thirty I think.'

'And walked back to Boulliers,' he added. 'Charles and Martine can tell you that.'

'Anyone see you that night?' asked Fatoussi.

It was Celia Murray who answered. 'The man in the pizza place. After that. Just me.' She cocked her head to one side and looked at Baptiste quite directly. 'Are we somehow under

73

suspicion? If so, can I just say you're wasting your time. Dan was out all last night looking for her. Unlike anyone from the police, I believe.'

'The Augustins didn't report her missing till this morning.'

'Ah. Apologies. I did say I was a bit grumpy and frankly this conversation isn't helping.'

Baptiste was struggling for the right words. 'Can I . . . would you like a coffee?'

'Had enough thanks. Are you going to ask me out for dinner next?'

Fatoussi stifled a laugh.

'Look, Baptiste.' She put a hand on his arm for a moment. 'If there's anything we can do to help, just say. I've got to go back to England tonight. Dan can stick around for a while.'

Her brother kept quiet, looked sullen for some reason.

'Really,' she added, 'you're barking up the wrong tree as we say in English. Does that work in French? Does it make any sense?'

'Did you hear anything?' he asked. 'In your camper van?'

'Voices,' Daniel Murray said. 'Music. Old-fashioned. I don't know where. Maybe the river.'

'I thought the music came from somewhere else,' she added. 'But . . .' She winced. 'The wine. I wouldn't swear to it.'

Baptiste could think of nothing more. He thanked them and went outside with Fatoussi. Celia Murray followed them to the car.

'I do hope I didn't sound too bad-tempered in there. Sorry.'

'Why are you here exactly?'

'Passing through.' The family had a travel business that ran holidays for the English on a camp site in the Loire. She'd been delivering new supplies there and decided to stop on the way back to see her brother.

'Have you been to Clermiers before?'

'No. And to be honest I doubt I'll be coming here again. The place has that backwater feel to it I don't like. Give me cities any day. You?'

'I'm from Paris. Étienne is from Marseille.'

She laughed. 'Poor things. What did you do to deserve a sorry place like this?' Celia Murray handed over a business card, a phone number in Folkestone for a company called Bouverie Camping. 'If you need me . . . do call. And please find that poor girl. From what Dan said she seemed a bit of a mystery in some ways. I hope she sees sense and doesn't come to any harm.'

The police station was only three minutes away. It was simpler to walk than find somewhere to park.

'An interesting woman,' Fatoussi said as they went up the hill towards the square. 'An attractive one, don't you agree?'

'I hadn't really given it much thought.'

'Of course not, Julien. We are professionals, nothing personal must come into our working hours. Still ...' He nudged Baptiste's arm. 'She gave you her phone number.'

'Across the Channel. In Folkestone.'

'Love knows no boundaries,' Fatoussi declared with a theatrical sweep of his hands. 'Look at the Augustins.'

'No love for you tonight, I guess. Bernadette's working, isn't she?'

He looked briefly guilty.

Baptiste groaned. *'Isn't she?'*

'The thing is . . . a friend from Marseille insisted on driving up to stay a few nights. Mimi. She's a hairdresser. You'll like her.'

'I liked Bernadette.'

'Me too. We won't make much noise, promise. She's not like that.'

Baptiste swore and rolled his eyes. Fatoussi looked offended.

'You may be a solitary man. I'm not. Mimi was desperate to come. I didn't have the heart—'

'Does Bernadette know?'

Étienne Fatoussi stopped and stared at him, mouth open, eyes wide, speechless, quite horrified.

'Fine,' said Baptiste then took out the business card Celia Murray had handed him. He'd never been to Folkestone. He wondered what the place was like.

22

Dupont was at the front window of the principal office of the Mairie. Portraits of Fabrice Blanc's predecessors lined the walls going back more than a century. The first was a daguerreotype from 1853. The police captain frowned at it.

'He was an evil-looking bastard. Could do with a haircut and a bath if you ask me.'

'You didn't come here to look at the walls,' said Blanc.

'Do you lot still like dressing up?'

The mayor of Clermiers grunted a low curse.

'I mean . . .' Dupont laughed. 'Grown men putting on fancy gowns. What's the world coming to?'

'We have traditions. It's entirely your prerogative if you wish to ignore them.'

'Best for both of us, I reckon. Oh look. Here they come.'

Baptiste and Fatoussi were striding up the hill towards the police station. Blanc joined Dupont at the window, far enough back so they might not be seen.

'I still don't understand why they're here,' he grumbled.

'I still don't understand why I have to keep explaining. They were sent. We're down on numbers. I may not like it, but I have no choice.' Blanc was a chubby bachelor, always immaculately dressed, fond of pomade on his hair and a finely brushed moustache. 'I doubt I can get rid of them for a month or so. By then I'll have Chastain back from his stupid caravan and with any luck Allemand will be out of the nut hutch. Allemand can man the desk and spend most of the day talking to himself. I'll get Bonnay off his fat arse onto the street along with Chastain. Full complement. *Au revoir* to our unwanted visitors.'

Blanc nodded. 'This sounds promising.'

Dupont jabbed a finger in his direction. 'In the meantime, you and yours need to keep your heads down. I don't want to see anything that's going to make this pair curious. It's bad enough with the black girl . . .'

'You have news?'

'Nothing.' Baptiste and Fatoussi were going into the station. 'I've checked out that pair. The kid from Marseille I can deal with. He's the bastard offspring of one of the local politicians there. Daddy got him a job in the police because sonny boy couldn't cut it anywhere else. Playboy with more money than sense.'

'I hope you're right.'

'The other one, Baptiste, is different. Very. His mother's holed up in the police house. Some little bastard from Boulliers left broken glass in the grass. She cut her foot on it. Bad.'

'Christ!'

'She'll be fine. Just can't walk far for a while. I spent some time with her.' Dupont turned back from the window. 'Julien Baptiste is a complex character. Father was a left-wing professor at the Sorbonne. Mother as good as dammit a commie too. The son's response was to be a renegade as well, against them. So, he joined us. He's smart. He's ambitious. He's worked in several departments in Paris – intelligence, forensic, fraud.' Dupont hesitated for effect. 'Homicide for a while too. An educated man with a future, or so he hopes. You understand what this means?'

Blanc shook his head. 'This is immaterial. There's nothing you need worry about here. I've asked around. Nothing at all.'

Dupont headed for the door. 'I hope so. You're no problem. Too much invested in this . . .' He glanced around the office. 'Wearing that chain around your neck.'

'Thank you . . .'

'Laurent I'd trust with my life. I mean, he owns it, doesn't he? He owns us all. And Chauvin, your tame priest, is a naive idiot who wouldn't see trouble coming if it had a neon sign over its head.'

'Perhaps . . .'

'But Gaillard . . .' He waved a finger in Blanc's face. 'He's a cowardly little snake. He'd dump you in the shit, any of you, if he needs to. If it means he walks away scot-free.' He hesitated for effect. 'And he's missing.'

Blanc sighed. 'You know what he's like. It happens.'

'If it's just another of his weekend benders then fine. So long as no one's going whining to anyone above me. Anything worse . . .'

'You have my word, Philippe.'

He walked over, his face so close Dupont's nicotine breath wafted all over the man. 'If you want me to keep a lid on this little carnival of yours, stay low, stay quiet, and let me deal with it the way I want. Find that fool Gaillard and make sure he keeps his head down and his mouth shut. Julien Baptiste is not a man to walk on by. We don't want people like him prying into things that are none of his business.'

'Such as?'

Dupont laughed. 'Where would we begin?'

The mayor nodded. 'You've nothing to worry about, I assure you.'

'Good,' said Dupont. 'Now you can get back to whatever you were doing that passed as work.'

23

Charles and Martine Augustin had barely spoken since the police left. He'd made one call to Laurent's office. She'd sat on the sofa in the living room, Noémie's scrapbook in her hands, glued to the cuttings and the photos, tears streaming down her cheeks. The dog was fed but still the creature kept whining, picking up the strange atmosphere in the house, Noémie's absence most of all.

'I need to take her for a walk,' Augustin said eventually.

'You don't enjoy spending time here, do you?'

She'd been wanting to say that for a long time. Now was probably the worst moment.

'Laurent's a hard taskmaster. I told you when I took the job. It got us out of Calais. Got us . . .' He waved around the room. 'A house, not an apartment where we could barely move.'

That much was true. There was still something strange about Bruno Laurent and his offer of a job for her husband, provided he start work immediately. Even if it meant leaving them alone for months on end in Calais, waiting on news of when they'd come to live in Clermiers.

'He treats you like—'

'Don't say it!' His voice was loud now. 'Not again.'

She took his arm and he seemed to freeze. 'I know what it's like, Charles. I know what you've been through. I've seen it.'

He glared at her. 'You've no idea. You've seen nothing. Noémie knows just a fraction. Not you.'

'What do you want me to say?'

He closed his eyes. 'I'm going to lie down for a while. Give it an hour or two then I'll take the dog out. If the police aren't back with news, or that English kid, maybe I'll take a look around myself. Might take a while.'

'Huh,' she snorted. 'There you go again. Wanting to get out of the house. Get away from me.'

He swore under his breath and rolled back on the sofa.

'I still don't understand why you couldn't come to the phone. In a hotel.'

'How many times am I supposed to explain?'

'As many as it takes to get to the truth. There's something you're not telling me, Charles. I'm your wife. I've known you twenty years. A wife can tell.'

'A wife can have an overactive imagination.'

'I think there are things you're not telling me.' Say it, she thought. Even if there was no going back afterwards. Even if this was a point where everything, their relationship, their life together, the future of Noémie wherever she might be, would turn on this moment. 'I think that, in all these long hours, these nights away from here, you're not working at all, at least not every time. You're seeing someone else. That instead of making you happy, it just makes you more miserable.'

Augustin got to his feet. 'Everything I've done, all the years I've spent trying to make things better, I've done for you both. This is what I get in return.'

She put a hand out to stop him. 'We could talk about it. I'm not trying to judge you. I'm just trying to . . . understand.'

'Understand what?'

'This dancing thing, for one. That black woman. Noémie never mentioned that to me.'

'Maybe you weren't listening.'

'I always listen.'

'Then . . .' he shrugged. 'I don't know. It was just some ridiculous thing girls have. It wasn't serious. Maybe you forgot . . .'

'Charles . . .'

'Enough,' he said. 'I'll walk the dog later. I need that lie-down.'

24

Dupont came through the door of the police station moments after Baptiste and Fatoussi.

'I went to see your mother since you were busy. Took her some food.'

Baptiste looked surprised.

'No big deal,' the captain added. 'I didn't want her to be hungry. She seems. . . settled.'

'Thank you.' Baptiste brandished the photos then placed them in front of Bonnay who looked as if he'd just woken up from a nap. 'These are good pictures of the girl. They need to go on the wire to all the major cities and their missing persons departments. Tell them she fancies herself as a dancer. May be worth checking night clubs, revues, those kinds of places.'

Bonnay looked up at Dupont, waiting on orders. The captain nodded. 'Take the spare car.'

Baptiste shook his head. 'I need this doing now.'

'We don't have a wire machine. Not in Clermiers. He'll have to drive to Millot.'

'Wait,' said Fatoussi. 'That's like nearly an hour.'

'If you don't meet a tractor,' Bonnay said, reaching for his jacket. 'Anything else?'

'Get them to put it out to the media,' Baptiste added. 'All the usual contacts the press officers have. If—'

'Wait, wait, wait,' Dupont cut in. 'I didn't agree to that.'

Baptiste was half-expecting a problem. He went through the reasoning. If the girl had run away to a big city, she had to take a train or a bus. Someone must have sat near her. They'd remember. She's a striking kid.

'She's black,' Dupont retorted. 'From a family on the wrong side of town. Don't you know how newspapers work?'

'Tell us,' said Fatoussi.

'First, she's missing. Probably a runaway. Second, if it's a pretty white girl with a good-looking middle-class mother and father who'll talk about it on TV then maybe it makes the news. You saw what the Augustins are like as a couple. Even if they were willing to sit down with a hack, how do you think that would go?'

Baptiste kept quiet. There was something in what Dupont was saying, much as he hated the thought.

'We put out the photos internally like you asked,' Dupont went on. 'With any luck someone in Paris will pick her up in one of these dance halls or something.'

'You knew about the dancing?' Baptiste asked.

'No. You just mentioned it. I'm trying to help. Like I tried to help with your mother. If we get any inkling this isn't just a runaway teenager . . .'

'And let's face it,' Bonnay said, 'she wouldn't be the first.'

Dupont glowered at him, and the man never noticed.

Fatoussi screwed up his eyes and said, 'You mean this has happened before?'

'There was the Hubert girl last year. Lili. She was from Boulliers too. One night she ups sticks and—'

'The Hubert girl!' Dupont looked mad. 'What more do you need to know? She couldn't put up with that bastard father of hers. No great surprise there. God knows what he was getting up to.'

'Do they have a son?' Baptiste asked. 'Didier?'

'He's an evil little sod.' Bonnay took out his car keys. 'Just like his old man. No idea where Lili Hubert went but it's got to be better than living with that pair.'

Dupont tapped his watch. 'You've done your shift. See you in the morning. I'll be routing all calls to Millot once I shut up shop here.'

25

An old soft-top Fiat was parked outside the police house when they got back. Mimi's it seems. She was out to greet Étienne Fatoussi the moment they turned up. A cheery woman, mid-twenties or so, with long, brightly dyed blonde hair and a figure and mode of dress she might have modelled on a young Brigitte Bardot. Mimi had already met Marie Le Gall. The two of them had talked, mostly about men it seemed.

Fatoussi kissed her tenderly and winked at Baptiste as they went upstairs.

Baptiste's mother seemed settled in his old flat. 'Your captain was round here for ages wittering on. At least he brought some food and drink.'

'That was kind of him, I guess.'

She waved a dismissive hand. 'The man was fishing. About you.'

'What did you tell him?'

'Nothing that wasn't the truth.'

The foot wasn't so bad, she said. In a day or two she'd try driving and if it went OK make her way back to Paris. Some things had turned up from home on Dupont's orders.

'No need to rush.'

'You mean you want me here?'

A loaded question, and one he was tempted to answer . . . yes. He liked bouncing ideas off her from time to time. She was honest, a sideways thinker, never tackling a problem head on. And, unlike him, never impetuous.

'You're welcome for as long as you want to stay. Now . . .' He retrieved Noémie's diary from his jacket pocket. 'If you'll excuse me, I have some reading to do. I may be back with questions later.'

She raised her glass. 'I'll see if I can fit you in.'

He poured himself some of the cheap red and stepped across the hall. There were voices from upstairs, girlish laughter, Étienne Fatoussi telling a story Baptiste couldn't hear. He liked the man from Marseille, even if his private life seemed a little exotic. After their long and curious day, there was no doubt whose side Fatoussi was on. It wasn't Philippe Dupont's.

At least he had a bed now. It was baking in there. He threw open the window and wondered whether that would make it better or worse. The night was alive with buzzing, biting insects. Somewhere not far away a tractor was working, its low, rattling engine cutting through the insect noise. They must have been doing something in the fields that seemed to stretch in every direction outside Clermiers, beet and grain from what he understood. The air was speckled with the kind of dust that came with harvest, one in the driest season for years.

There was an ancient bedside lamp to read by, a bare bulb, the shade long gone. Baptiste settled on the hard mattress and took out Noémie Augustin's little diary, the cover the kind of image you might expect of a girl of ten, not a young woman of nineteen. Her writing was adult though, as, for the most part, were her words. While it might have said 'Diary' on the cover this was really anything but. More a way of setting down a series of dreams, a collection of disorganised, almost random fantasies about the life another Noémie might have led if only . . .

If only she wasn't trapped in the grim, dull prison of Boulliers. She never said that, but he could read between the lines. The notebook was divided into stories, each no more than a few pages long. Imaginative descriptions of the life another Noémie Augustin might have enjoyed. Playing at Wimbledon, losing in her second match but gaining the admiration of her heroine, Évonne Goolagong, so much so she invited her to form a doubles team. Thanks to a quite extraordinary change in the rules, they were allowed to compete in the same tournament, and, after a series of gruelling matches, each described in a single breathless sentence, reached the final which, with great drama, they won. After that . . . the American Open, success on clay in Paris at Roland-Garros, trophies aplenty, success, travel, fame. The money she always mentioned last, but that too.

Then another life with Josephine Baker, taken under the wing of the legendary dancer in retirement at a château in the Loire. Learning the secrets of her performances, the costumes, the tasteful display of near nudity, the need for rehearsal and constant practice, for a regime of fitness much like that of the alternative Noémie, the tennis player. A residency at the Folies Bergère, adulation in New York, a Royal Variety show at the London Palladium. All, like the dreamt-of sporting experiences, described in passionate detail as if each had really happened, even down to the odd, invented note about some real individual from show business or politics, and how this fantasy Noémie Augustin had found them.

Lots of teenagers dreamt of fame, Baptiste guessed. Many wanted to escape the tedium and deprivation of the life fate had dealt them. Yet there was something he thought unique in this inventive redrawing of a life. At the close of almost all the entries there was a conclusion, often a single sentence but a consistent one. There it was after she'd won Wimbledon by the side of the great Evonne Goolagong.

And Evonne was kind enough to allow me to keep all the prize money — she had quite enough herself she said — so I could bring it back to Mum and Dad.

Again, in London, when she performed in front of the Royal family.

The look on Mum and Dad's faces when they met the Queen! Everything was worth it then. All the pain, the sacrifices I made, and they did too. We'll never forget London. I'll never be able to thank Josephine enough for her friendship and kindness.

After a while he couldn't take all the detail, could do nothing but skim read through the repetitive entries as they became shriller, more grotesque, more desperate, childish daydreams more depressing in that they were recounted in a voice so clearly on the cusp of an adulthood Noémie Augustin must have dreaded. A young girl fervently wishing to escape the misery and hopelessness of her life in the ghetto the locals called *Merdeville*. Shit Town.

There wasn't a single entry about boys, a family of her own. No sign of an ordinary ambition in that direction. Only those unattainable fantasies of escape.

Baptiste closed the little book. He felt guilty sneaking it out of the house like that, but Noémie must have kept it secret for a reason. Perhaps because there was such naive hope in those pages. It would have broken the hearts of Martine and Charles

Augustin to read the very private and pointless aspirations of their daughter.

Though maybe their hearts would be broken in any case.

He finished the glass of wine and told himself he needed another, and that was why he headed back across the hall.

26

It was dark now, nothing to see but a cloudless, starlit sky and the occasional shadowy figure scuttling in and out of the alleys of Boulliers. Still, Martine Augustin couldn't pull herself away from the living-room window. All conversation had died with her husband. Perhaps she shouldn't have said what she did. Perhaps she should have made her suspicions plain earlier. Perhaps Noémie had mentioned dancing and that American woman, and it had slipped her memory, though that she doubted. Sometimes, she thought, there were no good decisions or bad ones. Only hard choices that might reveal their consequences later. The way Charles hadn't responded – not a word wondering why she asked what she did, let alone a denial – made her think she was right. Something had happened to him in Clermiers, and the more she ran things through her mind, the more she was convinced it had occurred during the time he'd spent here on his own. Those months learning what Bruno Laurent expected of him, and supposedly looking for somewhere for them to live while she and Noémie tried to wrap up their lives in Calais, a place that no longer seemed so bad.

The dog, sensing something, came to her side, whimpered, brushed her leg.

'I'll take her out.' Augustin came to the window, a lead in his hand, bent down and fastened it to the terrier. He had a torch in his left hand.

'Where are you going?' she asked.

'I'll walk her. She needs it. I'll take a look around. Can't sit here doing nothing.'

'Where, Charles? Where do we begin? Where?'

He touched her arm. For a moment she thought he might try to kiss her cheek and wondered what she'd do if he tried. But no. Before that happened there was a knock on the door and they both rushed to get there.

It was Daniel Murray looking pale and exhausted. There was a conversation she thought might be repeated over and over, like a record stuck on the needle.

Any news?

No.

You?

No.

Where did you look?

Everywhere I could think of.

What did you find?

Then silence.

Except he did have something to say. And in his hand a wad of notes. He had to go back to England, that very night. His sister was in town and could give him a lift. Something urgent at home. Their father was ill. He had to cut his stay short.

'I'm sorry.' He handed the money over to Martine. 'This covers all the time I was supposed to be here. I don't want you to be out of pocket.'

Another time she'd have been grateful. But it didn't seem right just then.

'Noémie . . .' she whispered.

'I've done all I can. I talked to the police. I don't know what else.'

'It's not far off midnight,' Charles Augustin said, his tone not friendly at all. 'Are the police aware you're leaving?'

'My sister's spoken to them. They don't seem . . .'

He didn't want to say it.

'Don't seem what, Daniel?' she asked.

'They don't seem to think it's anything suspicious. Just that Noémie's run away for some reason.'

Charles Augustin grunted something about finding his jacket and wandered off inside with the dog.

'What reason might that be?'

'I can't imagine. Sorry.' He glanced at the stairs. 'If I can just get my things . . .'

She let him in, folded her arms, watched as he dashed up to the tiny spare room. When he came down with his rucksack her husband was ready to go out with the young terrier.

'I'm sure there'll be good news before long,' Daniel told them, and she thought he was doing his best to say those words with some conviction. 'Thank you for your kindness.'

Once more that night she wondered if she was about to be kissed, and what she might do if it happened. But it didn't, and Daniel Murray was off into town to meet his sister.

'We won't see him again,' her husband said. 'Won't have any more lodgers. Don't need the money that badly.'

She glared at him. 'Will you be long?'

He didn't meet her eyes. 'I don't know.'

'Like you told Daniel . . . it's nearly midnight. Another stock take, is it?'

He rarely lost his temper, but it looked as if he might just then. 'I'm going looking.' He waggled the dog's lead and the terrier whined again. 'Who knows? I can't just sit here climbing up the wall.'

'With me?'

'With you,' he said and left.

27

Baptiste's mother was in bed and looked as if she was sleeping. Eyes still closed, she said in a low, tired voice, 'What is it?'

'I'd like to talk to you.'

A sigh. 'Are you sure?'

'I'd appreciate your opinion.'

She did look at him then. 'You mean I'm not just here to listen to you complain?'

He grabbed a chair and parked it by the bed. 'Did you ever run away from home?'

She burst out laughing. 'Christ! You want to know that now?'

'Yes. It may be important.'

Marie Le Gall shuffled up in bed, intrigued. 'Now and again. From when I was maybe . . . I don't know, fourteen. Till I turned sixteen and started thinking about things more.'

'You never said.'

'You never asked.'

'Why? Why did you do it? Where did you go?'

'Mostly I wanted attention, I think. I always thought they loved Aline more than me.'

'Because Auntie Aline was younger?'

'I guess. And prettier. Not smarter but sometimes in a family being smart isn't always an asset. Sometimes you're just a smartass and nobody likes one of them. That was me. I didn't even like myself.'

'Where did you go?'

His mother peered at him. 'Why do you want to know? What business is it of yours?'

'There's a young girl. She's gone missing. It's . . . odd. I'm trying to understand.'

'Usually, I went and stayed with some boy I knew. Your mother had a colourful adolescence. We'll leave it at that. Could this girl have—?'

'No. I don't think so.'

She waved a hand at him. 'Anyway. Who are you to talk about running away? You did. Just the once. Which makes it worse. I was pulling my hair out until you turned up, all bruised and bloody, not even looking me in the eye.'

'That was just after Dad died.'

'I know exactly when it was, thank you.'

'Some kid I knew started talking about him. Like it was a joke. Like Dad deserved it somehow. We got into a fight. I stayed out in the park. One night. That's all.'

A confession of a kind. 'You got into a fight and some kid beat you up. Then you stayed out all night and drove your mother frantic. The Y chromosome all over.'

He shook his head. 'No. I won. I beat him up. It was bad. I was ashamed. Losing my rag like that . . . it wasn't me.'

'If it wasn't you, you wouldn't have done it.'

'Which is why I was ashamed.'

'Has a single word we've exchanged here,' she asked, 'revealed a thing about this missing girl of yours?'

'Ask me later.'

Marie Le Gall rearranged her pillow, a sign this awkward conversation was coming to an end. 'It's late. I'm tired. I'm grateful your friend upstairs doesn't seem minded to play the great lover tonight. If there's nothing else . . .'

'Perhaps I'm looking at this the wrong way round. Is there something common about running away?' he wondered. 'Something universal that might stop a kid doing it, however much they dreamt of being somewhere else? Someone else?'

'You came back after one night. You tell me.'

Baptiste shrugged.

'What's this girl's name?'

'Noémie. Noémie Augustin.'

'It's a nice name.'

'She sounds a nice kid.'

'Do you think Noémie Augustin felt wanted? At home? Felt loved?'

He didn't have to think about that for long. 'I'm pretty sure she did.'

'In that case the girl would never run away. Not unless something extraordinary – something I can't even imagine – happened. You came back, didn't you?'

He laughed, got up, walked over, kissed his mother on both cheeks, got a half-grateful grunt in return.

'And I always will,' he whispered.

28

Everyone in Boulliers knew Eric Hubert. Martine Augustin, always more at ease with strangers, warned her husband about the man not long after she arrived. One of the neighbours had, in couched terms, talked of him as a man well familiar with the police, a jailbird, though lately he always seemed to avoid prosecution. For what, Augustin's wife never said. Drugs, she guessed. Stolen property. Poaching. The man had no job that anyone spoke of but never looked impoverished, unlike some of those around him.

Most of the streets in the neighbourhood were named after writers. Hubert had an end-of-terrace house in the Rue Verne. It was one of the few places where the lights were still on. Augustin stood outside, hesitating, the dog twitching at his ankles. Not scared. He was a man who could handle himself if needed. That had happened from time to time in Calais. But there were decisions to be made, more so now Martine was asking awkward questions. He was about to knock when the door opened and Hubert was there, a hulk of a man in long shorts and a vest stained with sweat marks, straggly beard, muscled, a few centimetres taller than Augustin, someone with the physique of a dissolute boxer or wrestler. Behind him lurked the son who'd been hanging round the estate, watching Noémie.

'If this is about my brat,' Hubert said in a voice full of grit and menace, 'he's got nothing to do with your daughter. I'd advise you to listen to that. I don't want to say it again.'

'Can I come in?'

'Why?'

Augustin took out the notes, most of the cash he'd saved over the past few months. 'I think maybe we could do business.'

Hubert gazed at the wad then opened the door. 'Be my guest.'

29

It was almost four hours from Clermiers to Boulogne, hard driving, though at night the roads were empty. Celia Murray had planned the route in advance. Her brother sat in the passenger seat of the camper van with the directions she'd written down, checking them against the AA European atlas they had, two years out of date.

Most of the journey had been in silence since she picked him up at the petrol station, filling the camper van for the journey home, moaning about the price of fuel. It was only when they were passing through the quiet streets of Millot that she asked, 'What did they say? About you leaving early?'

'Not much.'

'Don't be like that, Dan. You know we've got to go.'

'Suppose so.'

'No suppose, is there?'

'I told them Dad was sick.'

'What?' she shrieked.

'I just thought . . . they wanted a reason.'

'Christ! We went through that, didn't we? You were getting depressed. About Noémie. About the fact you might have stuck with her instead of coming to see me. I thought we'd agreed—'

'We did. I forgot.'

'You *forgot*?'

He turned over the pages she'd given him and said something about the crossroads coming up. 'I didn't know what to say. They looked so bad. Like the world had ended.'

'Dan. Just keep your eyes on the map.'

'The map's old. I'm sure some of these roads are wrong. We could still turn back . . .'

'I told you. The sooner we're out of France the better.'

30

Hubert ordered his son to look after the dog then took Charles Augustin into the kitchen. The place smelled of game, raw meat getting old. Pheasants, rabbits and a hare hung on a washing line strung across the back wall. Dirty plates were stacked in the sink. A litre bottle of Nicolas *vin rouge ordinaire* was on the table, some of it poured into a glass tumbler. Alongside was an expensive-looking SLR camera with a long lens, a Nikon.

'I didn't know you were a photographer,' Augustin said.

'A man needs a hobby. Doesn't have to advertise it.'

Hubert waved the bottle and asked if he wanted some. Augustin shook his head. The place reminded him of the hovel he'd had to himself those first few months alone after Laurent had tempted him to Clermiers. Somewhere that hadn't seen a woman in a while.

'You got any idea where she is?' Hubert asked.

'None.'

'Is that bastard Dupont doing anything?'

Augustin shook his head. 'He seems to be leaving it to two new men. They don't know Clermiers. Dupont thinks she just ran away.'

'They do that.'

'Not my Noémie.'

Hubert leaned over the table, grabbed the tumbler, took a swig, rolled it round his mouth. 'Listen to me. Kids. You raise them. You think you know them. You don't. They've got little fantasies playing right there . . .' He tapped the side of his skull and Augustin noticed a tattoo on his neck, a serpent curling upwards towards his ear. 'Voices telling them to do things, stupid things sometimes, and you never get to know till it's happened.'

'If you . . . if you hear anything . . .'

'Why would I hear anything? Why me?'

'I-I-I don't know. I just thought you might . . .'

That got no response.

'And if you do . . . tell me first. Not Dupont. Me. Deal?'

Hubert chuckled and took a swig from the glass of wine. 'Don't need a deal for that. You think I'm walking into Dupont's grubby hands willingly? Not me.'

Augustin was fiddling with the wad of notes.

'Also, you're not waving all that cash in my face to ask me for rumours. Are you?'

'No.'

'What else do you want then?'

Crossroads, Charles Augustin thought. Life always came to them somewhere along the way. Go forward, go back. Turn left, turn right. He'd been lucky with some. That was how he met Martine. Then there were others, occasionally the ones that looked most promising, that turned out to be nothing like he expected.

He rustled the notes, looked directly at the man across the table and said, 'I was hoping you'd sell me a gun.'

31

Five in the morning, dawn was just starting to cast warm light on the chalk cliffs of Dover as the *Hengist* pulled into Folkestone Harbour, the Murrays' camper van in the ferry's belly, *Celia* at the wheel, her brother head down in the passenger seat. Daniel had thrown up halfway across the Channel. She was used to the ferries, liked them, even when the sea was rough. This was one of the gentlest crossings she'd known. It wasn't the waves that made him vomit his bacon sandwich into the grey waters off Cap Gris-Nez.

Even so her heart was in her mouth when they went through French customs in the early hours. The policeman she'd spoken to, Baptiste, seemed an interesting man. An intelligent one. If she'd gone to him and said her brother wasn't coping well with the disappearance of Noémie Augustin, that he needed to go home to recuperate, the man would doubtless have questioned the two of them closely. Perhaps even forbidden them to leave Clermiers at all. She'd no idea if French law allowed him to do that. No desire whatsoever to find out. She wanted her brother home. The French could deal with their problems themselves.

She'd been over the Channel so many times for work. It was a crossing she always made from Folkestone to Boulogne, a little slower than the Dover-Calais route, with fewer sailings too. But closer to home and over the previous two years she'd got to know some of the customs and immigration men who worked in the Folkestone terminal. A friendly face always helped.

There he was, waiting by the barrier when she finally got through the queue to the road, waving her into the side. She had her passport out of the window before he even asked.

'Miss Murray of Bouverie Camping.' He doffed his cap. Fred, that was his name. She was sure. 'What a pleasure to see you again. Anything to declare?'

'I'm knackered after lots of driving, Fred. No fags, no booze, no duty free. Work trip as usual.'

'All work and no play makes Jill a dull girl they say.' He grinned. 'But you never look dull to me.'

'Thanks. Can I . . .?'

'Someone's been asking after you.'

Her heart leapt.

'Who?'

He pulled a notebook out of his pocket, cleared his throat,

gave her a theatrical scolding look. 'Your mother. She said you're going to have to turn round and go back to France. Apparently, those new tents didn't work or something.' He waved the notebook. 'I don't know the details and they're none of my business. But it seems she and your dad have to go to London. They won't be back till Thursday at the earliest. She wants you to call her there and fix a return ferry as soon as you can.' He nodded at the ticket office behind the barrier. 'You could just do a U-turn and go back on the next *Hengist* if you wanted.'

'Stuff that. I'm bushed.'

He was squinting at Daniel. 'So's he by the looks of it.' He glanced at the passports. 'Your brother? Not seen him before.'

'Dan's been on an exchange visit. He can get seasick in the bath.'

'Ah . . . well . . .' He waved them on. '*Bon voyage* as they say across the puddle. See you again very soon by the looks of it.'

Her brother was staring at her as she drove through the open barrier, past the train station, out towards the ugly concrete bulk of the Burstin Hotel.

'Don't worry,' she said as they headed for the hill. 'I'll deal with it.'

Dawn breaking over Clermiers, harvest dust speckling the air. Martine Augustin sat at the window, staring out at the empty street. No sign of Charles again. No word. Maybe she'd chased him off with her sudden outburst. Maybe she should have stayed quiet and kept it all to herself.

Noémie gone. Now her husband.

And all the while she kept asking herself . . . was there something I missed? An errant word? A hint of the ruptures to come? Was Noémie so unhappy in Clermiers she might run after some daydream in Paris or beyond? Did Charles feel so unwanted he sought solace elsewhere? What kind of mother, what kind of wife, wouldn't even notice?

It had never occurred to her to wonder what it might be like to see a child go missing. That kind of thing happened to other people, ones you didn't know. Families who had to be living with some kind of fault line running through them like the sly and subtle tremors of a coming earthquake anticipating the moment of its deadly strike.

There were no fault lines, not that she'd seen. Only a day so ordinary it would otherwise have passed unremarked before everything turned to doubt and fear and agony.

'Where are you?' she whispered at the dusty glass.

Early morning in the petrol station. As usual Gilles Mailloux was anticipating the end of his shift with a coffee and a pastry past its eat-by date. The night had been quiet, one customer only, the English woman in her camper van, anxious to get away, her silent, miserable brother in the passenger seat saying nothing at all.

Mailloux would normally be organising the paperwork, the list of customers on account, money due. But, when he went to the filing cabinets to add that night's records, there was nothing there. Every sheet he and the day man had set down, names, registration number, fuel taken, price due to be paid, was gone.

It was inexplicable. His first thought was that Laurent would be furious. How could anyone be billed after that? Mailloux could probably remember most of the customers. But what they'd had in the way of fuel . . . there was no means of recovering that. Perhaps Augustin or Laurent himself had taken the records early for some reason. But if that happened, he would have been told. Setting them up for collection was his job, no one else's. Which meant, surely, that someone must have entered the garage the only time it was closed, Sunday night to Monday morning.

He had a key. Augustin as well. Bruno Laurent, obviously. Was there anyone else? He wasn't sure.

There'd be hell to pay, surely. Mailloux wasn't looking

forward to that when he saw a figure shambling up the road, a dog with him, limping on a lead.

Gilles Mailloux felt his blood run cold. He walked outside.

'Jesus. What the hell happened to you?'

Augustin was weeping and for a little while could hardly speak.

Étienne Fatoussi's radio had just come on, a breakfast show, loud pop. Till then Baptiste hadn't heard anything except for some farm traffic outside and the hooting of a pair of talkative owls. In Paris, on a case of any seriousness, there'd be an active night team he could talk to when he felt like it. Call in at any time and get an update of what was happening. But this was Clermiers and Captain Dupont remained reluctant to see the disappearance of a young black girl from a grim estate as serious at all. Baptiste hoped he was right, even if his instincts told him the opposite. There was something disturbing about Noémie Augustin's disappearance, just visible in the odd, almost hostile relationship between her parents, barely hidden beneath the unconvincing dreamy optimism of those fairy stories in her diary.

The unexpected sound of a loud phone disturbed his thoughts. It was the one in the hall. He dragged himself to the door, his mother already crying out for someone to answer 'the damned thing'.

'Got it,' he yelled as Fatoussi, half-naked, appeared at the top of the stairs.

'Is that you, Baptiste?' asked a shaky voice on a bad and crackly line.

'It is. Who's this?'

'Gilles Mailloux. From the petrol station.'

'I know who you are, Gilles. I'm pretty good with names.'

Silence. Baptiste could feel bad news waiting down the line.

'What is it?'

A moment then Mailloux said, 'I've got Charles Augustin here. The man's in a hell of a state.'

Another *longueur.*

'Because?'

'He says he's found a body.'

Part Three:

In the Bois de Mortery

32

12:32 p.m. Douai Prison, 15 November, 1976

There wasn't a sound from the prison yard. The guillotine, Baptiste guessed, was ready. All they were waiting for was the order.

'Let me try again,' Baptiste said. 'If you were to tell me somewhere we might look for Noémie. Anything. I can call Paris . . .'

Mailloux perked up. 'You mean you want another feather in your cap?'

'I didn't want this one. I was thinking of the girl's mother.'

'How considerate. Is she here? Is Martine standing outside demanding my head?'

That was one of the many curious aspects of the case. The woman had vanished.

'I haven't heard from her in months.'

'Do you not find that odd?'

'There's little about this case that isn't. Perhaps there were too many bad memories in Clermiers. Who's to know? Grief isn't a mathematical equation. People aren't machines. They respond to misfortune in different ways. Anger. Desolation. Blame, of others, of themselves.'

'Which do you think was hers?'

'The woman never let me close enough to know.'

'Then why are you throwing her name at me now?'

Baptiste couldn't stop looking at the cell door, wondering when it might open again, what the news would be.

Mailloux lounged on his hard bed, looking ready to sleep again. 'A more important question. Why do you think this is taking that corrupt fool in the Élysée Palace so long? Am I meant to believe he's agonising over the decision?'

'I wouldn't want a man's death upon my conscience.'

His eyes opened and Mailloux stared across the cell. 'He's a politician. What's conscience got to do with it?'

'All the same—'

'My death will be on yours. I can see that. No need, Julien. As you said. All you did was your job. Putting me in that court. The rest . . .' He waved his arm around theatrically. 'That's entirely of my own doing, and I remain immensely proud of the fact.'

After the sentence was passed, Baptiste had taken it upon himself to try to understand the process, how he might influence it in some way, perhaps get a stay of execution or, better, a change to a custodial sentence. It was clear the president's name on any reprieve was a formality. The real decisions lay among the labyrinth of bureaucrats within the Ministry of Justice, faceless men – all men – none of whom wished to speak to a lowly detective. The press had had a field day with Mailloux's behaviour in court, his arrogant silences, the way he laughed at the judge, at witnesses, at the evidence. As if the entire judicial process was a joke.

The verdict had been predictable from the moment Mailloux waved a dismissive hand at the bench and refused to plead. Still, the sentence . . . it was only towards the end that the reporters began to talk in whispers about the guillotine. It had never occurred to Baptiste the case might end this way.

'Why do you want to die, Gilles?'

That wave of a skinny hand again. 'You said yourself. People aren't machines. They respond to misfortune in different ways.' He leaned forward. 'Why do you alone wish to save me? Is that

101

mercy? Pity? Or for your sake, your precious sense of right and wrong?'

Perhaps, thought Baptiste, a little of all three.

He got up. 'I'll phone Paris and try to find out what's happening.'

33

Clermiers, Tuesday, 20 July

No one went for leisurely walks in the Bois de Mortery. No one could. Behind its high brick walls the place was a morass of brambles, sycamore, chestnut and fallen, rotting trunks, inhabited by nothing but foxes, badgers, and rabbits. The forest ran, unmanaged for decades, down the hill from the château, part of an estate long abandoned. It was in the reluctant ownership of the municipality by default. Clermiers couldn't afford to repair the place. No one was interested in buying a wreck that might cost millions to bring back into any kind of use. And so both château and its ramshackle surroundings, once the preserve of the local aristocracy, a place where the Marquis de Sade stayed while on the run from the authorities, rotted, unloved, unseen, a blemish invisible to the world outside.

All this Baptiste learned from Gilles Mailloux as he drove the police Simca down the track to the boathouse again, a weeping Charles Augustin crammed in the back with his puzzled little dog and Étienne Fatoussi now in smart casual clothes, not a well-pressed police uniform. Augustin left the talking to Mailloux. Noémie's father had turned up at the petrol station just after daybreak, inconsolable, barely able to speak. Mailloux had to feed him coffee, sit him down in the office, wait until he could talk.

Piece by piece it came out. The man had had an argument at home and gone out with the dog, thinking that perhaps that

102

might help him find something, anything to do with Noémie. Close to the boathouse the animal had become excited, yapping, frantic, tugging desperately at the lead. When Augustin let the terrier go, it scampered through a gap in the wall and vanished into the brambles and the undergrowth. The animal wouldn't come when called. He went after it, as best he could in the bright moonlight. Minutes later, fighting his way through the wood, he heard the dog whimpering, tried to find it, and stumbled into something.

In the back of the Simca, Augustin began to weep, his head in his hands, the dog puzzled on his lap.

'He said it was a body,' Mailloux added. 'Hanging from a tree. He . . . he bumped into the legs. Couldn't see properly in the moonlight. Turned and ran.' A shrug. 'All the way to me. I guess no one else would be around just then.'

They stopped at the end of the track, near the boathouse. Augustin looked lost, his head somewhere else altogether. Mailloux reached over and nudged his arm.

'Charles. You have to tell the policemen where to look. That place is a jungle. There's just us here.'

Augustin handed him the terrier. 'She can take you there. Keep her on the lead. I'm not . . . I can't.' Tears streaked his dark cheeks, his mouth hung open, slack, dead. 'I saw as much as I wanted.' He glanced outside the window. Another scorching summer day, cloudless, a pristine blue sky, beckoned. 'That was enough.'

Baptiste got out and tried to raise someone on the police radio. Nothing. Fatoussi came to join him. Then Mailloux.

'I think we're going to need you, Gilles,' Baptiste said. 'We don't know where to begin.'

He had the dog on the lead. 'Me neither.' Mailloux nodded at the estate wall. 'I've never set foot in that place in my life. Why would you? Maybe a few poachers go there. That's all.'

'You said you heard music. The other night.'

He hesitated over that. 'I was thinking maybe that was here.

103

Where you found things. The château, the forest. I don't know.'

Fatoussi took the lead from him. 'Enough chat. Let's go.'

34

The gate they'd seen before was ajar. Was it like that before? Baptiste wasn't sure. Maybe. They'd never checked, and perhaps that was an omission. Beyond was what they'd been promised: a jungle of brambles, fallen trunks, rampant sycamore and chestnut trees dying in the shade after so many decades of neglect. But there was a path of a kind, narrow, the grass well worn. A fox track, or perhaps that of a badger, Mailloux suggested, and neither Baptiste nor Fatoussi, both city men, were inclined to argue.

The dog kept pulling. It knew where it wanted to go. Fatoussi stopped at one point, turned, and stared at Baptiste. 'I never like seeing dead people, Julien.'

'Who does?'

Mailloux seemed disappointed in both of them. 'If the police don't deal with things like this . . . who does?'

'Yeah, yeah, yeah,' Fatoussi grumbled then let the terrier lead on. After a while they diverted from the fox track. It was easy to see someone had been here recently – Augustin they presumed. Nettles, brambles and tall, thick grass, all dry in the summer drought, had been bent over by someone making an awkward, zigzag path. Ahead was an upturned tree blocking the way, a gigantic oak blown over in a distant storm, broad trunk on the ground, next to it a pit full of debris where the roots once grew.

The terrier stopped. The bent grass and undergrowth marking Augustin's presumed route had vanished.

'I don't see anything,' Fatoussi said. 'Anywhere.'

The dog was whining.

'I think it misses Augustin,' Mailloux suggested. 'You should have made him come.'

Baptiste walked round the fallen oak. The path picked up again there. He took it, they followed.

A hundred metres on and they stopped.

'Christ,' Fatoussi muttered then wandered over to a patch of nettles and began to throw up.

She was hanging from the low branch of a sprawling sycamore, one that appeared to have grown up from an earlier fallen trunk like a twisted, unwanted weed.

The smell was faint and vaguely sweet. Old. Fading, like the corpse itself. Baptiste had little experience of long-dead bodies but this one must have been here a year or more. Time and weather and animals had taken their toll. It was not Noémie Augustin, though perhaps her father, stumbling into those bony, dangling legs, panicked, terrified, the yelping dog at his ankles, nothing but moonlight to see by, wouldn't know.

It was a girl, though, teenage or early twenties he guessed. A noose round her shrivelled neck, skull cocked to one side, mouth open showing yellow rotting teeth. She wore what looked like the costume of a church choir girl, white tunic with a scarlet collar ragged round what was left of her neck, black skirt that stopped just above what was left of her knees.

'Étienne. If you've finished getting rid of your breakfast, please take the dog back to the car and tell Augustin this is not his daughter.'

Fatoussi wiped his mouth. 'I told you I don't like this kind of thing.'

'Then perhaps Gilles has a point and you're in the wrong line of work.'

There was the briefest moment of conflict between them. Then Baptiste realised he was being too harsh. 'I'm sorry. I should never have said that. Leave this to me. Go and tell Augustin the good news. We've no reason to believe Noémie isn't still alive somewhere.'

Fatoussi nodded and went back the way they came.

'Looks like she hanged herself,' Mailloux said when they were alone.

'It would seem so.'

Gilles Mailloux crossed himself and shook his head. 'Lili never seemed happy. That father of hers. No mother. I've lived in Boulliers all my life. I learned early you stay away from the Huberts. Maybe I should have said something.'

'Wait—'

'When she went missing. When her father, and Dupont, said she'd run away. I wondered.' He grimaced. 'Sometimes she used to hint at things . . .'

Baptiste blinked against the sudden harsh sunlight breaking through the canopy of trees.

'You know who she is?'

'Lili Hubert. Not far off a neighbour. She used to do odd jobs around town. Cleaning for people. I believe . . .' He scratched his head then pointed out the torn, dirty gown she was wearing. 'Lili used to sing in the church choir as well. Not that the Huberts are religious you understand. Anything but. She had a good voice, or so the priest told her. It paid when there was a wedding or a funeral.' He grimaced. 'Probably the only honest francs that family earned.'

'You're sure it's her?'

Mailloux had something in his hand. He passed it over. A *carte nationale d'identité,* a photo of an unsmiling young girl with lank, greasy hair. A name. *Liliane Hubert.* Date of birth 13th September, 1957. A tiny notebook too with writing, faded and stained from dirt and rain. A kind of diary, though all this one seemed to have in it were single line entries for dates.

'I found them on the ground while you were having a go at your colleague,' he said. 'In this.'

A faded yellow plastic purse, very cheap. He opened it up. Inside a few coins and three condoms in their foil packs.

Mailloux cast a brief glance at the grisly sight above them

and wrinkled his nose. 'Poor Lili. You must excuse me. I can't take this any more.'

35

Charles Augustin's grim discovery of a young girl's corpse hanging from a tree in the Bois de Mortery was not welcome in the sleepy Clermiers police station. Bonnay, the only local on duty that morning, had no idea what to do. Only the captain could decide that. But Dupont was away for some kind of personal appointment, not expected back until late afternoon if at all. There was no coroner in Clermiers, no process or apparatus for dealing with a dead girl in the forest. After interrogating Bonnay about the possibilities, Baptiste took it on himself to call the regional police headquarters in Millot and ask for a coroner's officer and a recovery team. It was clear Clermiers' larger neighbour was expected to handle serious cases beyond the town's resources. Theft, traffic issues, unruly behaviour were matters Dupont probably relished taking on. Anything more complex, requiring work, time, and effort, he was happy to pass to the larger station whenever he could.

The officer who answered in Millot sounded used to this idea and said they'd be there when they could. Baptiste got the clear impression they couldn't give a damn about what happened in Dupont's tiny fiefdom. An apparent suicide on someone else's territory counted for little. The coroner would be responsible for any medical examination and report back to Clermiers. From that point on they would, it seemed, wash their hands of the dead Lili Hubert and wish to know little except who would take away the autopsied corpse.

Dupont's name came briefly into the conversation. It was not mentioned with any warmth. In the meantime, the girl would have to hang there in the Bois de Mortery as she must have done for the fourteen months since she went missing.

With a pained sigh, Bonnay found the file in the station's metal cabinets. Two pages only. Reported by a woman called Francine Lamarr who employed her once a week as a cleaner. When the girl failed to turn up, she'd gone round to the house, had an argument with the father who'd told her to mind her own business. Then come to the police.

'Accusations were made which could not be substantiated,' the report added at the end. Bonnay had typed it.

'What kind of accusations?' Baptiste asked.

The officer scowled. 'What kind do you think? That family's never been quite . . . normal. Boulliers scum.'

'What *kind*?' Fatoussi repeated, with a heat and anger that took Bonnay aback.

'The keep-it-in-the-family kind. Do I need to spell it out?'

Fatoussi swore then said, 'I hate men who mess with kids.'

'We all do,' Bonnay replied. 'You try bringing that kind of thing to court. Who's going to testify? Who's going to believe a messed-up kid against a grown man? Especially her father.'

Baptiste had been going through the file. There was little of use there, not even a mention of Hubert's demeanour.

'Was he surprised she'd gone missing?' he asked.

Bonnay scratched his chin. 'If I remember right, he didn't give much of a damn. He thought she'd gone to Paris to work as a whore. Which is what her mum did. Better than living at home with that animal, I guess.'

There was no address for the mother, no way of contacting her at all it seemed. Nothing but a name: Valerie Vartan. The couple weren't married.

Baptiste called his old station in Paris and asked them to look out for a woman of that name, perhaps working in the sex industry. Until Millot came back with an opinion on the corpse, there seemed little else he could do. Noémie Augustin was a more pressing matter. She, at least, might still be alive.

'Someone has to tell the father,' Fatoussi said. 'Bring him in here for a little chat. Let me do it, Julien. You've enough on

108

your plate. And Bonnay here looks ready to go for his coffee break.'

The local man glared at him. 'If you think you can take in that evil bastard on your own . . .'

'Oh, I do.' Fatoussi clicked his fingers. 'Keys?'

'Maybe we do this together,' Baptiste said. 'Safer . . .'

'I can handle myself.' Fatoussi clicked his fingers again. 'Don't worry.'

Bonnay leaned back in his chair and for once looked as if he was trying to make a serious point. 'Eric Hubert's an evil bastard. God knows what he's got up to that we haven't found out about. The things we did were bad enough.'

Fatoussi smiled. 'Sounds my sort of guy. Keys . . .'

Baptiste threw them over. 'Go easy on him, Étienne. He was still her father.'

'And you?'

Another young girl's diary. A very different one to that of Noémie Augustin. All the same Baptiste wanted to go through it, line by line.

'I'll go round the corner for a coffee. If, by chance, anyone wants me . . .'

Bonnay reached into his desk drawer and took out a fresh radio. 'Here. I found another one. It seems to work. You can both call me when you want.'

He watched them go, Fatoussi to the Simca, Baptiste to the café across the square.

When he was sure he was alone, Pascal Bonnay picked up the phone.

'What's this?' Dupont snapped down the line. 'When I say I don't want to be disturbed, I mean it.'

'The black guy, Augustin . . . he found Lili Hubert hanging from a tree in the Bois de Mortery this morning. He's back home now, weeping his heart out.'

Silence, then, 'Shit.'

109

'Millot are going to recover the body. Provide the coroner. They don't seem so interested.'

'What the hell was Augustin doing there?'

'Looking for his daughter. The dog smelled something.'

'Any news about his kid?'

'Not a thing.' Bonnay chuckled. 'That Fatoussi idiot has gone out to bring in Eric Hubert all on his own.'

'Any luck, Eric will put him in hospital. That way we get one of them off our backs.'

'It was suicide, boss. Lili Hubert was a basket case. They all said that. She hung herself. An inquest in Millot. A couple of paragraphs in the paper. Who cares about some little bastard from Boulliers?'

Dupont hesitated. 'I've a feeling our new recruit Baptiste thinks he does. Where is he?'

'Out there. Snooping. I gave them both radios so they can keep in touch. I'll tell you if they come up with something.'

'Good. *C'est tout.*'

36

There was barely a single sentence in Lili Hubert's diary. Just small and very careful scribbles next to dates written in a childish hand. Most appeared to be appointments for cleaning work. Baptiste could tell that from the regular entry against the name Lamarr: a little drawing of a mop. The mop appeared elsewhere too, once a week on Fridays, next to a crucifix. He was puzzled about that one until he found an entry that also included the observation, 'Chauvin is a pathetic old bastard.' The priest then. And there were others here and there, usually for Sundays, with a rough scribble of a singing mouth and a cross. Choir, he guessed, at the Église Saint-Vivien.

Only one seemed beyond interpretation. It was infrequent, but always written in an angry, bold hand, with an exclamation mark behind. It looked like a crucifix again, but smaller, to the right the number four.

Baptiste finished his coffee then used the place's public phone to call Millot. There was a new duty officer, one who seemed a touch more helpful. He said a team was on its way to the Bois de Mortery to recover the body.

'Dupont's dealing with it,' he added.

That threw him. 'I don't even know where Dupont is.'

'He's in the Bois de Mortery. With the body.'

'But he didn't know where it was.'

The man laughed. 'He said you lot left a track like an elephant stampede. It was easy enough. Suicide, eh? Never pretty, is it? We'll do the business here. The coroner's in the loop. You found the parents?'

'On it.'

'Never liked doing the death knock, myself. Especially for a youngster. Someone has to. Boulliers, Dupont said.'

'You know the place?'

'Only by reputation. Did station relief at Clermiers a couple of years back. Couldn't wait to get out of there. Good luck to you, chum.'

The line went dead.

He asked at the café counter for directions to the priest's house. Two streets away, a detached, three-storey mansion, big for one man, even a priest, he thought.

Christian Chauvin was short and stout, in his late forties, round, forgettable face, black trousers, white shirt, sweat stains beneath the arms as he carried a shopping bag up the path towards the door. The heat was intense already, the air full of insects and the tiny, glittering shards of wheat or grass that seemed everywhere that summer.

Baptiste caught up with him at the door, took out his police ID and said, 'Father Chauvin?'

'Oui?'

The man looked alarmed.

111

'May I come in?'

'Why?'

'I'd like to talk to you about Lili Hubert. And Noémie Augustin.'

Alarm turned to anger. 'What is this? I know nothing about those girls. Lili vanished ages ago. A sad, disturbed child, I'm afraid. As for the Augustin girl . . . they weren't church goers. I never knew her.'

He walked in and started to close the door. Baptiste stepped up and held it open.

'Charles Augustin went looking for his daughter last night. He found Lili's body in the estate of the old château.'

The priest looked shocked to the core. He'd surely no idea Lili Hubert was long dead.

'It appears she took her own life. If I could have a minute or two of your time, I'd appreciate it. Please.'

'Of course,' Chauvin said, shaking his head. 'This is dreadful. Would you like a drink?'

'No.'

The priest opened the door for him. 'Then do not judge me if I do.'

37

Fatoussi had just about buried his fury when he rolled up outside the Hubert house in the Dumas. He never talked about it to anyone, but there were reasons he could barely control himself when it came to sex crimes against juveniles. His younger sister in Marseille had been raped on the way back from school when she was just fourteen. That was the year before. The bright, cheerful kid he'd known had been stolen away one balmy July evening that was so warm and lovely she chose to walk home from youth club instead of taking the bus. One night was all it took.

The Hubert house was a miserable-looking two-up, two-down, older than the rest of the estate, another farmworker's place from when the area was agricultural. Curtains closed on all the front windows, downstairs and up. No woman would have put up with that.

He went to hammer on the peeling paint of the front door but before he could get there it was open. The weedy Hubert kid stood on the doorstep looking scared.

'Nicked yourself another bike yet, Didier?'

Fatoussi didn't wait for an answer, just pushed him aside and went into the narrow grubby hall. It was ill-lit and smelled of damp and mould. Something else from the back, an aroma he knew. Blood.

'Where is he? Your father?'

'Dunno.' The kid's voice sounded even more whiny and annoying than before. 'You can't barge in here like that.'

'You don't say . . .'

He walked on, towards the smell of meat, raw and rank, getting stronger.

On the kitchen table lay the skinned corpse of what must once have been a hare, front legs broken and severed, dark blood and even darker guts leaking onto stained wood.

'What did that?' he asked, pointing at the eviscerated animal.

'Dad can go hunting when he wants.'

'Not with traps, unless the law's different here.'

There was a yard and an outbuilding, brick with a flat roof, no windows.

He turned and crouched down in front of the terrified Didier.

'Tell me about your sister.'

The kid's face went bright red. 'Nothing to tell.'

'Oh. I think there is. I think there's lots. How did your old man treat her? Why'd she run away if this was all happy families?'

More than red, his cheeks were crimson.

'You shouldn't be here, mister. If my dad gets back he'll break your neck.'

'He can try. Now. About Lili—'

'I don't know anything.'

He put a hand to Didier's shoulder. 'I'm sorry. Never any easy way to say this. She's dead. They found her in the woods this morning. Hanging from a tree. Been there a long time. Not a pretty sight. Lost my breakfast over that.'

Didier Hubert started crying, shoulders chucking up and down, eyes pouring, nose soon snotty.

'Did she ever talk about killing herself?'

Nothing.

'Didier. Whatever happened . . . it's going to come out. Trust me. Best you let go of whatever it is you've got hidden down in your guts right now. Leave it any longer and it festers. Trust me. I know.'

Still silence.

'Not a lot to ask, is it?'

Fatoussi made the boy sit at the kitchen table close to the corpse of the hare. 'First things first. Let's go back a bit. Did you hide all that broken glass outside the police house? Or was it him?' Nothing. 'Don't worry. I'm not going to tell. I'm not going to nick anybody for it. I just want to know. So we've got it clear. My mate's mother's not hurt bad. We can keep it a secret between us—'

'He says don't trust the *flics*.'

'Right.' Fatoussi nodded. 'Do you trust him? Your own father?' A pause, to make it hurt. 'Did Lili, do you think? And if she did, why did she hang herself from a tree in the Bois de Mortery?'

Didier Hubert was weeping, no control over the sobbing, just a face full of misery, tears and snot and hurt. Fatoussi could feel every shudder.

'He'll belt me. Can't . . .'

'You said you were in Lille. For the football. Staying with Uncle Franc.'

'We did go. Came back.'

'What time was this?'

'Dark. Middle of night. I don't know.'

'And you stayed here?'

'Yeah.'

'Both of you.'

'Yeah.'

'There. Now the glass. The bike . . .'

The kid looked more terrified than ever.

'Lili. Your dad. Tell me the truth now. It's important. What did he do?'

The boy's eyes shifted to the back door, then the outbuilding, a sizable one, in the yard. After that he got up and took a keyring from a hook by the oven.

'He'll kill us both,' Didier Hubert whispered.

Fatoussi patted him on the shoulder, grabbed the keys and went outside.

38

There were four men from the Millot force, none of them Dupont knew. They'd taken the corpse down from the tree, stashed it in a body bag and were about to carry that to their van by the boathouse.

'Jesus,' moaned the one who'd dealt most with the corpse. 'Here we are doing Clermiers' dirty work again. How do you people pass the time?'

Dogs were barking somewhere further in the wood.

'I got no backup,' Dupont replied. 'Just me. One local buffoon. Two others they sent me for replacements. One from Paris. One from Marseille. You think I like this any more than you?'

The man juggled the frayed rope in his hands. 'I think you're lazy bastards if I'm honest. We put a dog team out to see if you've any other surprises lurking here.'

115

'Thanks.'

'No need. We don't want to come back and be getting you out of a hole again.'

The three others took hold of the body bag, lifted it, and began to walk along the track the recent human traffic had made, bent dry grass and thistles, treacherous brambles trying to trip someone with their snaking shoots.

'Fair enough.' Dupont shrugged. 'I'd feel the same if I were you.'

'That's done then.'

The Millot man set off without another word. Dupont followed.

'You're sure it's suicide?'

'What do you think, Maigret?'

'The kid was a nervous wreck. Her father's a local criminal. Probably not the kindest of men. She went missing . . . I don't know . . . more than a year ago. We did what we could.'

The man laughed as he struggled to shrug off a clinging bramble. 'I don't doubt that.' He held out the rope. 'Want this? As a keepsake?'

'I think the coroner might—'

The dog team, three men, two German shepherds with their tongues lolling, thirsty from the heat, emerged from a thicket to the left. Nothing else anywhere in the Bois de Mortery they said, except for a couple of badger setts and a fox den.

'Listen, Dupont. We've got work enough of our own. Staff shortages too. You write us a report about this kid saying she was just the kind to hang herself in the middle of some shitty jungle of yours. I pass that on to the coroner. The medics cut her about as best they can, given the shape she's in. If they don't find anything – and I took a good look, I'm like that, they won't – then we wrap this up and add it to the list of shit you people owe us for.'

'A thorough job then.'

He didn't like that. 'If you think you can do better . . .' No

116

answer. 'Thought so. Just write us that report. And find someone who'll dispose of this kid once we're done.'

39

Hubert's outbuilding was recent, new, big, almost industrial. It
took Fatoussi three goes to find the right key.

There was a light inside and a dividing wall halfway along
the room. This first section was Hubert's poaching base. Traps
of all kinds and sizes, shotguns hooked on the wall, packs of
cartridges stored below, more neatly than anything he'd seen
in the house. Eric Hubert knew his priorities. Another line of
dead ducks and pheasants, gutted but still unplucked, hung
from a wire set across the room.

Didier kept looking at the door ahead. That was locked too,
a smaller mechanism and fiddly, but Fatoussi got there in the
end. Ahead lay nothing but darkness until he found a switch
on the wall. A low red light came on slowly. He could scarcely
believe what he was seeing. A darkroom, smaller than the one
they had in police HQ in Marseille, but properly equipped, developing tanks, an enlarger, trays, and that smell of chemicals
he always associated with the process of turning silver halide
into first negatives then photos.

A row of prints was drying on the line. It only took one look
to understand what kind of industry Eric Hubert was running
hidden away behind the Rue Dumas.

There was a filing cabinet at the end of the darkroom.
Another key needed to unlock that. Fatoussi took out a stack
of prints from one of the dividers. A young girl, very young,
another hidden man. The same old, dismal story, pain and
violent sex.

He didn't show them to Didier Hubert. No need. This was
the miserable girl he'd seen on that ID card Gilles Mailloux
had found beneath the body in the woods. This was the source

of the misery drawn on that skinny, sad face.

A cry. A scream. Then the light failed and there was a shadow blocking the door, Didier squealing, crying, terrified.

'What the hell is this?' Eric Hubert grunted, fist out, face demonic in fury and the red light of the room.

With a sigh, Fatoussi casually drew out the revolver he kept in the holster beneath his jacket, raised it, pointed the barrel straight across the dark room.

'It's called a Ruger SP101. Five shells. How many you want, Eric? Just turn round, hands behind your back. You know the routine, I'm sure. Oh, and by the way. Not that I imagine you care. Your daughter's dead.'

A long pause and both men waited.

'Fuck you,' Hubert muttered then, and the light went out, the door slammed shut. A key turned, and a young, high voice shrieked with pain.

40

Christian Chauvin, priest of the Église Saint-Vivien, had gone to the kitchen to get himself a bottle of cognac, leaving Baptiste in what he assumed to be a study. Two walls were bookcases, full to the brim. Religion and philosophy mainly, as he flicked through the titles. A man's taste in literature always interested him. There was much to learn.

A third wall bore religious ornaments set around a landscape of Chauvin's church, a handsome, Norman building. Not a good painting but then he saw the signature in the bottom right and understood. This was the priest's own work, a record of the place Christian Chauvin would surely spend all his life as a servant of the Catholic Church.

The priest returned with his glass and a half bottle of cognac and settled in an old-fashioned, high-backed leather armchair by the open window.

'You're an enthusiastic reader, Father.'

Chauvin appeared to bridle at that. 'Why shouldn't I be?'

'No reason. Not everyone has the time.'

'Any more than I. Most are at best browsed through. Gifts and titles left behind by my predecessor. A priest works harder than most civilians appreciate. What can I do for you?'

'Tell me about Lili Hubert.'

He was a short man but muscular like a retired rugby player, though his face was ascetic, calm and quite without character. Chauvin's hair was as black as his priestly trousers, with a precise geometric cut, like a monk's lacking the bald patch of a tonsure. He took a sip of the drink, shook his head, and started on a story Baptiste found familiar from the time he'd worked in one of the poorer Paris suburbs. Lili was a troubled child, with a single parent only, and Eric Hubert hardly a man to set an example. She'd left school as soon as she could and worked across Clermiers doing odd jobs: barmaid until she was caught with her hands in the till, a waitress for the *Amis*, the charity set up to aid those who were struggling. Lili cleaned the priest's house once a week and didn't do the job so well. But he hadn't the heart to fire her. She sang in the church choir too, had a nice voice, might have earned more money there if she'd only been better at timekeeping.

'She was wearing what I think was a chorister's outfit when she died.'

Chauvin's mouth fell open. 'Oh my goodness. Why?'

'I've no idea. We found her in the wood. It looks as if she hanged herself. It's very remote. I can't blame anyone for not finding her.'

'Then how?'

Baptiste hadn't wanted to move on so quickly, but it seemed inevitable. 'Charles Augustin, the father of the girl who's missing from Boulliers, went looking. His dog detected something it seems.'

Chauvin closed his eyes and appeared to wipe away a tear.

'Clermiers is such a quiet, peaceful place. Two girls missing. One kills herself. Quite unbelievable.'

'These are assumptions only,' Baptiste added. 'When did she last sing in church?'

He had to think. 'Quite some time before she vanished. We didn't pay much. She said her father told her it wasn't enough. She had to find something better.'

'Such as what?'

'How would I know? She wasn't interested in the church, you understand. That father of hers . . . he'd only think of us as a place to steal some lead from the roof.' He winced. 'That was unforgivable. I apologise. Even a man like Eric Hubert must feel the loss of a child.'

'Does it surprise you she seems to have taken her own life?'

Chauvin seemed appalled by the question. 'Absolutely! If I'd thought that was likely to happen, I'd have been in touch with the authorities. Lili was miserable, angry a lot of the time. Hardly unique in that dismal place she came from.'

'Angry about what?'

'About being stuck in Boulliers I imagine. With a father like hers. Everyone thought she'd run away like her mother. To Paris. To do lord knows what. Instead, you say, she was here all the time.' He looked up. 'I'll arrange a funeral if the father allows it. At our expense. The *Amis* will pay, I'm sure.'

'This . . . charity.'

'*Oui.* Mostly we help with more cheerful matters. But needs must. Will you ask Hubert for me?'

'When I can. Noémie Augustin . . .'

The priest shook his head from side to side very slowly, the way he might have done at the bed of the dying perhaps. 'I never knew the girl, I'm afraid. There's some prejudice in a town like this. There shouldn't be, but habits change slowly. The father came here in Bruno Laurent's employ a few months back. Then the mother, who's white I gather. And the girl. Who isn't. None of them came to church.'

'She worked as a waitress for the *Amis*? In the clubhouse?'

'Well, yes. She served food and drink from time to time. I don't recall her being particularly talkative. Or grateful for the job if I'm honest.'

'And Lili Hubert was a waitress too.'

Chauvin stared at him. 'The *Amis* exist to help those less well off. Inevitably that means we employ people trapped in the lower realms of life. Which in our case means Boulliers. Not just dining staff. The washers up. When maintenance work is needed. It's why we're here.'

He got up and poured himself another half glass of cognac. 'You're sure you don't want something?'

'Very.'

'Do you really have no idea what's happened to the Augustin girl?'

Baptiste thought for a moment, wondering what to say. 'One always hopes they've just run away and found safety somewhere. Perhaps after an argument at home. Or there's a boy involved.'

'And?'

'We're not aware of any argument. Or a boy. The longer this goes on without news, the more I feel we should be concerned.'

'Dupont should seek help. From outside.'

'He's the captain here, not me. I've circulated her description. Hopefully we'll find the girl.'

'She may not be a child of the church, but I'll pray for Noémie Augustin. Things like this shouldn't happen in a peaceful town like Clermiers.'

'They can happen anywhere, Father. A police officer soon learns that.' The radio buzzed. 'Excuse me.'

He went to stand by the window for a clearer signal. It was Bonnay. The man sounded harassed. Étienne Fatoussi had called from the Hubert house. Something had happened. He wanted Baptiste there as soon as possible.

'What?' Baptiste asked.

'He wouldn't say,' Bonnay admitted. 'You're going to have to walk.'

Christian Chauvin watched him set off down the hill towards the bridge across the Chaume. From this distance Boulliers didn't look so bad. Just an unattractive sprawl of housing that had grown over the years with little regard to town planning or design. When Baptiste vanished round the corner past the church, he picked up the phone.

Bruno Laurent's wife answered.

'Véronique. Is he there?'

There was a silence that somehow seemed filled with resentment. They were far from a happy couple. Everyone understood that. Then, 'I'm not his bloody secretary.'

'It's important.'

'He's out riding his damned horse somewhere. I think, anyway. Tell me. I'll pass it on.'

'Something terrible has happened. They've found the Hubert girl. The one who vanished last year. It seems she hanged herself.'

Véronique Laurent gasped. 'Jesus . . .'

'I knew she was a sad little thing. If only I'd understood how much.'

'Don't be ridiculous. It's not your fault. That father of hers . . .'

'Tell Bruno. I advised the police the *Amis* would cover the cost of the funeral.'

That got a wry laugh out of her. 'You mean he's paying?'

'If he's so minded . . .'

'I'm sure he will. He's a soft touch for everyone but me. Why's it taken so long? Why now?'

'You know this girl who's missing? The black girl?'

'I don't *know* her. I heard at the hairdressers.'

'Bruno never mentioned it?'

'Why would he?'

'The father went looking in the Bois de Mortery. Poor Lili was there all along.'

'Ah. The château.'

That was all she said. Chauvin could only wonder what was on her mind.

'Bruno can call me if he wants. Not that I know anything more than I've said. We won't need the money quickly. There'll be formalities, I imagine. I will, of course, offer the service for no fee and the interment at cost.'

She laughed at that. 'How noble. What would the world do without the *Amis*!'

41

Étienne Fatoussi was outside the Hubert house, trying to calm a distraught Didier. The kid was in tears, bleeding from a nose that had clearly been punched, squawking about his father, about Fatoussi, about how he didn't know what to do. Baptiste got the story in a minute of rapid, clear but furious explanation from his colleague. It was obvious the kid couldn't stay in the house any longer. Fatoussi had no idea where Hubert had headed but if he returned and found his son there things might turn worse.

'OK,' he said, when Didier stopped wailing for a moment. 'Wait in the car. We need to talk.'

'Did Dad do it? Lili?' the boy asked. He looked about ten in this state, all bluster, all cockiness gone.

'I don't think so. It looks as if your sister killed herself.'

Nothing.

'Would that surprise you?'

He shook his head.

'Sit in the car,' Baptiste said again. 'I don't think he's coming back. If he does, tell us. We'll keep you safe.'

They watched him head off to the Simca.

'Jesus,' Fatoussi grumbled. 'This place really is *Merdeville*. Shit town through and through.'

'We'll find the father. We'll keep him away from the boy.'

'I didn't call you here to talk about Didier Hubert,' Fatoussi said. 'It's worse than that.'

The Hubert place was an odd mix of grubbiness and apparent money. The place wasn't so clean, but the kitchen was modern, the oven recent and not cheap.

Baptiste followed Fatoussi to the building in the yard, the outer door open, an inner one broken and off its hinges.

'Bastard locked me in there,' Fatoussi said. 'Had to kick it down. Gone by then and whacked his son on the way out.'

Dead birds, dead hare, dead rabbits, and again the rancid sweet smell of decomposition.

Three shotguns, all twelve-bore, one with a shortened barrel, hung on hooks, boxes of cartridges on a table beneath them. Something else too that didn't fit. Baptiste picked it up, a box of shells, brand name 'Fiocchi', half empty.

'You done here?' Fatoussi asked. 'Because—'

'These are for a handgun.' He looked round. 'Can you see a handgun anywhere?'

There wasn't one. It wouldn't be unusual for Eric Hubert to have a hunting licence to own the shotguns. A pistol, a revolver, that was different. They weren't allowed except on special conditions, usually to do with a shooting association where they had to be kept.

'It's not about guns,' Fatoussi said and pointed at the room ahead.

The light was scarlet, the smell familiar from the photographic labs in Paris. Baptiste followed him into the darkroom and found the switch for another light, a normal one. A fluorescent tube stuttered into life.

Prints were spread out over the light table where Fatoussi

had left them. Some were the daughter. Others, women they'd struggle to identify. The shots were heavily cropped, tight into head or groin or breasts, the only part of the men involved the predictable one with predictable results. No faces. Nothing that could be used to identify the other side. One odd thing seemed to link them all: the background. They'd been taken in what looked like a rich man's bordello. Even in black and white it was easy to see the money there: velvet drapes, a chandelier visible in some, a chaise longue, whips, sex toys, blindfolds and handcuffs, a bottle of expensive Bordeaux wine. A grand dining table with four stately chairs around it.

Baptiste went to the filing cabinet. It was all prints, maybe another thirty or more in there.

'There should be negatives. He's cropped the men out quite deliberately. Cropped hard sometimes, you can see that.' He pointed to a shot that was so grainy it was hard to make out in the end quite what was going on. 'The way the detail breaks up. If we had the originals . . .'

There was an envelope at the end of the table. Baptiste picked it up and shook out the contents. Six frames from a 35mm negative, the rest discarded. And a contact sheet, tiny images the same size. He grabbed the photographic loupe parked at the back of the bench, bent down, groaned as he looked at the picture magnified many times over, then passed the thing over.

Fatoussi took one look and began to swear, sweeping the darkroom bench with his arms, scattering tanks and trays and bottles of chemicals. The stench of spilled developer fluid and the sound of breaking glass filled the little room and still he went on. 'I will hang that filthy bastard myself. . . This shit . . . Christ . . .'

'Étienne . . .'

He wasn't listening.

'*Étienne!*'

He stopped then and in the anaemic light of the tube he

looked lost, younger suddenly somehow, as well, almost vulnerable.

Baptiste took his arm. 'One step at a time.' He took the prints from his shaking hand. 'What do you think?'

Fatoussi couldn't speak for a moment, and then seemed to find himself. 'Sorry . . . what?'

'This!' Baptiste waved the contacts.

'Oh yeah.' He didn't even look at them. Just closed his eyes and then muttered, 'Obvious, isn't it? The dirty bastard used that long lens of his to spy on Noémie through her bedroom window. Night. Or twilight.'

There were trees in the shot, full of leaf. And a near-full moon in one too.

It was hard to make out through the eyeglass, but what he saw was enough. Noémie was in her fantasy land, seeing herself as a new Josephine Baker, hands held high, eyes closed, near naked, just a skimpy bra and that circlet of fake bananas round her waist.

Taken recently, Baptiste thought. While she was . . . dancing. Dreaming.

Options were running through his head. The first was to scale up the case beyond sleepy Clermiers and Philippe Dupont, a police captain who craved a quiet life and nothing else. If Hubert was on the run, they'd need to put out a national alert. Photographs, descriptions, any vehicle details they could find.

'Let's go . . .' he started.

Then the door opened and the Hubert kid was there whimpering, terrified, tugging at Baptiste's jacket.

'He's back. My dad . . .'

Fatoussi ran for the door, gun out, yelling.

The house was empty, the front door open, Fatoussi walking round, weapon out, on edge. Dangerously so, Baptiste thought. He walked over, put a hand on his arm. 'You need to put that thing away. Won't help.'

'What will?'

Baptiste made him point the gun at the ground. 'Keeping your wits about you.'

'Where's the boy?'

The kid was curled up in a ball in the corner, shaking.

There was the racket of a motorbike getting kicked into life. Then the falling tone of its engine as the thing vanished up the road.

Fatoussi was still twitchy. 'I'll get the car . . .'

'No! You want a pursuit? In that thing?'

He pointed back to the yard. 'You saw what that son of a bitch was up to.'

'I did. And we'll find him. We'll get to the bottom of this. Just not by racing around god knows where in Dupont's old Simca.' Once more he pointed at the weapon. 'Put it away. I didn't even know you were carrying one.'

'We are police, remember.'

He was starting to appreciate the fact that Étienne Fatoussi was rash, unpredictable, didn't much care about the rules. Which made it all the more important Baptiste did his best to stick to them.

He bent down over the boy. 'Didier. You need to come with us.'

Eyes full of fear and hate, the kid said, 'Why? He'll kill me. He always said he would if I talked to you lot. That what you want?'

'Not at all.' He grabbed him by the arm. 'Let's go.'

42

Ten minutes later, back in the station, Fatoussi had calmed down a touch. Or just decided to stay silent.

Bonnay was up from his desk, getting ready to leave, Dupont

in his captain's office. Baptiste was outlining what he wanted: a motorcycle registration for Eric Hubert, a demand for the man's immediate arrest on suspicion of abduction, issued as an alert throughout the north.

'I'm knocking off soon,' Bonnay said. 'The bike won't be his. Can't it wait till the morning?'

'What the fuck . . .?' Fatoussi was on him in a flash. 'The Augustin girl's missing. This creep's been taking secret photos of her in her room . . .'

'You didn't mention that,' Bonnay snapped back. 'All the same . . . I can't get through to the vehicle licensing people till tomorrow. Like I said it'll either be nicked or have fake plates.'

'Where might Hubert go?' Baptiste asked.

Bonnay laughed out loud. 'Wherever the hell he likes. Could be Douai. Lille. Anywhere. That man . . . roams.'

Dupont's door opened. 'Get in here,' he said. He glared at Didier Hubert. 'Bring that with you.'

The captain's office smelled of stale tobacco and sweat, even with the windows open, the intense and humid night heat wafting through them. Fatoussi sat back and fumed while Baptiste told the captain what they'd found, the pornography, the weapons, the illicit snaps of Noémie Augustin half-naked, shot through her bedroom window. He left out the part about the missing negatives for most of the shots. That still troubled him.

'We need to put out an alert for Eric Hubert. Get a number for his motorbike.'

Dupont kept staring at Didier Hubert, a look of naked, bullying aggression on his face. When Baptiste was done, he lit a cigarette, came closer to the boy, blew smoke straight into his eyes. The kid squinted, rubbed his face with his arms. The elbows were out on his scruffy cotton shirt. He looked ready to cry.

'What do you have to say for yourself?' Dupont grunted.

Fatoussi was getting red in the face. Before the man from Marseille lost it, Baptiste butted in. 'Didier helped us. He told

Fatoussi there was something out back. Got punched by his old man for his pains.'

'Pains . . . huh.' Dupont put his cigarette in the ashtray, and leaned down until he was an inch from the boy's face. 'This one don't know his place. Never has. Where's your father, scummy?'

'Don't . . . know . . . sir . . .'

'Captain!'

Before Baptiste could do a thing, Dupont had swiped the kid around the cheek. A quick slap, hard, and a hurt, shocked shriek filled the little room. The man had his arm back to hit him again when Baptiste got there, took Dupont by the throat, backed him up against the wall. The man was probably good at beating up suspects, picking on little kids. But against someone younger, stronger, more determined, all he could do was flail with his hands until Baptiste squeezed further, pushed him harder against the partition.

'Touch the boy once more and Bonnay will have to drive you to hospital,' Baptiste said, quite calmly while Fatoussi took Didier to one side, wrapped his arms round him. 'Do you understand?'

Dupont's eyes were blazing, a torrent of vile curses coming out of his mouth.

'Do . . . you . . . understand?'

The man nodded. Baptiste let go.

'I could have your badge for that,' Dupont muttered, clutching at his throat.

'Take it. When we're done. When we've found Noémie Augustin. Alive, I hope. But Étienne and I will find her. And you will not touch this kid again.' He turned to Fatoussi. 'Call social services in Millot. Tell them there's a boy here in danger from domestic violence. They need to take him into care. Tonight. If they won't come and fetch him, drive him there. Didier . . .' The boy had watched it all, wide-eyed, astonished. 'Go with my friend. Don't worry. No one's going to hurt you.'

The kid couldn't wait to get out of there, though Fatoussi wasn't so keen.

Dupont went back to his desk, picked up his cigarette again. It was almost finished. Baptiste took out his pack of Disque Bleu lit one for himself and offered the pack.

'They're the kind of shit Parisians smoke, are they?'

'Seems so.'

'I want you gone. Both of you.'

'You never wanted us here in the first place.'

'Wasn't my choice. Don't need you.'

'There's a young girl missing! The longer this goes on the more I start to think . . .' He didn't want to say it.

Dupont smirked. 'You don't understand Clermiers. I do. Things happen here. We deal with them. In our way. Don't need a pair of smartass city jerks thinking they know better.'

The door opened. Fatoussi stuck his head in and said he'd persuaded Bonnay to drive Didier Hubert over to a safe house the council had in Millot.

'How the hell did you manage to get the lazy bastard to do that?' Dupont asked.

'I'm very persuasive when I feel like it, Captain.' He came back in and took a seat. 'Are we getting anywhere here? Pornography. Snooping. Noémie Augustin. Hubert ran for a reason. Any ideas?'

Dupont leaned back and checked his watch. Then opened the little fridge behind him, retrieved a bottle of Choulette Ambrée, popped open the crown cap and took a long swig.

'I'd offer you two . . . but you didn't earn it.'

'Jesus,' Fatoussi said. 'You've got god knows what going on over the river in Boulliers and all you can do is gulp down a beer.'

Baptiste tried to calm things. 'We need to find Eric Hubert. We need to talk to him.'

Another glance at his watch. 'Give it five minutes. Then you can ask him yourself.'

'What?'

'Hubert called just before you got back. Why do you think me and Bonnay are still here? Said he thought there'd been a misunderstanding. He wants to come in and clear it up. Hell . . .' He turned, got three bottles out of the fridge, and placed them on the table. 'We can sort this out right now.'

43

Martine Augustin was at the front window, a place she'd spent hours of late.

'I thought I heard something.'

Her husband joined her. 'It's Boulliers. What do you expect?'

'What was she like? This girl you found?'

'I didn't look too closely. Who would?'

'They're sure it wasn't Noémie?'

'Too old. Too . . . far gone the police say. They say it's Hubert's daughter. Teenager. Been missing for more than a year. She was depressive apparently. They think she killed herself.'

'Did you know another girl had gone missing?'

'No. It happened before Laurent gave me the job here. If I had, I'd have said. It's just coincidence. Noémie would never . . .'

He couldn't finish the sentence.

'Never what?'

'I don't know. If we hear nothing from the police by tomorrow morning I'll go and talk to them,' he said and tried to take her hand.

She shook him off.

'What's the point?'

'It's just . . .' His eyes were glassy, tears waiting there. She knew she ought to feel guilty about that. But she didn't. 'I can't keep sitting here, doing nothing.'

'Go back to work then. I'm amazed Laurent hasn't been on

the phone asking. There must be accounts to reckon up.' She hesitated. 'Stock takes to be done.'

That was part of the gulf between them. He really couldn't wait and wait. While she felt herself paralysed just thinking about their daughter. The immediate worry that dogged her to begin with was . . . where might she be? Now it was transforming into a simple question . . . was Noémie alive or dead?

'If you want me to go,' he said in a low, hurt voice, 'just say.'

'All I want is Noémie back.' That came straight out. 'Does you being here make any difference to that? At all?'

He hesitated for a moment then said, 'And if it did? If there was something I could do?'

She glared at him. 'Then I'd wonder why you're still here, all talk, nothing else. Do I know you, Charles? Did I ever? Or was this all some kind of piece of theatre? Is that what got into Noémie's head with her dancing round half-naked? She was just walking into the same fantasy world as you? While I just sat here like an idiot and never noticed?'

There were voices outside, loud, young, drunk or stoned maybe. The usual night-time chorus of the Boulliers estate.

'I'll sleep in the English boy's room.'

It just came out. 'You'll sleep wherever you want. Won't you?'

He went upstairs after that. The phone rang. Augustin rushed down, but Martine was there first, stony-faced, listening, not saying a word.

'Well . . .?' he asked as she put it down.

'Wrong number.'

'We're going to jump every time someone calls, aren't we?'

'Guess so.' She went for her jacket. 'I need some fresh air.'

He looked worried. 'Not at night, love. Not round here.'

Martine Augustin opened the door. 'What does it matter any more?'

44

Eric Hubert turned up pink-eyed, weeping as he stumbled through the door. He ignored Fatoussi and Baptiste and fell into a chair opposite Dupont.

'Is it true? Is my little Lili dead?'

The captain nodded and handed him a beer.

'Jesus Christ.' Hubert took it then swiped his rheumy face with a filthy handkerchief. 'I thought she'd run away to Paris to be with that whore of a mother. I tried to find her there, you know.'

'How hard?' Fatoussi asked.

Hubert ignored him. 'She was never quite right in the head. Made stuff up all the time. I asked the social people for help but . . .' He groaned. 'We're Boulliers trash to them. Who gives a shit?'

Fatoussi pulled up a spare chair and sat close to him, at the end of the desk. Baptiste stayed leaning against the wall.

'This . . . man . . .' Hubert jerked a thumb at Fatoussi. 'I didn't know he was one of yours. How could I? He never said. No uniform. Just breaks into my house, helps himself to whatever he wants. Pulls a gun. Jabs it in my face and says she's dead.'

'I was arresting you.'

'Huh!' Hubert didn't take his eyes off Dupont. 'What was I to think? Do cops do house-breaking now? I come home. There's some stranger there, pointing a barrel right at me. What am I supposed to do? Stay there and get shot?'

Dupont turned an icy stare on Fatoussi. 'What's wrong with you? What the hell did you think you were doing? You can't just break into someone's house . . .'

'Don't give me this crap.' Fatoussi looked ready to snap. 'I went there to tell him about his daughter. The boy let me in. I was concerned about – what was it Bonnay wrote on that report when she went missing? Oh, yeah. Accusations that couldn't be substantiated. Maybe they could, after all.' He pointed at Hubert. 'If this piece of shit got pulled in and talked to like he should have been years ago.'

Dupont looked dumbfounded. Baptiste felt a little that way too. It was an extraordinary way for Fatoussi to behave.

'You've been here five minutes,' Dupont spat back. 'Now you're behaving like a lunatic and telling me how to run things. Are you right in the head?'

Fatoussi was the one who couldn't find a word to say just then. Baptiste leapt in.

'Hubert. You hit Didier on the way out.'

'It was an accident. I didn't see him. Where is he?'

'Somewhere safe. He won't be coming back for a while. If at all.'

Hubert appealed to Dupont. 'What the hell is this? My daughter's dead. Now they've abducted my son?'

'We saw your photos,' Baptiste said.

He threw his arms wide open, a gesture of innocence. 'So what? A man's entitled to a hobby.'

'It's porn,' Fatoussi said. 'Kids in some of it.'

He shook his head. 'No kids. I guarantee it. That was private art. Not for anyone else. Just me.'

'Where are the negatives?' Baptiste asked.

'I don't keep them. I just want . . . the moment.'

'Lili was in those pictures. Who else?'

Hubert shook his head. 'I told you already. They were private. Not for the likes of you.'

Baptiste left it till last. He wanted to see the reaction. 'You took pictures of Noémie Augustin as well. Snatched ones. From outside. Now she's missing.'

That shrug again, a cocky protestation of innocence. 'A pretty girl stands by an open window and starts dancing with barely a thread on. What's wrong with a man watching? That's what the girl wanted, isn't it? Why else do it? I took a couple of snaps. Nothing special. Where's the harm in that?'

'Where were you Sunday?'

'Me and the boy went to a football match in Lille. Came home. Stayed home.'

Fatoussi muttered a quiet curse. 'This is all bullshit. Didier told us you stayed with his Uncle Franc that night.'

'We didn't. Like I said. We came home. We stayed in.'

'Then why did the boy say it?'

Hubert leaned towards him. 'He's a kid. He lies as easily as he breathes. Ask him. Now what's the story with my Lili?'

All down to Millot, Dupont said. They had the coroner, the morgue, the facilities. Little Clermiers would always hand over heavy lifting to the people there when they could. There'd be an inquest. Unless something odd cropped up she'd be listed as a suicide pretty soon. 'Chauvin has offered to bury her for free with Bruno Laurent's help.'

Hubert sniffed. 'Don't like charity. Still, a man like me's in no position to turn it down.'

'A man like you . . .' Fatoussi murmured.

'Look. There was a misunderstanding. That's all it was. Can I go now?'

Fatoussi kicked off. Porn. Noémie Augustin. The boy. The daughter. He spat it all out and he'd still not finished when Dupont yelled at him to shut up.

'You two wait outside,' the captain ordered. 'I'll deal with this myself.'

Baptiste had to take Fatoussi by the arm. They went back into the front office. Baptiste lit a cigarette, said nothing.

'We're going to get fucked, aren't we?' Fatoussi grumbled.

'For now. Do me a favour.'

'What?'

'Go along with it. Just for a while.'

'Dammit! You saw her in the wood! You saw those pictures! You know what men like that do to girls?'

He nodded. 'I do. But we're here to find Noémie. That can come later. Patience . . .'

'*Bof.* Patience is for mugs.'

Baptiste went to the window. Night was falling. Clermiers looked quiet, empty, the kind of place nothing much ever happened. He wondered where she was. If they'd ever find out.

'Well?' said Hubert, taking the offered cigarette. 'What do we do now?'

'You think she killed herself?'

A frown, that shrug again. 'Said she was going to do it often enough. Got quite tedious in the end.'

'And this black girl—'

'I took some pictures. She was dancing in her room. Hardly a thing on. What's wrong with that?'

Dupont sat back, closed his eyes, closed the window too, so many insects around in the heat of the night. The room stank of the pair of them. 'Baptiste is a smart bastard. He's seen the rest of the pictures.'

'They didn't have my permission to be in there, Philippe. Nothing they can use in court.'

'Don't call me that in front of them. I told you. He's smart. Got your number already.'

'Oh, I doubt that. And even if he has . . .'

'What?'

Hubert laughed, walked to the door, peered through the partition glass, making sure they couldn't hear.

'Even if he has, you know this is going nowhere, *Philippe.* Who wants to see the mayor with his dick in a teenager's mouth? For starters . . .'

Dupont stormed up and grabbed him by the throat. 'We went through this. They paid. You don't have the pictures. Or the negatives.'

Hubert shook him off, grinned in his face. 'You think I'm stupid? You think I don't keep back a little insurance for a rainy day?'

'I think you're living dangerously.'

'Then there's the small matter of a police captain asking me to arrange a welcome present for his unwelcome guests.'

Dupont almost exploded. 'I didn't ask you to hurt anyone. Just—'

'Just what?' Hubert looked amused. 'Anyway, the idea was the brat's. He put it there. You don't want me to crush his spirit, do you?' He prodded Dupont in the chest. 'The lesson is very simple, *Philippe*. If I go down, I do not go down alone. And you and your friends wouldn't like Douai jail, believe me. I speak from experience.'

He waved his hands around the room. 'Are we done now?'

Baptiste was on another Disque Bleu by the time they emerged, the smoke so thick and rank Étienne Fatoussi had opened every window to try to get it out.

Dupont didn't look at them as he ushered Hubert to the door.

'M. Hubert will receive a caution over this photography. I have his word it's a hobby he will now abandon. In the circumstances—'

'The circumstances?' Fatoussi bellowed. 'Pictures of his own kid having sex? God knows what else when we go back and take a closer look.'

Dupont stopped and glared at him. 'I'm the captain here. There'll be no going back. The man receives a caution. And you . . .' A stubby finger jabbed at Fatoussi's face. 'Will follow procedure from now on. If I tried to prosecute this man, you do realise I couldn't use a thing you found when you broke into his place?'

'And Noémie Augustin?' Baptiste wondered when there was no reply.

'You heard his explanation. Do you have any reason to doubt it? The man took some unfortunate photographs. He regrets it now.'

'I do,' said Hubert with a smile. 'As I regret running away

137

from this fellow. But he had a gun. He scared me. I'd no idea—'

'This is bullshit,' Fatoussi snarled. 'I will see you again.'

'Now this one threatens me!'

'Go home!' Dupont cried. 'The pair of you. This man's just learned his daughter's dead, not lost as he believed. I think we have room to show a little mercy.'

'As you see fit,' Baptiste said. 'Étienne . . .'

They waited outside in the battered Simca. A few minutes later, Dupont locked up then pointed Hubert to his car.

'He's giving the bastard a lift home.' Fatoussi opened the window and spat at the cobbles. 'What the hell is going on here?'

Baptiste was tapping the fuel gauge. The needle didn't move.

Then it came out in a rush. Fatoussi and his sister. The attack, the effect it had, not just on her, but the whole family. He listened to his younger colleague pouring his heart out as Philippe Dupont drove Hubert down the hill back to that house in Boulliers, with its horrific collection of photographs, those dead animals rotting away on wires, the weapons, that strange box of pistol shells that didn't seem to belong to any of them, the boy who was so terrified of his own father, so desperate to get away. Just like his sister Lili, Baptiste guessed. That was a suicide by the looks of it.

Fatoussi finished his story. He was in tears, but Baptiste didn't look his way. With any luck he'd think it had gone unnoticed.

'We need to put some fuel in this rusty tin can, Étienne.'

'Sorry. I just needed to get that out.'

'You did.'

Ten minutes to the petrol station. It occurred to Baptiste, for the first time, that the place was a kind of guard post for Clermiers, the first thing anyone saw when they came in from the main road from the south. More than a garage too. When he walked into Gilles Mailloux's night-time home there was almost a small grocery store there, bread and cheese and packs of meat. Booze too, wine, beer, brandy, whisky.

'Baptiste,' said a now-familiar voice from out the back. It was hard to believe he'd only been there since Sunday. Gilles Mailloux emerged. 'I'll come and fill your car in a moment. But you must write your name and address in my little book and sign it. I'll add the price when I'm done. No choice. As I think I said, I don't have the books any more so it's something in writing for everything on account. Petrol. Booze. Cigarettes. Until Laurent comes back with a new set of ledgers.'

It rang the faintest of bells. 'Where did they go?'

'I don't know. Augustin comes in each week and picks up the names and numbers.' He hunched his shoulders, baffled. 'All gone. You want some beer and cigarettes on the police account too?'

'Er, no.'

'Your choice.' He smiled. 'It doesn't stop anyone else.'

Baptiste scribbled down his details on Mailloux's pad and followed him out of the door.

There was someone there outside a camper van parked in the yard at the back of the lot by the edge of the Bois de Mortery.

'Miss Celia Murray,' he said. 'I thought you were leaving.'

45

She seemed startled to see him.

'I . . . I was just putting the van in the siding. Gilles said it was OK. Like before.'

'This is where you were on Sunday?'

'Yes. Have you found her? The girl?'

'No.'

'Are you close, do you think?'

He frowned and said nothing.

'God. That poor mother.'

'There's a father too.'

'Of course. Him as well.'

Mailloux was filling up the Simca. Fatoussi sat in the passenger seat, face like thunder. The day had changed the man from Marseille. Or perhaps revealed something he'd kept hidden before. Baptiste liked him, but there was an unstable side to the man that needed to be checked. Not that he was going to say it in front of Dupont, but the man was right about Hubert's porn collection. They'd have a devil of a job persuading any court to accept it as evidence after the way Fatoussi broke in.

She smiled in a wan, nervous way. 'I'm sorry about Daniel.'

'What about him?'

'That he had to leave.'

'Leave?'

'Go home, I mean. I drove him. Then turned straight round. Work. Trouble on the camp site.'

'I thought you said you didn't want to come back to Clermiers. Something wrong with the place.'

A nod of the head and he couldn't stop looking at her. 'Work. Had to do a quick turnaround. I've got to stay somewhere for the night. Can't make the Loire all in one go and it's on the way. Gilles lets me park here for free. He's got food. I'm having dinner in my van. Cheese, beer and bread.' She glanced at Fatoussi. 'I'd invite you in. But your colleague doesn't look so happy.'

'No . . . I mean, no thank you. I'd have liked to talk to your brother again. It's not good he's gone.'

'I understand. That's your job. But I'm his big sister and my job's to look after him. He was going crazy here. Cursing himself for not doing something. Not staying close to Noémie that night she vanished. Unlike me, he's a gentle, fragile soul. Dan's better off in Kent. Phone him if you like. I gave you our office number, didn't I?'

'I don't do interviews by phone. You can't look people in the eye.'

140

Celia Murray smiled again, a little embarrassed this time. 'So I see. Shame about the cheese and beer.'

Fatoussi stuck his head out of the car window and yelled, 'This rusty tin can's full.'

'I'll be gone tomorrow first thing,' she added. 'Next time it'll be an earlier ferry. Won't be passing this way again.'

Back in the car Fatoussi asked, with an edge, 'What was all that about?'

'The Murray kid's gone back to England.'

'Huh? Why?'

'Seems he was upset. Couldn't take it any more. Blames himself for not sticking close to Noémie.'

Fatoussi slammed his hands on the dusty dashboard. 'Screw that. He should have cleared it with us first.'

'He was under no obligation. And he didn't.'

A nod at the camper van. 'But she's back?'

'Passing through. Work.'

Fatoussi snorted. 'Every last bastard round here's jerking us about. You realise that? Playing us for fools.'

Baptiste started the car.

46

Marie Le Gall was eating supper outside with Mimi when they got back. Fatoussi lightened a little at the sight of his Marseille girlfriend. They made small talk as Baptiste joined them, picking at the crackers, the bread, the ham and cheese she'd bought from the shop in town. He didn't say much, and barely listened. It was hard to get Celia Murray out of his head. And that invitation to her camper van, a humbler supper, but company he'd find more intriguing.

Fatoussi and his girlfriend didn't linger. Mimi was looking concerned as they left.

'Your chum seems downcast,' Marie observed, pouring

herself the last of the wine. 'What have you done now?'

'It was a . . . difficult day.'

One that began with Fatoussi throwing up beneath the long-dead corpse of a local girl in the Bois de Mortery. And ended with them watching her abusive father, whose grief was surely for show, allowed to walk free.

'Any more on this missing girl?'

He wondered how often he'd hear that.

'No.'

'Nothing?'

He picked up the wine bottle and squeezed out the last dregs. She poured him a little from her own glass to top it up.

'Julien . . .'

'We bumped into a dodgy guy on the rough estate. Who seemed very active when it came to taking dirty pictures among other things. But rather lax about keeping the negatives.'

'Is that unusual?'

He wasn't sure. Perhaps Hubert made a living by selling on the negs and keeping prints for his own entertainment. The sex trade was the province of a specialist unit in Paris, one he'd never gone near. All the same it sounded odd. Hubert couldn't claim in one breath his mucky pictures were for his private pleasure alone then say he'd destroyed the original film for the sake of 'the moment'.

'I don't know. That's not my field. It isn't black and white it seems to me. If a woman's happy being pictured that way, if she wants to sell her body, is that really the business of the police?'

'Lot of ifs there.'

'I'm aware of that.'

She looked interested. 'Julien Baptiste having doubts about his job. That's new.'

He raised his glass. 'Not really. I just haven't raised them with you before.'

'The trouble is you're never totally comfortable about things that happen beneath the waist. The rest of us tend to live with it, mostly. This is your problem. Or your girlfriend's when you have one.'

She never missed an opportunity. 'Can we leave my private life out of this for a while?'

'Such as it is . . .'

'We also found a body. Or rather someone did. A young girl. Hanging in the wood.'

Her hand raced to her mouth. 'Oh my god, Julien. I'm sorry. I didn't mean to sound flippant . . .'

'You rarely do.'

'Another girl?'

Another. They had to be connected. Though how – other than through Eric Hubert's snatched pictures – was that possible? Lili died, by suicide probably, long before Noémie moved to Clermiers. Fatoussi had good reason to hate Hubert, given his own background and the depressing tale he'd told about the attack on his sister. Nevertheless, Baptiste was inclined to believe that, in Noémie's case, Hubert was nothing more than a voyeur. If he had been involved in her abduction, would he really have walked into Clermiers' police station so openly, shedding crocodile tears for his own daughter?

'She'd been dead more than a year.' He nodded at the ceiling. 'It affected Étienne quite badly.'

'It would affect most people.'

'The girl was dressed like she'd just come from church. White tunic, a scarlet collar. But the priest says she hadn't sung in the choir for ages before she vanished. I'm struggling. What could have been going through her head?'

'You're a man, Julien. You're bound to struggle. You've no idea what women go through. Not a clue the crap we have to deal with.'

'You . . .?'

'All of us! There's not a woman alive who hasn't had something happen she'd rather not share. Even with her son.'

143

'Why?'

She laughed. 'Only a man could ask that. Because you're not believed. Or people don't care. Or they just think . . . that's how the world is. Why complain?'

'I can't fix something I don't know about.'

'Oh dear. In one ear, out the other. Anyway, struggling is good. It's how we get places. Much better than giving up. One of your finer virtues is you're never going to do that. However much it costs. Come here.'

He did. She kissed him on the forehead just as she had when he was little. That hadn't happened much after his father died. A loss that had pushed them apart in a way neither understood or knew how to question.

'Sleep on it,' she whispered in his ear. 'I recognise the moment that brain of yours starts turning. I see it now.'

'I don't. There's something odd, something dark about this place. Something I can't quite grasp. And there's just me . . .' Another glance at the ceiling. 'Étienne . . . Dupont, the captain and an idle sidekick.'

'Dupont's a sly man,' she said. 'I should have spotted that earlier.'

'I think he may be more than that.'

'Such as?'

'I don't know. I don't know how to find out either.'

'Then call Paris! Tell them.'

He gestured with his hands, a sign of despair. 'Tell them what? I'm stuck in the middle of nowhere with a police captain who's bone idle at best and maybe . . .' He didn't want to say it. Was it possible the police house was bugged?

'Maybe what?'

'Maybe I'm talking too much. It's late. I'm tired. My head's not on quite right.'

'Your head's just fine, love.'

He kissed her and got up. 'I wish. Good night.'

47

Charles Augustin spent the rest of the evening in his daughter's bedroom, staring at the posters. A tennis player from Australia. Then the cuttings Baptiste had found. A black woman, rich, adored, famous.

All part of Noémie's dreams.

He'd hidden the handgun he'd got from Hubert, six shells in the magazine the man said. Not that Augustin knew enough to doubt him. The thing was tucked in the shoebox Noémie kept beneath the bed alongside a couple of recent postcards from the south of France posted by the one friend she had. The girl who'd invited her there with her family, not that they could afford to let her go. He didn't know if a gun might solve anything. Might prompt answers out of nothing. But tomorrow he'd see Dupont and his temporary cops from Paris. He'd find out whether they really were making progress. If not . . .

There were footsteps on the stairs. Light, slow, familiar. Martine's. He could recognise every squeak. She was on the landing, getting a suitcase out of the little room they'd rented to the Englishman. Still wearing her jacket.

'You've been out a while,' he said.

'Not as long as you. Do I need your permission?'

'I was worried.'

She opened the case and started to fold some clothes in there. He had an icy ache in his stomach just watching.

'I can't stay here any longer.'

He didn't know whether to feel more angry than upset. 'Where do you think you're going?'

'Tomorrow you'll drive me to the station in Millot. I'm taking the train back to the coast. I'll stay with my sister for a while. You know the number.'

He reached out for her. She shrank back.

'I need you here. With me.'

'Why?'

'You're my wife!'

'And that gives you the right to tell me where to go? What to do?'

'Noémie . . .'

'Do you not know who we are, Charles? Impoverished strangers in a ghetto that never wanted us.' She waved an angry hand at the window. 'If we were from Hauteville, a nice, bourgeois family, white and with money, there'd be police crawling all over this place looking for her. Dupont at their head. But we're not. We're little people. Unimportant people in their eyes. And Noémie has the misfortune to be black. *They do not care.*'

'I think the Parisian does. Baptiste. And maybe the one with him.'

'Then they'll be gone soon enough. Dupont will see to that. You were a fool to come here. To swallow the promises of Bruno Laurent. But I was the bigger fool to believe you. Now look where we are.'

His voice fell close to a whisper. 'I saw a dead girl this morning. Hanging from a tree. In the dark I thought it might be Noémie. Then I ran away and all the time I thought, I prayed, I hoped, it wasn't. That she'd be someone else's daughter. Dead, out there in the woods. And that made me hate myself even more.'

Her face was stony, unforgiving. No words at all.

'Can you not understand, Martine?'

'All I understand is this place you led us to is bad . . . *Merdeville*. Shit Town. They call it right. I won't stay here any longer.'

There was the start of tears in her eyes as she carried the little suitcase into their bedroom and closed the door behind her.

Augustin went back to staring out of Noémie's window into the empty darkness, thinking about her, thinking too about that gun beneath the bed.

48

Two at the table in Celia Murray's camper van. Gilles Mailloux, grateful for the food, for company too. The night was stifling, pierced by owls screeching and hooting as they sought their prey in the Bois de Mortery, the rustle of animals, foxes, badgers, feral cats, stealing through the thick brambles and the hard, dry grass.

She was exhausted after spending so much time on the road, in England, in France. Then, when the last of the cheese and ham was gone, she said she needed to turn in for the long drive south the following morning.

'Did you tell Baptiste you won't be back?'

'I did.'

'A shame. I think he has an eye for you.'

'Maybe he's shy.'

'No.' Mailloux waved a piece of bread in the air, so vigorously his hand touched the low van ceiling. 'It's not shyness. He lacks the courage. I suspect because he fears you'd say no. Or matters would end in disappointment. Failure affects him. Perhaps he's over-familiar with it.'

'Quite the character judgement, Gilles.'

'I've been thinking about it. I've been thinking about a lot.'

'I know. Well, it isn't going to happen. What's the point?'

He thought about that. 'What's the point of anything? I've no idea. Any more than I know why I'm giving you advice on anyone's love life. You may as well ask it of a monk.'

She smiled and he knew he'd said enough, perhaps too much, already. 'It's late. A very long day. I'm tired. We've talked . . . talked a lot.'

Gilles Mailloux climbed out of the camper van, closed the door behind him, watched her silhouette behind the curtains as he walked back to his office. Celia Murray peeling off her clothes.

Back behind his desk he picked up the book he'd been

reading, a rare and old one the public library had taken months to find. A life of Apollonie Sabatier, courtesan, mistress and muse to his favourite poet Baudelaire. On an inside page she was depicted as a statue, nude, writhing with an agonised, erotic grace. *Woman Bitten by a Serpent*, by a sculptor called Auguste Clésinger who, the book said, had also made the funeral mask of Chopin.

Sex and death, Mailloux thought. The two so often went hand in hand.

49

Dupont never liked calling Bruno Laurent at home. His wife, Véronique, was a snotty bitch, always asking questions, forever trying to poke her nose into places she wasn't wanted. Why Laurent put up with it, Dupont could only guess. The man had bottomless pockets. He could heave that mouthy woman out of the window with a fat divorce cheque and it would still be petty cash.

As luck would have it she was the one who answered.

'Dupont. Is he at home?'

'Ah, Captain.' He could hear the amusement she got from knowing he'd wanted Laurent to pick up the phone. 'How nice to hear from you. I imagine you must still be at work. What is it . . . one girl missing? Another dead?'

'A runaway teenager and a kid who killed herself while the balance of her mind was disturbed. The first a mystery I'm sure will soon be resolved. The second a tragedy. They happen. Life goes on.'

'My . . . you are all sympathy.'

'Your husband . . .'

There were voices at the end of the line. Not friendly it seemed to him. Then Laurent saying he'd take the call in his office.

Dupont waited. After a while there was a click and Bruno Laurent was there sounding stressed and angry.

'Before you utter a single word,' Dupont said quickly, 'tell me she can't be listening.'

'Do you think I'm an idiot?'

'No. But I think you're careless from time to time. On a bad day that's as good as idiocy. Maybe worse.'

Laurent mumbled a low curse. 'You're not as important as you think, Dupont.'

'Really?' His voice rose, fury in it. 'Allow me to inform you, sir. Right now, I'm the most important man in your fucking life. Your priest, your saviour, your life raft out of this sea of shit you've got swilling all around you. I've two strangers sticking their noses in where they're not wanted. Neither of them looking ready to get tamed.'

'Then move them on.'

Dupont rolled his eyes. 'Let me reconsider my previous remark on the subject of idiocy. If it was that simple, don't you think I'd be doing it right now? Your wife just reminded me. One girl missing. One dead. Even the dumbest desk jockey in Paris would notice if I was trying to ship officers out of an undermanned station at a time like that.'

There was a weary groan on the other end of the line. 'What's the purpose of this call exactly?'

'Burn everything. I mean . . . everything. I don't care what it costs. I don't want to find one tiny tinfoil pack of dope, one record from the garage, a single photo I never wanted to see, *anything* if they come looking. Burn everything.'

'Done already.'

'Good.'

'And?'

'If you can find that moron Gaillard, get the message to him. I can't raise him at home. His office. Anywhere. His dumb sister says she's no idea where he's gone.'

'I am not Louis Gaillard's keeper.'

'I don't want Baptiste near him.'

'But you *are* that man's keeper, aren't you?'

'You haven't met Baptiste.'

The line went quiet, for so long Dupont thought he'd hung up. Then, Laurent asked in a voice marked by uncertainty, 'Do you think she's still alive? The black girl?'

'Do you?'

'I've really no idea. She was very pretty. If you like that kind of thing. I seem to recall you don't.' The tone changed. Turned more severe, more arrogant. 'But I'm interested. Tell me, Captain. What are *you* going to burn?'

'Every last thing if I have to.'

Dupont hung up, poured himself another drink and walked to the window.

Clermiers went to bed early. Just past eleven and there was hardly a light on anywhere. A quiet, insignificant town that was as good as invisible to the world at large. It needed to stay that way.

Part Four:

Departures

50

Paris had nothing to say about the chance of a reprieve. Baptiste couldn't get beyond a lowly desk officer in the Ministry. When he was allowed back into the cell by the warder Joel, with a grin and a wink, Gilles Mailloux was slumped against the brick wall by his simple bed, eyes closed.

'There is no news,' he said without stirring.

'How do you know?'

'Because you're alone.'

Baptiste took the chair again. 'What would you like to talk about?'

He opened his eyes. 'Are you out of questions then?'

'I only came with one. Where is she?'

'Ah.'

Then nothing.

'If, for some reason, you don't know . . .'

'You think that?'

'I don't know what to think any more.'

Mailloux shuffled more upright then leaned forward on his skinny arms. 'Do you know why the estate's called Boulliers? *Merdeville* to its inmates, of course, but to the world beyond . . .'

It was the last response Baptiste had expected. 'Tell me.'

151

'It's all in the library in Hauteville. I went there a lot. It's warm in winter. You can stay comfortable for free. Henri Boulliers was an architect. He studied with Le Corbusier and worked on a project of his in Moscow. A Marxist as a result, some said. But the man's long dead and our brutalist estate is his one legacy. Such as it is.'

Baptiste had never heard of the man. 'So?'

'I'm endeavouring to give you a little insight. Henri Boulliers, being both a Marxist and a devotee of his master, believed that the working class deserved better than to live in hovels rented from their bourgeois masters. Like the proletariat of the Soviets, they were to be housed in new communities, designed by the likes of him, owned by the state. Or in our case, the town council of Clermiers. Inspired by Le Corbusier, so naturally they would look like concrete shoe boxes stacked one upon one another. But each would be identical because, in Boulliers' ideal world, every man and woman was equal, allotted the same amount of space to eat, to sleep, to shit. Those few cottages you see apart – and they're not publicly owned, but in the hands of men like Bruno Laurent – everyone in Boulliers lives within the confines of the prison he created. Trapped there. Devoid of ambition, of hope, of the energy to escape.' He glanced around the prison cell. 'This will sound strange since you think me incarcerated. But in some way, for the first time in my modest little life, here, for once, I'm free.'

'That does sound strange.'

Mailloux stared at him, disappointed. 'What does your father do?'

'He's gone. He was a university lecturer.'

'And your mother?'

'The same. She still works, part-time.'

'We come from different worlds. Different planets, as good as. My father was Algerian, an engineer for a shipping company. Oil tankers mainly. He'd be home for a few weeks then vanish for months on end into the bowels of ships oceans away in parts of the world I was never going to see. When I was three, he packed his bag and never came back.'

'I'm sorry.'

'I'm not. How could I be? I never knew him. My mother . . .'

Collette Mailloux had refused to talk to Baptiste, even when he went round to the house in Boulliers and begged. As far as he knew, she'd never visited her son in Douai jail. He'd assumed the storm of publicity and Gilles's notoriety had deterred the woman, perhaps understandably. The press would surely have been on her the moment she appeared.

'What about her?'

'When I was old enough to be left on my own and got that job through Laurent in the petrol station, she signed up for a post on a ship too. Purser on long tourist cruises out of Le Havre and Cherbourg. Gone for months on end. Good money for the likes of us. She told me she hoped she'd see him somewhere and tell his new woman – there had to be one – what a shit he was. I'm not sure I believe that. She just wanted to be out of Boulliers. Out of the cage. She escaped. Not many do.'

'Did Lili Hubert want to?'

He laughed. 'You really don't understand, do you? Anyone with half a brain wants to flee that place. But where? How? With what?'

'You're an intelligent man.'

'It's nothing to do with intelligence,' he said, a sudden chill in his voice. 'It's about opportunity. Where was a feeble-minded child like Lili to go? To Paris where her mother was a whore? To pick up tricks in the Bois de Boulogne instead of hanging herself in the Bois de Mortery?'

Mailloux was well-read, self-educated as Baptiste had come to appreciate as the Augustin case came to its shocking conclusion. 'You're anything but feeble-minded. You could have got out of there.'

'I fear you're wasting your time here, Julien. I know I asked you to come but if you choose to leave, I won't be offended. The last thing I want in my final few hours is tedious company.'

Baptiste shook his head. 'No. I'm not leaving. There are things I want to hear.'

'Lili Hubert was so desperate for money she came to my petrol station one night and offered to suck me off for pocket money. That kind of thing?'

He stayed quiet.

'You know you want to ask.'

'She's dead. It's of no consequence.'

'I declined the offer. Then put a few coins in that little yellow purse of hers and asked her to clean the place.' He winced. 'When she'd finished, she pulled out one of her condoms, grinned at me, hoping. Free, she said. She didn't want screwing. She craved affection and that was how she thought you got it. Poor Lili. Such a sad creature. Boulliers through and through.'

'And Noémie Augustin?'

'I read somewhere a gentleman never tells.'

Baptiste was ready to snap. 'A gentleman doesn't leave a dead girl's mother in purgatory. Martine Augustin loved her daughter. As did her father.'

'Ah, yes.' He sat back again. 'The father.'

There was a commotion outside. The sound of steel being raised once more. Then the swoop and swish of it falling and reaching its target with a loud thud. Another practice. A successful one judging by the cheer from someone in the yard.

'Don't look so glum, Julien. The blade will always fall. It must. That is in the nature of both gravity and these insignificant lives we lead.'

Clermiers, Wednesday, 21 July

There were no noises from upstairs, no night-time interruptions from his mother across the hall. Still, Baptiste could scarcely sleep. Around six thirty he crept out of the front door, closed it as silently as he could, and walked along the road, lighting the first cigarette of the day. It was still cool, the air relatively fresh and free of the agricultural miasma that would soon rise as a dusty mist alongside the dry and searing heat.

The police house was set on a hill at the back of Clermiers. From the bend below he could look down on the town; the tall, old houses of Hauteville, running in a curving line from top to bottom; the spire of Saint-Vivien piercing through tiled rooftops just after the square with the Mairie and the police station; the winding road down towards the Chaume, tree-lined and dotted with flower beds, dry and wilting in the scorching summer; the stretch by the river where, on the town side, a couple of men were fishing already; then, across the single bridge, the Boulliers estate, a line of older cottages closest to the bank, and behind, crammed together in tight ugly squares, the concrete and cement blemish where the town's underclass seemed fated to live. Beyond those, in the desiccated fields of sugar beet and stubbles of wheat and barley, stood the outline of some kind of factory, half-fallen chimneys, corrugated iron roofs, industrial equipment, all derelict, like a rusty alien monster long dead.

A pair of buzzards cruised idly on the warm air over the river. Crows and magpies danced and cawed and chattered down the hill. To his right lay the sprawling abandoned estate of the Château de Mortery where a young, distressed girl called Lili Hubert had decided to end her life some fourteen months before. What led to that, Baptiste could guess. But not whether it might help him discover anything about the fate of Noémie Augustin. The place looked even more impenetrable from a distance, a jungle of trees and scrub and ivy. He'd never have known there were the remains of what was once a substantial château in there if he hadn't been told. Little was visible behind its high walls save for the snag-toothed remains of a single tower that rose like a broken stone incisor above the treetops a good half a kilometre in.

He remembered something Gilles Mailloux had said: de Sade had stayed there when he was on the run. The young man from the petrol station seemed unlike anyone else he'd met in Clermiers: intelligent, helpful, literate, intellectual in a way, unafraid of strangers, though naturally cautious of being close to the police. Quite why someone like that was working behind the counter of a garage at night was beyond Baptiste. People made odd choices about their lives. Perhaps he was waiting for his mother to return. Or he just liked the lazy, casual life he had. Ambition, which Baptiste knew he possessed in a directionless and uncomfortable excess, did not lead to happiness in many cases. Even when those aspirations came to be fulfilled.

A sudden urge to talk at greater length with Gilles Mailloux seized him. But before he could think about that a hand grabbed his arm and a now familiar gruff southern voice said, 'Julien. I have *pains au raisin* and *au chocolat* and a couple of *chaussons aux pommes*. Fresh from the baker. Best thing about this dump. The only good thing, come to think of it.'

Fatoussi was taken by the view then. 'This place should be nicer than it is. Shame about that concrete wart across the river. What's that thing over there?'

The agricultural plant, rusty amid the fields. 'I suspect an old beet refinery. For sugar. You can thank Napoleon for that.'

'What?'

History, Baptiste guessed, was not on his companion's agenda. He gave him a quick rundown of how Napoleon had introduced beet farming to northern France to beat an English blockade on cane sugar from the Caribbean.

'You do fill that head of yours with some strange stuff. I wonder there's room for anything else. Come. The ladies will be outside at the table waiting on their *petit déjeuner*.'

Baptiste didn't move.

'Come! Come!'

'Étienne. Today you leave the gun at home.'

His face fell. He didn't like that.

'The gun stays here. Along with your anger, which is justifiable I might add. If we happen to meet Eric Hubert, you leave the talking to me.'

'That thug should be in jail.'

'Very probably. But Dupont was right. We could never use those photographs against him. Not the way you found them. His son's safe for now. His daughter's dead. There's nothing more to be done. We need to find Noémie Augustin. Every day we don't I fear more for her life.'

Fatoussi winced.

'What is it?' Baptiste asked.

'She vanished on Sunday. It's Wednesday now. Face it. You don't need to be a genius to realise. She's gone from here. Or else she's . . . she's dead.'

They began to walk, in an awkward silence. As they approached the police house Baptiste could see his mother and Mimi chatting at the table on the dry grass, coffee cups and orange juice on the chequered cloth from the kitchen.

He lit another cigarette.

'Am I wrong?' Fatoussi asked before they were within earshot.

'No. Any more than I'm wrong about you leaving that gun behind. We do this my way. Not yours. Not Dupont's.' He stopped and looked Fatoussi in the eye. 'Then maybe we find out what's happened to that girl.'

He seemed to take the point. 'Of course. You're right as usual, Julien. You lead. I follow.' Mimi was waving at them

157

demanding food. 'I'm glad she's still here. I need a woman to keep me sane. You?'

'Normally works the other way round.'

Fatoussi's head went from side to side. 'One day. I'm out of my depth here. Back in Marseille the job meant street hoods. Dope. Gangs. Bad guys. We knew who they were. They knew us. The only question was whether we got the drop on them. You didn't have to find the bastards. You just had to work out which one to try and put in jail.' He sighed. 'This place is different. That Hubert creep apart.'

'Which means what?'

'It means I'm used to the idea bad people do bad things and when they drop their guard we pounce. But this place is full of people who think they're different. Above all that. We're not meant to be here, going through their dirty washing. They don't think they're bad at all.'

Baptiste laughed. 'Bad people don't think they're bad either, lots of the time. They believe they have their reasons. Sometimes they do.'

'Three days in and we don't have a clue. Don't have anyone to turn to for help. Just a captain who keeps saying it's a teenager who decided to run away. None of our business. What if he's right? What if she did just get the hell out of this dump? Dreaming of being a dancer like that American woman she seemed to think was god? Who'd blame her?'

Baptiste had been there already. 'And never so much as called home to say she was safe?'

'Fair point. That's the difference between us. You think then do things. I just try stuff and look to see what happens.' Fatoussi shook the bag of pastries. 'I think we're wanted.'

Mimi and Baptiste's mother fell on the food. Half the coffee and orange juice was gone already.

'Busy day ahead?' Marie asked.

Fatoussi glanced at Baptiste. His to answer.

'We'll see.'

'And this missing girl?'

'I said. What are you up to today? Sightseeing? Not that there looks like much round here.'

'Well . . .' Mimi wiped some jam from her lips. 'I'm going to Paris.'

'With me,' Marie added.

Baptiste was shocked. Disappointed perhaps, he couldn't work it out. Fatoussi looked outraged.

'What is this, Mimi? What have I done?'

'Who said you did anything?'

'I thought you were here for a couple more days.'

'We talked,' Marie said. 'While you two were out doing whatever you were doing just now.'

'We did,' Mimi agreed and patted her hand.

'And?' Baptiste asked.

Marie answered. 'We decided we don't like this place. And we don't like watching what it's doing to you two. You look lost. Angry. Wondering who you can turn on next. We'd rather it wasn't us.'

That hurt and she knew it.

'I'll help you pack,' Baptiste said.

'No need. I'm not a cripple. We're taking both our cars. Hope that isn't inconvenient.'

'It is a bit.'

'They are our cars, Julien.'

The two of them got up, said thanks and sorry in the same sentence, then went inside.

'Women,' Fatoussi grumbled. 'They conspire.'

Thirty minutes later they were gone, Marie first, Mimi after, both with the briefest of goodbyes.

Baptiste climbed behind the wheel of the police Simca and waited.

'We're on our own then,' Fatoussi said as he climbed into the passenger seat. 'Abandoned.'

159

'My mother was never going to offer much in the way of advice when it comes to criminals, Étienne. She thinks the whole country, the French state is a criminal enterprise.'

'You mean she's a Commie?'

'Kind of. My dad was too.'

'Oh. She seemed quite normal and sensible to me.'

He started the car. 'She is.'

A tinny voice barked at them from the radio in Fatoussi's pocket. Pascal Bonnay sounding touchy, saying Dupont wanted to know where they were, what they were doing.

Baptiste clicked his fingers. When Fatoussi passed the handset over, he turned the thing off.

52

Christian Chauvin had never seen much of Hubert over the years. But there he was on the doorstep that arid, overheated Wednesday, taking off his beret, offering a freshly skinned rabbit in a sack by way of introduction.

'May I come in?'

Chauvin took the bag, ushered him through the door, then left the bloody gift in the kitchen. The housekeeper could deal with that later. A casserole. Or a pie. He liked pie.

'I'm sorry for your loss,' he said as they sat down in his study. Hubert had dirt on his boots, dirt on his country trousers. There'd be some sweeping up to be done once he was gone. The man's bearded face looked unwashed, sunburnt, more that of a man of sixty than the forty or so Hubert must be.

'Ah, yes. Poor Lili.'

Hubert looked around as if expecting an offer of coffee. Chauvin demurred.

'We'll handle the interment. I'll officiate at no cost. The *Amis* will cover the expense of the sexton, a place in the cemetery. You need have no financial worries.'

Hubert stretched his legs and opened them wide, the posture, Chauvin thought, of a peasant. 'You think? I've no daughter to bring me money. No son I can send out to work now the social people in Millot have taken him away. Just me.'

He got up and went to stare at an image of Christ on the cross, pinned to the wall. A memento from Lourdes it said beneath the crucified figure. 'You get all this for free? From God? A house? A wage? A woman to cook and clean and who knows what else?' He crooked a finger and patted the head of Jesus. 'There, there, son of God. Soon be Christmas when you get to be born. Then Easter when we kill you all over again.'

Hubert laughed then sat down.

'Every Easter he rises,' Chauvin said. 'That's the point.'

'Not going to happen to my Lili, is it? Or that black girl from what I hear.'

'You hear what?'

A shrug. 'Just mutterings.'

Chauvin went to the door, made sure the housekeeper hadn't turned up, closed it all the same.

'The widow Ducasse will be here soon. If you have something to say—'

'How much money is Laurent – sorry, the *Amis* – putting on the table to bury my girl?'

'I'm not aware of the exact—'

'Guess.'

Chauvin shuffled on his chair. 'Ordinarily, with the service, I imagine you don't want anything fancy, I'd say around eight or nine thousand francs.'

'And for me?'

He shook his head. 'I'm sorry? This is for the undertaker. The sexton. The grave space. I give my services for free but others . . .'

Hubert groaned. 'There are debts to clear. Lili left them. Little horror when it came to spending money. I've been putting them off . . .'

'To whom was she indebted?'

'That's my business. Not yours. The point is . . . now they know she's dead they're asking me for payback. With interest. If I can't find the money somewhere, I'll have to sell something. A few valuable items I've retained for a rainy day as it were.'

Chauvin knew it was coming. 'What sort of things do you have in mind?'

'Oh, all sorts. Did you know our beloved mayor has an occasional taste for boys? No wonder the man never married.' He stared across the room and there, Chauvin thought, was the real Eric Hubert. A bully and a thug. The man grinned. 'I wonder if he mentions this in that private box of yours. Probably not . . .'

Like most men of the cloth, Chauvin was familiar with prying questions. 'What happens there lies between me and the confessant.'

Hubert laughed out loud, heavy shoulders chucking up and down. 'Oh, man! You should see your face. Such an innocent. Bad enough he doesn't tell you. Worse, you don't even suspect . . .'

'I fear this conversation is improper. I don't expect to be threatened by a grieving father.'

Hubert waved his arms in protest. 'No, no no! I never meant to threaten anyone, least of all you. I've no reason to doubt what you say. But your peers, well . . . They're just men like me. Untouched by holiness. All I desire is a quiet life, free from worry, where I may mourn my little Lili without fretting whether the bailiffs are going to turn up on my doorstep demanding their pound of flesh. Not that such a thing would turn a head in Boulliers, would it?'

There was only one question to ask. 'How much is this . . . debt of your daughter's?'

'Twenty thousand with interest.'

Chauvin gasped. 'Such an amount of money.'

'Lili had expensive tastes. She did it behind my back with

one of the bloodsucking loan sharks from Millot.'

'I still don't know—'

'Then find someone who does.' He winked. 'Anyone talked to our holier than thou local councillor lately?'

Chauvin felt twitchier than ever. Gaillard had gone off on one of his lost weekends before. But never for so long.

'Louis . . .? What's he got to do with this?'

Hubert frowned. 'Maybe nothing. Who knows?'

Chauvin stayed silent.

'Cat got your tongue, Father? Listen to me. I'm done with this shithole. No family, no son to keep me now, is there? Getting picked on by the law to boot. Pay me my money. I'll tidy up every last thing that may worry you and your mates. Leave you a little parting present if you're lucky. Then I'm gone.'

'Where?' Chauvin wondered.

'Somewhere you don't need to know because you and your *Amis* will never hear from me again. South, I think. It's warmer. The girls are prettier. Somewhere I can start again. All I need's the money. In cash. Today.'

Chauvin asked him to wait for a few minutes while he made a call.

When he came back Hubert was back at the wall looking at the pottery Christ from Lourdes. It was an ugly, garish thing, something Chauvin had inherited from his predecessor.

'One of Laurent's minions can bring it round my place,' he said before Chauvin could open his mouth. 'Just not the black guy. Something wrong with that one.'

'I was told to say . . . this must be an end to everything. No more . . . surprises.'

'Oh . . . Father! You think I like the surprises I've got of late? A dead daughter? A boy stolen from me? I'm a man of my word. You doubt it?'

'No, no. I'm sorry about Lili. The loss of a child . . . I can't begin to imagine.'

'True,' Hubert said and nothing more.

'I rather wished she'd confided in me.'

Hubert threw back his head and howled with laughter. 'Oh, that I very much doubt. An innocent like you wouldn't have understood a fraction of it.'

Chauvin wished he wasn't so frightened of the man's sweaty, muscular presence. 'One does not need to be soiled by the physical world to be aware of the perils it poses. I might have helped.'

Hubert tugged at his ear. 'You're burying her for free. Buy her some flowers as well. Say they were from me.' He clapped his hands. 'That'll do.'

He chucked the pottery Jesus under the chin and went, 'Coochie, coochie coo, pretty boy. Hope those nails don't smart.'

Then he strode over to Chauvin and grabbed him by the collar of his black clerical jacket. 'Tell your masters they're walking on broken glass. And I'm the one who can strip them naked.' He snapped his fat fingers. 'Just like that.'

53

Down in Boulliers Martine Augustin was waiting outside the house, with her bag and Fifi the terrier, miserable on a lead. She'd packed everything she could manage. Her husband had watched in grim silence. There was a finality to the act they both recognised. Those underclothes squeezed together into tiny bundles, that wash bag with its toothbrush and de-odorant, the everyday clothes, the same ones she'd worn for years in Calais, all this signified an end to a marriage that had lasted twenty-two years, impoverished for the most part, but happy too. Until he took Bruno Laurent's money and moved to Clermiers. Those months her husband had spent there changed him, and it was only after Noémie vanished that she accepted what she'd silently recognised all along.

Charles Augustin stared glumly at the whimpering dog. 'What will you do?'

'I'll go and see my sister. Look for work. I won't be asking you for money if that's what's bothering you.'

'It never entered my head. Martine . . . do I have to beg?'

'You can try but it'll make no difference. Clermiers was a mistake. What's happened here we can't undo. Can't turn back.'

She picked up the bag. He took it from her and watched as she led the dog to the back of the car. Always polite, always thoughtful. That hadn't changed. It was one reason she felt guilty for being so harsh towards him at that moment. Not that there was a choice. The decision was made.

'When there's news . . .'

'You think there will be? Soon?'

He held out his arms like a supplicant. 'How the hell would I know?'

She checked her watch. 'Don't make me miss that train.'

The drive was almost an hour. Augustin stopped outside the station, lost for words, staring through the windscreen.

'It's hurtful to do this,' he said in the end. 'To leave me when she's god knows where. I never thought you were capable of such unkindness.'

'Twenty-two years and still we're strangers in some ways.' She reached for the car door. 'Maybe all marriages are like that. I've no idea. You know Annette's number?'

He nodded.

She squeezed her eyes tight shut and perhaps that was to stop the tears. All the same she reached out and touched his arm, just for a second. The last time that would happen she felt sure. 'I'm sorry, Charles. There'll come a point where we need to talk about lawyers. If either of us has the money. Not now.'

The terrier whimpered by her side. Martine Augustin didn't move. It pained her to see the flicker of hope in her husband's face.

165

'Don't go . . .' he started.

She got out of the car with her case and the little dog. Fifi was whining, aware of the odd atmosphere.

Then she was walking into the station. Never turning to look back.

He sat at the wheel of Laurent's car, Laurent's name stamped on the side, watched the train pull in. Watched it leave, vanish down the line. A journey he'd made himself all those months before when he'd been promised a new life, prosperity, reward for all the ambitions his passive nature and the colour of his skin had long suppressed. A fool, and Bruno Laurent surely knew it from the start.

54

Baptiste pulled onto the forecourt of Clermiers' filling station. No other car there. No camper van either. Celia Murray was gone.

'You missed her,' Fatoussi said.

'That's not why we're here.'

'Do I get to know the reason then?'

He couldn't work out what had affected Fatoussi most. The episode with Eric Hubert and the fact the man walked free. Or Mimi's sudden decision to leave.

'Because this place is a kind of nexus for Clermiers. Everyone's got to come through here at some point or other. Maybe there's something to learn.'

'Huh.'

'You don't sound convinced.'

Fatoussi raised a finger. 'You're a smart fellow. I'm not. What I do know is that sometimes you can be too clever for your own good.'

Baptiste laughed. 'Now that's what I call cryptic. Do I get an explanation?'

'You like this young guy here.'

It was a statement, not a question. 'Christ, Étienne. He's just about the only local who's given us the time of day since we turned up.'

A sigh. A shrug. 'Yeah. I know.'

'Then . . .?'

'Just . . . the not clever, suspicious part of me wonders . . . why? It all goes back to Boulliers, doesn't it? And where does Gilles Mailloux live?'

Baptiste threw up his hands in despair. 'Yesterday it was Eric Hubert. Today it's the one person who actually talks to us.'

Fatoussi nodded. 'It's possible it's both. Or neither. Or more. What the hell do I know? And anyway . . . what are you going to ask him?'

'Watch.'

Fatoussi put a hand to his arm as he was about to climb out of the car. 'This is what I mean about being too clever. Mailloux works nights, remember? Not everyone's on the job twenty-four hours a day like you.'

Baptiste wondered why he hadn't thought of that. Too little sleep. Too much to occupy him.

Someone they'd not seen before walked out of the cabin. A balding man in his early thirties, chubby in an oil-stained mechanic's boiler suit.

Baptiste wound down the window and flashed his card. 'Who are you?'

'Roland Noyer. Might ask the same of you. Where's Dupont? Bonnay?'

Fatoussi leaned over. 'They're busy. Paper clips to count.'

'Ah.' He pointed at them. 'The smartasses. I heard about you. Want some fuel? Some fags and booze . . .' He winked. 'On account?'

A dismissive wave, a look around him and then Baptiste wound up the window and gunned the little engine. Noyer

167

shrugged, mouthed something they couldn't hear and ambled back to the cabin.

'We can't go after that bastard Hubert because he's nothing to do with Noémie, according to you.' There was a touch of sarcasm in Fatoussi's voice Baptiste hadn't expected.

'Correct.'

'And we don't have anyone else in our sights, anything to chase at all?'

Baptiste grabbed the radio, turned it on and called into the station. Bonnay was there sounding grumpier than usual.

'Dupont has been asking after you.'

'The handset went on the blink,' Baptiste said. 'Any news?'

'Millot confirmed Lili Hubert strung herself up. No sign of anything else. It's going to the coroner as a suicide.'

'That was quick.'

Bonnay muttered something they couldn't hear. Then, 'They're busy. They wanted it out of the way.'

'Noémie Augustin. The description we circulated. Paris? Dance halls? Trains? Buses?'

'Not a thing. Dupont wants to know where you are. What you're going to do.'

Baptiste made a crackling noise down the radio then switched the thing off. Then someone rapped on the glass. A middle-aged woman in a lurid red shirt and bright blue trousers, grey hair pulled back in a bun.

'Why does your captain not answer my calls?' she barked the moment Baptiste wound down the window.

'I'm sorry . . .'

'My brother. He's been gone since Sunday. He rarely misses dinner. We have it every night, seven on the dot. I cooked a hare for us. Never came. Never called.'

'Really I . . .'

'Dupont doesn't phone me back. What's going on? And who the hell are you? Why isn't that fat fool Bonnay out doing the rounds?'

'Madame . . .?'

'Gaillard. Alice Gaillard. My brother . . .'

'I can give you a lift to the station.'

'He's not a nobody, you know. Louis is our representative on the regional council. A stalwart of the *Amis*. If it wasn't for him those idle sods in Boulliers would be worse off than they are. Bruno Laurent always likes to take the credit. Him and that stuck-up mayor of ours. But it's my brother who gets things done round here. And Dupont won't even listen now he's missing.'

Fatoussi was out of the car in an instant, smiling in that way women always seemed to admire.

'Madame Gaillard,' he said, opening the back door of the car. 'May we drive you into town ourselves?'

'Don't be ridiculous. We only live round the corner. We can talk there.' She wagged a finger from side to side. 'This is not like him! Louis is normally the most cautious of men.'

55

Charles Augustin parked outside the Mairie and marched into the police station. Bonnay was at his desk as usual, scruffy in a uniform that hadn't seen an iron of late.

'He's not here,' he said before Augustin could utter a word.

'Who?'

'Dupont. That's who. The captain has business.'

Augustin pulled up a seat, unasked and sat down in front of him. 'I have business. A missing daughter.'

Bonnay's head went from side to side. 'We've circulated her description far and wide to everyone we can think of. Nothing's come back. I advise patience. When teenagers go missing, they often wish to stay under the radar as it were. They're afraid they'll get into trouble when they finally realise home wasn't so bad.'

'Her home wasn't bad!'

Bonnay tried to swat a mosquito buzzing round in front of him. 'Her home was Boulliers. No need to take this personally.'

Augustin closed his eyes and whispered a foul curse. 'Noémie is missing. You people are doing nothing to find her. My wife has left me.'

'She has?' Bonnay looked interested finally. 'At a time like this?'

'At a time like this.'

'Women get hysterical. She'll come crawling back. Your daughter too. Go home. Go do some work for Laurent. He surely wants that too.'

Except he didn't. One call between them since Noémie went missing and work was never mentioned.

'Where are the other two? Baptiste and whatever his name is.'

Bonnay licked his lips then muttered, 'Out.'

'Out?'

Nothing.

'Out where? Looking for my Noémie?'

The policeman reached into his desk and took out a notebook and pen.

'I don't like your attitude. It sounds aggressive. And threatening.'

'Fuck it!' Augustin banged his big fist on the desk. The pen jumped and fell on the floor. 'What are you doing to find my daughter?'

'Everything in our power. Every last thing. Baptiste and Fatoussi are on the case right now. Perhaps they'll wish to talk to you later. I'll suggest that when I see them.'

'You don't even know where they are, do you?' He nodded at the little office. The fading posters on the walls about home security, traffic advice, agricultural diseases and a local election long gone. 'This place, all of you, it means nothing. You just sit

170

on your fat arses, fill your face and your pockets and let the rest of us go to hell.'

Bonnay picked the pen off the floor and tapped it on the desk.

'In the circumstances I'd rather not have to arrest you for threatening behaviour . . .'

'Would you be saying that if I was white?'

A frown. 'Probably not. I'd give you a couple of minutes more. But you're not white, you're not Clermiers, and you don't have a friend in the world round here.' He grinned. 'Not even a woman now it seems.' Bonnay nodded at the door. 'So get your black arse out of here. We've only got one cell and I haven't cleaned it in a while. When we've got something to say, we'll be in touch.'

Two minutes later Augustin was back in his car, cursing behind the wheel. Bonnay got up from his desk, stretched his back, watched him drive off down the hill towards Boulliers. Where else could he go?

'Cheek of it,' he muttered then went back to his much-loved chair and called Dupont.

'Augustin's been in again. He's not a happy little minstrel.'

Dupont swore. 'What did you tell him?'

'We're working on it.'

'And Baptiste?'

'He called in briefly. Says the radio's playing up. Conveniently when I ask where he is and what he's up to. The bastard's turning it on and off when he feels like it.'

'Huh.'

'You want me to tell him to get his arse in here?'

'Nah. Let him chase his tail. The black kid's run away, hasn't she? No one's seen her anywhere. End of story.'

'Teenagers,' Bonnay said and made it sound like a swear word. 'She'll be back whining like a baby when she's broke and hungry.'

'Exactly,' Dupont agreed.

'And if she doesn't . . .?'

'One thing at a time,' Dupont said. 'Got a meeting of the *Amis* executive at three. The shop's all yours.'

56

Louis and Alice Gaillard were twins. That much was obvious from the moment Baptiste and Fatoussi stepped through the door of their three-storey mansion opposite the rusty iron gates of the château. Photos of the two of them, as infants in identical sailor's costumes, in school uniform, as adolescents smoking cigarettes and trying to look cool, with little success. Then later as they travelled into their thirties, so alike, so miserable, so anxious to have their image stamped on the walls of their home. There, a good decade before, the camera stopped. Perhaps they no longer wished to be reminded age came to them as well. All the same, these framed pictures, ranged up and down the wall, were so atmospheric, images from another world, a different way of life, wealthy, privileged, insular, Baptiste could only stare.

'I don't see any of your parents,' he said as she led them towards an expansive living room at the back. A grand piano stood on one side, dusty, unused for ages he imagined. On the other side, in front of a frayed and ageing sofa, stood an ancient gramophone alongside a fastidiously arranged library of classical LPs. It might have been the France of decades before, just after the war.

'They're dead,' she said and sat down.

The place had the fusty smell of somewhere the windows weren't often opened. Dead flies had collected beneath the doors to a conservatory full of fleshy plants, orchids he guessed, exotic, quite out of place so far north.

Fatoussi took out a notebook and glanced at Baptiste . . . *all yours* his look seemed to say.

'When did you last see your brother?' Baptiste began.

'Sunday,' she said with a firm jab of her finger. 'That afternoon when he went off for a meeting of the *Amis*. Louis said not to expect him back for a while. Maybe not that night. He had work. Business.' She crossed her legs then lit a cigarette. 'My brother's a man with much on his plate. The expectation is he will soon be a *député* in Paris. People recognise his talent. His hard work. His expertise.'

'Expertise in what?' he wondered.

'In ... in ... administration. He's been on the regional council since our dear father passed on the seat. Thankless work, poorly rewarded. Fortunately, we have private means. The hoi polloi, Boulliers in particular, hate us, of course. No matter all the good work Louis does down there.'

'And you've heard nothing from him since Sunday?'

'One night or two I would allow to pass. He has his own life. No need to feel answerable to me. But no more than two. It's unthinkable.'

'He has a girlfriend?'

She laughed, very briefly and with little in the way of humour. 'He's discreet about his private life. With reason. He nearly got married once. Me too. We saw sense before the fatal blow.'

'You have a name for any of his friends? Male or female?'

Her eyebrows arched in anger. 'What are you suggesting?'

'Nothing, madame. When someone disappears, we always try to ask around the people they know.' He smiled. 'Which we would have done with this missing girl from Boulliers, Noémie Augustin, if only she had some friends.'

'My brother would not be acquainted with a black child from that place I can assure you. This isn't like him.'

'He has enemies?' Baptiste asked.

Her eyebrows rose in tandem. 'Of course not. He works for the good of society. How can one earn enemies like that?'

He bent over and murmured something in Fatoussi's ear.

'It's rude to whisper,' she said.

'It is, Madame Gaillard. I apologise. I was asking my friend to take over the questioning here. I'm afraid I ate something that disagreed with me last night. If you could direct me to the toilet?'

A wave of a skinny hand and a plume of cigarette smoke towards the hall. 'Third along. Leave it as found.'

On the way in he'd seen what looked like a small office on the left. Baptiste opened the toilet door, then, quite noisily, closed it and went into the adjoining room. A gentleman's study: an old oak desk with a typewriter, grey metal filing cabinets on both sides. Next to the Olivetti was a pile of papers, council documents to do with planning applications and housing policy.

Every drawer of the first cabinet was unlocked, inside, neatly filed, council documents, some going back more than a decade. Tedious, uninteresting material. Nothing there concerning the organisation that interested him, the *Amis*, the charity that ran the club by the tennis courts, and put money into Boulliers from time to time. And had, it seemed, employed on a casual basis both Lili Hubert and Noémie Augustin.

He turned to the next one. There, at least, was something. The top drawer contained the minutes of *Amis* meetings, the list of people attending. Most seemed to consist of a dozen or more locals, names he didn't recognise. But in the middle drawer were the records of the 'executive committee'. That appeared to comprise the mayor, Fabrice Blanc, Bruno Laurent, the businessman, Louis Gaillard as the representative of the regional government, Chauvin, the priest. And Philippe Dupont, on behalf of the local police.

The documents were dry and tedious, records of donations for a playground, the renovation of a social centre, grants for minor groundwork and tree-planting projects. Indications, too, that some of the money came through Gaillard's council contacts, but most were handouts from Laurent's companies, carefully timed and organised to be as tax efficient as possible. Nothing Dupont said in any of the meetings was recorded.

The bottom drawer was locked.

Baptiste went back to the door. He could hear Fatoussi talking rapidly down the hall. Occupying the Gaillard woman as best he could. Not much time. He went back to the desk, picked up a paper clip from the tray, wound out one end, started wiggling it in the drawer lock. He could only hope. After the third failed attempt, he picked up a letter opener from the desk and levered the drawer open with some force. The Gaillards would know. He didn't care. Inside, again neatly filed, was a series of blue separators each with a large manila envelope, full to bursting.

Baptiste took out the first three and scattered the contents across the desk.

'What in god's name do you think you're doing?' Alice Gaillard snapped from the door.

Fatoussi was behind her, shrugging, apologetic.

'I said . . .'

'I heard, Madame Gaillard. Would you care to look at these and tell me what you think?'

They both came to the desk. Étienne Fatoussi's face turned scarlet, furious. Alice Gaillard had her hands to her mouth, eyes wide, shock obvious.

'That, I believe,' Baptiste said, pointing at a set marked April the previous year, 'is Lili Hubert. With your brother.'

Before she could say a thing, he took out the rest of the envelopes and scattered the photographs across the desk. All black and white, Hubert's work he imagined. All of Louis Gaillard naked with a succession of women, engaged in a variety of positions.

'I am, naturally, guessing here,' he went on. 'But I would venture the opinion that most of these women are professional, as you might say. While Lili was not, or at least not in quite the

175

same league.' He turned and watched her. 'A reward for all that good work in Boulliers, do you think?'

'I don't believe this. Any of it . . .'

Fatoussi came and grimaced at the pictures.

Baptiste pulled out a sequence of four, Gaillard taking a naked woman from behind, his face a picture of anxiety and desperation, while she, turned to the camera, mouth open, winking in one, as if she knew the game. 'What is this place?'

There was furniture, a velvet couch of a distinct design, made for sex of a certain kind, erotic paintings on the walls, velvet drapes. Just like the photos they'd found in Hubert's darkroom.

No answer.

'You have a room like this here?' Baptiste asked.

'Don't be ridiculous!'

'Then where?'

'I don't know. Put those things away. I refuse to look at them.'

'We'll take them.'

'You will not!'

Fatoussi ignored her and began to put the pictures back in their envelopes, glancing through them.

'Nothing here of the Augustin girl I can see.'

'They would date from Sunday,' Baptiste said. 'Too soon perhaps. And Louis Gaillard is, of course, missing. Just like Noémie.' He turned to the woman. 'Do you think it's possible your brother has run away with her? Willingly on her part? Or perhaps not?'

'That's preposterous. My brother's a leading light of this community. One day soon he'll be in the National Assembly. Why would a Gaillard run away from Clermiers? We've lived here, honoured citizens, for generations.'

'Honour's a funny thing,' Baptiste murmured, glancing at the photographs on the desk.

'The Augustin girl's black!'

Fatoussi gave her a filthy look. 'It seems your brother has broad tastes. She was very pretty.'

'*Is*,' Baptiste corrected him again. 'Until someone shows me otherwise. You'd no idea Louis engaged in behaviour like this?'

Alice Gaillard was fast recovering her composure. 'I want you to leave this house now.'

'We'll go when you've answered my question.'

'A man's a man! Is sex illegal now?'

'Lili Hubert is young . . .'

'I believe the age of consent is fifteen. And in Boulliers largely ignored. If you want to find criminals and this girl you're looking for, I'd suggest you start there.'

A common refrain, Baptiste thought. Philippe Dupont had been singing that song from the start. He hadn't listened because there'd been so many distractions along the way. Perhaps Louis Gaillard's private life was another.

Fatoussi had all the photos in the box, and from the look on his face was thinking there wasn't much left to be found in the curious home of the Gaillards.

'We'll need these photographs for our inquiries,' Baptiste told her. 'Your brother's description will be circulated to all the relevant agencies. If you hear from him, I expect to be told immediately.'

'You're not to make those public!' she bellowed. 'I forbid it. They don't belong to you. Louis will be a *député* come the next election. Perhaps a *sénateur* one day. A minister. He has friends in the Élysée. I will not see a man of his calibre damaged by the likes of you.'

The harangue continued as they headed for the door. Then from the patio as they left.

57

Dupont collected the money from the mayor's office. Fabrice Blanc counted out the bills. Arpin, the bank manager, was there looking deeply uncomfortable. No paperwork, no signatures, no traces left.

'This surely has to be an end to it,' Blanc said as the last of the notes went into a thick courier's envelope. 'For pity's sake let's have some peace.'

Arpin shook his head and said, 'I don't want to hear any of this. You have your money.'

Blanc ignored him. He was only a bank manager. 'Hubert told Chauvin he's leaving?'

'For the south it seems,' said Dupont. 'For good.'

'That brat of his . . .?'

'He's in the care of the Millot social workers. Given the circumstances, we won't see him here again.'

Arpin looked ready to scream. A quick excuse and then he marched out.

'The boy has stories to tell,' Blanc said.

'He's a Hubert. From Boulliers. Who the hell's going to believe him?'

'I would rather he didn't open his filthy mouth at all.'

Dupont grinned. 'That's not what I heard.'

Blanc glared at him.

'Fair enough,' Dupont said. 'I'll tell them we had problems with him telling fairy tales.'

'Will it work?'

A dismissive shrug. 'My clairvoyant powers are limited. Perhaps.'

Blanc squinted at him. 'I'm not the only man in jeopardy here. Remember that.'

Dupont smiled and waved the envelope. 'If you'd rather be the delivery man . . .?'

No answer.

'Thought so,' the captain said and walked to his car.

Hubert had left instructions on how he could be found. Even without them, Dupont would have had a good idea where to look. Not the house, he'd surely stay away from there. It was the old beet processing factory three kilometres east. A place Dupont knew very well. The young of Boulliers went there to smoke dope and shoot up, much as they used the old boat-house of the château for screwing and drinking. All pit stops on the local entertainment scene.

The boathouse was quite public though, so there they were mainly content with being a nuisance, the source of occasional complaints about noise and unruly behaviour. The abandoned beet plant was more private, down a potholed single track dirt lane from the narrow winding back road that led eventually to Millot. Dupont visited from time to time to make sure they all knew he was watching and might act if matters got out of control. There would always be mischief in Boulliers. It was best it happened somewhere he knew. Besides, there were more adult activities from time to time. Hubert would arrange the odd cock fight or bring in vicious fighting dogs from one of his pals outside Lille. An evening of drinking, laughing, betting and watching the birds and the dogs tear each other apart was something a good few of the agricultural men in and around Clermiers enjoyed. Dupont and Bonnay too on occasion.

A battered rusty BSA motorbike sat on its stand next to what was once the factory office. Next to it a shiny blue Renault 12. No sign of Hubert. Dupont called out his name. No response.

'Make me work for it, you bastard,' he muttered, then set about walking round the plant. It covered a good couple of hectares, corrugated iron buildings falling to pieces, old processing machinery, pipes and pumps and boilers reduced to rusty hulks. After five minutes he turned the corner by a dumper truck sitting on its wheel rims, tyres long stolen, and there the man was next to a makeshift fighting ring made from

179

tyres and old planks, the place Dupont had last been a few months before, watching a mastiff rip a pit bull to shreds.

Two brightly coloured cockerels were in there now, clawing at one another, blood on the dry summer dust, feathers everywhere, flesh too. Hubert watched them, shoulders heaving with laughter.

'You like my children? I call them Louis and Bruno.'

One of the birds looked ready to drop. The thing was hobbling, barely able to lift its claws, to stab at the other with its beak.

'Bah.' Hubert swore under his breath, climbed into the ring, picked it up, wrung the thing's neck. The other cockerel, furious, started to claw at his ankles. Hubert threw the dead bird to one side and grabbed the living one by the throat and swung it round till its torn and bloody body went limp.

He held it out. 'You want dinner? Yours to pluck and gut. No charge. Never is for my friends in the police.'

'Here.' Dupont held out the envelope. 'Take this and fuck off forever.'

Hubert dropped the bird, opened the envelope, peeked inside. 'I won't bother counting them.'

'Nice to know we have your trust, Eric.'

He laughed. 'Oh, you don't. It's just that if you screw me around, I'll come back for more. You all know that.'

One of the birds wasn't quite dead. Limping across the bloody dust. Hubert stamped on the thing.

'You're leaving now?'

'Couple of loose ends to clear up. Packing. Lying low.' He waved the envelope. 'Nothing that need concern you. Saw my new car on the way in? Swish, huh?'

'Don't tell me you nicked it. Not again. Got enough loose ends to clean up.'

'I really don't know what you mean there, Captain. I'm a man of my word . . . see for yourself.'

Hubert walked across the yard into what looked like a barn,

180

roof half-off. At the end a small bonfire was petering out. He ran his foot through the ashes and melting negatives. Film, 35mm by the looks of it, and the burned edges of blackened prints.

'All gone. You've nothing to worry about.'

There was a noise. A voice, pained, a cry, what sounded like a mumbled plea for help.

'Oh yeah. One more thing.' He leered. 'You'll never guess.'

58

'This place gets lovelier with every passing second,' Fatoussi said as Baptiste leaned back in the driver's seat and lit another cigarette. He opened a window and waved out the harsh Disque Bleu fumes. 'You smoke too much.'

'My lungs.'

'Mine too. I guess Louis Gaillard thought his mucky pictures would never come back to bite him. What did the little perve get out of keeping those things? Was he whacking off at the desk while he went through his planning applications, putting a cross against the ones where nobody gave him any money? This one passes. This one fails. Whoops . . . where are the tissues?'

Baptiste made his best attempt at an admonitory scowl.

'OK, OK. A step too far. But you know what? She did have a point.'

'What point?'

'There's nothing here we can take him for, even if we do find the man. Private orgies may not be what the electorate of Clermiers expect of their representative – or maybe they do and don't care. But if we tried to nick every politician who's got an exotic love life, there wouldn't be many left to pretend they're running the country.'

'True.'

181

'Thank you! A word of praise, finally. And, may I add, she also had a point about Boulliers. The only solid piece of information we've gleaned about Noémie Augustin came from there. Those photos of Hubert, snatched through her window. Found, as it happens . . .' He jabbed a finger at his chest. 'By Étienne Fatoussi, none other.'

'Which we can't use. Because of the way you stole your way in there.'

Fatoussi kicked the box at his feet. 'You think you can use these?'

Baptiste picked out a couple of the photos of Lili Hubert with Gaillard. 'Did you notice what she's wearing?'

In some she was naked. In others she wore the white tunic and collar of a choir girl. The same outfit she had on hanging from a tree in the Bois de Mortery for more than a year.

'That wasn't taken in a church.'

'No. At least,' Baptiste said, 'I doubt it. I'd guess that usually he liked to buy his women. But sometimes he wanted a young local girl. And he wanted her to dress up.'

'Plastic bananas,' Fatoussi said. 'A black dress. Dancing. The English kid said Noémie had them in her tennis bag.'

'Quite.'

'We need to search that place, Julien. Turn it upside down. Find that dress. Find those things and we're there.'

Baptiste shook his head. 'You think we have enough to ask for a warrant to go in there? That Dupont will allow it? There's nothing that connects him with Noémie.'

'Then what do we do?' Fatoussi snapped. 'Isn't there someone you can call in Paris and say . . . we're stuck out here in turnip land, no support, no interest from a captain who looks like he'd overlook a murder if it interfered with his lunch break? Can't they come in and . . .?'

'And what? Is there someone you can call in Marseille?'

'Paris! You come from Paris!'

'I doubt they'd be interested. Dupont would tell them . . . it's a missing teenager. A black kid from a rough estate. Probably run away like they often do.'

Fatoussi sighed. Baptiste gestured for the radio and called in.

'He's not here,' Bonnay said before he could even ask about Dupont.

'Where is he then?'

'Out. I think he'd like to ask that of you.'

'Same here.'

'He has a meeting with the *Amis* at three. I don't know if he'll be in here at all today.'

'The clubhouse?'

'I guess. Don't disturb them. They wouldn't like that. Important people.'

'Louis Gaillard among them?'

A long pause then Bonnay said, 'None of my business. Or yours.'

Then he was gone.

Fatoussi kept staring out of the front window, absorbed.

'What is it?'

'We need to go back to Boulliers.'

'Why?'

'Someone has to talk to the Augustins. Make it look like we're trying.'

Baptiste started the Simca and edged it down the road. 'True.'

'Also, I'd like to see your friend from the petrol station again. If he's home.'

'Why?'

Fatoussi tapped his nose. 'Intuition. Something's funny there. You like him, so you don't notice.'

183

59

Louis Gaillard was on the ground in the barn, back against the wall. Dried blood black and caked around his nostrils, hands tied behind his back, hair filthy with grime, cheeks scratched, eyes bright and terrified, what looked like chicken shit marking his creased and grubby business suit. A filthy rag was round his mouth. Hubert walked over and ripped it off. The man was screaming straight away, demanding Dupont get him out of there, straight to a hospital.

'The bastard's had me here for a whole night. Beating me up. Letting his fucking cockerel take a go at me.'

'Bested by a chicken.' Hubert chuckled. 'Says it all.'

'For god's sake, Dupont . . .'

The captain sniffed, said nothing, just stared at Hubert.

It was a kind of explanation. After they found Lili dead Hubert had thought about the pictures he had again. How Gaillard had promised to treat his daughter. Mostly though, about how little he'd paid given what he'd done with Lili exceeded the father's expectations.

'I was in an emotional state,' Hubert said without an ounce of emotion. 'Saw him pulling up outside that fancy house of his and something snapped.'

'You were waiting for me!' Gaillard shrieked.

'Well.' Hubert wiped his nose with his sleeve. 'We came back here for a chat and, I dunno, it didn't go so well.'

'You waited—'

'Where've you been all this time?' Dupont asked.

'Drove to Amsterdam Sunday night. Needed a break.'

Hubert snorted. 'A smoke, a visit to one of those ladies with their red lights. Or a couple of little kiddies, huh?'

'A break . . .' Gaillard whispered.

'Never tipped my little girl. Never came round when she went missing.'

Hubert walked over and kicked him hard in the gut.

184

Gaillard yelped and screamed and began to cry.

'Enough,' Dupont said when he saw Hubert drawing back his foot for one more boot.

'If you say so, Captain.' He pointed a grubby finger at the weeping man on the floor. 'But I tell you this, Councillor. I'm taking that tip now. It's a blue Renault. Mine. My ticket out of *Merdeville*. And if anyone wants to complain, well . . .' He winked, at Gaillard first, then Dupont. 'I doubt that's going to happen.'

'Give him the keys,' Dupont ordered.

Hubert pulled them out of his pocket and mouthed, 'Mine already.'

'Then get the fuck out of here.'

A bow, a grin. 'As you wish, sir.'

One minute later, round the corner, a car started.

'Don't touch that,' Hubert yelled, pointing at the motorbike. 'I'll be back for it. On my way out.'

Really gone? Dupont wondered. Hubert looked like a man who still had business left. He just hoped that happened out of sight. As it had with Louis Gaillard.

'Forget hospital. Take me home, Philippe,' the man on the floor bleated. 'Alice can manage.'

Dupont groaned and closed his eyes.

'For god's sake . . . take me—'

'You're not going home!' Dupont fetched him a kick then, not as hard as Hubert's but enough to start the whimpering again.

'Philippe . . .'

'*You're not going home!* There's all manner of shit flying round this place. Some Parisian bastard and his *pied-noir* mate looking to cause us pain. I'm not having you with your trap wide open getting near that pair.'

He bent down, yanked him up by his roped arms. Saw a flicker of defiance in his eyes.

'Alice won't like this at all.'

'Your sister can go to hell.'

'And me, Dupont? I am the regional councillor for Clermiers! I have friends who count. A seat waiting for me in the National Assembly before long.'

'Chances of that happening are on a par with me being the next pope.'

'Where—?'

'You're upset, Louis. Under a lot of stress. You need peace and quiet, not that bitch of a sister yammering in your ear.'

'I demand to go home!'

Dupont grabbed his filthy jacket and pulled him close. 'Listen, you ungrateful little shit. You'll do exactly what I say. Stay exactly where I tell you. Until I've got rid of Baptiste and his pet monkey and we can all go back to living the way we like. *Compris?*'

A moment, then, terrified, Louis Gaillard nodded.

'*C'est tout,*' said Dupont as he half-dragged, half-kicked him past the dead cockerels, the old motorbike, the ashes and the melted film strips, the detritus of the dead beet works.

60

Charles Augustin was locking his front door as they turned up. The man looked more downcast than ever. Baptiste got out and tried to talk to him, Fatoussi watching, hands in pockets, suspicious. It was obvious Augustin wasn't interested.

'Don't you want to know what's happening?' Fatoussi asked.

'I talked to Bonnay. Nothing's happening. You people don't give a damn. Black girl from Boulliers. Runaway he says. Why bother?'

'Does Martine feel the same way?' Baptiste asked.

Augustin looked shifty. 'She's gone to stay with her sister for a while. Can't take the atmosphere round this place.' He jingled his keys. 'Got to go.'

'Back to work?' Baptiste wondered.

No answer.

'Charles. The records at the petrol station. Mailloux says they're gone. All of them. Names and number plates, times and dates. Just vanished.'

Augustin sounded interested. 'Are you sure?'

'We're sure. We've no way of knowing who passed by there last Sunday. Did you take them?'

'It wasn't me.'

Not another word, then he walked off to his car. Fatoussi was staring hard at Baptiste.

'I know you think we should be chasing the landed gentry here, Julien. But let me tell you . . . the keen antennae of Étienne Fatoussi are twitching right now. It's Boulliers we should be looking in. Not uptown.'

'Hello!' said a cheery, young voice. Not what they expected. Gilles Mailloux ambling down the Avenue Laval, looking round, maybe checking to make sure he wasn't seen. 'Afternoon, officers.' A quick salute. 'Anything I can do?'

'A coffee and a biscuit would go down well right now,' Fatoussi said.

'Sure. The coffee's instant and the biscuits are past their eat by date, liberated from my little office up the hill. *Bon appetit.*'

Before Baptiste could say a word, Fatoussi had Mailloux's arm, and they began walking down the street.

61

Thirty minutes out of Clermiers, Gaillard finally found the courage to speak.

'You need to tell Alice I'm safe.'

'All in due time.'

'I've a planning meeting in Millot on Monday. Important.'

Another half hour and they'd be there. A private sanatorium, a place for alcoholics to kick the booze, the suicidal to be kept away from knives and pills, and the dying to be told they might live a little longer if only they kept on paying. Dupont knew the director and had done him some favours in the past. Time to call in old debts.

'I said . . .'

'I heard. You'll be staying out of sight until I say so. It may be a couple of days. Or longer. You can forget about your council meeting. The National Assembly. Whose backs you can scratch, and hope you climb another small rung of your very small ladder.'

Gaillard grunted, angry. 'You don't understand. I am a man of influence . . .'

Dupont took one hand off the wheel and slapped him hard around the face. The car lurched, hit the verge, pitched back into the centre. A farm truck coming in the opposite direction sounded its horn and a furious fist waved out of the window.

'You're a fucking idiot, Louis. A slack-mouthed, no good, shit-for-brains idiot. The last thing I want right now is you popping up your stupid head and saying something that gets us all in trouble.'

Gaillard whimpered, 'I can be discreet.'

A laugh, and Dupont said, 'Where you're going that's guaranteed.'

'What?'

'It's a medical facility. For people who need to be kept out of circulation for a while. They can look you over for broken bones. And maybe stitch that face of yours . . .'

'Stitches? I mean . . .'

Dupont's icy stare shut him up.

'Tell me, Councillor. Which would you prefer? A comfy sanatorium stay for free? Or jail?'

Silence then. Dupont put his foot down. With luck there'd just be time to get back to Clermiers for the meeting he'd demanded of the *Amis*.

62

The coffee was bad, the biscuits too. But Gilles Mailloux was talkative, and his home – three bedrooms in a cottage that preceded the estate – tidy, clean, different. There were posters on the walls Baptiste recognised, mostly grotesque and decadent images from the late nineteenth century. Aubrey Beardsley's *Salomé*, a woman bending gleefully over a severed head seemed to have centre place.

Fatoussi didn't look impressed and asked to use the toilet. He winked at Baptiste as he followed Mailloux's directions. A trick he'd maybe just learned.

'Your friend doesn't seem to appreciate my taste,' Mailloux said as a door closed down the corridor.

'It's different,' Baptiste admitted. 'Not what I expected round here.'

He was squinting at another Beardsley, another severed head, that of Medusa about to be kissed. Alongside a few smaller works, erotic drawings with giant cocks and farting women, horned demons and hints of rape.

'I'll take that down before Mum gets back. Not sure she'd appreciate them. Couple of months to wait for that. The cruise ships work her hard. Did Charles Augustin tell you? About his wife?'

'Gone to stay with her sister.'

'She's left him. Won't be coming back.'

'How do you know?' Baptiste asked. Fatoussi returned, a sour expression on his face.

'A little bird. You'd be amazed the gossip you overhear when you're behind the counter. I think I get to listen to as many secrets as the priest sometimes.'

'Any about Noémie Augustin you haven't told us?' There was more than a shade of animosity in Fatoussi's voice when he said that.

'I heard noises Sunday night. As I said.'

'But she wasn't the kind of girl to run away?' Fatoussi asked in the same hard tone.

'I'm not sure I could make that judgement. I've tried to help—'

'What is this shit?' Fatoussi was going red in the face, gesturing at the posters, voice loud, a sudden anger in him Baptiste had come to recognise. 'Young girls. Men with giant cocks. Jesus. What—'

'It's art.'

'Art?'

'An eccentric Englishman called Beardsley,' Mailloux went on. 'A sad genius, died young, tragically, wanting all this . . .' He pointed at the more lurid drawings. '. . . destroyed after he was gone. Thankfully, his friends ignored him.'

'It's disgusting.'

'I believe some art is meant to be, not that I'm an expert.'

Fatoussi tapped Baptiste on the shoulder. 'You should see this.'

He headed for the back.

'I thought you needed the toilet.' Mailloux seemed unbothered.

No answer. Fatoussi tried the door at the end of the short corridor. It was locked.

'What's in here?'

'My mum's things. She likes to keep them private.'

'Bullshit.' Fatoussi opened the door on the right. 'This is your mother's room.'

A double bed, some dresses on an open hanger.

'Gilles?' Baptiste said.

'I said they were her things. Not where she slept. Why are you doing this?'

'Because . . .' Fatoussi pushed open the door on the left and walked in.

A male bedroom, obviously. On the wall a poster of a black woman scantily dressed. It took Baptiste a moment to realise.

This was Josephine Baker, dancing when she was young.

'Where did you get that thing?' he asked.

'Noémie. She said it was a famous American dancer. I don't know about dancing but she's beautiful. Don't you think?'

Fatoussi muttered something inaudible then turned to the opposite wall. Two verses of poetry there, hand-written in a neat, flowing script, with a paint brush, the letters all a hand high so they stretched from ceiling down to either side of the bed.

On the left . . .

C'est l'Ennui! – l'œil chargé d'un pleur involontaire,
Il rêve d'échafauds en fumant son houka.
Tu le connais, lecteur, ce monstre délicat,
– Hypocrite lecteur, – mon semblable, – mon frère!

'It's boredom!' Mailloux read out, amused. 'Eye burdened with an involuntary tear. He dreams of gallows while smoking his hookah. You know him, reader, this delicate monster. Hypo-critical reader, my fellow, my brother!'

On the right . . .

Si le viol, le poison, le poignard, l'incendie,
N'ont pas encor brodé de leurs plaisants dessins
Le canevas banal de nos piteux destins,
C'est que notre âme, hélas! n'est pas assez hardie.

Baptiste took that one.

'If rape, poison, dagger, fire, have not yet embroidered with their pleasant drawings, the banal canvas of our pitiful desti-nies, it is only that our soul, alas! is not bold enough.'

'What in god's name . . .?' Fatoussi demanded.

'Poetry,' Baptiste said. 'Famous. French. Baudelaire.'

'Rape, poison, dagger, fire, gallows, a hookah and a delicate fucking monster . . .'

191

Mailloux seemed amused. 'I take it Marseille isn't big on verse. Baudelaire and Aubrey Beardsley. They kind of go together like . . . like coffee and biscuits.'

'Fuck this,' Fatoussi snapped. 'I hate all this weird shit.' He went back into the corridor. 'I want that door open.'

'Étienne . . .' Baptiste took his arm.

'I want it open. If there's nothing there, what's the problem?'

Mailloux shook his head. 'The problem is you're not asking nicely. I think it's time to leave. I think it's time for me to go to work.'

'Étienne . . .'

'Can't you see this guy's taking you for a ride? All the smiles and fake friendliness. Don't fool me.'

'We need to go.'

'Fuck this.'

Baptiste didn't say it again. He stood between them until Fatoussi cursed once more then turned. A litany of profanities followed all the way back to the Simca. Not a word exchanged between the two of them until Baptiste was back behind the wheel.

'Are you all right?' he asked.

'Those pictures. Those girls . . .'

'They're just posters. You see that kind of thing on the walls of student bedrooms all the time.'

'Well, there's the university guy talking. I'm just the stupid *pied-noir* too dumb to appreciate them.'

'I didn't say that. Gilles Mailloux is the only one who's given us the time of day in this damned place.'

'He's also got a poster of a half-naked black woman. The same one Noémie worshipped. And all that weird stuff.'

'You're seeing things that aren't there.'

'You think?'

'I do. Are we going to find Louis Gaillard or not?'

No answer for a moment. Then, a little calmer, Fatoussi turned to him. 'Your mother told me she was a Communist.

192

Your father too. You as well, Julien? Is that why you want to put all this on the town up there? Not the scruffy, downtrodden paupers of Boulliers? Is someone like Gilles Mailloux, poor but clever, a kind of hero for you?'

Baptiste didn't understand where all this came from. Since Mimi left, Étienne Fatoussi had seemed quite adrift. 'I'm as familiar with politics as you are with poetry. And no, I think Mailloux is an intelligent, solitary guy with not a clue how he escapes this hellhole. Not a hero. Or with any ambition to be one.'

Fatoussi waved at the windscreen. 'Poetry and painting. Bullshit. On with it then, boss. I follow in your footsteps. But I'm telling you. There are more answers here than in Hauteville.'

They headed down the Avenue Laval towards the bridge over the torpid, muddy waters of the Chaume.

Just then, Baptiste thought, he'd settle for any answers at all.

63

Roland Noyer was still on duty at the petrol station when Augustin drew up and came into the office.

'Sorry to hear about your girl, Charles. Any news?'

Augustin just glared at him and nodded at the car. A shrug, then Noyer went and filled it up. 'On the account?'

'You have the books?'

Noyer blinked then stuttered, 'N-no.'

'Why not?'

'You're not due the books yet.'

Augustin came close, threatening. 'I asked if you had them.'

'No need to be like that. Laurent took them. They're his, aren't they?'

'When?'

'I don't know. I asked Mailloux. He said they were here when he shut up Sunday. Gone when I opened Monday morning. I guess he came in overnight. Who else has the keys? He's the boss. He can do what the hell he likes.' A quick laugh. 'Where he likes. Owns it all, doesn't he?'

If that was the garage man's attempt to lighten the tone it didn't work. Augustin swore, spat on the asphalt forecourt then climbed back in the car.

'Charles! I need you to sign a receipt. You can't just drive off.'

Augustin started the engine.

Noyer went and stood in front of the bonnet. 'Laurent will hear of this!'

Head stuck out of the window, Augustin yelled back, 'The bastard may own you. Not me.'

Then threw the thing in reverse and screeched out into the road.

64

There were three men in the *Amis* clubhouse, one Baptiste didn't recognise. Middle-aged, tanned, aristocratic in pink trousers and a Burberry check shirt, smug. Bruno Laurent looked the part of the local magnate. The shiny scarlet Jaguar E-type in the car park outside was surely his too.

Fabrice Blanc appeared embarrassed. Chauvin, the priest, puzzled as usual.

'We're having a meeting,' the mayor said. 'We don't want to be disturbed.'

'About anything in particular?' Fatoussi asked.

Baptiste glanced at him. They'd agreed he'd do the talking. Fatoussi didn't seem minded to stick to anything at that moment. The incident in Mailloux's home and the brief, angry conflict that followed still burned.

'The *Amis* is a charitable organisation,' the priest said in a calm and amicable tone. 'The executive committee get together at regular intervals to—'

'To decide where to spend my money,' Laurent cut in with a quick grin. 'How can we help?'

'Louis Gaillard's a member of your committee?'

'He is indeed,' Laurent agreed.

'Where is he?'

'A good question, officer. One I wish I could answer. But . . .' A frown and nothing.

'I need to talk to him,' Baptiste said, then took the envelope out from beneath his arm and began to spread the photos across the table.

The room went quiet apart from Christian Chauvin's pained gasp as the priest averted his eyes. The others looked then turned aside too.

'I believe,' said Laurent, 'I speak for all here when I say we've seen enough. Kindly tell us where you got these things then put them away.'

Baptiste left the pictures where they were and took them through a few details. The locked drawer in Gaillard's home office. The obvious fact that the man was having sex with several different women, the young Lili Hubert among them. Presumably, he said, for money.

'And what,' asked the mayor, 'has this to do with us?'

'I don't know, sir. You tell me.'

'Tell you what?'

'If you knew Gaillard had such habits. If you were aware he had a relationship with the Hubert girl who killed herself, perhaps as a result. Where and when this might have happened. If Gaillard had connections with Noémie Augustin, missing, presumed dead in all probability, much as I regret to admit it.'

Chauvin raised a finger. 'The Augustin girl worked as a waitress here from time to time. Louis would have met her then. As we all did. I know no—'

'She waited on tables once a week,' Blanc snapped. 'I never saw him paying the girl any attention whatsoever. I doubt . . .' He hesitated for a moment then said it anyway. 'I doubt Louis would be interested in her. He has strongly held views on immigrants.'

Fatoussi snapped, 'She's not an immigrant. She was born here.'

'You know what I mean. As to where he is, ask Alice . . .'

'I did,' Baptiste said. 'She's no idea. She's worried.'

They all looked at one another. Laurent scooped up the photos and pushed them back across the table. 'You take these. We don't want that kind of thing here. The *Amis* is an organisation about charity, about helping others. If this is what Louis Gaillard does in his spare time, I believe I can safely say we want no more to do with him.'

'And,' added Fabrice Blanc, 'he can forget about a place in the National Assembly. I won't support him for the regional elections. Not now. It's a disgrace. The fellow must resign, from the *Amis*, from the council as well. In return we should all agree to keep this private. No need for scandal. Any objections?'

They nodded.

Fatoussi looked ready to explode. 'This isn't about your pervert chum, gentlemen. We've a young girl missing. One dead already.'

No answer. There was the sound of a car crossing gravel in the drive outside. Laurent got up and looked. 'Ah, the very man. Excellent timing.'

Baptiste held a finger to his lips and glanced at Fatoussi: *shush*.

Dupont breezed in, apologised for being late, looked the two men up and down. 'I didn't know you'd been invited.'

His eyes fell on the photos on the table. Briskly, unmoved, Dupont went through a few then pushed them to one side.

'I imagine that explains it.'

Baptiste struggled to work out what that meant. 'Explains what?'

'I've just come from the sanatorium in Cambrai. Gaillard's in there, raving, quite mad. Seems he took himself off to

Amsterdam for entertainment, ingested some drugs along with god knows what else. I always thought the chap a little unbalanced, to be honest. But now . . .'

'We need to talk to him,' Baptiste said. 'About Noémie Augustin.'

Dupont screwed up his eyes. 'What? How do they connect?'

'We don't know. But he was paying Lili Hubert for sex. She worked here. Noémie too . . .'

'Lots of young women work here. Are you saying Gaillard was screwing them all?' He laughed and looked at the others. 'I believe if that was the case we would have heard by now.'

Fatoussi was sighing and shaking his head. But at least he kept quiet.

'We have to interview him.'

'It's not illegal to have sex.'

'We need to ask him some questions.'

Dupont frowned. 'You can't. The doctors wouldn't let me in there for more than a few minutes. They say he's very sick.' A finger pointed to his face. 'Up here. Psychotic or something. Louis Gaillard won't be out of there for some time. Even if you could talk to him, he's just babbling nonsense. Drugs. They let anything go, the Dutch.'

'Come, Julien,' Fatoussi said and nudged Baptiste's elbow. 'We're wasting our time. These . . . gentlemen have work to do. Charitable business.'

'True,' Dupont agreed. 'Also, it's the end of your shift and I'm not paying overtime. Any progress with the Augustin kid?'

'Not yet . . .'

'The girl's run away, obviously,' said Laurent. 'It's desperately sad but that place, Boulliers, it destroys some of them. Which is why we in the *Amis* try to offer a little in the way of hope.'

Baptiste went to scoop up the photos. Dupont stopped him.

'I'll take those. We don't want that kind of material going walkabout, do we? Lock and key. My lock. My key.'

*

Outside, the heat had begun to fade. A mixed doubles match was in progress on the furthest court.

'We're screwed,' said Fatoussi. 'They're all laughing at us. That bunch. Éric Hubert. Your mate Mailloux. Everyone.' He grabbed Baptiste's arm. '*Merdeville*. They got that right. There's got to be someone we can call. Tell them this place is rotten, top to toe.'

All Baptiste could think about just then was that troubling conversation with his mother the night before. What she'd said about why women kept quiet about attacks, rape sometimes, even with those closest to them.

'For that to work, someone would need to care.'

'Just you and me then?'

'Seems so.' Baptiste took out the keys to the Simca. 'What do you want for supper?'

Fatoussi looked worn out, staring at the clubhouse, hands in pockets, a tense and twitchy stance. Dupont was grinning at them from the long windows that gave out onto the courts. 'Whatever you like.'

65

The red Jaguar sports car was nowhere to be seen at the back of the family mansion eight kilometres north of Clermiers. Augustin knew where to wait. The guest bungalow where Véronique now lived, lonely she said. In need of company. Something her husband, with his own life to lead, encouraged.

One more secret he'd lacked the courage to share with Martine.

One more demand he hadn't dared refuse.

Burning with anger, at Laurent, at Clermiers, but most of all towards himself, Charles Augustin waited as a sultry summer evening sank into twilight, the chatter of songbirds turning to the hoot of owls hunting the nearby chestnut coppice.

Clermiers, beyond Boulliers and Hauteville, out in the fields and woods around the Laurent estate on the borders of Millot, could pass as beautiful.

There was a light on in the cottage. Véronique, watching TV, drinking, wondering where next to spend her husband's loot. Who to take to bed. Whether Bruno Laurent would want to know, to watch.

'I am the biggest fool in the world,' Augustin whispered to himself as he sat in the car. Laurent's. Like the little house in Boulliers. The prize that had lured Martine and Noémie from the austere but settled poverty of Calais to the promise of a better life, advancement, the hope of becoming middle class one day.

A sound. The roar of a V12 engine. Laurent gunning his E-type down the private drive towards the mansion.

Augustin watched him get out and walk through the front door. No servants. Only a cleaner and maid who worked days. He'd be alone and there was no sign Véronique, in her little bungalow, was moved to join him.

The gun was in the spare tyre compartment in the boot. Along with spare shells, Eric Hubert had offered him an ancient army holster, khaki canvas, a few pieces of peeling leather around the strap.

That went under his jacket with the weapon. Charles Augustin set off for the house.

66

Half a chicken and an old baguette was the best Baptiste could find in the grocer's before it closed. They drove back to the police house in silence. Fatoussi tore off a leg and a chunk of bread then poured himself a coffee cup of red wine and went upstairs. Loud music from the radio again. Rock didn't much interest Baptiste, but he recognised this one. He'd seen the band on French TV and they were hard to forget. Thin Lizzy, 'Jailbreak'. Wailing sirens and violent lyrics. The way crime and the breakdown of law were so often portrayed. As if evil was confined to the dark, not the sunny, apparently peaceful world where people thought themselves ordinary and innocent, undeserving of scrutiny and attention.

Baptiste barely ate a thing, but he did manage two cigarettes and a couple of tumblers of wine. Still, he felt restless. Étienne Fatoussi was starting to worry him. First, there'd been the incident at Hubert's and the gun. Now he seemed to be withdrawing inside himself, upset by what they'd seen in Gilles Mailloux's home. Artwork and poetry. Nothing much to remark on if it had been Paris. But in Clermiers . . .

He went into the hall and called his mother.

'You want to know how I am,' she said before he could get out more than three words. 'What a good son you are.'

'Maman . . .'

'A lot better, thank you. The foot doesn't hurt so much. I managed to walk upstairs without howling.'

'Good—'

'Mimi's a delight. Such a lovely young woman. I hope Étienne appreciates her.'

That, he thought, was said within earshot. Since he suspected his mother, always judgemental, had already decided that Mimi, while pleasant, lacked the character and intelligence of her predecessor in Fatoussi's bed, Bernadette.

'Are you any closer to finding this girl, Julien? Oh. I apologise. I'm not supposed to ask, am I?'

'Not much. Do you know any reporters who might be interested?'

'In a teenage black girl who's probably run away from home in a little town most people have never heard of?'

'I thought we'd agreed she hadn't run away.'

'Can you prove it? Can you prove *anything*?'

The radio had gone straight into another song from the

same band. 'The Boys Are Back in Town'. Baptiste felt as if the thing was mocking him.

He asked if he could have a word with Mimi. His mother was so thrown by that she didn't say another thing, just passed the phone over.

'Julien? How is he? Is everything all right?'

'Not really. He seems upset. This missing girl. There are things we've seen . . . they disturb him, I think. His sister. He told me a little about what happened. Is she OK?'

Silence.

'Mimi. Are you still there?'

Her voice was soft and low and pained. 'What did he say?'

'Just that she'd been attacked. They couldn't find the bastard who did it. She's still affected . . .'

Another long wait. Then she said, 'Eléa hanged herself last Christmas. Étienne found her in the garage. They know who did it. Some gang lord's kid from Felix Pyat. They just couldn't get him in court.'

Baptiste nearly dropped the phone.

'I thought he was starting to get over it. But then it turned out he has . . . he had . . . a habit. That's why they wanted him shipped out of Marseille for a while.'

It was his turn to stay silent.

'I assumed it was the same with you. That you had some problem. Did something bad.'

'This habit . . .'

'I was telling myself he'd kicked it. He seemed clean enough when I turned up.'

Upstairs the music was getting louder.

'Leave it with me,' said Baptiste.

The door was locked. Baptiste hammered hard until Fatoussi came to the other side and said something about being washed out and needing to sleep.

'Open up. I want to talk.'

'Are you deaf?'

'I can kick this thing down if you like. Give Dupont another reason to hate us. Damaging police property.'

'What's so important?'

He waited for effect then said, 'Eléa.'

A curse. He heard Fatoussi walk away from the door, do something, then return and let him in.

First time in the upstairs flat. The place looked neat and cleaner than his own.

'You talked to Mimi?'

'See. You can work things out if you try.'

'And she stitched me up.'

'If telling the truth amounts to that . . .'

The food was on the table untouched, the coffee mug empty. A cloth was placed over something on the draining board by the sink. Probably just before Fatoussi opened the door.

He strode over and took it off. A syringe, a spoon with burn marks, a plastic bag half full of white powder, a lighter.

'Well done, Detective,' Fatoussi muttered. 'Want to charge me?'

Baptiste was getting mad. He turned, grabbed him by the shirt, slammed him up against the wall. Fatoussi's eyes were wide with shock.

'Is this what your dead sister would want? Her brother out of his head on dope, drowning in some pointless remorse when there's a girl out there, maybe in the same kind of trouble, maybe dead, who knows . . .?'

'Sympathy's not your thing, is it, Julien?'

'It's not sympathy you're after. It's pity. That's different.'

A nod at the door. 'Just leave, will you?'

He let go, shrugged. Went back to the draining board and stared at the things there. Fatoussi must have been getting ready for a fix. Something told him this was the first time in Clermiers. The presence of a woman had kept him together. The absence of one and the day's events changed all that.

'I suppose you're going to confiscate that now. Like a school-teacher punishing a naughty pupil.'

Baptiste threw the cloth back in place. 'Not at all. What's the point? If this is your way out, do it. Come the morning you can find your own way home and drown yourself in more junk when you get there.'

Fatoussi was starting to tremble, ready to break.

'Or you could help me find Noémie Augustin.'

'Boulliers. I told you. Not Hauteville. There's something there.'

'There's something everywhere, Étienne! Hubert, Gaillard, Dupont, those creeps in the *Amis*. I want to take them all apart. I think . . . I think I've been a touch too nice around here. Time to change.'

Fatoussi was shaking, weeping. Baptiste came up, took his arms, held him, felt the agony, the pain, the weariness. He pulled back, placed his hands on his damp and bristly cheeks. Kissed them quickly, once each side.

'I need you. That girl needs you. Maybe just to bury her properly, I don't know.'

'I couldn't . . .' Weeping, choking, lost. 'I couldn't even nail the bastard who ruined my sister's life.'

'This isn't a game of football. Ninety minutes, win, lose or draw.'

'Meaning . . .'

'Meaning it goes on. And on. And we don't give up. We don't stop. Not till there's no door left to kick open, no corner not to turn. You know what we do?'

The tears were rolling down his face. 'Huh?'

'*What do we do?*'

'I don't understand—'

'We find things that are broken. We try to mend them. That's it. The beginning and the end. All this job is. Hoping to fix bruises and lacerations others don't want to look at, don't dare think about.' A pause, and he hoped this was going in. 'Then, if it works, we can maybe heal those same wounds inside ourselves.' He glanced at the tea towel and the draining board. 'But it's your choice. Not mine.'

Baptiste was at the door when Fatoussi came over and stopped him.

'I know why they banished me to this dump. What the hell did you do to deserve it?'

That had been bothering him too.

'I guess I'm just an awkward bastard no one wants around.'

'Ah.'

'Can you imagine?'

No hesitation in the reply. 'Yeah. I can.'

67

Bruno Laurent answered the door in shirt and underpants, a glass of brandy in his hand. He didn't look pleased.

'What the hell is this?'

Augustin walked past him and looked around the hall. In all the months he'd been working for the man he'd never been invited to set foot inside Laurent's home. It felt like a palace, fine carpets, fine wallpaper, fine furniture. Paintings, a chandelier hanging near the entrance, a winding staircase with a plush red carpet rising up to the floor above.

'I said—'

'Where is she?' Augustin demanded, with as much control as he could muster. 'Where's my daughter?'

He sniffed and took a sip of his cognac. 'Why are you asking me? I've no idea.'

'Don't believe you. Where—?'

'Get out.' Laurent nodded at the door. 'Get out now before I lose my temper.'

'Tell me—'

A half smile then and that only made Augustin madder. 'If

you think I know something, Charles, go to the police.'

'Ha! Dupont? You think I'm stupid enough to waste my time on him?'

'There are two new men, aren't there?'

'Running round and round, getting nowhere.'

Laurent shrugged. 'What am I supposed to do about it?'

'Tell me where she is . . .'

'Jesus.' He rolled his eyes, spilled the drink. 'I don't know. That's the truth.'

'You told me all she had to do was dance!'

'Seems to me,' Laurent said with a quick wink, 'you're having a bad case of parental guilt. Looking to shift the blame on others. A touch of naivety too. Seems to me—'

'Shut up! *Shut the fuck up!* You lured us here. You . . .' The memory was so bad it stung. 'You wanted Noémie in the interview. I should have—'

'Standard practice. We're a family firm. Seems I chose wrong this time . . .'

'Fuck you!'

Laurent laughed. 'Oh, come on. You were begging for it. You came willingly. Did everything I asked.' Another wink, a grin. 'Gave you a house, a car, a good job. How many people round here would do that for the likes of you?'

The weapon came out. Augustin held it in his trembling fingers. Laurent glanced at the gun and burst out laughing. 'Good god. Now you really are being ridiculous.'

The words just happened, bellowed, angry. Accusations, fears, suspicions. Augustin had barely finished when they both heard a sound at the door. Véronique Laurent was there, wrapping a skimpy nightgown round her, puzzled, mad too.

'This is quite the argument. You woke me.'

Laurent nodded at Augustin. 'Well, you know, if you two feel like it . . .'

She pouted at him. 'Want to watch, Bruno? Let's face it. That's all you can do.'

'Fuck you, s-slut.' There was a slur to his speech and it occurred to Augustin the man was half-drunk already. 'Get this moron out of here.'

Véronique stormed over, took the tumbler from his hands, threw the drink in his face.

'See?' Laurent yelled, glaring at Augustin. 'See what you've done?'

'I want my daughter back.'

'Then go look for her. Get the fuck out of my home while you can.'

The gun rose. Véronique Laurent stared at it, wide-eyed, scared now.

'Tell me . . .'

'Leave.'

'Tell me.'

'To hell with this . . .'

Laurent lunged for the weapon. Augustin struggled to hold it. He didn't know what happened next. Who pointed the barrel, which of them reached for the trigger. But the sound that came was loud and shocking as their hands wrestled over the grip. Laurent's fingers loosened, a shower of something hot spilled across Charles Augustin's chest.

'Jesus,' Véronique whispered, backing against the wall beneath a painting, an idyllic landscape, fields of wheat, windmills, a horse pulling a plough, a bucolic farmer at the rear. 'You shot him, Charles. You . . .'

He was on the floor, hands flapping by his side. A pool of blood building beneath his shirt, the red tide running down to his waist, to his naked legs. Then he was still, mouth open, eyes too, staring up at the ceiling, no expression there at all.

'You killed him,' she yelled. 'Christ, Charles. *You killed him.*'

He wiped his face with the back of his hand, looked at it, red with blood, just like the gun, slippery in his fingers. Eric Hubert's gun. Or whoever it belonged to before Hubert stole it. Such a simple thing, capable of so much. He wondered what

Martine would think now. What Noémie might if she was still alive. This was the last thing he could think of to try to find her. And, like everything else, it ended in failure, turned to agony and dust.

'Don't point that thing at me,' Véronique whispered, eyes wide, scared now. 'Charles . . . please . . .'

The place reeked of gore and booze and a noxious, dusty stink he could only put down to the discharge of a weapon.

Augustin stared at the terrified woman backed up against the wall opposite, the bloody corpse between them, and felt he'd stumbled into a dream.

'Charles . . .!'

A second explosion tore through the airless night.

Part Five:

'Noémie Augustin is Dead'

68

2:15 p.m. Douai Prison, 15 November 1976

Gilles Mailloux wriggled on his prison bed. 'Did you never, at any stage, question the character of Bruno Laurent?'

'There wasn't the time. Or the opportunity.'

'Because he was the local lord? An aristocrat? The monarch of our tiny corner of the glorious republic?'

In that last phase of the case, events moved so quickly. Baptiste hadn't felt in control at all. There was still so much he didn't understand. Not that Mailloux had done a thing to dispel the mist.

'I see this is not a subject you wish to discuss, Julien.'

'I've nothing useful to say. You, on the other hand . . .'

'Don't be repetitive. It's tedious. What time is it?'

Baptiste checked his watch. The light was going. Sometime soon they'd hear the chime of church bells. 'Almost three.'

'Only murderers kill people in the dark, surely?'

'I've really no idea how these matters work. It had never occurred to me the case might end this way.'

'Ah.' Mailloux was amused by that. 'You thought your conscience would be eased by putting me in jail for life. In solitary, of course, since they'd never dare allow the Monster of *Merdeville*, a perverted killer of a young girl, to mix with

208

ordinary criminals, for fear they'd slit his throat the moment they could.'

'The path you took was of your own choosing, Gilles. Your attitude. Your lack of remorse . . .'

'I feel no remorse. Why should I feign it?'

Again, he had to say it. 'The fact you won't tell us where she is.'

Mailloux leaned back on the bed, placed his skinny arms behind his neck and yawned.

'I would rather die in daylight,' he said quite casually. 'If it's night they'd have to have floodlights or something. Which makes it sound like sport. Perhaps, to some of them, it is.'

Baptiste felt like screaming. 'It's not a game. Anything but.'

That laugh again. 'Are you sure?'

'Very. It's not too late—'

'But it is, Julien. It was too late that night you arrested me. The path was fixed. The end settled. I repeat, the blade must always . . .'

There were footsteps outside, loud, several men, voices, not that their words were clear.

Gilles Mailloux fell silent. For the second time, Baptiste thought he detected a sudden flash of fear on his narrow, bloodless face.

69

Clermiers, Thursday, 22 July

Again, Baptiste slept badly. The heat. The mosquitoes. The night birds calling. A new worry too. Étienne Fatoussi, a bright, enthusiastic, promising young cop, felled by a personal tragedy he was unable to shake off. A damaged man with a needle and a gun. Perhaps he should have taken away both the previous night. Though something told him that would only have made matters worse. Fatoussi would not relish being treated like a disobedient child. The man was on the edge. It would be so easy to push him over with a simple mistaken decision made with the best of intentions.

He went into the kitchen, got coffee, took out yesterday's bread, put it in the toaster, found butter and the half-eaten jar of fancy strawberry jam Fatoussi had brought with him from Marseille. Then called up the stairs, wondering.

A shout back, incomprehensible, and Fatoussi came down, two steps at a time, full uniform on, buttons shiny, well-pressed, immaculate, shoes too.

Baptiste, scruffy in plain clothes as usual, looked at him and burst out laughing. 'Are you trying to show me up?'

'I like uniforms. They say who you are. I know you enjoy being anonymous. Invisible. I don't. I never will.'

'Fair enough.'

'Dupont can live with it.'

'He can.'

Fatoussi had a paper bag with him. He dumped it in the bin. Baptiste didn't ask, just offered him some bad coffee and half-burnt toast.

They sat at the table.

'Is there any chance we get out of jail early, Julien? This could be the longest two months of my life. And you?'

That was left up in the air. Baptiste had simply been told he had to spend some time out in the sticks in Clermiers as part of his career development. Paris would call him back when they felt like it.

'They didn't say.'

'If I don't arrive home clean, I'm out. I guess . . .' He frowned. 'I guess Mimi told you. I spent a little too much time with the wrong people.'

Baptiste brushed some toast crumbs off the sleeve of Fatoussi's police jacket. 'You'll be fine. We'll find out what happened to Noémie Augustin. Once that's done, I'll get Dupont to release us early. I doubt he's going to object.'

Fatoussi's eyes were on him. 'He could ask for that now. But he won't. Why, do you think?'

'Doesn't want to draw attention, does he?'

'Too many nasties lurking under too many rocks. Do you think we can get to speak to Councillor Gaillard in this sanatorium of his?

'Doubt it.'

A nod, then, 'Any ideas at all?'

He had. 'We look at places.'

'Like Mailloux's house?'

He should have seen that coming. 'If you want. We'll go back. We'll ask him to open up that last room. If you really feel—'

'I do. There's something wrong about that guy.'

'But first . . .' He took a bite of toast. 'Nice jam.'

'It's from the market. It should be. First . . .?'

Lili Hubert's tiny notebook continued to bug him. Especially that cryptic symbol, the little crucifix, next to it the number four.

'Gaillard lives opposite the château,' he said.

'True. And it's a dump of a place no one ever visits.'

'Mailloux and the English woman said they heard music coming from there.'

'The boathouse, Julien. Where Dupont kicked that condom into the water.'

'Lili Hubert was nowhere near the boathouse. She was in the woods. I just think we should take a look.'

'Going to let Dupont know where we're going?'

Baptiste fetched the radio. Bonnay answered straight away for once, sounding anxious and stressed, not his normal idle self.

'Everything OK?' Baptiste asked.

'Why wouldn't it be?'

'Is the captain there?'

'Busy.'

None of the usual . . . *What are you doing? Where are you going?*

'Fatoussi and I are going to check out a couple of locations. Boulliers. The Hubert place. I want to see Charles Augustin again.'

Nothing.

'We're going to check out the old château.'

'Pointless. There's nothing there.'

'Maybe. But we should have taken a closer look after Lili Hubert was found.'

'Millot went over the place with dogs. You needn't waste your time.'

'Ah. Thanks for the tip. We don't expect to be in the station unless we're needed.'

A moment, then Bonnay said, 'Fine.' And that was it.

Fatoussi finished his coffee. 'That was remarkably easy. Sounds like we're off their radar screen.'

Yet there was something odd in Bonnay's manner.

Ten minutes later they were headed for the car. On the doorstep the phone rang. Leave it, Baptiste said. Fatoussi didn't move.

'Julien. It's someone trying to call us. How often does that happen? Why in god's name wouldn't you want to answer it?'

He rushed over and got the phone before they rang off. Listened, cupped his hand over the mouthpiece, said, 'It's for you. Your mother. Sounds . . . bad.'

70

Fabrice Blanc was back in Dupont's office along with Christian Chauvin who was clucking like an old hen that had lost its chicks.

'What on earth is happening?' the priest whined. 'First, we

have this dead girl in the woods. Now Laurent. The Augustin fellow with him.' He glanced at the door. 'Where are your men, Captain? Who is dealing with this?'

Dupont told them. Laurent's estate straddled the border of Clermiers and Millot. That gave him a way out. Millot was bigger, had more manpower. Facilities he would have to beg and borrow. After he got the call at home from Véronique Laurent the previous night, he was able to dash out there, see the mess for himself, do his best to deal with the hysterical woman, then ask Millot to take the case. They leapt at the invitation. Easy work and they liked dealing with the newspapers. Dupont was happy to leave them to it.

'We don't have to be involved at all?' Blanc asked.

'You might get a call with some condolences. And asked to say a little something at the funeral. That'll be in Millot too. No need to trouble anyone here.'

'Poor Bruno . . .' the mayor lamented. 'The irony of it. The man who paid for so much in Boulliers, shot dead by one of those he sought to help. He'd no need to employ Augustin, you know? Let's face it . . . who else would give that sort a job around here? I did warn him.'

The priest looked lost. 'Warned him about what?'

'About dealing with foreign strangers, of course.' It seemed a given to Blanc.

'I don't understand. You're sure this was nothing to do with Augustin's missing daughter?'

'Not at all,' Dupont insisted. 'It was the old story. A disgruntled employee with a gun. Augustin picked up the takings from Laurent's businesses. It seems he'd adopted the habit of liberating a little for himself. His master found out and . . .' A brief shrug. 'That's all there is to it. I've told Millot. They'll mark it down as a murder suicide. Madame Laurent is understandably distraught, as one might expect. Even though I gather the couple were no longer close. I've given orders no one will disturb her from here. It's Millot's case.'

Chauvin stumbled to his feet. 'It's all too upsetting. I must go home. This is the end of the *Amis*, I imagine.'

'That would be an insult to Bruno's memory,' Blanc insisted. 'We must go on. The work is too important.'

Dupont narrowed his eyes. 'I agree. Far too important.'

'We'll institute some kind of memorial to him,' said Blanc. 'A prize, perhaps. A . . . a scholarship to a college somewhere.'

'You'll get the wife to pay, I hope,' Dupont added. 'Don't think that'll go down well if you try to stick it to the taxpayers here. I'm not chipping in a cent.'

'All in due course. And your unwanted visitors? What are they up to?'

'Jesus Christ. I've been up half the night dealing with two dead bodies. You think I've time to chaperone that pair as well?'

Blanc started to leave too. 'I think it would be wise.'

'All too shocking,' Chauvin mumbled. 'I'll say a prayer for poor Bruno and his widow.'

'I'm sure that'll help,' Dupont said and opened the door.

Bonnay was on his own as usual, looking stuck to his chair with sweat. Even with most of the windows open the station felt like an oven.

The two policemen watched the mayor and the priest leave.

'They look shell-shocked,' Bonnay noted.

'What do you expect?'

'I don't know any more.'

'Bruno Laurent and the man who killed him are not our problem. They're outside our jurisdiction. If anyone asks, tell them to call Millot.'

'OK.'

'And Baptiste?'

'He called in. Said he was going to nose around.'

'You didn't mention Laurent?'

Bonnay's eyes flashed. 'Of course not. You said.'

'Good.'

'Nose round where?'

'Boulliers. The Hubert place.' He laughed. 'Lot of luck they'll have there.'

He went quiet.

'And?' Dupont asked.

'They mentioned they wanted to take a look inside the château.'

'Shit . . .'

'I told them . . . I told them there was no point. Millot have been all over it with their dogs. Nothing to find. Boulliers. Go to Boulliers.'

'You think they listened?'

'Yes. I do.'

'First time for everything,' Dupont muttered.

71

Fatoussi went outside as if he knew Baptiste's conversation with his mother was going to be awkward.

'How are you doing, *Maman*?'

He could hear the intake of breath down the phone. 'Stop going on about that. I told you already. It's getting better. What I—'

'How's Mimi?'

A sigh. An angry one. 'Mimi left for Marseille this morning. You upset her.'

'*I* upset her?'

'I just said that.'

'How?'

'Poking your nose in where you're not wanted. You're good at getting things out of people they'd rather not say.'

He glanced at Fatoussi in his uniform outside the door. The syringe, the spoon and the pack of foil were in the kitchen bin. If he'd done nothing . . .

215

Before he could begin to explain she said, 'Have you heard the news? God. That place. What it must be like beneath the surface.'

'What news?'

A pause. 'Are you serious?'

'I usually am.'

'It was on the radio this morning. The father of that poor missing girl. He went and shot his boss last night. Then turned the gun on himself.'

Baptiste felt something move inside him, wondered for a moment whether he was going to lose his balance.

'I can't believe they haven't told you.'

'You're sure?'

She yelped, a quick curse. 'Why do people always ask that question? You think I'd make something like this up? It was on the radio. They said the father had fallen out with the man who employed him. An argument about money or something.'

'Money? They said it was to do with money?'

'Yes! Why are you asking me this?'

'What else?'

'Wait. I scribbled down a note. If I can read my own writing . . .' A moment. 'They said the case is being investigated by the police in Millot. They're sure no one else is involved. The incident was witnessed by the wife of the man he shot. A tragic murder followed by a suicide. Oh, and the killer was a black immigrant. That'll stir a few comments in some quarters.'

Fatoussi was watching now, intrigued.

'They never mentioned a missing daughter?'

'Not that I heard. I thought that seemed odd. They interviewed a police captain from Millot. Leclerc. He seemed to think it was an open and shut case. Laurent, the boss, was quite the local figure it seemed. Big on charity. Employed lots of people. A benefactor. Is that right?'

'So they say.'

'Haven't learned much while you've been in Clermiers, have you?'

'I think I've learned quite a lot. Anything else?'

She hesitated. 'I'm worried about you, Julien. You have an obsessive nature. It does you no good.'

'We're looking for a missing girl called Noémie Augustin. When I've found her, I leave.'

'And if you don't?'

'I will.'

Baptiste walked outside and lit a cigarette. Fatoussi was starting to sweat in his uniform. That was his choice.

'Well?' he asked.

'It seems last night Charles Augustin visited Laurent, his boss, and shot him dead. Then killed himself.'

Fatoussi's jaw dropped. 'Christ . . .'

Neither of them knew what to say. Then Fatoussi lost it, started stomping round the Simca cursing wildly, only stopping to give the rusty old wreck a boot.

Back to the way he was the previous night. Baptiste gave him a moment or two then said, 'Cut that out.'

'What? *What?*'

'I said cut it out—'

'Cut what out? This is those fuckers all over. Making you do things like you're someone else. Turning you . . . Jesus . . . He didn't seem a bad guy, did he?'

Baptiste came close and gripped him by the shoulders. 'Étienne. Don't lose it. If we're going to find Noémie, I need you. Straight. Sane. Can't do this on my own.'

A hard stare and then, 'You think the two of us can?'

'I don't know. But no one else is going to try, are they?'

He lost a little of the anger. 'You got all this from your mum?'

Baptiste waved away a persistent fly. 'She listens to the news. Bonnay didn't mention a thing. Not even when I said we were going round to talk to Augustin. They've handed the whole thing over to Millot. The captain there's told the press it's an

217

open and shut case. Murder suicide. Charles had been on the take and Laurent found out.'

'Oh, for god's sake. There was something odd about the guy, but he didn't look like a thief.'

'No. He didn't.'

'Boulliers. We need to look at Boulliers.'

'Later. First, we pay a visit to the petrol station. I want to find out if Augustin really was fiddling the books.' Baptiste took out the car keys. 'After that we need to talk to the widow. While we still can.'

72

On the Pas de Calais coast, a hundred and thirty kilometres away, another widow sat at a balcony window, phone in hand, weeping as she watched the windsurfers on the beach, for what precisely she wasn't sure. Her sister brought a cup of coffee and a brioche, put an arm round her shoulders. The two weren't so close, perhaps because their lives had been very different. Martine working as a school cleaner, Annette getting a job at a car hire firm in Boulogne, then marrying Davide, a chef, the two of them living childless above Au Bord de la Mer, his upmarket hotel-restaurant in the elegant resort of Le Touquet.

Through the open balcony windows came the sound of a busy kitchen prepping for the day, knives being sharpened, hobs being fired, the ranks of Davide's staff getting ready for another hectic session feeding well-heeled visitors from Paris, London, Brussels. Annette had become used to money early on. If she pitied her poorer, plainer sister she never showed it. All the same she had been shocked when Charles Augustin came on the scene. It seemed so unlike Martine, a quiet, cautious woman with little in the way of ambition, to fall in love with an immigrant, a big and muscular man, more reticent and shy than his sometimes forbidding looks hinted.

What misgivings she had faded when she saw the genuine love between them, the way the two became even closer with the arrival of Noémie. When they were seeking an escape from their impoverished lives in Calais, Davide had offered Augustin a job in the restaurant. But that, it seemed, was too much like charity for a man who had a well-developed sense of pride. Charles Augustin wanted to make his own way, not wait on tables, chop vegetables, or wash dishes.

And now he was dead, after murdering the man who'd lured him out to Clermiers in the first place.

With the cruel sleight of hand that came with hindsight, Martine Augustin could mark the decline in their happiness and their fortunes from the moment they'd been summoned, Charles, her, and Noémie too, for an interview. An odd request, one she'd found puzzling at the time though Charles' enthusiasm – no, desperation – to win Laurent's favour, a job, more money, the prospect of a house not a cramped apartment, all these factors weighed upon her so much she'd stayed silent.

Bruno Laurent had eyed her up and down and found her wanting, she thought. He didn't seem to take much notice of Noémie either. If the man had leered at her there was no way Martine would have stayed silent. In some strange way it was Charles who seemed to engage his interest more. But this was, at heart, a job interview, and he was the one seeking employment. So perhaps, she'd convinced herself, that was only natural.

That the best thing to do was trust the man with all the money, position, importance, a pillar of society.

Trust.

She'd placed that in Charles too, and never questioned the decision. Yet there was the catch. The only way to discover if one's belief in a person was deserved was to place that confidence, then await the possible moment of disappointment. Martine Augustin wondered if she would ever trust another man again.

Windsurfers raced across the perfect golden sands, sails billowing, happy on their holidays. Fifi was slumbering in a basket at the back of the kitchen.

'An early lunch,' her sister said, breaking into Martine Augustin's dismal reveries.

'Not now.'

'Do you want me to drive you back to Clermiers?'

'I'll never set foot in that place again,' Martine said, her eyes fixed on the fast-moving figures dashing across the beach.

'OK. Millot. That's where the police seem to be dealing with things according to the news.'

'Have they tried to call?'

'Martine! They probably don't know where to find you!'

'Fine with me.'

Annette hesitated before going on. Finally, she said, 'That will be where they've taken him, I imagine. There'll be arrangements to be made. A funeral.'

'Charles is dead and gone—'

'Noémie then! The police are still looking, surely.'

Martine gazed at her sister and wondered if there was any way she could explain the gulf between them. It wasn't money. More that in quiet, affluent Le Touquet, Annette and Davide enjoyed security, a safe passage into the future. Freedom from worry and need.

'They think she ran away.'

'Noémie would never do such a thing!'

'That's what parents always say. Or so they told us.'

'Oh god . . .' Annette threw her arms around her sister. Martine felt damp tears smudge against her face. 'Tell me what to do.'

'All you're doing now. That's enough. Being kind. Being patient. Let me stay a while until I can work out what comes next. If the police call, tell them I've nothing to say. Charles and I were separated. There's nothing I can tell them about him or Laurent they don't already know.'

220

Annette let go and stared at her in shock. 'You think they'll be happy with that?'

'I'm pretty certain of it,' Martine said and kissed her back.

73

Roland Noyer was behind the counter in his greasy garage overalls, munching on a chocolate bar.

'Laurent's dead. Charles shot him then killed himself,' he said the moment Baptiste and Fatoussi walked in. 'No petrol on account today. Cash only.'

'Are you the local newspaper too?' Fatoussi asked, picking up some sweets for himself.

'People got the right to know.'

Baptiste put his elbows on the counter, watched as the garage man stepped back. Then grabbed a pack of cigarettes and threw some coins in the empty ashtray.

'I mean,' said Noyer, 'they do, don't they?'

'Has someone been dipping their fingers in the till?'

The garage man started going red. 'Not me. No.'

'Anyone?'

'No! Laurent would have known. He went through everything. Got money, and money makes money. Got no money, you get to work for it.'

'Capitalism!' Fatoussi cried. Then he patted Baptiste's arm. 'My friend's a Communist. Watch out.'

Noyer stood there, jaw flapping open, no words.

'You are, I trust, surprised by this turn of events,' said Baptiste.

'Well, yeah. Who wouldn't be?'

'Did Augustin strike you as violent?'

'Big guy. Black as coal.'

Fatoussi sighed and tore open the wrapping on the bar he'd picked. 'Did they get on? Him and Laurent? Did they argue?'

It seemed the question was ridiculous. 'No one argues with Bruno Laurent. He owns everything. Charles was OK. Not my kind but I never had problems with him. He picked up the books. He was polite. Respectful.'

'Respectful?' Baptiste repeated.

'Yeah. I mean, he wasn't local. Nobody knew him or wanted to. That wife of his never came out much, did she? As to the girl . . .'

'The girl who's missing,' Baptiste said. 'What about her?'

'I don't know. Barely saw her. They didn't mix. That's all I'm saying.'

'And now he's dead.' Fatoussi waved a chocolate-covered finger in the air. 'And his daughter's missing. Maybe dead too.'

'What? I don't know anything about that. Don't you two have work to do?'

'Funnily enough,' said Baptiste, 'this is work. Where did Bruno Laurent live? I want the address. And directions.'

Noyer scribbled down something with a pencil and a pad.

Baptiste checked it over. 'This is Clermiers, right? Not Millot?'

'The house is in Clermiers. Like a palace. We used to get invited there once a year for a staff summer party. Lots of food and drink. The garden only. Didn't let us go inside.'

'Not Millot?'

'Big estate. Maybe some of it is. How would I know?'

'And the wife . . .'

'Véronique. Hot stuff.' He winced. 'I don't think she and the boss got along too well.'

Fatoussi leaned on the counter too. 'Ladies' man, was he?'

'Got money, looks and a fast car. Unlike me. What do you think?'

Baptiste tapped the ashtray. 'I think I want my change. Not going to fly a flag half-mast? Wear a black arm band or something?'

Noyer threw some coins his way. 'He was my boss. Not my friend. Maybe Mailloux will do that when he comes in this afternoon. Got to take over from me early. I'm off to see the doctor.'

Fatoussi was interested suddenly. 'Mailloux? Why would he do something if you wouldn't?'

'Ask him.'

Back in the car Fatoussi finished the bar and threw the wrapper out of the window.

'Go pick it up. Put it in a bin,' Baptiste ordered. 'I don't like litter.'

Fatoussi grunted something then did as he was told.

'You're just pissed off your mate Mailloux came into that,' he said when he got back.

'I said already. One more line of inquiry. A dead Augustin and Laurent are more promising, don't you think?'

'It wasn't about money, was it? Whatever they rowed about.'

'Seems unlikely.'

'Dupont's going to go mad when he hears.'

'True. You're fine with that?'

'More than fine. Delighted.'

Baptiste didn't start the car. Fatoussi was puzzled by that.

'What did I do now?'

'Nothing. You just did everything right.' He nodded back at the petrol station cabin. 'We sounded like a team in there. Finally.'

Fatoussi grinned. 'You're kidding me?'

'Why?'

'You're not a team man, Julien. Just pretending. A part of you wishes I wasn't even here. That you could just go out there on your own, a lone wolf on the hunt.'

Baptiste was opening his new pack of cigarettes.

'Gitanes now?'

'They didn't have Disque Bleu.'

'You'll smoke any old shit then?'

223

Baptiste just stared.

'OK, OK,' said Fatoussi. 'Who am I to talk?'

74

The Millot town sign was by the gate to the Laurent estate, the house the Clermiers side, most of the grounds, from what Baptiste could see, in the territory of its larger neighbour. Three marked police cars, all Simcas but newer and cleaner than their own, were parked in the drive when they arrived.

The place reeked of money. A three-storey classical mansion for the main house, a cottage to the right, stables, a formal garden with fountains and designer flower beds still in good form in spite of the drought. Laurent could obviously afford to ignore the water restrictions that affected everyone else.

They were hardly out of the car before a tall man, mid-fifties, upright athletic build like that of a retired footballer who'd kept himself fit, was over, demanding to know who they were. Baptiste was glad of Fatoussi's uniform just then. The officer from Millot was called Leclerc. He didn't seem impressed by their presence.

'Did Dupont send you?'

'Not exactly,' Baptiste said.

'Then what the hell are you doing here?'

'Looking for a missing girl. Noémie Augustin. Her father, well, you know . . .'

Leclerc sighed. 'He's in our morgue along with the man he shot. Bruno Laurent. Kind of royalty for Clermiers I guess.'

'We just . . .'

'Wait,' Leclerc ordered. 'Let's get this clear. Dupont asked us to take on this case. I'm fine with that but I don't want any interference. It's straightforward. Augustin came here last night. They argued. He shot Laurent. Then himself.'

'Over some kind of boss worker argument?'

'That's what we're assuming. Laurent's wife caught the tail end. They were fighting. Laurent tried to grab the gun. Maybe the whole thing was an accident to begin with. We can leave all that to the coroner.'

'Noémie. The daughter . . .'

Leclerc waved a hand. 'She's yours. Bad enough we had to pick that dead girl out of the woods for you. Clermiers needs to deal with some of its own shit from time to time. *Compris?*'

'All that interests us is the daughter. The rest is yours. I'd like to talk to Véronique Laurent. Just to check . . .'

Leclerc was looking at him, interested. 'You're the two new-comers I heard about. The pushy pair. Not the usual country bumpkins he gets.'

Baptiste smiled and nodded. 'Julien Baptiste from Paris. Étienne Fatoussi from Marseille. A delight to meet you, the circumstances apart.'

'Nice uniform, Fatoussi.' He laughed. 'As to you . . .'

'Below the radar,' Baptiste said.

'And how do you find Dupont?'

'With difficulty.'

Leclerc didn't laugh. He jerked a thumb at the house. 'She's in there. Follow the smell of booze. We're just about done here but don't mess anything up.'

There were blood stains on the carpet in the entrance hall, marked off with yellow tape and two silhouettes in blue chalk. A couple of bored officers waiting there didn't say a word, just nodded directions when Baptiste asked where she was.

Véronique Laurent wasn't drunk. Not quite. Not yet. But it was only eleven in the morning. Give it a little while, Baptiste thought. He was happy with that.

The room was interesting, large, leather furniture, a desk with a typewriter, filing cabinets to the side, pictures on the walls. Cocktail bar built by long windows that led to a patio covered in shrubs and flowers, all very much alive. A place for work and leisure, brash, masculine, lacking the softness of a wife's touch. But it had a bar, which was why, he guessed, Véronique Laurent was there.

She was a striking woman, maybe forty, in a grey silk shirt and white slacks, perched on a tan leather sofa, legs up beneath her like a model, a half-empty pack of Royale cigarettes on the coffee table alongside a bottle of Gordon's gin, a half-full glass, neat, no ice, no lemon. From the state of her eyes – pink and watery, free of make-up, which was maybe rare – she'd been crying, but not for a while. The shootings happened just after eleven the previous night. There'd been time to get used to the idea. Time to sort and arrange her story too. Perhaps with a little help from Dupont.

It seemed simple enough. She and Laurent had been living apart, him in the house while she took the cottage, ahead of a slowly approaching divorce. Just as she was getting ready for bed, she heard a car outside. Then loud voices, shouting.

'They were having the kind of half-hearted stupid brawl men like. I thought nothing much of it. Then there was a shot. Bruno on the floor. Charles . . . he seemed crazy. I thought for a moment he was going to turn the gun on me. Instead . . .'

She reached for the glass and another cigarette as if that explained everything.

Fatoussi got up and began stalking round the room, looking at the walls. Baptiste had spotted that already. Nudes, women in garish costumes, paintings mostly, but a few were crude erotic photographs, black and white, a long way from Bill Brandt and Helmut Newton.

'What were they arguing about?' he asked.

'I didn't really hear.'

'You told Dupont it was about money.'

'Yes, yes.' She brushed away a hank of hair that had strayed from her forehead. Then lit the cigarette. Menthol. The smell of tobacco and mint wafted through the room. 'I think there was something about that.'

'What exactly?'

'How do you mean?'

'I mean . . . what did they say?'

She shook her head. Her hair looked matted, sweaty. 'I don't remember the words . . .'

Fatoussi pointed at one of the photos on the wall. 'This is you, isn't it?'

'Who was accusing who?' Baptiste went on. 'Was your husband claiming he'd been robbed? Was Augustin protesting his innocence?'

'They were angry. Very angry. I said. I didn't hear the details.'

'There's another!' Fatoussi cried.

'What was Charles Augustin's reaction? When you turned up?'

She shook her head. 'Nothing. It was all so quick.'

'He shot your husband dead. Then killed himself. And you never exchanged a word?'

Véronique Laurent glared at him. 'What kind of conversation do you feel was appropriate in the circumstances?'

Fatoussi walked over with three photographs he'd taken from the wall, handed them to Baptiste and sat down.

'Do you two enjoy seeing me naked?' she asked.

'Not at all,' Baptiste said.

'Wipe that look off your face. It's not pornography. It's art.'

'Ah.' He took a good look at them, one by one. 'I knew Eric Hubert was a thief. A poacher. A man who pimped his daughter to anyone who'd pay. A daughter Charles Augustin found hanging in the Bois de Mortery a few nights ago when he was searching for Noémie. But an artist, that I never guessed . . .'

She was going red, and the glass was shaking in her hands.

'Here . . .' Baptiste pointed to the background of the most lurid photograph, one in which Véronique Laurent was naked, draped over a chaise longue, hair down her back, one hand to her breast, the other lower down, a handcuff hanging from her wrist. 'This piece of furniture. These velvet drapes. The cuffs.

Black and white. Grainy. Quite crudely developed and printed in a home darkroom, nothing professional. We've seen the like before, madame. In the shed where Hubert kept his darkroom, with women who look perhaps not as elegant as you. Women from a different kind of background. There not out of duty, let's say, but because they were paid.'

Sucking on the cigarette, hand trembling, face full of fear and misery, she said, 'I think you should leave.'

'We leave,' Baptiste went on, 'when we've heard your story. The real one. Not before. I still harbour a hope, a faint one, that Noémie Augustin may be alive somewhere. Who knows? Maybe in this place where Hubert photographed you, on your husband's behalf, I imagine.'

He leaned back. Fatoussi copied the gesture. The two men stared at Véronique Laurent.

'We're waiting,' Baptiste said. 'And we are the most patient of men. But Noémie . . . you could help us find her. Could you not?'

'My husband's dead. A little sympathy wouldn't be out of place.'

'You were getting divorced anyway. Now all this . . .' He waved a hand around the room. 'Is yours. Besides, it's Thursday, and we don't do sympathy on Thursdays, do we Étienne?'

'Once in a blue moon,' Fatoussi replied. 'If you're lucky. And the moon isn't blue, Véronique. So, you're not.'

She was shaking, grabbing for the bottle. Baptiste pulled it away.

'Talk first,' he said. 'Drink later.'

75

Dupont was in his office, listening to Fabrice Blanc whining down the line.

'I'm getting calls from the press. People asking why you're not in charge. Bruno was one of ours. It looks bad.'

'I told you already. It's Millot's. Half his estate's there. They've every right to take the case.'

'He was Clermiers. Through and through. It's the principle.'

He laughed. 'Oh. Principles. We're fond of them now, are we?'

'I don't appreciate the sarcasm.'

'You don't appreciate anything. This is a puny little country police station. Two resident officers only at the moment. Two pushy outsiders I'm having to watch like a hawk.'

Blanc stayed silent.

'I mean . . . if you want . . . I can ask Baptiste and his mouthy sidekick to look into Bruno Laurent as well. Try to find out why Augustin was so mad. Where he got the gun. I've my own ideas there, but you wouldn't want to hear them.'

'Are they getting anywhere with the girl?'

The truth was Dupont didn't know and didn't much care.

'How many times? She's long gone. Run away to become a dancer. Or a cocktail waitress. Or a whore. What black kid with a brain would want to live in Boulliers?'

'You sound very sure of that.'

'Any reason to doubt me?'

'The newspapers . . .'

'Millot's problem. I fed a couple of hacks the story too. Augustin was on the take. Bruno found out and wanted his money back. He'd mentioned it to me but didn't want anything done out of sympathy over the missing daughter.'

'I wish you were as good at police work as you are at fabricating fairy tales.'

Dupont swore under his breath. 'The biggest fairy tale anyone's fabricated round here is yours. The idea this is some quiet little rural paradise where everyone gets along, everyone knows their place. Every penny of the public purse goes where it should with no . . . leakage. We are a community of angels.

What was it they said in that stupid story? All's for the best in the best of all possible worlds.'

It was Blanc's time to curse. 'I never put you down as a bookish man.'

'We all have hidden depths. Except you. I think they're shallows, and not well-hidden at all. Be grateful for what I bring you, Mayor Blanc. Do as I say without question, and this will all blow over in a matter of weeks. Bruno Laurent will be buried. A black girl from Boulliers will be forgotten. Our two awkward visitors will be dispatched back whence they came, none the wiser.'

Bonnay was at the door looking anxious. He lifted an imaginary phone to his ear and mouthed something that looked like, 'Millot.'

'I don't have time for this shit,' Dupont said and cut the call.

It was Leclerc, the captain from Millot he half knew and didn't much like.

'Thank you for your help in this matter, Alain. As always, I'm grateful.'

'No need. A dead rich guy. A dead immigrant. No work involved. Just a couple of corpses and some reports for the coroner. More our kind of thing than yours.'

'True.'

'I heard that councillor of yours, Gaillard, has lost the plot and gone into a sanatorium or something.'

'Who told you that?'

'Can't recall.'

'Councillor Gaillard has always been of a nervous disposition. It's not the first time. I doubt it'll be the last. That's between the two of us, of course. Discretion is in order.'

Leclerc chuckled. 'Oh, discretion is always in order in Clermiers, isn't it?'

Dammit, Dupont thought. The man could be infuriating.

'It's always a pleasure to talk. Is this a social call?'

Again, a laugh. 'Ah, no. I forgot. You told me this business was ours. You'd have nothing to do with it.'

'Exactly.'

'Then why have your two cocky visiting officers just turned up demanding to speak to the grieving widow who's now well in her cups?'

Think fast, say little.

'Did you hear me, Philippe? Did you send them?'

'No. I did not. I made it very clear to Véronique Laurent she was to speak to your officers and no others. The woman has been through quite enough already.'

'Very compassionate of you, I'm sure. Well, she's speaking to them now. At length it seems. Been in there a good half hour already. I thought you ought to know.'

Dupont put down the phone. Bonnay stuck his head through the door and asked if everything was all right.

'Everything is absolutely wonderful.'

Bonnay blinked, said nothing as Dupont stormed out of the door.

76

The bigger the dam, the faster the flood when it burst. Véronique Laurent, when she broke, had quite a story to tell. They sat, they listened as it came out piece by piece, loosened by the drink.

Bruno Laurent, it seemed, was a success at most things except being a husband. Not long after they were married, he went hunting, was thrown by his horse, spent four months in an expensive hospital in Switzerland recovering and undergoing extensive, painful surgery.

'It as good as killed him,' she said with a resigned sigh. 'The man who came back from Geneva was not the one I'd married. True, he could run companies. Be even more ruthless when it came to business than he was before. But . . .' She raised the glass as if in a toast. 'He couldn't get it up. Impotent. Irreversible. God knows I tried.'

'What's this to do with Noémie Augustin and her father?' Baptiste asked.

'I'm getting there. Can you imagine how a man like Bruno might feel? Knowing he could never father a son? That this . . .' She rolled her eyes around the room. 'This *palais* would never be inherited by another Laurent, after god knows how long in the family! We'd seemed made for one another, in and out of bed before he went on that idiotic hunt.' She closed her eyes for a second or two. 'After a while he decided the best he could do was watch. Watch others. Watch me with whoever he brought home. Even that wasn't enough after a while.'

Three years before it began. One night Laurent announced he might not be home till dawn, perhaps at all. There was a private club he'd formed in Clermiers. The details she wasn't to know. That wasn't like Véronique Laurent. After it became a monthly event, Sundays always, she demanded to go along.

Her bleary eyes ran to the walls and the photos there. 'That's where they took them. Some coarse man called Hubert I didn't know. An occasional extra when they wanted him.' A laugh, dry and hollow. 'Him and four men. They wore masks. Stupid papier-mâché ones like you see in Venice for the carnival. Not quite full face, there had to be room for food and drink you see. I got drunk. Took some kind of dope they offered. Went along with whatever Bruno demanded. Wasn't much choice. Their blood was up. They wanted satisfaction.'

'Names . . .' Fatoussi demanded.

She cocked her head to one side. 'Did I not say they were wearing masks?'

'All the same . . .'

'I knew my husband was there. The others . . . I couldn't tell. I got . . .'

She stopped, stumbling over something.

'Got what?' Baptiste asked.

'I got the impression Bruno used to go there with two men he knew. The fourth place went to a . . . a guest. Someone different every time. There used to be phone calls. From Paris. Abroad sometimes. Strangers. He always turned vile if I asked questions. Bruno's little secret. Four men. Three local. One invited. All masked. And that pig of a photographer when they wanted him.' The eyes again, pain from a returning memory. 'That night, me, and the girl. The one you found in the woods. Hubert, the bastard with the camera, was her father. I didn't know at the time. I might have said something.'

Fatoussi looked ready to scream.

'What did Lili do?' Baptiste cut in quickly.

'She wore a choir girl's outfit, white top, red collar, black skirt. I guess that turned them on. After my turn was over, it was hers. I didn't stay to watch. I'd had enough. Only went the once. Not my kind of thing.'

A pause at that moment, embarrassed, Baptiste thought.

'Madame Laurent, we need to find Noémie. Last Sunday . . . where was your husband?'

'Where do you think?'

'Was she there?'

'How the hell would I know?'

'Where were you?'

'Here . . .'

'Alone?'

Another humourless laugh. 'You're quite sharp, aren't you? No wonder they don't like you in Clermiers.'

'It's not my job to be liked. Who were you with?'

She sniffed, screwed up her eyes again, eyed the bottle on Baptiste's lap. 'I was here most of the night with Charles. After I failed the test with the *Amis* and objected to my husband fetching in some gigolo he'd found god knows where, Bruno decided he wanted to get his kicks seeing me with someone regular. There were a few earlier specimens. But a black man piqued his sense of humour and what little was left of his libido. We, by which I mean the two of us, interviewed the entire family. Bruno had a sly eye on the girl, not that the mother noticed. Or the father guessed. He arranged it so Charles was here for quite some months on his own to establish the routine. When his wife and the daughter arrived, we'd fit it in when we could. Not always with Bruno around, you understand. Charles and I got along. He was a nice man. Desperate to be accepted. Willing to do whatever was necessary. He wanted work and work meant doing whatever Bruno wanted. I'd no intention of taking him away from his family. It was just . . . harmless fun.'

Fatoussi stared at her, wide-eyed, speechless.

She glowered back at him, defiant. 'Don't you dare look at me like that. I did nothing wrong. Charles was fine with it in the end. Enjoyed himself, I think. His wife was a bit of a frump I gather.' She leaned forward. 'Do you have any idea how fucking boring this place is?'

Baptiste placed the gin bottle back on the table. She poured herself a shot and spilled half of it on the Persian carpet.

'Last Sunday?' he asked.

'Charles stayed until four or so. There was always some excuse about having to work nights. Bruno was out doing . . . whatever . . .' She put the glass on the coffee table, remembering something new. 'The following morning, I found him burning things in the yard. Papers. Records. Photographs. All gone. I wondered at the time if something had happened. But he wasn't going to tell me.' The drink again. 'Charles was furious when he came round. I've never seen him like that. He had a gun. Kept screaming . . . *Where is she? Where is she?* Bruno was ada-mant he had no idea. They did that stupid grappling thing that men do and . . .' She pointed at Baptiste. 'Bang.' Then raised a finger beneath her throat and said more softly, 'Bang . . .'

Baptiste sighed. 'Nothing more?'

'She was only supposed to dance. Charles said something like that, and Bruno snapped back something about him having a bad case of parental guilt, being naive, whatever that meant. How he gave him a house, a car, a good job, and he ought to be grateful. Not many people round here would do that for the likes of him. Which is true. But I don't think Charles enjoyed being reminded of it.'

There was something else. Baptiste waited.

'My husband was never violent. Just . . . rough sometimes. What happened in that club of theirs, it was meant to be consensual. Or to put it more precisely, I believe it would have stopped if I'd asked. If the Hubert girl had too. The Augustin kid if she went there. They chose that place because it was connected with that evil old bastard. But it wasn't rape, it wasn't sadistic, as you might say.'

A light went on in Baptiste's head and he wanted to curse himself for being so slow.

'De Sade. The Château de Mortery.'

'Quite.' A quick smile. 'Where exactly I can't tell you. Bruno insisted I was blindfolded, before and after I demanded someone get me out of there. They say the place is ruined and most of it is. But not everything. When they let me see again, I was at the boathouse. That place of theirs can't have been far away. Though who *they* were exactly I'm not sure.'

'Guess,' said Fatoussi.

'I told you. Two men Bruno seemed to know. One guest.'

Baptiste got up and said it was time to leave.

'You have to look hard,' she said as they left. 'They're good at hiding things.'

'Any clues?'

'You're the detective. Not me.'

77

They parked opposite the house Louis Gaillard shared with his sister. Curtains moved in the front room as they turned up. A rusty chain was keeping the gates closed. But a crowbar

Fatoussi found in the boot of the Simca dealt with that. Ahead lay a dense wilderness unspoilt by the trample of feet. Whatever way Bruno Laurent's party took into the château, it wasn't this.

Baptiste took along the map of the area he'd bought when they first sent him to Clermiers. This indicated the château estate covered a vast area, running down the hill to the boathouse on the banks of the Chaume, towards the bridge to Boulliers, then, on the other side, the road out east. The boathouse apart, the only building indicated merited just a few lines that seemed to signify ruins at the centre.

Twenty minutes it took and they were there, on a rare patch of bare grass and paving stones, next to the wreck of what was once a fountain, the remnants perhaps of a small courtyard. Fatoussi, his neat uniform filthy and torn from the brambles, stood back, put his hands on his hips and said, 'You can see why no one ever bothered to do up this place.'

A single brick tower with what looked like the remains of a monumental fireplace on the first floor was all that remained of what must have been the main building. Around it, stones and shattered walls ran out in a fractured rectangle, all scavenged for building material over the years. It was impossible to imagine what the château must have looked like in its prime. Old, like a Norman fortress? Or more like a smaller version of the country palaces found in regions like the Loire? Baptiste had no idea. Yet the infamous Marquis de Sade had once hidden from the authorities here and would later spark a sordid private gathering in his name.

'It's all been pillaged, Étienne. This stone, this brickwork . . . you see the same in some of the houses in Hauteville. A lot must have come from here.'

'Jesus,' Fatoussi moaned. 'They steal from their own. What did we do to deserve being exiled in this dump?'

'What did Noémie Augustin do?'

Fatoussi had gone so quiet when Véronique started talking.

Buttons getting punched again, and all the wrong ones.

'What are we assuming, Julien? You tell me because my head's all over the place.'

He ran through it. A group of local men met somewhere in secret on the château grounds. They organised a sex party, three regulars, Laurent and two men he knew, if his wife was correct. And a guest, a different one each time. Prostitutes were brought in, perhaps organised by Eric Hubert who took pictures when required. Sometimes, there was a local girl as well. Lili Hubert on more than one occasion. Noémie perhaps just the once. Charles Augustin, it seemed, knew about that too, which explained his odd reticence when the investigation began, and perhaps why his wife had left him.

Fatoussi didn't look convinced. 'You believe everything that woman told us?'

'What else do we have? Why would someone make it all up? The photos on the walls were Hubert's. There was a predictable amount of shame in the way she spoke. And a predictable amount of gratitude to get it off her chest, I thought.'

'You're a more forgiving sort than me. All I saw was a woman who thought she was better than the rest round here. Some kind of natural superior lording it over the likes of the Augustins. Happy to use them anyway they want. What did they call it when the local lord used to demand to sleep with any peasant virgin before she got married?'

That had run through Baptiste's head too. '*Droit de seigneur.* Or *de cuissage.* Or if you like the Latin . . . *ius primae noctis.* The right of the first night.'

'You do know your history.'

'It's what I studied. That whole thing's probably a myth by the way. A folk tale told for entertainment.'

Fatoussi picked a couple of ripe blackberries from the nearest bush, peered at the fruit, broke it open, showed Baptiste the maggots wriggling there.

'You think they look on it as a myth round here? People like

Laurent? Our friendly police captain? All these important men who really don't want to talk to us?'

Baptiste walked to the edge of the paving stones and peered into the thickets ahead. 'If we find something, I'll make them talk.'

'And how do we do that?'

Étienne Fatoussi was a man made for maintaining law and order, not sifting through half-facts and lies trying to discern the scent and colour of truth. Baptiste had met plenty of officers like that. They were, in many ways, the backbone of the police service, while the inquisitive, the suspicious, the obsessive like him were a minority.

'A group of men came here on Sunday night. It was a full moon. I remember. They could see their way without torches if they wanted to avoid detection.'

'With you there.'

'Still, they would leave a trace. We know they didn't come in the way we did. So how?'

Fatoussi cottoned on quickly. It took them thirty minutes, scanning the perimeter. At the far corner, a good two hundred metres behind the fractured remains of the fireplace, the grass and brambles weren't just trodden down by recent feet. Someone had been through there with a brush cutter and carved a path from the other side of the estate.

They walked downhill first.

'I can't see a thing,' Fatoussi moaned. 'It's just jungle.'

All around them, brambles, elder and sycamore that hadn't been cut for decades. Yet towards the river end there was ivy. A thick bank of it, climbing up towards the treetops. Beneath, just visible, something more solid. A wall.

It was obvious when they got there. This was a building, small, hidden in the forest. After a while Baptiste found a rusty iron ring handle poking through the tangle of green. He turned it and pushed. A hidden door, the same colour as the ivy, opened with a slow creak on unoiled hinges. One step forward and he nearly tripped. At his feet was an oil lantern, clearly recently used, smelling of fuel. He took out his lighter, put a flame to the wick and carried on.

78

Roland Noyer was still on duty at the petrol station. Dupont pulled onto the forecourt and ordered him to fill the car and put a couple of bottles of wine and forty Gitanes on the police account. Noyer saluted, head down, and scuttled about.

'Busy day?' Dupont asked, following him at every step.

'Not so much.'

'People asking about your late employer?'

'A few. Word gets around.'

He slapped Noyer on the shoulder. 'And if doesn't, you're guaranteed to give it a helping hand.'

Silence.

'I take it my two temporary colleagues from elsewhere paid you a visit?'

A quick shudder. 'They told you?'

'Some things I don't need to be told. What did they ask?'

Noyer shoved the pump into the tank and wiped his greasy hands on his overalls. 'Was Charles violent? Stuff.'

'What did you say?'

'Not so much.'

'Stuff?'

The pump clicked off. Dupont's car was almost full when he turned up. This wasn't about fuel.

'They wanted to know if anyone had their fingers in the till.'

Dupont watched him stow the pump then walked back to the cabin and lit a cigarette.

'Shouldn't be doing that near petrol just after I poured it, Captain,' Noyer warned, voice aquiver.

Dupont put his lighter back in his jacket, then, as if puzzled

239

by the find, withdrew his police revolver, eyed it, and stashed the weapon back in its holster.

'Shouldn't I?' He grabbed the jittery mechanic by the collar of his oily overalls. 'Fuck things up around here, Roland, and I'll be bathing you in it and flicking a match.'

'No need to talk that way, Captain. I didn't . . . I didn't tell them anything.'

'About what?'

'I don't know. Whatever.'

Dupont let go, smiled, and said, 'Good.'

'They wanted to know where Laurent lived.'

'And, of course, you said.'

'Christ! It's not a secret, is it? If it wasn't me . . .'

Dupont held up his cigarette, stared at the red, smoking end for a while, and made a little jabbing move in Noyer's direction. The mechanic whimpered.

'Just kidding, Roland. Yeah, they were going there anyway. Not that there's a thing to find. An outsider got caught messing with the books. Killed one of our own, a big man, when he was confronted. Then shot himself. End of story.'

'End of story,' Noyer agreed.

'Better be. When's Mailloux due here? Don't tell me it's hours. Last thing I want is a trip down to that dump you all live.'

'Thirty minutes. I have to see the doctor.'

'Nothing serious I hope.'

'I don't know maybe it is. Gilles said to get it checked out. He uses the same guy and says . . .'

The cigarette jabbed again, and he fell silent. 'Never for one moment think I care. Now . . .' He nodded at the shelf. 'Give me a Kro', a cold one, on the house. A plastic cup. Peace and quiet while I sit in my car and . . . meditate.'

Noyer passed over a bottle of Kronenbourg from the fridge.

'The other thing I want is for you to concentrate on your job, nothing else. Bruno Laurent is gone. His widow's going to

240

struggle to keep all his many plates in the air. The last thing she needs is for one of his lackeys to let her down.'

'I won't . . . I won't do that, honest.'

'Nothing you see here this afternoon need be committed to memory. You understand that? Nothing.'

'I never saw anything at all.'

Dupont reached over and patted him hard on the shoulder, spilling cigarette ash over his filthy overalls. 'Good man.'

79

There were more lanterns inside, and lamps on the walls. Baptiste walked round lighting every one he could find, all freshly used and still with oil. Their smoky yellow light began to illuminate the room and soon they realised what they'd found: a small chapel, centuries old, hidden away in the depths of the Bois de Mortery. At the end of the nave was an altar with an image of the Virgin and behind, a statue of Christ in agony on the cross. Ivy had crept in everywhere, crawling through the roof, bursting through shattered stained-glass windows, trailing down the walls.

Gravestones in the floor dated back to the early seventeenth century and bore the names of priors and lords, barely visible from all the feet that had passed over them. There must once have been pews, perhaps a pulpit. But now the place had a different purpose. A large and recent oak table was set before the altar, around it four tall and stately chairs. A pile of plates on the table, pewter or silver, goblets of the same and three candelabras, one leaking wax as if someone had forgotten to extinguish the flame. Velvet drapes and erotic paintings on the walls. Between table and crucifix was the chaise longue they'd seen in the photographs, a pack of condoms placed by the bolster.

A small crucifix and the number four. Now Baptiste

understood that little drawing against dates in Lili Hubert's notebook.

'Julien . . .'

Fatoussi had been exploring the corners, not the centre of the chapel. A dark, hurt note in his voice gave Baptiste some concern.

Behind the altar there were two chests, old, wooden with metal fittings. Inside the first were long robes, velvet, rich, medieval-looking, or costumes from some old horror film. Masks too, half-face, the mouth open just as Véronique Laurent had said, leaving the wearer to eat and drink. The contents of the next were as grim as anything he'd seen. Whips and instruments of torture, different masks, leather, cruel with studs and spikes, chains and handcuffs, a metal contraption for the mouth he guessed, and any number of gaudy plastic objects Baptiste didn't want to think about. He couldn't help going back to de Sade's *The 120 Days of Sodom*, four men, wealthy libertines, locking themselves in a distant castle with drink, prostitutes, slaves and the kidnapped sons and daughters of local families, all there to be abused, tortured, killed. An unfinished work de Sade had scribbled out while imprisoned in the Bastille, presumably after his brief attempt to flee jail while hiding in Clermiers.

'In that story . . . they murdered people?' Fatoussi asked when Baptiste mentioned this.

'In the end. They locked themselves away for months with an army of victims, some willing, some not. Male and female. Young and old.'

'Why would someone write something like that?'

'Perhaps to see how far they could allow their imagination to travel.'

He scowled. 'This isn't imagination. Also . . .' He gave Baptiste a cold look. 'It reminds me of the poetry we saw on Mailloux's wall. That was sick too.'

'Anyone who reads French literature will know about de Sade, Étienne. It's not a secret.'

Fatoussi's voice went up a couple of tones. 'You'd read that filth?'

'Not now. This isn't an out of the way castle in the Vaucluse either. It . . . It feels more like an amateur tribute act. A sex club for the debauched, out of sight, never, they'd hope, discovered. De Sade as an excuse, more than an inspiration.'

That, he thought, was why Dupont has done his utmost to keep him and Fatoussi away from any lead or hint of a clue that might direct them to this secret lair in the depths of the Bois de Mortery. Why Louis Gaillard had hidden himself away in a sanatorium. Fear of being found, exposed. Perhaps Noémie Augustin and Lili Hubert were a tiny part of that story, in their eyes, incidental details.

The wan oily light caught something in the corner as he moved his lamp. Baptiste's heart sank. Fatoussi saw it too and was over before him, picking the thing up, and the scrap of black that came with it.

Something so banal, so cheap, so childish. A single plastic banana and ripped shiny fabric from a dress. Baptiste groaned and reached down into the shadows beyond. There he picked up a pair of ballet pumps, pale pink and cheap, old and worn. All Noémie Augustin could afford he guessed.

'What the hell did they do to that poor kid?' Fatoussi muttered.

Baptiste wished he'd keep quiet. He was trying to think. Noémie came here from the tennis club that bright moonlit Sunday night he and his mother drove into Clermiers. Four men were waiting here, three familiar with one another, the last a guest. No Eric Hubert. That, at least, seemed certain if the son was to be believed. Yet, nowhere in the chapel showed any sign of violence, not a drop of blood, even on the instruments of torture in the box.

'Maybe she just danced for them,' he whispered, mostly to himself. 'Maybe . . .'

'And left her shoes behind?' Fatoussi retorted. 'And tore

her dress? And vanished?' He was getting more furious by the minute. 'What do we do? Shouldn't there be some kind of forensic team we can call in? Go over this place with all that stuff they've got? I told you. I never did this kind of work . . .'

'Can't say it's something I know a lot about either,' Baptiste said. 'We can ask Dupont . . .'

Fatoussi swore. 'I need some fresh air.'

Outside, clouds of insects swarmed down from the green canopy, hovering, buzzing, biting. Fatoussi cursed as he tried to swat them away, but there were too many. Baptiste thought of the syringe and the tinfoil package he'd thrown in the bin. Wondered if the right thing to do might have been to dispose of it entirely. But there'd always be another waiting somewhere. The solution lay with the man himself, not depriving him of opportunity.

'Back to the car?' Fatoussi said.

'Not yet.'

He strode to the narrow path they'd found, cut into the brambles, the one thing that seemed to be maintained in the wilderness of the Bois de Mortery. Baptiste needed to know where it went.

Fatoussi followed. The route from the château's secret chapel was straight for the most part, steadily rising. Dead vegetation from the last turnout with the brush cutter lay on both sides. This way in was established, kept clear for months, all year round perhaps. His head kept working, trying to make sense of that, until after half a kilometre or so they saw a high wall ahead, red brick stained with algae, yet more ivy creeping everywhere. Nothing visible above. He'd no idea where they were in relation to the car, to Gaillard's home, to Clermiers itself. In the deep green wasteland of the wood all bearings, all connections to the world outside, had vanished. As they had, perhaps, for those – four men only judging by the chairs

– who locked themselves in the chapel with the women they'd chosen for the night.

There was a door in the wall, plain brown wood, like the entrance for a workman or gardener. No lock. The circular handle turned easily when Baptiste tried it as if recently oiled.

He walked through, Fatoussi behind, and stopped, amazed, wondering how his sense of location could have failed him so badly.

They were in the last place he'd expected. At the back of Bruno Laurent's garage, standing on an asphalt area broad enough to park several trucks, empty apart from some storage boxes for bottles and a few heating gas canisters stacked against the back of the cabin.

Fatoussi came and stood next to him. 'They parked here, didn't they? Your mate Mailloux knew all along. What's the betting Laurent got him to cut that path for them? I told you he was jerking your chain.'

'He's not the only one who works here.'

'He's the only one at night.'

Baptiste was trying to cast his mind back to the previous Sunday. They must have been in place already. Parked at the back before walking down to the chapel along that freshly cut track. He'd never have noticed. None of this was visible from the road. But Fatoussi was right. Gilles Mailloux surely knew.

'What do we do, Julien?'

The only thing they could. Walk back the long way down the road, pick up the battered Simca, drive to Clermiers, confront Dupont.

'If he doesn't let us bring in forensic to tear that chapel apart, I go over his head. The two of us drive to Paris, go and sit in headquarters until someone listens. Sends in a team to clear up this mess.'

Fatoussi said nothing.

They headed for the road. As they passed the garage office a door slammed somewhere. A figure emerged from behind the workshop. Dupont, moving quickly for once.

'My car's round the corner. Get in.'

'You can take us to the rust bucket you gave us,' Baptiste said. 'Game's up, Captain. We're going back to the station. Time to talk.'

Dupont pulled a service handgun out of his jacket, waved it in front of them.

'I told you. Get in the fucking car. One word I don't like and I'll cuff you.'

Fatoussi made a move to lunge at him. Dupont pointed the barrel at the sky and fired.

Somewhere in the trees behind birds squawked at the racket. A head stuck out from the garage office. Gilles Mailloux. Then swiftly vanished.

'Not asking twice,' Dupont said. 'Baptiste drives. I'll tell you where.'

80

It took fifteen minutes, Fatoussi in the back alongside Dupont, gun in hand, driving along narrow country lanes lined with wilting cow parsley and scorched grass. Finally, they came to a halt down a dead end, a circular parking space, nothing more. Ahead, a derelict office and the rusty skeleton of what looked like an old mining wheel.

'Guess someone from Paris doesn't know what a place like this is,' Dupont said when they came to a halt. There was another car there, a recent Peugeot Baptiste recognised.

'You've got pits?' Baptiste said.

'Not much of one. It didn't last. Bruno Laurent's father. Never had the business nous of his son. Get out. Don't argue. You're here to listen not talk.'

Baptiste popped open the door.

'Lots of mine shafts around here,' Dupont added. 'You know

what? I once asked our friendly local coroner from Millot if he had any idea how you'd carry out the perfect murder. Easy, he said. Make sure no one ever finds the corpse. Drop it down a mine shaft. Gone for good.'

Baptiste watched the two of them climb out of the back. 'You can still prosecute a murder without a body. Ask any lawyer.'

'Pedantic piece of work, aren't you? Walk on. Someone wants a chat.'

Round the corner, by the derelict office and a scrapyard of old colliery equipment, Fabrice Blanc, the mayor of Clermiers, sat at a portable picnic table, wine and pâté, cheese and fois gras, laid out on paper plates. Three spare collapsible chairs, dainty silver knives and forks, four glasses.

'Gentlemen,' said Blanc. 'Will you join me for a little picnic? Philippe. Do put away that stupid weapon. There's no need for it.'

Baptiste sat down and motioned for Fatoussi to do the same. Dupont was last, and placed the pistol back in his shoulder holster.

'I'll pass. No appetite right now,' Baptiste said.

'Oh.' Blanc's mood seemed jovial. 'On the contrary. I think you and your colleague are starving. Famished for what you think of as facts. A truth that will show you to be knights in shining armour, delivering justice out of the darkness.'

'Fat chance of that,' Dupont said then picked up a fatty piece of foie gras in his stubby fingers and dropped it into his gaping mouth.

'Noémie Augustin was in that chapel. She danced like her heroine Josephine Baker. There are traces of her costume . . .'

'Traces, Baptiste,' Dupont said, mouth half-full. 'The tiresome labour you two have been putting in this long and weary week. All you have are traces.'

'Traces are a start.'

Blanc waved that away with disgust. 'They're nothing. Look

247

what we have instead. Clermiers' most generous benefactor murdered, shot dead by a black incomer we never asked for. The discovery of a tragic suicide, a young local girl from a troubled family who took her own life, god knows why.'

'Noémie Augustin,' Fatoussi said, furious. 'You never mentioned her.'

'Another black incomer we never asked for. Bruno Laurent was a victim of his own generosity. Lord knows he's paid for it.'

'The Augustin girl's gone,' Dupont added. 'She's on the missing persons register. No one has a clue where she went, you included. There's nothing more to be done than have her on the national files. Which I have arranged. *C'est tout.*'

Baptiste shook his head. 'I'm not happy with that. I want a scene of crime unit to go over that place. Find out what happened.' He looked at the two men. 'Who used it. See what a proper forensic examination will reveal.'

Dupont picked up a glass of wine and knocked half back in one. 'Anything else? A helicopter? Divers? A couple of unicorns?'

'There's a young girl missing. Strong evidence she was subject to sexual assault.'

Blanc looked baffled. 'What evidence might that be, officer?'

'Her dress, or what I assume to be her dress . . . there's a torn piece of it there. A part of her costume.'

'Clothes tear. People lose things.'

'I want, I demand—'

'You're in no place to demand a damned thing,' Dupont snapped. 'Still. We'll fill you in on the Chapelle de Mortery. Fabrice? Would you like to start?'

It was Laurent's idea, the mayor said. A decent man ruined by a terrible accident. The château was unused, unwanted, too expensive for the town council to restore. But it had some history in its stones, the Marquis de Sade most of all.

'Bruno, as his wife may have confessed, was a man who was no longer a man. He could only watch where once he was

248

quite the fellow. He proposed what I imagine you'd call a gentlemen's club.'

Fatoussi snorted. 'The one thing I've learned about gentlemen's clubs is they're never patronised by gentlemen.'

Blanc glared at him. 'Be that as it may. This was his creation, his money on the line, his to run.'

'Four men,' Baptiste said. 'Three who knew one another. A guest, a different one each time.'

They glanced at one another, then Blanc carried on. 'I am unaware of such details. Mostly, I gather, Bruno and his company enjoyed the pleasures of ladies of the night, brought in from Lille, Brussels, Amsterdam even.'

Dupont poured himself another glass. 'Nothing illegal in that. Everyone's entitled to their private amusement.'

'Lili—' Fatoussi began.

Dupont waved at him to be quiet. 'May I remind you the age of consent is fifteen.'

'We're aware of that,' Baptiste said. 'The age is not the issue. It's that word . . . consent.'

'And who are you to say the girl denied it? She's dead.'

'Noémie—'

'Tell them, Fabrice.'

Blanc topped up his glass of wine and gestured again at the food and drink on the table.

'Fuck you,' Fatoussi growled.

'Not the conduct of a police officer, I'd say,' Blanc complained. '*Eh bien*. We've made our own inquiries. It seems the Augustin girl was there at the suggestion of her father. As you know, she was a fan of the Baker woman, a dancer with quite a reputation. Let's face it. She was Folies Bergère not the Bolshoi. Near as dammit naked most of the time. I imagine Laurent was expecting much the same. He'd offered a lot of money. Ten thousand francs it seems. You'd want something . . . memorable for that.'

'And?'

'It seems they didn't get it. When the young lady was pressed and asked to provide the performance required, she became angry. Upset.'

'With her father, mostly,' added Dupont. 'Apparently the word "pimp" was used.'

'Which was unfortunate and quite inaccurate,' Blanc continued. 'As far as I understand it, she was only paid to dance and be as accommodating as she felt like. Though now the man's dead, that's best forgotten I imagine. The girl ran away from the chapel of her own accord. Unharmed. Untouched. In furious tears but, I repeat, more with her father than the gentlemen of the club.'

'And still she took her money,' said Dupont. 'Which, in the circumstances, is tantamount to theft, I'd say.'

Baptiste held up four fingers. 'Four men. Bruno Laurent one. Louis Gaillard another. Where were you on Sunday night, Mayor Blanc?'

He waved away the question and picked up a slice of meat.

'And you, Captain?'

'None of this is relevant,' Dupont insisted. 'I interviewed Bruno Laurent myself the day after. He filled me in.'

Fatoussi cursed again.

Baptiste rocked back on his heels. 'And you never told us?'

Dupont's eyes narrowed as if the question was idiotic. 'Why should I? What was there to say? I established that nothing illegal or remotely suspicious occurred in the Chapelle de Mortery that evening. I told you, repeatedly, the girl had simply hot-footed it out of town for her own reasons. Nineteen. Not a minor. She could go where she pleased, and it was none of our business. If you wished to waste your time looking for her . . . *tant pis.*'

'And then,' added Fabrice Blanc, 'you march in here like avenging angels. Looking for trouble. Determined to find it, and if you can't, invent it. The girl has simply taken to her heels. As Dupont says, she's of an age where she can do whatever she likes.'

'Names,' said Baptiste. 'I want them—'

'For Christ's sake,' Dupont yelled. 'This is like talking to a damned infant! Noémie Augustin picked up her things, her bag, her clothes, then scampered out of there, with more money than she'd seen in her sad little life. Pissed off with her father and yelling she never wanted to see him again. And still you refuse to accept that simple fact.' He gestured at them, with open hands. 'It's obvious. She ran. I don't know where. You don't. Maybe we'll never know. But her old man's dead. Her mother's vanished. Millot can't even find her to come and pay for his funeral. Who, in the great swing of things, gives a damn?'

Silence. Then Dupont laughed, patted Baptiste on the shoulder. 'Oh, apologies. A pumped-up, arrogant young *flic* from Paris. Who thinks he's smarter than everyone else and can't wait to prove it.'

'Give me the chance . . .'

'You had your chance. And yes, you're quick. But you don't listen. It's not in your nature. Listen to me now. This is over. Tomorrow you can start handing out parking tickets until the morons who sent you see sense and take you back.'

'Étienne?' Baptiste said.

Fatoussi laughed. 'Are you kidding me? Forget it, Captain. We're going back in that place. We're not stopping.'

'Oh.' Dupont shook his head. 'I'm so disappointed. A man tries to help a fellow officer and—'

'We're not stopping,' Baptiste repeated.

There was a jar of cornichons on the table. Dupont picked out a couple, munched on one, pulled a face, and spat the things onto the dead, dry grass. 'Then you leave me no choice. This is most unfortunate.'

He left it there.

Fatoussi looked worried. Baptiste said, 'I don't understand . . .'

'Today's the day the cleaner deals with the police house. The woman called me earlier. She found something in the bin.' He raised an eyebrow in Fatoussi's direction. 'Heroin. A filthy drug. I was warned that you had some kind of problem. I never knew it was dope. Unless, of course, the package is yours, Baptiste. Who's to know? No matter. You're both suspended. In the morning I'll be in touch with your home stations and inform them of the circumstances. I think we can close this without prosecution. Provided you pack your bags and I don't see your smug faces again. Fabrice?'

Blanc was putting the food back into the hamper. 'What is it?'

'Will you run these two back to their car? I'm afraid there's nothing I hate more than a rotten *flic*. Don't want them stinking out mine.'

81

One hour later, back in the police house, Fatoussi's room. Baptiste didn't want to leave him on his own for a while. The remains of Blanc's hamper were on the table. The mayor had passed them over when he took them back to the Simca. Best not to be seen around town before they left, he said. Clermiers was a small place and gossip soon got around. People weren't fond of those who used drugs.

They'd talked idly about what to do next. Fatoussi was desperate to go home to Marseille and his family, to try to get Clermiers out of his head. Or so he claimed. Baptiste wasn't so sure.

'And you?'

Paris, Baptiste said. Where he'd go to police headquarters, to the Justice Ministry if need be, and sit there until someone listened and agreed to take a look at what was happening unseen in Clermiers to the north.

'But we don't know what's happening, do we?' Fatoussi objected. 'Dupont's right. We're as much in the dark now as we were when we first found out Noémie was missing. All we found was a place hidden in the woods, somewhere for dirty old men to play out their dirty old fantasies. Not against the law. Not unless there's something we missed.'

Baptiste poured himself half a glass of wine. Fatoussi waved away the offer.

'I've never been good at giving up, Étienne,' he confessed. 'Problems. Wine from time to time.' A wave of the packet of Gitanes, now nearly empty. 'These. You must have noticed.'

'Better than my problem. Sorry. I screwed it all up, didn't I?'

'Nothing to apologise for.'

'What? I brought that junk here. Ridiculous.'

'And I didn't get rid of it. Which was worse. Go home. Put it all behind you.'

'And do what?'

Baptiste had no answer to that. His mind was working again. There was another possibility when it came to the missing Noémie Augustin. He hoped it hadn't occurred to Fatoussi.

'Julien. You're thinking.'

'It happens.'

'Me too. What if that's all it was? A club for sad old bastards. What if Dupont's telling the truth? Noémie hit the roof when she found out what they wanted was some kind of sex show. Got mad with her father for sending her there. All that money. Ten thousand francs.'

'Then what?'

'She storms out. Only one way to go. Up that path. To the garage. To Gilles Mailloux.'

'I went there Sunday night. He said he was closing early.'

'Did he? He wasn't alone either. That English woman, her brother. They parked up there too. All that stuff about they heard something. Damn right they did. It was on their doorstep, right next to that van of hers. And Daniel Murray

253

conveniently scampers back to England the next day.'

Baptiste had been there already. 'He was back at the Augustins at ten. Murray went out looking for her. The timing doesn't work.'

'That pretty sister of his was there, wasn't she? And Gilles Mailloux. What's the betting there's a brush cutter in that garage? That Laurent got Mailloux to carve that path through the wood for them to take? Face it. He must have known what went on. Who was parking in the lot behind his cabin. Maybe made a note of their numbers. Certainly did if they bought fuel. We screwed up. We lost two potential suspects. God knows where they are now, but Dupont isn't going to let you go looking.' He reached out and patted Baptiste's arm. 'I can try and put this behind me. If I get back to Marseille. Can you?'

All good points. Ones that had occurred to Baptiste already, though he'd kept them quiet.

'Let's sleep on it,' he said. 'We've still got the car. If you want to leave in the morning, I can drive you to the station.'

'You told Martine Augustin we'd find her daughter. Now we don't even have a clue where the hell *she* is.'

Baptiste got to his feet. 'True.'

Downstairs, he phoned his mother from the hall. She sounded sleepy, bored, until he said he thought he was coming home shortly.

'Oh dear. That sounds ominous. Fallen out with the local yokels?'

'You might say that.'

'Any nearer finding that girl?'

He didn't answer.

'You're talkative tonight I must say. Was there any point to this call except to tell me very little indeed?'

It was a long shot. She knew some left-wing politicians. Perhaps there was one somewhere who'd take up an issue of police and local council corruption.

'I may do,' she said, 'but if you blab, you'll lose that precious job of yours, won't you?'

'Some things are more important.'

A brief silence and then, with a different, softer tone, she said, 'Yes. They are. Let me think about it. Goodnight.'

Ten minutes later, on his bed, sleep still far off, Baptiste heard the front door close very gently. With the cruel rapidity of every unwanted thought he'd ever had, it struck him: Fatoussi had thrown his syringe and tinfoil in the rubbish bin, but he still had the gun.

Outside, beyond the open door, the light was weak beneath clouds scudding across a moon now waning gibbous.

Étienne Fatoussi was back in uniform at the wheel of the old Simca, firing up the engine as he released the handbrake and started rolling down the hill.

Boulliers, Baptiste thought.

The house of Gilles Mailloux. That locked room. Étienne Fatoussi was right. They should have looked.

82

It was six kilometres from the police house, a winding road, lit by nothing more than the occasional flash of moon. Owls murmuring in the dark, the ever-present buzz of insects, the occasional drone of a jet starting its descent to Charles de Gaulle. Four times Baptiste tried to flag down a rare passing car. But no one stopped for a desperate stranger running as fast as he could down the hill towards the river and the bridge. It didn't matter how much he yelled he was police, or when, with the last driver, a white farm pickup with what sounded like animals in the back, Baptiste walked out into the road and waved his arms.

They just drove past as quickly as they could.

Exhausted, sweating, he stumbled on, falling once so he

tumbled into dust and filth, came up, knuckles grazed, knees bleeding from the feel of it.

Then, getting closer, the meandering line of the Chaume, a silver ribbon ahead.

There were people around in Boulliers, mostly ambling pointlessly by the river. Not that Étienne Fatoussi cared. He had a gun. One thing on his mind. No stopping. Ever since he'd turned up in Clermiers he'd had people telling him to take it easy, to quit, to stay calm. Not any more.

The Simca slammed over the kerb as he was trying to park. A tyre burst and it sounded like a rifle shot. Clumsy. *Tant pis.*

No lights on in the Mailloux house. Curtains closed. Not a sign of life.

'Yeah, Gilles,' he muttered. 'Fine.'

He leapt out of the car, marched up the cracked concrete path, took a flying kick at the green painted door.

A couple were walking past with a young kid. They stared at him as if he were crazy, hurried away, back into the alleys behind.

Somewhere a motorbike engine gunned, got louder, closer, moving down the avenue. Not that he bothered to look.

'Gilles!' Fatoussi bellowed, then got out his gun and hammered on the frame with the butt. 'I am here and I am curious. *Gilles* ... '

Maybe the place was empty. Mailloux worked nights. Or maybe he was waiting inside, staying quiet. Waiting. Hoping Fatoussi would give up and walk away. Something had been wrong with the guy from the beginning. From the moment he started talking about how pretty, how *striking* Noémie Augustin was. People, normal people, didn't try to get close to a missing girl case like that. Sometimes it almost seemed people like that wanted to be found.

Fatoussi stopped, tried to think. No way of kicking down

something like that. As to shooting off locks . . . that was one for the movies.

He dropped his arm, let the gun hang at his side.

Felt stupid. Knew he'd have to go back to Baptiste, apologise, and try to talk him round. Maybe . . .

The rumble of the motorbike died on the street.

'Gilles.' He could hear the defeat in his own voice, stamping on the door with a futile fist.

When he stopped, he realised someone was near, behind him, a sweating, panting presence.

As he was about to turn, a bony fist hooked him under the jaw and clawing fingers stole the weapon from his hand.

'No . . .' he mumbled as a knee caught him in the groin, sent him tumbling to the ground. 'This . . . this is a mistake.'

A grinning face out of focus through teary eyes. Closer, the barrel of a gun. Fatoussi's own.

Breathless, panting, rolling on the filthy, dusty ground, he closed his eyes and waited, but not for long.

Across the river a siren wailed and, not long after, a flashing blue light raced along the Avenue Laval.

By the time Baptiste got there a small crowd had gathered at the roadside, locals gossiping, some with hands to their mouths, a couple weeping, others shaking their head in shock.

The siren came from an ambulance, light still flashing, doors closing after a stretcher was lugged inside by a couple of burly paramedics.

'Shot,' an elderly man cried in a sharp falsetto. 'He got shot.'

Baptiste grabbed him by the arm. 'Who? Who was shot? Police.'

He clutched for his card, realising it was still back in the house, that he'd run all this way in nothing more than a shirt, trousers, and bare feet inside old shoes.

'Police?' the man spat back and turned away.

The ambulance was moving down the narrow street,

back to the bridge, still screeching beneath that electric blue light.

It was Gilles Mailloux's home behind the crowd. Of course it was. He should have known. When he elbowed and pushed his way through the milling, mumbling mass of gawkers, he saw Mailloux there, seated on the doorstep, head in hands.

'Gilles,' he said, and dragged him to his feet. 'Talk to me. What's happened?'

Mailloux lifted his head and glared at him, damp-eyed. There was a gun at his feet, not that he made a move to reach for it. 'You mean you don't know?'

'No! I—'

'Your friend. He was trying to break into my home.'

'What . . .'

'They're taking him to hospital. You'd no idea?'

Baptiste was lost for words.

'What kind of *flic*, are you, Julien? To not know? To let . . .' His hand ran to the crowd then rose to point at Hauteville. 'To allow all this to happen?'

'I've done my best.'

'And it was inadequate. Come.' He took Baptiste's arm. 'This has gone too far already.'

The house inside was as Baptiste recalled, tidy, bare, the lair of a lonely man, an abandoned one in some ways, and again he thought he should have taken more notice.

They walked past Mailloux's bedroom with the scrawled verses from Baudelaire on the wall.

He dreams of gallows while smoking his hookah. If rape, poison, dagger, fire, have not yet embroidered with their pleasant drawings, the banal canvas of our pitiful destinies, it is only that our soul, alas! is not bold enough.

Then to the end of the corridor, the locked door, his mother's things, he said, not that Étienne Fatoussi was happy to accept that.

'Your friend so wanted to see. Now I give it to you. Perhaps if he lives, you'll tell him. He was right. Not you.' A pat of Baptiste's arm. 'I'm sorry.'

The key was now in the lock. Mailloux turned it, pushed open the door, reached for the light. It was little more than a box room, for storage mostly, an old collapsible bed against the back wall, cardboard chests full of books.

But not the nearest.

Gilles Mailloux lifted it with his skinny arms and began to rifle through the contents.

'See. A black dress. Torn and stained with blood and who knows what else?'

It was ragged fake silk, low cut at the neck, in tatters below, dark patches where something had corrupted it.

'Her underwear.' Mailloux picked out a bra and pants. 'And this.' A tennis racket, a bag and some balls. A broken waist-band with a few plastic bananas dangling from threads.

Finally, he retrieved a small pink purse decorated with a cartoon of a smiling cat and turned it inside out. Empty.

'I took the money. Noémie Augustin is dead. That is all I have to say.'

Part Six:
The Blade Must Fall

83

2:50 p.m. Douai Prison, 15 November 1976

Once Étienne Fatoussi was in hospital, close to death, once Mailloux was in custody, silent, refusing to speak, all the endless dangling threads concerning the missing Noémie Augustin began to fade, as if lost in a mist that came from a kind of certainty. For everyone except Julien Baptiste. In Clermiers, a town desperate to return to its previous anonymity, Philippe Dupont, out of convenience, not kindness, quietly disposed of the heroin stash his cleaner had found in the police house. The murder-suicide of Bruno Laurent and Noémie's father moved to a swift conclusion.

Deprived of any useful information from Mailloux, Baptiste had tried to assemble his own sequence of events. From the outside, they appeared much as Fabrice Blanc had suggested over that picnic table at the abandoned mine. Noémie had performed for four men, three regulars and a guest, all still unnamed, in the chapel of the Château de Mortery. Then she fled when they asked too much and encountered Mailloux near the garage. What happened after that the world could only guess, filling in the blanks Gilles Mailloux seemed to have quite deliberately provided.

'You kept a list,' he said as Mailloux lounged back in his cell, waiting, waiting. 'For Laurent. All the names, the car registration numbers, those who turned up for their meetings.'

A question he'd put in the interview room in Millot more than once, only to be met with silence. But now Mailloux nodded.

'It was my job. Roland Noyer kept the path clear with his brush cutter. I did the paperwork.'

'The paperwork?'

He laughed. '*Oui*. I noted down the details of the guests. You should have seen them. Men from Paris, Brussels, London once. Bankers, industrialists, politicians, musicians. An actor the public believe to be a happily married man and deeply religious. People Laurent had dealings with. I imagine their presence in his little chapel helped him . . . negotiate, shall we say?'

'Blackmail?'

'Your word not mine.'

'And the regulars?'

He waved a nonchalant hand. 'Laurent apart, I wasn't to know. They came with him. I never saw and he'd made it clear I wasn't to look.' Something struck him. 'That last night, with Noémie, I never saw a guest at all. Which can only mean the invitee arrived with Laurent too. Which was unusual. Anyway . . . let's speak of happier matters. Your friend from Marseille? How is he?'

Étienne Fatoussi spent two months in a coma in Douai hospital, attended to by a watchful Bernadette and an equally distraught Mimi. The two women got on and were close friends within days. Baptiste had visited as much as he could, though by then he was back in Paris. There was so little to do or say, but he sat by the unconscious Fatoussi anyway, talking out loud about anything that came into his head. Anything except Clermiers and Noémie Augustin.

'He's back with his family in the south. Recovering, I believe. They say he should be fine within a few months.'

'And he can go back to being *un flic*?'

That was a question Baptiste had wanted to ask not long after he regained consciousness. But it seemed too prurient, and in any case Fatoussi soon got that obstacle out of the way himself.

'He can't wait. I don't know. Something happened to him. He seems . . . renewed. Keen to do a good job this time round. Funny what a brush with death can do to you.'

The spider in the corner had gone back to its web and was spinning its threads further out to the damp rungs of the window. Mailloux couldn't take his eyes off the little creature. Something alive, determined, indefatigable.

'If Étienne had never woken up, if he'd died, you'd have stood trial for his murder.'

Mailloux scowled. 'So what? I've only one head. You can't remove it twice.'

To begin with, he'd been charged with the rape, abduction and murder of Noémie along with the attempted murder of Fatoussi the night of the shooting. This was all in Millot. The case had grown too big, too violent for little Clermiers. Dupont was glad to be rid of it, as he was glad to see Baptiste side-lined then summoned back to Paris. It was only when Étienne Fatoussi woke that they learned the truth. He had been trying to break into Mailloux's home to investigate the locked room. But it was Eric Hubert, prowling his old territory before fleeing, who saw him that night, stole up on him, grabbed the gun as they fought, shot Fatoussi once then fled as Gilles Mailloux returned.

'You could have told us it was Hubert.'

'Oh, Julien. You seem determined to assume I know so much I keep from you. I found him on my doorstep, the gun underneath him. I called the ambulance. That seemed enough. Then . . . you came along.'

Far from being his assailant, Mailloux may have saved his life. In more ways than one. The Étienne Fatoussi Baptiste had last seen was a changed man, clean, sober, engaged, someone who'd reached a turning point in his life that made him look to the future not the past. Whether that was with Mimi or Bernadette, Baptiste was as unsure as the man himself. The first Étienne Fatoussi he'd met, sparky, amusing and attractive to women, hadn't vanished with that bullet.

'I still don't understand why you never spoke of it. Not a thing. Not even why you were there. Why you'd left the petrol station early . . .'

A shrug. 'Bruno Laurent was dead. I was bored with standing behind the counter of a petrol station all night. Also, I'd no idea who was going to pay my wages.'

It was Baptiste's turn to laugh. 'See, Gilles! That was so easy. Why tell me now? Why not then?'

No answer. Footsteps in the corridor again. More men this time. The door burst open. The prison governor, a cold man with horn-rimmed glasses whose name Baptiste had never learned, stood there, a telex in his hand, all capital letters, a few brief paragraphs. He began to read it out, legal jargon, long words for a simple message.

Mailloux sat hunched on his single prison bed, staring across the room directly at Baptiste, no one else.

'If I shiver, Julien, it is only because I am cold.'

A group of burly warders marched in.

Baptiste stood up and in a stuttering voice that sounded like pleading said, 'I've not finished interviewing this man. We require more—'

Two guards pushed him to one side and another clamped Mailloux's hands behind his back. Perreault, the executioner stood behind them, black gloves, black coat, black scarf.

Gilles Mailloux was bundled out of the door, towards the yard.

They tried to stop Baptiste following, but when he fought back, thrust his police ID in their faces, Perreault intervened and said to let him through. He could watch, nothing more.

Out into the freezing corridor, grey November light at the end, that curious wooden contraption casting its long shadow over the black and glistening cobbles of the prison courtyard of Douai.

All Baptiste could think about was the distant prelude to this final act, the aftermath of that baking summer night in Clermiers, a world away.

Gilles Mailloux in an interview room in Millot, Baptiste there along with two tired local detectives who could outsmoke even him. Amidst the thick fug of Gitanes and Disque Bleu fumes, Mailloux sat impassive, silent, except to ask for a glass of water from time to time or someone to lead him to the toilet.

I took the money. Noémie Augustin is dead. That is all I have to say.

He repeated that once and then came the long silence. A week that went on. A week in which a professional forensic team finally got to look at the dress and the belongings found in Mailloux's locked room. And, at Baptiste's insistence, to examine the secret chapel in the Bois de Mortery where nothing of great interest was found. Though how hard they looked – Dupont insisted on being there, and Baptiste was most definitely excluded – he'd no idea. No one spoke to the *Amis*. No point, Dupont insisted. They had their man already.

The case built on blood and traces of what looked like semen on Noémie's dress and underwear. Just as much, too, on Mailloux's constant and infuriating silence. Baptiste attended every interview he could, from nine in the morning until midday, by which stage his fellow interrogators grew bored with their prisoner's insolence and gave up for lunch.

'I can make him talk,' said one that last day, and brandished a fist.

Gilles Mailloux blinked and said, 'If it'll make you happy . . .'

Baptiste got there just in time to stop a second blow. All the same Mailloux was left with a fat and bloody lip and smiled through the rest of the day without saying a single word.

The same when he was moved to jail.

The same when, one last time before his first appearance in court, Baptiste begged him again for the whereabouts of Noémie's body, for the sake of her mother, now a widow too. For himself as well, in the forthcoming trial where contrition, sympathy, a willingness to cooperate finally with the police, might win him a more lenient sentence.

All he got was a strange stare in return, a look of doubt and disappointment. He was grasping at straws.

Outside, the light was fading and a small crowd in uniform had gathered for the spectacle of Gilles Mailloux's death. Police and prison guards, a priest carrying a bible, assembled to mark the ultimate punishment, the taking of a life. They formed three sides of a rectangle around the timber crane of the guillotine, a small and formal audience for a fatal piece of theatre.

Baptiste pushed through the nearest rank, elbowed his way towards the front, found himself blurting out a mangled, incomprehensible plea for delay, more time to speak to the captive, a final chance for redemption, some hint, the slightest clue to where Noémie Augustin might be found.

Some small chance this cruel dumb show might be halted too, a forlorn hope and he knew it, though that didn't stop Baptiste begging all the same.

Finally, it was the governor who grabbed his arm, stared fiercely into his face with those emotionless eyes glistening behind the heavy spectacles.

Mailloux stood in front of the guillotine, two officers on each arm, the priest saying something in front of him, words Baptiste couldn't hear, sentiments he knew the man for whom they were intended would regard as ridiculous.

'Don't make a fool of yourself,' the governor snarled. 'The reprieve has been denied. The sentence must be carried out.'

'I don't think he killed her,' Baptiste told him. 'I don't think this case is at an end.'

'Too late.'

'More time—'

'Time?' The man's voice rose above the murmur of voices and the shuffle of feet around the square. 'This monster had all the time in the world to tell us what he did with that poor girl! And what did he say? Huh? *What?*'

One week into the trial Baptiste started to realise the direction it was headed. From the moment he'd seen Mailloux charged, he'd assumed a life sentence was inevitable. The rape and murder of a young woman, a blank refusal to explain what had happened to her body . . . those two facts alone were enough to seal a custodial verdict that might see Gilles Mailloux incarcerated for the rest of his life.

Yet the courthouse was a theatrical device too, open to swings of emotion, the currents of public opinion. The law might be fixed in stone, but its implementation, and the cruelty of its punishments, lay with a judiciary willing, on occasion, to be swayed by popular mood and the outrage of the press.

Mailloux had refused to plead, to be examined by a doctor, had only allowed a rudimentary psychological examination to prove he was, as he insisted in one of his brief outbursts, 'as sane as any man in the room, and doubtless a good more so than a few'. A remark he aimed at the judges quite deliberately.

He'd seemed determined to inflame opinion from the start. It wasn't just his refusal to cooperate and talk about what had happened to the missing girl. The way he yawned from time to time, pretended to sleep when the prosecution began, how he twisted his skinny, almost emaciated body as if gripped by a terrible boredom, how he laughed at small, incriminating details, waved others away with a dismissive hand.

Ten days in, the defence lawyers assigned to his case by the court resigned on the grounds that, since he refused to speak to them, they had no way of arguing any case for clemency. The following morning, the forensic scientists who'd examined

266

Noémie's torn dress and underwear spoke of the evidence of a violent assault, keenly resisted, the possibility she might have been strangled or bludgeoned to death then buried somewhere beyond reach, perhaps in those endless mining tunnels Dupont himself had mentioned the day Étienne Fatoussi nearly died.

Mailloux had appeared to be listening intently. Then, in the middle of an explicit explanation of the physical evidence on Noémie's dress, he pulled out an Asterix comic book, started to read, chortling at the contents, holding up the pages, showing them, laughing, to the court. The principal judge was a florid-faced obese individual with a heavy dark walrus moustache, obviously dyed. Mailloux picked up a page that had a full-length depiction of Obelix, the overweight buffoon in the cartoons, and pointed between that and the bench, creased with amusement.

Baptiste had watched in horror. The judges ordered the comic book confiscated immediately and told Mailloux he had to take an interest in the proceedings, to treat the court with respect and the seriousness it deserved.

Outraged, bloodless face flushed for once, that was when he yelled in the hard, stern tone of a stage tyrant, hands outstretched and ripping the air like talons, 'If this world had a heart, I would reach through its ribs and tear the bloody thing to shreds.'

The day after, the newspapers began to speak of a possible death sentence for the man local wags, unfettered in their language, had dubbed 'the Monster of *Merdeville*'. A week later the trial concluded, the verdict taken for granted. For many, the sentence – the rare imposition of the guillotine – much the same, and deserved too.

Gilles Mailloux listened, rolled back his head, laughing out loud.

A line of black crows had gathered along the high prison wall, as fixed on the performance below as their uniformed equivalents on the cobbles. The guards had removed Mailloux's prison jacket. Beneath was a white shirt two sizes too big for his skeletal frame. It billowed on the chill November wind as he shivered, teeth chattering, gaunt face dreamy, as if none of this was real.

Still, Baptiste couldn't drag his mind away from all the many memories of that strange and steamy summer by the Chaume.

A picture shot into his head, Gilles Mailloux's bedroom, those quotations from Baudelaire scrawled on the bare painted walls.

Eye burdened with an involuntary tear. He dreams of gallows while smoking his hookah.

Baptiste could smell, could taste the bitter remnants of the last cigarette in his mouth and wondered if he was shaking more than the man now being led to the deadly apparatus in the centre of the yard.

Perreault was by the device's side, gloves reaching out for some kind of handle. From this new viewpoint Baptiste could see a coffin waiting a metre or so away, plain pine, no shape to it at all, just a box, a rectangle in which to place the unwanted, the soon to be forgotten.

He dreams of gallows . . .

'This is wrong,' Baptiste said, trying to barge through the line of armed soldiers. 'You need to stop. I have to speak to the prisoner. There are matters unresolved . . .'

Before he could say another word two warders had him by his arms, forced them up behind his back so hard he grunted in pain. The prison governor was glaring at him, eyes bright behind those ridiculous spectacles.

'Show some dignity,' the man spat. 'This is not a circus.'

'Dignity?' Baptiste almost wanted to laugh. He nodded at the wooden contraption five metres from them. 'You call this dignified? You're about to murder a man who may not deserve it.'

'You make a spectacle of yourself,' the governor replied, then shouted, 'Proceed.'

One guard only on Mailloux now. He wasn't struggling. No side glances, the doomed man looked up at the high frame of the guillotine, bowed as the lone officer guided him to the flat plank bed, moved his greasy hair above his neck then placed him on the semi-circle beneath the high blade.

Baptiste's legs failed him. The men with his arms let go, one chuckling with a cruel precision as he tumbled to the filthy stones. When he looked up, he was beyond the forest of uniformed legs, out in the open space by the guillotine, the glittering blade moving slowly for some reason, as if reluctant to submit to the heartless demands of gravity.

But it fell. It fell and there was a sickening sound, half bone, half flesh. The force was so powerful he saw Mailloux's body jerk as if touched by electric shock then tumble sideways off the frame, down to the grubby cobbles.

Something warm and liquid touched his hand, his wrist. Baptiste recoiled, then stared in disgust at the bright red line of spatter there, Gilles Mailloux's blood, a final stain, a last reminder of some doubt, some tear in the world he still couldn't name, let alone see.

Look, Mailloux demanded. *You have to watch.*

Yet tears so filled his eyes so he barely saw a severed head, a decapitated corpse, what was left of the young man from Clermiers, carried then dropped into the plain wooden box, then lifted from the yard like trash for disposal.

More harsh words from the governor. A few from the guards around him. The yard began to clear. Before long it was just Baptiste, a few men starting to talk about disassembling the guillotine as if it were a prop from the theatre or a piece of machinery from a construction site, the performance over, the job done.

The crows were still there on the wall, rapt, fascinated, watching his wretched form on the ground.

A hand came and lifted him to his feet, held him until he was steady.

Perreault, the executioner. He took out a handkerchief, wiped the scarlet stain from Baptiste's hand then handed over the cotton cloth.

'You had to be here, didn't you?'

'You shouldn't have killed that man.'

The shrug he got was that of a farmer regretting the slaughter of a prize beast. Something Perreault perhaps did frequently.

'I told you. If it wasn't me, it would have been another. You may have got the fellow convicted. From what I heard, he was the one who had himself condemned.'

'I still don't see . . .'

That shrug again. 'I presume you asked him.'

'He wouldn't say.'

'Then I imagine we'll never know. One cannot converse with the dead. Get out of here, Baptiste. Take a holiday. You look like shit.'

84

At nine the next morning he still felt like shit too, with good reason. The night of the execution he'd found himself a room in a flophouse round the corner, went out to every bar he could find, got stinking drunk, barely ate a thing. Soon he was in an argument with some loudmouth who'd been praising the beheading of a pervert and telling the tale of one of his brothers who'd been among the guard and watched with glee Gilles Mailloux's final moments.

Matters had developed and before long the two were out in the alley behind the scruffy little café. Baptiste, not given to violence but willing when provoked and in drink, beat the living daylights out of the man and left him broken in a pool of blood before staggering back to his bed. He woke with grazed knuckles, scabby elbows, thick head, furry tongue.

Breakfast was difficult. Two cafés refused him service after his drunken behaviour the previous night. In the end he had to go back to the grimy flophouse by the Pont d'Ocre and stomach the basic croissant, pots of jam and bad coffee, all they had to offer. Halfway through a woman walked in and, unasked, took the chair opposite. She was fifty or so, skinny, grey hair, lined face, calm in manner, with eyes that were dark and rimmed with pink.

'My name is Collette Mailloux,' she said, taking off her coat and placing a cheap handbag on the table. 'Yours is Julien Baptiste. We need to talk.'

Talk she did, slowly, carefully, struggling at times to contain her emotions. There was something about the woman that reminded him of her son. The intelligence, the steadfast, earnest determination to say what she wanted and nothing more.

Mostly she spoke about Gilles. How he'd grown after his father fled the house leaving them with nothing. How he'd supported her from the very beginning, taking any job he could find, even as a kid. The fields, the beet factory when it was working. Clermiers had no great love of restrictions on child labour. Gilles Mailloux helped keep them both in food and accommodation, labouring relentlessly through weekends and holidays, leaving school as soon as he could to take a job with a regular wage, behind the night counter of Bruno Laurent's garage. Then spending what free time he had in the library with his beloved books.

'I think that's what he liked most about the garage. Being left alone all night long with little to do but read.'

'He could have gone to college,' Baptiste said.

She gave him the same hard look her son had. 'We were never ones for pipe dreams.'

'Gilles could have escaped.'

'To do what? To go where?'

'I don't know. I—'

'He told me you could never understand.'

271

That was strange. From what he'd heard, Mailloux had refused to see his mother while he was in custody. The cruise ship she'd been working on was on the other side of the world when he was arrested. She couldn't afford an air fare back. Instead, Collette Mailloux had been forced to work out her contract which meant she didn't return to France until a few days after he was sentenced to death.

'I wasn't aware you'd seen him.'

'Once. Once only. That was what he wanted and who can refuse a condemned man? Four weeks ago. He said that was enough, to say what had to be said.'

'Which was . . .?'

She took out a tissue and wiped away a tear. 'I knew he wasn't well. I didn't want to go on that ship. But he insisted. We needed the money. Gilles had been seeing a doctor in Millot for a couple of years. He told me it was nothing serious, just a touch of asthma. They gave him the news after I set off on that last cruise.'

'What?'

A sigh, a sip of coffee. 'My son was dying. A heart ailment. Untreatable. Gilles had at most a year to live. Perhaps not that. Nor would it be quick. Or peaceful. I would have to give up work to look after him. Where the money would come from . . .'

For a moment Baptiste couldn't think straight. In his head so many hazy ideas and doubts were finally beginning to take shape.

'He wanted to go to the guillotine,' he whispered. 'He wanted to make some kind of . . . statement?'

Another dab of the tissue at her eyes.

'My Gilles was a kind boy. He never harmed a soul. Never would. Even the thugs in Boulliers, and god knows we have plenty, never troubled him. They realised he wasn't well, I guess. That he was different. Never a threat. Never one to be a weasel when it came to dealing with that creature Dupont.'

272

All the same, Baptiste said, Noémie Augustin's belongings were in their home. 'The evidence seemed overwhelming. Gilles confessed.'

Her eyes flashed at that. 'Did he? Do you recall the words?'

Just that one bleak statement: the money was gone, the girl was dead. Then nothing.

'What do you want of me, madame?'

'Me?' She frowned. 'Nothing. What could you possibly have that I might need? My son is dead. His name's mud. The Monster of *Merdeville* indeed. No one who knew him could think of him as that.'

'I couldn't and I barely knew him at all. But he wouldn't talk to me. Even yesterday we just went round and round in circles.'

She opened her handbag and took out an envelope. 'He liked you. He told me you were honest. Trying to do your best.' She passed the envelope over. 'He wrote this in secret in prison. For you, no one else.'

'What does it say?'

'I don't read other people's letters.' She placed a stubby finger on his name, written in a clear, flowing hand. 'That's you. Not me.'

'If there . . .' He was struggling. 'If there's something I can do.'

'They won't let me bury him in Clermiers. It's a prison grave. I have to make an appointment to visit. Can you change that, Baptiste?'

He grimaced. 'I'm just a cop from Paris. They won't listen.'

'What can you do, then?'

He had no words.

'*Eh bien*,' said Collette Mailloux, then tapped the envelope again and left.

273

85

Baptiste went to the dank, damp room where his bags lay packed for the journey back to Paris. There, through the dim, grey light of a greasy, bird-stained window, he read the letter, a single page. The writing was firm, confident, that of a self-educated man, articulate, punctuated with more care than Baptiste saw in the average police officer.

In a way, it was what he'd wanted to hear from him ever since the night Fatoussi was shot and Mailloux arrested. Answers of a kind, but general, vague, almost taunting at times.

The tone was set by the first paragraph . . . 'I was speaking the truth when I told you Noémie Augustin is dead, but a man as smart as you, Julien, surely knows I never said the one responsible was me. Nor can I give you a name. I simply do not know.'

What followed was the most puzzling part: Mailloux thanked him for his arrest, for the interest he'd taken in the case from the abortive interviews on. Said he was not to blame for the sentence the court imposed. That, Gilles Mailloux insisted, was his doing alone, and he scribbled a little smile in the margin as if to emphasise the point.

'You and Étienne Fatoussi were stumbling through an endless night. This is scarcely surprising, since darkness, it seems to me, is Clermiers' natural state. A curse I've now escaped. Remember the poet . . .

Il est doux, à travers les brumes, de voir naître
L'étoile dans l'azur, la lampe à la fenêtre
Les fleuves de charbon monter au firmament
Et la lune verser son pâle enchantement.
Je verrai les printemps, les étés, les automnes;
Et quand viendra l'hiver aux neiges monotones,
Je fermerai partout portières et volets
Pour bâtir dans la nuit mes féeriques palais.

Baptiste knew those lines well. They were from 'Paysage', one of his favourite poems in *Les Fleurs du Mal*. A lyrical Baudelaire far away from the bleak verses that made his name.

It's sweet, through the mists, to see being born,
Stars in the azure sky, the lamp at the window,
Streams of dark smoke rising to the heavens,
And the moon that gifts her pale enchantment.
I shall see the springs, the summers, and the autumns;
And when winter comes with dreary snows,
I shall close all my doors and shutters,
And build my fairy palaces in the night.

With a lump in his throat, Baptiste went through the final paragraph of Gilles Mailloux's letter.

'Now my doors and shutters are closed. Somewhere neither of us can imagine I build my fairy palaces in an eternal winter. All I ask of you is this. You have the makings of our dénouement. Now reveal what injustice means, even to those who bring it on themselves. Show how harsh and wrong this punishment is that they wreak upon their fellow citizens of the *République Française*. I can only tell you where to begin but that you know already. Not with a sickly bookish young man behind the counter of a petrol station, but where your instinct and your intelligence told you to look all along. In Clermiers, not Boulliers, in the *Amis*, not my poor neighbours. Behind the walls of the dismal, desolate chapel of the Château de Mortery. What happened there I do not know. Only that these are the people, these the locations you must begin with. There is your fairy palace, for you alone to build.

'I must apologise. At some point in the days ahead I will say I do not mean to haunt you. That will be the only lie I ever told.

'*Je vous envoie mes amicales pensées.*

'Gilles Mailloux, *décédé*.'

Baptiste had never wanted to return to Clermiers. Now there was no choice. Still hung-over, unshaven, scruffy in the clothes that bore the dirt of the Douai prison yard, he drove slowly, carefully, trying to think things through. The place was different on a dull November afternoon, the light beginning to fade, few people on the street. The Chaume was high after recent rains, its swirling grey waters almost reaching the bridge. Boulliers seemed as grey and miserable as ever. Even Hauteville with its fine houses appeared smaller, duller than he recalled.

The iron gates to the Château de Mortery were locked, a new chain there and a sign saying, 'Private Property: Keep Out'. The publicity that came with Mailloux's trial must have attracted the attention of a few ghouls. There was only passing mention of the chapel where Noémie had, in the words of the prosecution, 'performed' for a private event before being seized by Mailloux on her way home. But that, Baptiste guessed, was enough.

The town square was empty except for Fabrice Blanc's shiny Peugeot outside the Mairie and a recent marked police car in front of the station. The rusty Simca he and Fatoussi had been given was, perhaps, no more.

He parked next to the police car, sat back, wiped the sweat from his face, tried to tell himself he didn't feel so bad, with little conviction.

Pascal Bonnay was in the same chair wearing the same crumpled uniform, half a croissant on a napkin in front of him, the other half in the hands of an equally sleepy looking cop by his side.

'What the hell . . .?' Bonnay began.

'Good to see you too, Pascal.' He nodded at Dupont's door. 'Is he around?'

'The captain's busy.'

'He is now,' Baptiste said and walked right in.

It was cold in the station reception but not Dupont's office. There an old duck nest fireplace burned bright with coal, the heat and fumes sucking oxygen out of the room.

The man looked startled when Baptiste burst in, then amused. He rolled back in his chair and placed his boots on the desk.

'Did you watch?' he asked.

'I did.'

'Why?'

'Because Mailloux asked me to.'

Dupont chuckled. 'All that time you spent trying to get him to talk. And finally, the day he dies, you get there. You must be top of detective school back in Paris.'

Baptiste grabbed the spare seat and sat at the desk opposite him.

'I imagine there's some stupid reason you're here.'

'Were you there that night? In the chapel? When Noémie danced?'

That laugh again. 'Christ, Baptiste. Let it go. Yesterday they cut the head off the man who killed her. Job done. Go home. Piss off someone other than me.'

'Gilles Mailloux didn't murder her.'

Dupont feigned interest. 'Oh? Really? How strange, given you brought in the fellow to begin with. Didn't you see the way he behaved when he had his time in court?'

'It was an act.'

'You took his confession that night Fatoussi got shot!'

Baptiste shook his head. 'It wasn't a confession. It was a statement. Nothing more. I want this case reopened. I want forensic to take another look at the chapel. I want everyone who was there that night interviewed. That should have happened first time round.'

Dupont scowled. 'There was no need to put anyone else into the mix.'

'I want them all. Don't care who they are. If that includes you, so be it.'

'Not asking for much, are you? Correct me if I'm wrong but you're an officer in Paris now. Nothing to do with us here.'

'You can order it, Dupont. Or I can go over your head.'

'Who to? You think your masters give a damn about little Clermiers?'

'Millot.'

'You're wasting your time. And mine.'

Baptiste reached into his pocket and took out the letter. 'Mailloux had his mother deliver this to me after he died. It seems he was very ill. He wanted to be executed to make a point.'

'A point?'

Weak ground, and Baptiste knew it. 'That's not important. What is . . . we don't know who killed Noémie. It must be reopened.'

Dupont sniffed at that then took the one-page letter and read it very slowly.

'And?' he asked when he was done.

'There's reason enough there to look again.'

'Are you out of your mind? Some ridiculous poetry. An unconvincing denial though he never uttered a word of this while he was alive. Then a few vague accusations. Against what? Every man in Clermiers?'

'The *Amis*. It says.'

Dupont waved the page in the air. 'How do I know this is even genuine? You say it came from the mother?'

'It did.'

Another contemptuous wave of his hand. 'Maybe she wrote it. The woman's simply trying to convince herself her son wasn't the murderous creature we all knew. She may think you're mug enough to fall for it. Not me.'

Baptiste held out his hand for the letter. 'I gave you the chance. Now . . .'

278

'You're just looking for excuses for your own failures. It's pathetic. *You're* pathetic.'

'The letter . . .'

'This?'

Before Baptiste could move, Dupont swivelled on his chair and fed the single sheet into the fire. Gilles Mailloux's careful, lyrical handwriting vanished in flames and embers that flew up the chimney as soaring black ashes.

'Noémie Augustin is dead,' Dupont declared. 'So is that sad little bastard from Boulliers, thank god. And so, Baptiste, are your hopes of stirring up yet more shit in our peaceful little town.' He pointed to the door. 'I'd say *au revoir* but, for your sake, I hope I never see your ugly face again.'

Part Seven:

Dénouements

88

Paris, Thursday, 14 May 1987

'Are you happy, Julien? Eleven long years have passed between us. Are you yet content?'

There he was again in the prison yard of Douai, leaning against the guillotine looking younger, more robust than he ever had in life.

'There are different kinds of happiness, Gilles. Different kinds of contentment too.'

Even Baptiste thought it a glib answer. The words came too quickly, sounded inaccurate, banal, insincere.

Mailloux seemed amused. 'I'll take that as a "no".'

Crows looked down on them from all four high brick walls. The two men stood by the too-familiar creature that loomed over their encounter like a spindly timber stork. Baptiste and the man he'd brought to this place. Someone who'd failed himself in some ways but had been failed by others too.

'Eleven years . . .' Mailloux whispered again, and something liquid fell from his right eye, ran down his cheek, dripped to the blackened cobbles.

But it was not a tear, not even pretending to be one. What fell to the stones was blood, deep red and thick, congealing as it swam slowly to a nearby drain.

'Eleven years,' Gilles Mailloux repeated, more firmly. He

stood back. Baptiste blinked. When he looked once more, Mailloux was dressed like the old executioner Perreault. Black coat, black gloves, black scarf. Pale and regretful countenance.

'Sometimes it pays to be patient,' Baptiste objected. 'To await the right moment. The opportunity.'

Mailloux threw back his head and laughed. His teeth weren't quite right, too sharp, too yellow, and his throat was raw and red.

'What is this, Detective? You talk to a dead man of patience?'

Baptiste reached out to touch his arm. His fingers travelled through cold November air, dimming as they reached what should have been flesh, as if Mailloux's spectre stole away some of the light.

'Who better to ask? What's time where you are anyway?'

'It wasn't my time I was thinking about.'

Mailloux stepped to one side of the guillotine frame, looking up at the silver blade, then winding his long and skeletal fingers around the lever that protruded from its waist.

I do not mean to haunt you. That will be the only lie I ever told.

Baptiste knew what came next. He'd been here so many nights before. When he looked at himself again, he was shivering in a billowing white shirt and the skimpy thin trousers of a Douai prison uniform. Standing in front of the simple planks of the guillotine frame, Mailloux there, waiting.

No one to guide him forward. No need any more. He knew this routine too well.

Baptiste lay face first on the cold, splintered wood and edged forward until his neck fell neatly into the semi-circle beneath the blade.

'I am truly sorry, Julien,' said the black-clad figure above him and then it began, the slow descent, the shrill whine of metal travelling down the cables and the paths a long-dead carpenter had routed in the ancient oak, not knowing how many lives his work might come to steal.

I wonder if you die the moment the blade has done its work. Or live on a second or two after, watching the ground rise up to meet you.

Gilles Mailloux had asked that when Baptiste turned up at his beckoning the day of the execution. Now he knew or thought he did. A sudden savage blow, a twist to his vision and then, as if suddenly cut loose from gravity, he was staring back at the wooden crane above him where blood gushed beneath sharp metal and, to one side, a briefly thrashing headless corpse kicked hard in shock, gore streaming from a severed neck before it tumbled aside.

All the world, all of time, beginning to end, awash with blood, sticky, warm and streaming, torrents of it, wave upon wave, a scarlet flood tide in which Julien Baptiste swam and floundered and began to drown.

He screamed. He always screamed. Never knowing if any could hear.

Then he was awake, sweating in his striped pyjamas, bolt upright in his childhood room in the 7th arrondissement, the second-floor apartment in the rue de Bourgogne, where he'd lived with his widowed mother, an awkward, rebellious adolescent, wishing to escape.

'Poor boy,' said Marie Le Gall, her voice for once soft and sweet as she stroked his damp, hot brow. 'Not again?'

89

Breakfast, croissants from the bakery round the corner, jam and butter and coffee.

'You have to eat,' his mother insisted. 'Some vacation I must say.'

Baptiste's apartment in Montmartre was uninhabitable after a flood from the flat above. A further week or more of repair work before he could move back in. Not that he'd be spending them with his mother. He'd called in his holiday entitlement, ten days in all. No need to be back at work until Tuesday the 25th. Enough for what he had in mind. That had been months in the planning.

Her coffee was always good, as were the pastries.

'None of my business I know, but do you still see that Dutch girl?'

'Martha's returned home. She was on temporary attachment from Amsterdam anyway. I thought I told you.'

'No need to be snappy. A mother can inquire of her son's happiness. I did tell you never to go out with someone in the same job. At least I'm not nagging you to get married and give me grandchildren.'

He kept quiet. This was a conversation he didn't want at all.

'The twins in the flower shop, Chloé and Elise. They always ask after you. Chloé is the prettiest and Elise the brightest in case you're interested.'

'I'm well aware of Chloé and Elise, thank you. They were two years down from me at school.'

'Ah. I forgot. They're both like you as far as I know. Not spoken for, that is. Or rather occasionally spoken for but rarely for long.'

He smiled, raised his coffee cup, and said nothing.

'I take it the nightmare is the usual?'

'I've never told you about my nightmares.'

'You don't need to. You've been on the phone here non-stop since you turned up. I may be old but I'm neither deaf nor stupid. It's that damned place again, Clermiers, isn't it? The missing girl? What was her name again?'

'Noémie Augustin.'

She sighed. 'I'm sorry. I should have remembered. This was what . . . ten years ago?'

'Eleven.'

'Can't you put it behind you, Julien? Or at least try?'

He patted her hand and did his best to look nonchalant, diffident even. 'There may be developments.'

'Such as?'

Baptiste tapped his nose.

'You really are a detective, aren't you? All secrets and winks. I hope you're right. It would be quite annoying if I had to watch you spend the rest of your life with this sorry albatross round your neck.'

A short trip, he said. A week, ten days at the most. By then his apartment would be back in order, he'd return to Paris and work.

'And for this you must visit that miserable hole again? On holiday? Not official business?'

Baptiste raised his coffee cup in a toast. 'There's an old friend turned up. We need a reunion.'

90

One last call before he left. To Fournier, his contact in the advanced forensic unit at police headquarters in the rue des Saussaies across the river on the Rive Droite. The material he'd requested from the evidence store at Millot had arrived.

'And?'

'There's blood,' Fournier said. 'Maybe a trace of semen.'

'Good.'

'There's also no guarantee this is going to work. I warned you . . . DNA profiling is all very new. I'll do my best—'

'I know you will.'

'The dress is torn, and I imagine it's been handled by lots of locals out there. Same for the underwear.'

A picture flashed up in Baptiste's head. Dupont kicking the condom they'd found by the boathouse into the muddy swirl of the Chaume . . .

It's spunk. That's all.

'If there's still semen there, that's unique, isn't it?'

'As good as. Blood too. Though if there's contamination, more than one attacker . . .'

'I doubt that.'

'You have someone in mind?'

'Possibly. But I doubt this was gang rape. That would be beneath them. One man. One only.'

'You understand . . . even if I can get something from these clothes, you need to provide me with a match. A second sample. You understand, too, that even if this works, I've no idea whether you can take it to court.'

Fournier was a scientist, not a cop. A good friend of the forensic officers in England who'd developed the technique of DNA extraction. There, Fournier hinted, they were close to using it in a rape and murder case for the first time. The possibilities seemed extraordinary. The ability to link a suspect to a crime through a smear of blood, sweat or semen might revolutionise police work more fundamentally than the advent of fingerprints. But only if they could gain a sample for a match, and as things stood that was not going to be easy. There was no way he could force any individual to provide one. That, for the time being, was beyond the law.

'Have a car waiting at Clermiers police station at six this evening, Carl. There'll be something for you. How long—?'

'The question every detective asks of forensic. This case is a decade old, isn't it? What's the rush?'

'It's a decade and a year old. Who knows what the man has got up to in the meantime?'

'Fair point,' the forensic man said. 'If it's good news, maybe weeks. If it's bad, a lot less. Patience, Julien. And hope you're in luck. We're dealing with something that's half science, half witchcraft.'

'Never been fond of patience. Or much of a one to count on luck. But thanks.'

His mother let out a long, pained sigh from the dining room

when he came off the phone. Baptiste had packed his small suitcase. On the top, something he'd been keeping for eleven long, uneasy years. The secret notebook of Noémie Augustin, filled with the dreams of a teenage girl lost to the world one sultry summer night when he was no more than a kilometre or so away.

Clermiers was two and a half hours in the Renault, a faster journey than before. The roads were better, the world perhaps a little too. The weather was benign, warm, sunny, but not the debilitating heat of the summer of 1976 that had sucked the life and energy out of everyone.

The bridge over the Chaume had been freshly painted. Some of the houses in Boulliers too. The rusty iron gates of the Château de Mortery had a large chain and padlock across them, and what looked like an even wilder jungle of vegetation behind. Hauteville seemed much as it did before, perhaps a little grander. There was money in parts of Clermiers still.

He stopped outside the police station. There was a new sign, nothing else different. All the same it felt odd walking through the door to find Pascal Bonnay wasn't slumped in his chair toying with a pastry. Instead, there was a striking young woman in a plain blue dress who stood looking at the notice-board. New cork, recent notices, not like it was before.

She looked at him, smiled and said, '*Oui?*'

'Is the duty officer around? I have an appointment . . .'

'I am the duty officer, Baptiste. Though because of you, I gather, I am here in my off-duty clothes.' She had very red hair and green eyes and a sparkling smile. 'Don't you have women officers in Paris now?'

'We do. I . . .'

The door opened. It wasn't Dupont there but Étienne Fatoussi, older, a touch of grey to his hair above the ears, a neat moustache, the smart and recently pressed uniform of a captain.

'Don't let Anaïs scare you,' Fatoussi said. 'She's not as terri-
fying as she appears.'

She beamed. 'Too kind.'

The two men embraced, arms round one another.

'Do you want a moment to yourselves?' Anaïs asked.

'We do.' Fatoussi glanced at his watch. 'Thirty minutes, officer. Then the show begins.'

91

'You look older.'

'I am, Étienne. So are you.'

Fatoussi had a smart new chair behind a smart new desk.
The duck nest fireplace where Dupont had burned Gilles Mailloux's letter to ashes was now filled with a bouquet of flowers.
There was a photo by his telephone: two smiling children, a
boy of six or so, a girl of four, with them a beaming mother.

'It was Bernadette who brought you back then?'

He picked up the picture and kissed the figures behind the
glass one by one. 'Eventually. Mimi kept me in Marseille for
a while. Then I realised I couldn't get this place out of my
head. Bernadette doesn't take me too seriously. That's good for
a man. There was an opening in Millot. When they finally got
rid of Dupont, they wanted someone local and reliable to hold
down this little fort.' He laughed. 'Not much competition to be
honest. No one with a shred of ambition comes to Clermiers.
Except, it seems, you.'

'And a woman officer too?'

'Anaïs?' He leaned over to peer through the partition window
and make sure she wasn't listening. 'She's a marvel. Got most
of this place under her thumb. No wife for you, Julien? No
kids?'

Baptiste wasn't about to go there, so they ran through the
fate of a few mutual acquaintances. Dupont had remained in

287

Clermiers, a solitary, surly bachelor, after early retirement. The elusive Louis Gaillard had stayed in post despite a series of unsavoury rumours after he made a brief public apology and uttered a promise that 'lessons had been learned'. In spite of some dubious financial manoeuvres, Fabrice Blanc was still mayor, largely because no one else wanted the job. Véronique Laurent had remarried and moved to Nice. Pascal Bonnay was now part-time, replaced by two new officers Fatoussi brought with him from Millot.

'Our friend Eric Hubert, I trust you know about?'

Baptiste did. The man had gone on the wanted list after Fatoussi recovered following the shooting and told them Hubert, not Gilles Mailloux, was responsible. Two years later he died in a stabbing outside a drug café in Rotterdam.

'What about the son?' Baptiste asked. 'Didier?'

'Ah.' A sad shrug. 'Much as I'd like to say Boulliers has improved a touch since you were last around, those the place treated badly do not recover so easily. The kid turned out much like his dad. Currently in jail in Lille. Dope and protection rackets for hookers. Some of the kids there . . . it's not easy to escape.' He hesitated. 'And Noémie Augustin. You really think this fresh magic you have in Paris might tell us what happened to her?'

Baptiste opened the pilot's briefcase Carl Fournier had provided and began to take out the gloves, the plastic bags, the labels, the marker pens. 'It's worth a shot. You're sure they're meeting this afternoon?'

'The *Amis*? Every other Thursday now. Like clockwork. There will be familiar faces, some strange ones too. Why am I refused a part in the fun?'

'Just because—'

'Because your bosses in Paris have no idea you're playing these games.'

Étienne Fatoussi was as sharp as ever.

'If I strike lucky, you get the credit, you get to charge and arrest and I steer clear.'

'And if it all goes wrong and those people start whining about harassment? Maybe I escape. But Anaïs . . .'

'I'll take full responsibility and tell them I lied to get her to help.'

'And lose your job. Maybe worse.'

Baptiste kept quiet.

'That poor girl still eats at you, Julien.'

'It's not just Noémie Augustin. I sent an innocent man to the guillotine. What do you think?'

'Seems to me he sent himself. Besides, we've stopped all that now. No one will ever go through that horror again. I suspect some of the doubts about Mailloux, the newspaper reports that came out saying it wasn't him after all . . . they went some way to changing minds.'

Another long silence.

'I imagine you helped a little with those too. Talking to reporters. Running your own little private investigation. You do take risks. Is it worth it?'

Straight away, Baptiste answered, 'If I can find out what happened to that girl? For sure. I don't forget. I don't file people away.'

Fatoussi rapped on the desk with his knuckles. 'Very well. *Je touche du bois.* Anything else?'

Backup. He needed that. The DNA idea was a desperate stab in the dark. There was one more loose end worth chasing.

'If you could find out where Martine Augustin's living that might help.'

92

The home of *Les Amis Dans L'Adversité* looked different too. Bright new awnings, a modern porch, spruced-up tennis courts and extended gardens leading down to the river. Anaïs had the plastic bags, the labels, the marker pens and her instructions.

Baptiste nothing but his wits. The routine of the *Amis* he knew already from Fatoussi. They lunched, often heavily, on a meal from the town's finest restaurant, in the club dining room, then retired to the lounge overlooking the tennis courts to smoke, drink more and chat. Étienne Fatoussi had had cause to warn them about getting in their cars afterwards. Dupont might have turned a blind eye to their drunk driving. He wasn't so disposed. So, around five in the afternoon, pre-booked taxis would arrive to take home those unfit or unable to walk. Such was charity still in Clermiers.

It was past two and, from the shelter of the hedge of conifers outside, Baptiste could see the meal had ended, the plates of the last course were being cleared. Fabrice Blanc was there, along with the priest, Chauvin and a man he knew from file photographs to be the reclusive Louis Gaillard, seemingly recovered from his previous frail state judging by his ruddy cheeks and guffawing countenance. A merry lunch, perhaps ten people, the rest strangers, of no interest whatsoever. But there was Philippe Dupont too, now retired. Of all the faces there, he, alone, seemed downright miserable, as if the proceedings were compulsory but bored him deeply.

Baptiste beckoned for Anaïs to join him.

'Four only,' Baptiste whispered, pointing them out. 'The mayor, Dupont, Gaillard and the priest. You know them? You can see where they're sitting?'

She checked out the dining room then peered at him as if he was mad. 'Of course I know them. How big do you think Clermiers is?'

'The rest you can ignore.'

'You think one of them . . . that girl who disappeared?'

'Maybe.'

'There was the dead man too. Laurent. I remember him when I was growing up. He was rich. Not a lot of that round here. The kid's father shot him. Must have been a reason for that.'

Not now, thought Baptiste. 'As you said . . . he's dead. Just those four. I'll distract them in the lounge. You won't be disturbed.'

She took out a pair of latex forensic gloves supplied by Carl Fournier. 'Maybe they'll think I'm the cleaner.'

'I don't want them to know you're there. Be quick, get out and meet me back at the station. You understand what I need?'

Anaïs saluted. 'Yes, sir.'

The *Amis* were getting up from their chairs and shuffling into the adjoining lounge. It was easy for her to enter the dining room without being seen. Only a door between there and where the men would sit for their smoke and to eye four young women playing doubles on the nearest court.

'Me first,' said Baptiste.

He marched through the dining room and closed the connecting door behind him. The lounge was full of smoke and the smell of drink, the murmur of idle, alcohol-fuelled male chatter. A couple of men he didn't recognise were close up to the window, ogling the women on the court.

It didn't take long for the *Amis* to fall silent. Finally, Dupont swore, a furious look on his face, and snapped, 'What in god's name are you doing here?'

'Passing through. Thought I'd pay my respects.'

He took a seat, lit a cigarette, peered out of the window at the tennis players.

Fabrice Blanc looked angry too. Gaillard, maybe the drunkest of them all, baffled. Like the priest Chauvin, still in the same black suit Baptiste remembered.

Dupont pointed at the door. 'You've passed through. Now fuck off.'

Baptiste threw back his head and laughed, loud, theatrically. 'I thought this was a charity. Hardly sounds like it.'

'We're a private organisation,' Blanc said. 'You're not invited. You're not welcome.'

'Noémie Augustin is dead.'

He left it at that.

'I don't understand . . .' Gaillard mumbled.

'Noémie Augustin is dead,' Baptiste repeated. 'That's what Gilles Mailloux said after we thought he'd shot Fatoussi. Which I foolishly took as a confession.'

Dupont looked ready to explode. 'What is this? He had her clothes. He behaved like an idiot in court. Didn't plead. Didn't talk to lawyers. Didn't show the least respect—'

'All the same, he didn't kill her. Someone here did. Someone in this room. After she stormed out of your grubby little party in the chapel of the Château de Mortery.'

Dupont groaned. 'You're a sad obsessive.'

'If this world had a heart, I would reach through its ribs and tear the bloody thing to shreds. I wondered what Mailloux meant by that. Why he said it in court that way. It took me a while. The world, his world, was Clermiers. Mailloux was talking . . .' Baptiste waved his hand around the room. '. . . about you. He was hoping that one day I'd find out what really happened to that girl. Point the finger at someone here.'

A lithe figure in a blue dress dashed down the path by the side of the tennis courts. Anaïs, holding a supermarket carrier bag.

'Point it then,' Blanc said. 'Or get out. You're ruining a perfectly innocent, sociable afternoon.'

He scanned the faces, saw nothing that helped. Guilt was only visible with individuals who felt themselves culpable. The lounge of *Les Amis Dans L'Adversité* appeared to be home to men who thought themselves above those to whom they offered a *soupçon* of charity. This was their world. Gilles Mailloux's mistake – a fatal one, perhaps – was to believe it had a heart to tear out in the first place.

Baptiste got to his feet.

'Noémie Augustin may be dead, gentlemen. But let me assure you . . . she is not yet buried.'

*

Twenty minutes later he was back in Fatoussi's office. Anaïs had laid out her treasure trove on the desk. Four plastic bags with smeared glasses, each with a name. A further four containing napkins, labelled again.

Fatoussi puffed out his cheeks. 'You're seriously telling me this could put someone away for rape and murder?'

'In theory.'

'The theory being . . .?' Anaïs asked.

'The theory being there's a scrap of something physical here that some clever people in Paris can match with the stains on Noémie's clothes. Like a kind of invisible, unique fingerprint.'

'You don't sound very confident,' she added.

'I'm doing my best. Étienne?'

'Yes?'

'Martine Augustin. If she still uses that name—'

Fatoussi sighed. 'I'm sorry. If I had more time . . .'

'She never made contact with Millot after her husband killed himself?'

He shook his head. 'She didn't even go to the funeral. The council had to pick up the bill.'

'Les Amis?'

'Maybe.' He pulled out a notepad. 'All I could find is this.' An address for a hotel restaurant on the coast, Le Touquet. 'She has, or had, a sister. Married to the owner of this place. Annette.' He pushed the phone across the desk. 'If you want to call . . .'

'Sure . . .'

Baptiste did, but just to book a room and a meal for the night.

Fatoussi looked disappointed. 'I thought you'd stay with us. Bernadette was hoping to see you.'

Anaïs patted Baptiste on the shoulder. 'Your friend's a man with a mission. I don't think he's going to rest till he's done.'

93

Two hours it took to get to the coast. Two hours in which Baptiste tried to still the growing sense he was headed nowhere. Four dirty glasses, four napkins, all in plastic bags with labels. It was hard to believe he might have the makings of a successful murder conviction with that.

Though Le Touquet dubbed itself 'Paris Plage', he'd never set foot on the stretch of northern shoreline known as the Côte d'Opale. All he knew was that it attracted a certain type of upper middle-class tourist, from Paris, from England too. There were ornate art deco villas in the wood as he approached. Then the road opened out to a flat, golden beach where sunbathers were catching the last of the day's warmth. Au Bord de La Mer was a wood and brick Gothic building on the edge of town. Fifteen rooms, the woman on reception said, and he'd have to make do with the single because every larger one was booked. Lucky to find a vacancy, and lucky too to get the last table for dinner.

She was middle-aged, serious, and perhaps stirred memories of Martine Augustin. Then the porter addressed her as 'Annette' and Baptiste was sure. This was the right place, this the right woman.

At six, he called Fatoussi to make sure a car had arrived from Paris to pick up the material Anaïs had collected. Then he phoned Carl Fournier in Paris to tell him the goods were on the way.

'I know, Julien. I checked too. Enjoy your holiday. Relax. When I have news, you'll be the first to know.'

Baptiste could hear voices behind him. 'You're in the office.'

'I prefer to call it a lab. Yes. We like to work nights. It means we don't get disturbed by nagging policemen. Now if you'll excuse me . . .'

At seven thirty, he sat down for a long and excellent dinner of *soupe de poissons, choucroute de la mer* and *tarte tatin*, one bottle of Muscadet, a cigarette between each course, before and after too. Then, spirits sinking, a glass of *marc*.

The hunt for Noémie Augustin seemed a folly at that moment. An obsession as both Dupont and his mother had said. Four glasses, four napkins, and now the faintest of hopes that a woman he'd never spoken to before might spill some family secrets to a stranger, a police officer on a private mission, no authority to wield, no right to be told anything at all.

The woman called Annette was behind the bar when he retired there, the only customer she had. Baptiste got a look he recognised when he ordered another *marc*: one more, *c'est tout*.

She brought it over to his table by the window looking out onto a beach now deserted, shining silver under the summer moon.

'One night isn't much for Le Touquet. So much to do here. The sea. Golf. Do you play golf, *monsieur*?'

'No. I don't.'

'What do you play?'

'Nothing. Unless you count chasing phantoms.'

She harrumphed, got herself a small glass of neat Lillet then came back and took the chair across the table.

'That's a strange answer, I must say. Is everything all right?'

'It's kind of you to ask.'

She shrugged. 'Not really. You look . . . gloomy. Dissatisfied. The food—'

'The food was excellent, madame.' *Say it*, Baptiste thought. *Now or never*. 'My problem is eleven years ago I was briefly a police officer in a place called Clermiers. Noémie Augustin, a young girl, a stranger there, went missing. Presumed assaulted. Murdered. I caught a man I thought responsible. I believe now I made a mistake. What happened to Noémie is still a mystery. While her mother, Martine, your sister, has vanished.'

She swore, cast him a vicious look and he thought he saw the start of tears in her eyes. 'Police. What use were you back when my niece disappeared?'

'Very little. I'm trying to make amends.'

'Martine told me you never even tried.'

'Oh, we tried. Not the locals, true. But I did. My colleague nearly lost his life as a result. But we failed. I don't like failing. I hate mysteries. If you tell me where I can find Martine, perhaps she knows something that might help.'

'Noémie's dead somewhere. What help do you have to offer there?'

The booze had got to him. The cigarettes too. His head felt wrong, his voice was failing.

'You drink too much,' she said. 'You smoke like a chimney. You sit here like a sorry creature asking questions that break my heart.'

'All I want to do is to talk.'

'There's nothing to say. Martine stayed here briefly during those dreadful times. Then . . .' A moment of hesitation, one Baptiste might have been able to interpret if only it wasn't for the booze. 'Then we were back to the way we were as children. We never got along that well. After Noémie . . . she wouldn't talk to me. Not properly. She left. I haven't heard from her in years.'

'Left for where?'

A moment then she finished her drink. 'Who knows?' With a sweep of her hand, she cleared away the glasses, Baptiste's still half-full. 'Will you be leaving first thing in the morning? I think that would be wise.'

94

At quarter past six, while he was dosing his hangover and the remnants of another nightmare with aspirin and a cigarette, Fournier called.

'That was fast, Carl.'

'Remember what I told you.'

'Quick bad. Long good.'

296

'Precisely. There's nothing usable on these samples you sent us. Nothing sufficient for us to process. God knows we tried. If you could get me blood . . .'

'I can't. You think they'd volunteer?'

'Then I'm sorry. You're on your own.'

Bags packed by seven, he went down to reception. Martine Augustin's sister was there behind the counter, tapping away at a typewriter.

'Your bill's prepared,' she said without looking up.

An expensive night, but at least the food had been good. He rolled out some notes and a decent tip.

'I apologise if I offended you, madame.'

'You're police. You're never sorry about anything.'

That prickled. 'You're wrong there. I did my best. I'm still trying. They might fire me if they find out.'

'What?'

There was no reason why he shouldn't say it. 'This is just me. Without authority. Just one man. Tilting at windmills it seems.'

She got up and came to the counter. 'Are you sure you're all right?'

'Not exactly. A man went to the guillotine because of me. I never found out what happened to your niece. It nags. It . . . haunts . . .'

'You should get help. Obsessing about dead strangers is not healthy for a man.'

'I'm not concerned about my health. Did she . . . did Martine really give no hint where she might be headed?'

'No. She just went. I never heard from her again. Clermiers didn't just take poor Noémie. That sorry father of hers. It stole my sister too.' She scooped the money off the counter and said nothing about the tip. 'I'm sorry I couldn't do more when I thought she needed it.' He got a hard look. 'That's the problem with people in trouble. Half the time they're so consumed by their own misery they don't know they need help at all.'

'I must use your pay phone, if I may, and then I'll be gone.'

Science, he thought. Fine as far as it went, which wasn't far enough. Still, as he'd told the woman, he wasn't at that moment a police officer on duty. Just an individual, a lone hunter pursuing a mirage.

Time to resort to bluster and lies.

His old friend listened then went quiet.

'Étienne . . .?'

'You're sure about this?' Fatoussi sounded distinctly dubious. 'You could lose your job. Maybe they'll be telling me to charge you with something . . . I don't know.'

'Let the blame come my way. I'll take the fall. I'll deserve it.'

'And what career would Julien Baptiste contemplate next? You're a detective. I can't imagine you as anything else.'

Nor could Baptiste. 'Please. . . make those calls.'

95

Two hours later Baptiste was back in Clermiers. He drove past the Gaillard place where a sour-faced Alice was clipping a privet hedge, a cigarette to her lips. Past Dupont's small bungalow on the edge of town. Past the Mairie where Fabrice Blanc could be seen through the window, talking to someone at his desk.

Then to the priest's house. He was on the porch, taking a tray of eggs from a woman in a farming boiler suit. Baptiste waited for that encounter to finish then, as Chauvin was closing the door, walked up the path and faced the astonished priest.

'You've got a nerve.'

'Goes with the job,' said Baptiste then, uninvited, strode inside, straight to the study, where he waited, scanning the shelves of books.

The priest took the chair by the window. 'But this is not your job, Baptiste. Not for much longer. Your old colleague ratted on you. He told us about the idiotic game you played.

298

Your superiors won't look kindly on such a stupid escapade. You're screwed. There'll be consequences.'

'Consequences, Father, are exactly what I seek. And confession too.'

'Confessions are for the Église Saint-Vivien. Not my home.'

'I meant your confession. Not mine.'

The priest glared at him, a mix of fear and fury in his face. 'What nonsense is this? You fraud. We've heard it all. Lying to a junior officer, telling her it was her duty to stay silent because you were on some secret mission from Paris. Not a vendetta that was purely personal. Breaking into private premises. Stealing items from a charitable institution.'

'The door was open. Dirty glasses and napkins. Hardly burglary. As for the charity . . .'

'I told you,' Chauvin spat back. 'Dupont has connections. He'll have your head.'

'An unfortunate turn of phrase in the circumstances. Now if you could tell me what you did with Noémie Augustin . . .'

There was a sudden rush of heat to the man's cheeks. 'What? *What?* Why on earth do you think I had anything to do with that girl?'

This was a stab in the dark. The idea that one of them would relax, might even boast, if they knew the risky venture with the forensic people in Paris had failed, that Baptiste had placed his career on the line and now might be about to lose it.

'I didn't. I was going to approach each of you in turn. Then, when I came to think about it, you were bound to be first. I know the story now. I have it . . .' He raised a finger by his cheek. '. . . all assembled. In here.'

Chauvin gasped. 'This is madness. A story? What story?'

'Four men in the Chapelle de Mortery for a private, salacious performance. Three regulars. One guest. A man who came with them, with Bruno Laurent, not by himself as usual. A local fellow then. You.'

Chauvin snorted. 'You should take up writing fiction,

Baptiste. Fantasy. It seems more suited to your peculiar talents than police work.'

'There's fiction in this too. And fantasy. *Les 120 Journées de Sodome ou l'école du libertinage*. De Sade, a one-time resident of the Château de Mortery. Though he wrote that in the Bastille of course . . .'

'I know nothing of such filth.'

The slightest shrug of the shoulders. 'Let me jog your memory. Four debauched men lock themselves away with hired women and innocents, food and drink, and proceed to do whatever it is they wish, regardless of the mores of the world outside.'

'I do not need to hear this—'

'Four men, one a corrupt priest. Four chairs in the chapel of the château. Bruno Laurent's idea of fun, though as his wife told me, that was to watch others since he could no longer partake.'

Chauvin pointed to the door and ordered, 'Just go.'

'The leader was Laurent, of course. Two regular attendees. Louis Gaillard, which is why he ran to Amsterdam then hid in a sanatorium afterwards. The third, I feel sure, was your mayor, Fabrice Blanc. Those three were thick as thieves. I choose my words with care.'

The priest waved away the idea with a low curse.

'And the honoured guest?' Baptiste continued. 'I thought . . . I stupidly thought the fourth must be Dupont. But no. He hates you all, he holds you in the utmost contempt. I realised that yesterday with the *Amis*. Dupont's pleasure lies in taunting you, letting you all know how much you need him, and how little he cares in return. He wasn't the fourth man. You were.'

Chauvin went quiet for a moment and laughed. 'But this game you played . . . these tricks, getting Fatoussi's girl to steal our things . . . what did they tell you?'

'Nothing. The magic didn't work. There was no rabbit in the hat.'

'Quite . . .'

Baptiste sighed, got up, walked to the bookcase and pulled out an old leather volume. The life of an obscure Catholic saint with a praying figure, haloed, on the cover. 'You're a literate fellow. When I was here before, while you were out of the room, I took the liberty to investigate your tastes.' He retrieved an old-fashioned bookmark from the pages. 'An avid reader always leaves one of these in a title he likes to read more than once.' He slipped off what was nothing more than a cover to reveal a different, smaller volume tucked inside. 'As you know, this is not a religious title at all.'

For the priest's benefit, he flicked through the pages, show-ing him. It was De Sade's notorious work, an old and cheap edition, well-thumbed. With salacious illustrations.

'Had Gilles Mailloux not put his neck on the block that night I would have pursued this further. But then . . .' The memory still burned. 'We believed we had our murderer. There seemed no point. Just a churchman with a dirty book, a dirty mind to boot. Hardly news.'

Chauvin hesitated for a moment. Baptiste followed the shifting emotions on his face, from fear to anger and finally amusement.

'Yes. A book.' He smiled. 'Nothing more. Words on a page and a few risqué drawings. Oh, Baptiste! What a fool you are. To waste your time, to destroy your career, on such a pointless pursuit, no prize at the end, only shame. A book. You think that counts as proof?'

'Not at all.' He took the chair opposite. 'You're right. I failed. You win. You escape. I simply . . . wanted to know. The doubt, you see, it haunts a man. As does the guilt I imagine . . .'

'Don't treat me like an imbecile!' Chauvin bellowed. 'I have enough of that from them. Time and time again. Look at this pathetic old bachelor and laugh. A virgin by choice. No love. No pleasure in his existence. I'm here to service their births and deaths, to listen to their vile amusements in the confessional.

301

And in return? What? Invited to watch in silence while they feast and fornicate. Just the once. For them to laugh at me.'

'To watch and when the girl, an innocent girl—'

'Innocent? You didn't see her.'

'But I've built my own story, remember? An innocent girl runs in fury and terror after Bruno Laurent demands what he thinks he's owed. Who then to trust when she's outside the chapel, alone, frightened, furious with her own father for what he's done?'

Silence.

'Who else but a priest? Inside the chapel you wore a mask. She never knew you were there. Now you're a man of the church, wandering by the river. Someone who might help her. If only . . .'

Chauvin raised a single finger to object. 'Do not dare to judge me.'

'She fought. The blood . . .'

'One time I fall! One time only I'm tempted.'

Baptiste nodded, waited.

'What is it?' Chauvin demanded.

'The time you fell you remembered to take a condom with you. You knew what you were doing. You came prepared.'

'The girl was . . . was . . .'

He stopped. There was sweat on his pale brow, a mix of guilt and scorn in his face.

'A young woman of no importance?' asked Baptiste. 'An outsider? Different? Of no use at all except when you desired her?'

'All men have weaknesses. All of us sin . . .'

'You let Mailloux go to the guillotine for your crime—'

'No!' He was out of his chair, furious, spitting as he spoke. 'That's a lie! The girl was alive! Staggering up the path to the garage. Alive . . . I swear. Blanc stormed out of the chapel when she refused to do what she was paid for. But Laurent found us down there. Gaillard too. They saw.'

He touched the crucifix around his neck. 'What I did was

wrong, but that monster Mailloux was of a different order. He murdered her. Not me. Now . . .' With two hands, he pushed Baptiste towards the door. 'Leave. You said yourself your trick has failed. What's passed between us here is of no consequence. I'll deny every word, and since Dupont is laying an official complaint about your outrageous behaviour, I will be believed. A priest against a failed, dishonest *flic*. No contest.'

Baptiste shuffled the book back into the fake cover then placed it on the crowded shelves. 'Perhaps the contest is in your head. Your conscience if you can find it. The fact the only man you've confessed to is a failed, dishonest *flic*.'

'And God.'

'God?' Baptiste roared, shaking a fist in the priest's face. 'Where was your god for Noémie Augustin? For Gilles Mailloux when they severed his head from his body?'

The priest retreated, shaken by the force of the outburst. 'One last time . . . get out.'

Baptiste strode across the room, came with an inch of his face. 'On the day he died, Mailloux said to me . . . the blade must always fall. It's in the nature of both gravity and these insignificant lives we lead. I thought he was talking of himself. But no. It was about Clermiers. Men like you. Rotten to the core and thinking yourselves impregnable, all-powerful, lords of your putrid little paradise. The blade will fall. The truth will out. One day a different piece of science will come along. Or a young girl who survived your clutches will find the courage to speak your name. One day, your heaven will turn to hell. I will watch. I will wait. One day I will see . . .'

'She vanished up the hill,' Chauvin cried, his voice close to falsetto. 'The monster you seek is the one you sent to the guillotine. I followed her. In spite of Laurent's objections, I wanted to make amends. Then I heard them talking. Mailloux and her. Someone else . . .' He shook his head, trying to remember something. 'An English voice maybe, but the girl kept screaming and screaming. About her father more than anything. Hysterical.

Laurent and Gaillard saw. Gaillard could speak for me. He's still alive. They were terrified, for themselves naturally.' He groaned. 'What was owed to them was never for the likes of a priest. Hypocrites. Laurent demanded we had to leave by the boathouse, avoid what might be going on up the path. Burn everything. Every record of our meetings. Every photo.'

Chauvin stormed out into the hall, dragged the front door open so forcefully Baptiste could feel the walls tremble. On the step the priest glared at him. 'A man should know when he has lost, Baptiste.'

'A man should know when he is lost, Father. One time, you say, you fell . . .?'

'One time, Baptiste! Years ago. Is there no forgiveness in you?'

'And what of Lili Hubert? The child who sang in your choir. The girl who hung herself from a tree in the Bois de Mortery, still in the white robe, the scarlet collar of the Église Saint-Vivien? Stayed there rotting for fourteen months until Charles Augustin's dog found her?' He grabbed Chauvin by the neck and pushed him hard against the wall. 'Did your condom come from her pathetic little purse? What of all the other girls who've suffered? The ones who still live? Who one day will find the courage to tell their tales?'

The look on Christian Chauvin's face was that of fear and horror. 'You're a madman. Go back to Paris. See if you can save yourself when Dupont strikes.' He nodded at the street. 'There's nothing for the likes of you in Clermiers now.'

96

An English voice.

He'd thought to pack his passport, used just once for an expensive and unsatisfactory weekend in London with Martha, a break that only hastened the end of their brief and somewhat histrionic affair. Four and a half hours after confronting Christian Chauvin in Clermiers, he was showing it to immigration in Dover at the end of a queasy journey on a hovercraft called *The Princess Margaret* he'd just managed to catch in Calais. It was nearly five local time. After the last-minute ferry fare, he had fifteen hundred francs in cash, no idea where he might stay, what in truth he might do. Just a small piece of paper, the business card Celia Murray had given him eleven years before, an address in Folkestone, a phone number, the name of a company, Bouverie Camping. And a question that he thought might never leave him . . . If Christian Chauvin was telling the truth and he left Noémie alive after assaulting her, what happened when she walked up the path to Gilles Mailloux's garage?

There was an exchange booth in the ferry terminal. Four hundred francs got him just over £40. Then he brandished the business card.

The woman behind the counter smiled. 'Blimey, that's old, isn't it?'

'I was hoping to talk to someone who worked there.'

'Not Bouverie Camping any more. It's Bouverie Travel. Got quite big. All sorts of businesses. Lovely family, the Murrays. Very close. Big in Folkestone. Not Dover.'

'This address . . .'

She took the card then checked the phone directory. 'Don't know that at all. They've got an office down by the beach now. Past the Burstin. Marine Parade, near the Rotunda.'

'The Rotunda?'

'It's a fairground on the sands. Bit cheesy but . . .' The woman picked up a free tourist map and ringed the place then passed it over. 'Fresh doughnuts.'

'Sorry?'

'There's a stall that does fresh doughnuts, makes them in front of you. Lovely, they are. Well, for us Brits. What you lot are going to make of them . . .'

It was thirty minutes on the winding road that ran along the chalk cliffs, Baptiste struggling to adapt to driving on the left. He wasn't certain he was insured any more. How far the money might go. Whether he even had enough for the return fare.

Folkestone seemed a warren of streets, steep hills, confusing signs. Until finally he saw one that pointed to the harbour, rounded an odd hotel called the Burstin, and found himself driving past a fairground, a rollercoaster, dodgems and stalls, families wandering among them with ice creams, buckets and spades, going home as the afternoon drew to a close. The smell of hot fat wafted through the open window. The doughnut stall the woman had talked about. Then the road came to an end close to a funicular railway running up what was more hill than cliff.

Ahead was what looked like a small Victorian hotel converted into offices, a sign outside that read, 'Bouverie Travel Ltd'.

Baptiste stopped on the double yellow line, killed the engine and tried once more to think what he might say, whether it would be better aimed at Daniel Murray or his sister.

Or he could give up this strange, seemingly doomed quest, turn the car round, go back to Dover, try to get on a ferry across the flat grey waters of *La Manche* and hope once more to bury Noémie Augustin in his head for good. If Chauvin was right and Dupont was going to kick up a stink with his superiors in Paris, he'd be headed for dismissal in any case. A private citizen, no access to people like Carl Fournier, no right to ask questions of anyone at all.

He was about to start the car when he saw them emerging from the Bouverie Travel building, walking to the footpath by the funfair. Just one more couple among many on the beach that afternoon. A man, a woman, clearly pregnant, a young boy by their side holding the lead of a fat and elderly terrier waddling along, trying to keep up.

Daniel Murray looked heavier, with less hair, but unmistakable. The woman with him was just as tall but slender, beautiful, black and elegant, walking with the practised, precise gait of a dancer even with one hand on a bulging stomach.

Baptiste's fingers fell from the key as he stared at them through the windscreen. They looked so happy, the perfect family, the woman's free hand entwined with that of her husband, the little boy chattering as he walked with the ageing dog.

Just as he was about to climb out of the car, the passenger door opened, and someone fell into the seat beside him.

'Well, well,' said Celia Murray, 'if it isn't you.'

Every question he'd wanted to ask vanished from his head.

'Drive, Baptiste,' she ordered. 'Start the car now and get us out of here before I scream the place down.'

He glanced at the busy fairground, the rides, the coconut shy, the stalls, the arcades, people everywhere, young and old.

'No one would notice.'

'You haven't heard me scream. Turn this car round and drive.'

97

'Do you usually look this dishevelled?'

They were the only customers in the garden of a rural pub on the edge of dead flat farmland that seemed to stretch all the way to a blue-grey line of water on the horizon. Romney Marsh, she said. Roses were starting to bloom all around them, their fragrance drifting over air that bore the scent of countryside and the briny tang of the nearby sea. Gulls squawked overhead. A pint of warm flat beer sat in front of Baptiste, a glass of white wine for Celia Murray.

'I don't recall you being a snappy dresser back then. But . . .' She flapped a hand at him. 'You look terrible.'

Le Touquet. The encounter with Chauvin in Clermiers. Then a race to Dover and the uncomfortable, bone-shaking first experience of a hovercraft. 'It's been a long day.'

'No wife then?'

That took him aback. 'What makes you say a thing like that?'

'Sticks out a mile. No matter. Marriage isn't all it's cracked up to be. At least it wasn't for me the brief time I attempted it.' She sipped her wine. 'Eleven years and still you're looking. Talk about obsessive . . .'

He wondered how many times he was going to say it. 'I watched an innocent man go to the guillotine. I sent him there thinking Noémie Augustin was dead.'

'Gilles told you so, didn't he?'

That was in all the papers. No secret.

'Yes.'

'Because she is. She's Jo now.' A smile. 'Jo Boulanger. She chose the name herself. Josephine Baker, you see. Well . . . actually she's Jo Murray. Possessor of a British passport after quite a struggle with the Home Office and a few lies they never cottoned on to thank god. Married to my darling brother Dan. Little boy just turned four. Another baby on the way.' Her smile vanished. 'The little boy is called Giles. And here you are, ready to tear it all to shreds.'

'I just wanted—'

'To know. To find her. Well, you have. I suppose you feel you're owed an explanation.'

'That would be welcome.'

'Fine.'

She told the story in a flat, articulate monotone, like a reluctant witness in a tedious court case. The night it happened, she'd been about to go to sleep in the camper van by the garage, drowsy with wine after her brother left, when she heard voices outside. Mailloux was there with the distraught Noémie, shrieking, crying, cursing her father, though why they weren't sure.

'We got her into the van. Tried to calm her down. It was obvious what had gone on. The state of her. The dress. The blood. I don't need to spell it out.'

Baptiste raised a finger and was about to speak.

'Before you say a word, can I just say if you tell me we should have gone to the police I will scream for real and for a very long time.'

'I wasn't about to suggest any such thing.'

'Good. May I continue?'

Noémie was incoherent, barely able to speak rationally. It was only because Mailloux recognised her that they had a name at all. When he suggested they take her home, she turned quite hysterical.

'Her father, you see. In Noémie's eyes, he'd kind of pimped her. Sent her to a bunch of old men she barely recognised who expected . . . well, you know.'

'I might have been able to do something.'

'No, Julien. You're a decent man. Gilles assured me of that. But you're a man all the same, congenitally incapable of understanding what it's like for a woman, for a young girl particularly, when something like this happens. You think of the physical harm, the blood, the damage, the assault. All that's terrible, but what's just as bad, sometimes worse . . .' She pointed to her wayward fair hair. '. . . is up here. Bruises fade, cuts heal. The mind works differently. It preserves those memories and, unless you're careful, amplifies them over the years.'

He closed his eyes, rolled back on the hard garden chair, wanting so much to sleep. 'Trust me. I may be a man, but I appreciate that.'

'I hope so. I found her some of my clothes. Got her cleaned up a bit. It seemed obvious what we had to do. She was screaming she wanted out of there. We thought we might find her time to recover.' She winced. 'Stupid really. If they'd caught us at Dover god knows what would have happened. But we weren't thinking. We just thought it best to get her as far from Clermiers as we could.'

'You might have told her mother.'

Silence. Then she said, 'I'm hungry. Would you like fish and chips? It's very good here. Fresh cod from the Channel just over there.'

'*La Manche.*'

'*Oui. La Manche.* Do you want some or not?'

She vanished inside when he said yes and came back with a tray and a bottle of Muscadet Sur Lie.

'I said . . . you could have told her mother.'

'I brought malt vinegar. We sprinkle it on chips.'

Nothing more.

Baptiste blinked and swore in a whisper. 'Martine . . . she knew.'

'A lovely woman. She works for the company now, admin, very capable. Got a house of her own just down the road from Dan and Jo. Babysits and does something for Jo's dance studio too. Did I mention that?'

'Dancing? No.' His mind was racing back to that strange, convoluted July week eleven years before. 'You returned. The same day you left.'

'Correct.'

'You told Martine. Which is why she decided to leave her husband.'

'She needed to know her daughter was somewhere safe.'

'Then Augustin shot Bruno Laurent and killed himself.'

She groaned, squeezed her eyes tight shut for a moment. Celia Murray was just as striking as he recalled. An intriguing, sly woman who was, to some extent, playing with him.

'That was a nightmare. It was just when Noémie was starting to emerge from her shell. Back in she went. We paid for a private retreat where she could get professional help. Took months. Martine came over in . . . October, I think. Never went back.'

'I found her sister. She has a hotel in Le Touquet. I was there last night. She said they'd never got along. Martine stayed there for a while then disappeared.'

The smile again, so warm he felt it was in part for him. 'Annette? She and her husband keep a little plane. Sometimes they hop across the Channel from Le Touquet to Lydd, a few miles from here. They stay with us. I stay with them.'

Baptiste closed his eyes and murmured a mild but amused curse.

She poured two glasses of wine. 'Annette was doing what she thought was right. We all were. She phoned and told me you'd turned up out of the blue, asking awkward questions, looking sorry for yourself but very determined. You don't think I make a habit of hanging round Folkestone seafront, do you?'

A young woman emerged from the pub carrying plates. 'Oh, look! There's grub.'

He was ravenous.

She pinged a fingernail on his pint glass. It was hardly touched. 'English beer's a bit of an issue it seems, but I'm glad you like fish and chips. Now where are you going to stay? You can't possibly go back to France. You look shattered.'

He took out his wallet. 'I've only got £40 in English money. Is that enough? Normally I only travel in Europe.'

'England is Europe.'

'Are you sure of that?'

'Very. They're digging a bloody great hole in the cliffs just along from here. Starts in Folkestone. Ends in Calais. Called the Channel Tunnel. No problem. You can stay here.'

'How much will they ask?'

'Nothing.'

'But—'

She slapped her hands on the table. 'Julien! Listen to me! This place is part of the family business. My part. That cottage by the garage?' A small building, perhaps converted from a barn. 'That's where I live. These rose beds?' It was impossible to miss them. 'They're one of my little hobbies. Floribunda. Hybrid Tea. Some very old Grandiflora.' She pointed out a bush nearby, already in flower. Beautiful blooms, yellow with pink tinges to the edges of the petals. 'That one's called "Peace". The creation of a French horticulturist between the wars. Got its name the day Berlin fell. Peace. I find it here. Do you enjoy gardening?'

'I live in an apartment. In Paris.'

'Oh well. Pudding? Cheese and biscuits?'

'I'd rather hear why Gilles Mailloux was so desperate to go to the guillotine.'

A moment, then she said, 'All in due course. I'm going inside to sort your room.'

With that Celia Murray was gone, leaving Baptiste to stew for a good fifteen minutes, enjoying the quiet garden, admiring the splendid rose beds which seemed very professionally laid out. She returned with a key and a plate of stilton, cheddar and crackers.

'Stay as long as you like.' There was a yellow concoction on the plate too. 'That's piccalilli. We make it ourselves. The place is quiet at the moment. School holidays haven't started. You're very welcome.'

Baptiste tried a forkful of the yellow stuff and shuddered.

'Piccalilli requires patience like most anything worthwhile. Gilles was dying.'

'I know. His mother told me.'

'Less than a year left. It wasn't going to be easy. She'd have to give up work to look after him. No idea where the money would come from.'

'Gilles told you all this? The night you came back?'

She groaned. 'The second time I burst into tears in a day. I didn't understand quite what he had in mind. Not till later. But then I'm not sure he did at the time.'

'Collette Mailloux passed on a letter he'd written, for me to read after the execution. There was some poetry. Baudelaire. No real information. No name for who really attacked her. Just that I should look more closely at the *Amis*, demonstrate how wicked, how unjust, the guillotine was.'

'May I see it?'

He shook his head. 'Dupont, the captain then in Clermiers, burned it in front of my eyes. No one in Paris would let me reopen the case. If Gilles had given me a name . . .'

'He couldn't. None of us knew who attacked her.'

'You never asked?'

Celia Murray raised her clenched fists in exasperation. 'Your capacity to make me want to scream is quite remarkable. Of course not! That's why men are so useless in situations like this. Unless it's someone like Gilles Mailloux. But then he was different. Very.'

'The man who raped her—'

'We were trying to help Noémie heal. That was what mattered. Nothing else. Trust me, it wasn't easy. She never mentioned a name. Mostly if she talked, it was about her father. How she couldn't believe what he'd done.'

Baptiste remembered Augustin's sad and anxious face. So much was starting to make sense. 'There was something Laurent's wife said. About how Charles yelled at her husband . . . she was only there to dance. That was all. Maybe he really believed that. Or wanted to.'

'Men can be terribly naive at times. When it suits them.'

'I think he paid the price.'

She pulled at her hair, curly, a little unruly, the colour of the dried-up wheat he remembered from those fields around Clermiers that fateful summer. 'Agreed. The last thing Noémie needed was to be dragged into an interview room and inter- rogated by detectives who hadn't the faintest idea of what she went through. Then put in the witness box in court and asked to relive it all again. She was a wreck. We had to watch her day and night to make sure she didn't harm herself. To hell with

313

justice . . . we wanted her better. Starting with getting Martine here, the only piece of family she had left. As to the bastard who started all this—'

'It was the priest. Chauvin. He admitted it when I tackled him this morning. Only because he thought there was nothing I could do.'

There was a sudden flash of anger in her face. 'I didn't want to know that. I wish you'd never told me.'

'I said. Gilles left me that letter. He wanted me to look again.'

She hesitated for a long moment. 'Look . . . Gilles was dying, trapped in a game that got out of hand. As far as I can work out, he was lost, confused. Trying to make things right in his own way, the best he could. Eleven years on you're still playing his game. How many other *flics* are on the case?'

He grimaced then explained the sequence of events, the attempt to steal DNA samples, how Paris had rejected them as unusable. 'It's just me, on my holidays. I'll probably get fired when I get back. Not supposed to do this kind of thing. Chasing a phantom. Except it turns out it's that of Gilles Mailloux, not Noémie at all.'

'You told them you'd screwed up? All these people you suspected? For pity's sake . . . why?'

He wished he could say he'd thought it through. In truth it was a decision made in an instant, on impulse. 'It was the last card in my hand. All I had left. They think themselves invincible. Above the herd. Above everyone. Sometimes people like that, when you tell them they're untouchable, can't help but gloat. To let you know you were right and there's nothing you can do about it anyway.'

'And now you're going to lose your job!'

'I owed it to Gilles. And to Noémie, or so I thought. And myself. To quieten a ghost that's been haunting me for a decade or more.'

'Oh, Julien.' She reached across the table and held his hands for one short, warm moment. 'I talked to him again, just once.

On the phone. After they found that poor girl in the woods. After Charles Augustin died. He was going to pieces. All he wanted was to allow Noémie to start a new life of her own. Then he decided to give up his own, in a way he thought worthwhile. Like a martyr, I suppose. I tried to talk him out of it, but I think he felt responsible. For Augustin. For your friend too, for all I know. For not doing anything to stop what was going on. He was beyond logic. Beyond argument.' She winced. 'Not that I had any good ones if I'm honest. There were no easy answers. No ways ahead that wouldn't cause someone pain.'

That last night was still clear in Baptiste's head. Fatoussi storming away from the police house, determined to see inside Mailloux's locked room. 'Gilles left me reasons enough to be suspicious. I didn't take any notice. I liked him. I couldn't believe he'd do such a thing.'

'You were right.'

'But there were those clothes, the blood, what sounded like a confession. The missing money . . .'

'It wasn't missing. He gave it to Noémie.'

'The performance in court was so . . . . odd. So damning.'

'It was exactly that. A performance. His swan song.'

He wondered whether he dared say it. 'You could have saved him.'

That got him a filthy look. 'You're not listening. He didn't want to be saved. He didn't want to be condemned to a different kind of death. One he dreaded more. One that, in his eyes, would have achieved nothing and put his mother through an even greater hell. Not to speak of what it would have done to Noémie. Do you think any of this was easy?'

There were tears in her eyes. He felt bad for putting them there.

'I'm a police officer. I'm trained to think in straight lines.'

'Life's never composed of straight lines. They go all over the place, in directions you can never guess or control. Gilles must have held out some forlorn hope you'd tear Clermiers to pieces after he was gone. He hated that town. The people who ran it. The way they treated everyone they regarded as their inferiors, deserving of nothing. I imagine he wanted to make the judiciary feel guilty for killing an innocent man too. He thought it through. He was very organised that way. Though I imagine he hoped you'd be allowed to reopen matters rather more quickly than you managed.'

He poured her more wine, a little for himself. 'I have a name now. Christian Chauvin. If Noémie could face him in court . . .'

Celia Murray did shriek then. 'Oh god! I told you. She's called Jo. She came here illegally. Got married. A son. Another child on the way. She's happy. Settled. You want to take all that away? And for what?'

'Justice. To put the man who raped her in jail.'

'Or is that vengeance? Your way of getting back all the years you've spent with Gilles Mailloux's ghost inside your head? He was one of the bravest, smartest, saddest men I've ever met. But you tell me. If he was here now and we could ask him . . . what do you think he'd say?'

Baptiste smiled and looked at her plate. 'I think he'd wonder why you haven't touched your cheese.'

Celia Murray took out a tissue and dabbed at her eyes.

'There's something I need to show you,' he said and went to the car.

It was at the bottom of his suitcase. A young girl's secret thoughts. Stories about a dead dancer she idolised. A tennis player now retired. Adolescent dreams she would never begin to realise.

Celia read it wiping away more tears, which simply made Baptiste feel guilty twice over.

'I'm sorry,' he said when she finished and placed the notebook on the table next to the empty wine bottle. 'I shouldn't have showed you that. I shouldn't have come here in the first place.'

'Don't be ridiculous,' she replied, wiping her eyes with the sleeve of her shirt. 'People always go on about putting things behind you. Seems to me it makes more sense to accept them, let them be a part of who you are, and after that get on with life all the same.'

She opened the pages again, smiled for a moment at what she saw, then pushed the diary away. 'Gilles told you. That girl's dead.' Celia Murray picked up her wine and looked at him very directly. 'Thank you, by the way. We don't speak about any of this. Haven't for years. We pretend it didn't happen, I guess. But it did and talking helps you let things go somehow. Doesn't it?'

'A little, I guess. Not everything.'

'Cheers.' She chinked her glass against his. 'Everything would be wrong. A shameful kind of amnesia. An injustice in itself. These things make us who we are. And we talked. We enjoyed a few minutes of pleasant catharsis. That's worth a lot. There. We've something in common.' She closed her eyes for a moment, looked more placid, so at home among the roses and quiet of the garden. 'I'm glad you came, Julien. No, delighted. I never thought I'd be saying that when I kidnapped you outside the Rotunda today. Life's sometimes full of strange surprises.'

He laughed. 'I never thought I'd be in a beautiful garden, looking at the end of my career, perfectly content. Noémie Augustin – sorry, I'll always think of her as that – alive.' He hesitated, then said it any way. 'And with . . . with you.'

There was a gleam in her eye at that moment, and it wasn't just the remnants of a tear.

'My goodness, you really are the most unusual Parisian I've ever met. The best part of two hours we've been here and I'm inclined to think you finally made a kind of attempt at a pass.'

That took him aback. 'There is the small matter of context.'

'That doesn't stop your compatriots. I've twice been propositioned at a French funeral.'

'Well . . .' He felt sure he was blushing. 'If I may say yes to your kind offer and stay a few days . . .'

'Do you play golf?'

'Certainly not.'

'Ride?'

'Bicycles?'

'Horses, silly.'

He shook his head.

'How about fishing? I have a small boat. The Channel . . . *La Manche* . . . is full of mackerel right now. We could bring them back here. Smoke them. Barbecue.'

'It won't be rough out there, will it?'

She bent forward, creased with laughter. 'No, M. Baptiste. I'll always try to steer you away from the rough, I promise. You seem to be a man who finds it far too easily for your own good.'

'Then I would like that very much.'

She threw back her head, closed her eyes, murmured the softest sigh of relief. He couldn't take his eyes off her for a second.

'Will they really fire you?'

'If it was up to me . . . like a shot.'

Celia Murray yawned and stretched her arms behind her neck. 'No rush then, is there?'

98

It was Wednesday before he got back to France, driving straight to Clermiers, parking in the town square between the police station and the Mairie. He sat at the wheel for a couple of minutes composing his apologies. There were four officers inside that afternoon, two bickering over who was to use some new speeding gadget just turned up from Douai. To his surprise, Anaïs greeted him with a cheery '*Bonjour!*' and waved him to the captain's office. Étienne Fatoussi was behind the desk, immaculate in his uniform as ever, a fresh bouquet of flowers in the duck nest fireplace.

'Julien!' he cried, bright-eyed. 'You look different.'

'You mean guilty as hell for landing you all in it?'

'No. I mean sharp and smiley. Not . . . not the usual, you know . . . you.'

'Thanks. I think.'

'*De rien.*' He went to the door and asked Anaïs to bring them some coffee. 'News . . .?'

'Anaïs doesn't seem annoyed with me. Any more than you.'

'Why should we be annoyed?'

An odd question. 'Did you forget? I asked her to steal those things for the lab in Paris. Then got you to tell all the *Amis* what I'd done.'

'Ah. White lies to flush them out, you said. And they didn't work. Any more than this magic trick your friends in Paris promised.'

'Sorry. I was desperate.'

A wave of the hand. '*Bof!* Who cares?'

There was something disconcerting about Fatoussi's attitude.

'Dupont cares, for one. I gather he's kicking up a stink. Don't worry. I plan to go and confess everything when I get back to Paris. I'll carry the can. Say it was just me, chasing phantoms with a bunch of lies.'

Fatoussi dismissed that with another *bof*. 'You tried, didn't you? Find anything?'

A shrug. 'Noémie Augustin's dead, I guess. Where? How? I doubt we'll ever know. You can close the case.'

Anaïs brought in the coffee, still smiling, amused too for some reason.

Fatoussi waited till she was gone. 'It's on file anyway. Which is as good as closed. Unless . . .?'

Baptiste took a seat and found he couldn't look him in the

eye. 'If I can't get to the bottom of this after eleven years there's not much chance now, is there?'

'A wild goose chase then?'

'Without so much as a sight of the goose. Besides, I'm about to be suspended. Out of a job not long after. Maybe . . .' He'd been turning this over in his mind. 'Maybe charged with something or other. I'm done.'

There was a blue folder in Fatoussi's tray. He took it out, flicked through the pages and grimaced. 'It's true I had Dupont in here furious, demanding your head. It's gone no further for the moment.'

'Étienne. I don't want to get anyone else in trouble. If—'

Fatoussi picked up another file and waved at him to be silent. 'I'm captain here. Let me finish. The other development in your absence . . . the day after you left, I had a visit from the priest, Chauvin. He wished to make a statement admitting to assaulting Noémie that night. Though he insists, he swears – and who doesn't believe a priest who swears? – that she was alive when he left her.' He took out a couple of pages from the new file. 'Though quite why he should do this now he wouldn't say. Except that it was preying on his conscience.' He threw down the folder. 'Preying on it for a very long time it seems.' Fatoussi beamed at him. 'Coincidence, I imagine?'

Baptiste hoped he wasn't blushing. 'What else might it be?'

'I've no idea. In any case, there's precious little I can do. One man's hysterical confession to a crime without witnesses. No proof on our part it even happened. Only his word, for what it's worth. I hate to think what lawyers would make of that. Besides, the Church, as usual, looks after its own.'

He was struggling to keep up. 'I'm sorry ...?'

'The ecclesiastical authorities have pounced and decided Chauvin is undergoing some kind of mental breakdown. It appears he's confessed to having had fantasies about sexual experiences in the past. They've relieved him of his priest-hood and whisked the fellow off to a hospital or monastery, whatever. Somewhere that tends to put him rather beyond my reach.'

He took the two folders, emptied the pages onto the desk and began ripping them to pieces. 'The thing one must always remember about Clermiers is that a little place like this is always good at keeping its secrets. We have an accommoda-tion. I won't pursue Christian Chauvin. In return, Dupont's complaints will go no further than this desk.' He leaned across and took Baptiste's hands. 'Listen to an old friend. Forget about Noémie Augustin. Put her to rest.'

'Done.'

Fatoussi looked sceptical. 'That seemed remarkably easy. I do hope so. You're too decent a man to destroy your career over something like this. Go back to work. You're needed by the living. Let the dead rest in peace.'

'I don't know what to say.'

'Then for once in your life say nothing. Oh . . .' He picked up a notepad. 'I forgot. Your mother called. She'd no idea how to reach you.'

'Is she all right?'

'On top form from what I heard. Unlike your apartment. It seems the plumbers they used upstairs were cowboys and it's all flooded again. She's got your old bedroom ready for the duration. You will stay with us for dinner tonight? Longer if you feel like it. Take a break. Relax. Bernadette wants to see you again. You can meet the kids and—'

'Love to,' said Baptiste.

99

On Saturday morning, after a prolonged and pleasant stay with Fatoussi, Bernadette, and their two playful offspring, he drove back to Paris. As always it wasn't easy finding a parking space near the rue de Bourgogne. As always, his mother was in a prickly mood, complaining she'd no idea where he'd been, how to contact him, what he was up to.

Busy, was all he said, which didn't improve matters much at all.

'I have two messages,' she announced as he lugged his case into his tiny childhood bedroom. 'One personal. One professional.'

'The personal . . .'

'No. First, the professional. Your boss called and said he wants you to go straight to Vincennes on Monday. A man's vanished in the woods behind the château. He seems to think you're good with missing people for some reason. Can't imagine why.'

'Ah.'

'Is that it? Ah? I'm assuming you didn't find the Clermiers girl.'

He opened his case and began to unpack. 'I didn't.'

'Oh, Julien.' She touched his arm. 'Please tell me there'll be no more nightmares.'

He kissed her cheek and retrieved a jar he'd brought with him. 'A gift.'

'What in god's name ... it looks like puke.'

'They call it piccalilli. Home-made.'

'That could give *me* nightmares. Would you kindly answer the question?'

'No one dreams on demand. They wouldn't be dreams if you could do that. But I think Clermier's behind me.'

'Good.' She held up the jar. 'From England?'

'Yes.'

'Hmm.'

There was something Marie Le Gall was holding back, quite deliberately.

'And the personal message?'

'A woman called Celia phoned. An *English* woman. She said she's arriving in Paris on business this evening. Short notice.

Very short by the sounds of it. She asked me to pass on the address for her hotel . . .'

She handed him a note in her spidery hand. A place Baptiste knew, not far away, near the Eiffel Tower.

'Did she say anything else?'

Her cackle reminded him of a magpie's chattering rattle. 'Does she need to? I can only presume that, having run out of European women to disappoint, you now turn to our neighbours across *La Manche*.'

'The English are European.'

Another laugh, a little gentler this time. 'Ignore your grumpy old mother. You can bring her back here if you want. I liked the sound of her. A woman, it seemed to me, who knows her own mind.'

Baptiste was looking at his watch. Time for a shower, fresh clothes, perhaps a nap if his mother would leave him alone.

At five he called the hotel. She'd just turned up. And yes, to dinner. Le Suffren, a traditional Parisian brasserie, the other side of the Champ de Mars, not far from the hotel.

'Are you out of a job, then?' she asked.

'It seems not.'

'Oh.' She sounded disappointed. 'I've missed you.'

'It's only been a couple of days.' Silence. 'Me too. I'm glad you're here.'

'That's something.'

'I'll be there in an hour. If that's. . .'

'Can't wait.'

The flower shop was just closing. Chloé and Elise were behind the counter in their purple nylon housecoats, tucking away buckets of blooms.

'Ah!' cried Chloé. 'The great detective.'

'Yes! The very one!' Elise narrowed her eyes and peered at him as if scrutinising an unsatisfactory bouquet. They'd developed an infuriating tease whenever they saw him, talking to

323

one another as if they were quite alone. 'Remember what his *maman* said when we met her in the café?'

Chloé tapped the side of her nose and left it at that.

'I'd like some flowers,' said Baptiste.

'Right place to come,' Elise replied with a nod and a wink.

Chloé folded her arms and looked at her sister. 'I hear the great detective has an English girlfriend now. After the Dutch one slung her hook.'

Elise wiped away a theatrical tear. 'French girls not good enough for him, it seems.'

'Roses,' Baptiste said, anxious to get out of there.

Elise smiled innocently. 'A rose for his English rose. Ah. . .'

He harrumphed.

'What colour?' asked Chloé.

'You choose.'

Again, that glance between them. 'It seems to me,' Elise went on, 'our neighbour may be the great detective, but he's not a true romantic at heart.'

'It seems to *me* . . .' her sister piped up.

Baptiste slammed his wallet on the counter.

'Do you want to sell me these damned flowers or not?'

Credits

David Hewson and Orion Fiction would like to thank everyone at Orion who worked on the publication of *Baptiste: The Blade Must Fall* in the UK.

Editorial
Sam Eades
Sahil Javed

Copyeditor
Francine Brody

Proofreader
Linda Joyce

Audio
Paul Stark
Jake Alderson

Contracts
Dan Herron
Ellie Bowker
Alyx Hurst

Design
Charlotte Abrams-Simpson
Tomás Almeida
Joanna Ridley

Editorial Management
Charlie Panayiotou
Jane Hughes
Bartley Shaw

Finance
Jasdip Nandra
Nick Gibson
Sue Baker

Marketing
Hennah Sandhu

Production
Ruth Sharvell

Publicity
Aoife Datta

Sales
Jen Wilson
Esther Waters
Victoria Laws
Toluwalópe Ayo-Ajala
Rachael Hum
Ellie Kyrke-Smith
Sinead White
Georgina Cutler

Operations
Jo Jacobs
Dan Stevens